T0208535

This "38 Dark Days" is his sixth book and second novel.
His first novel is: "Cha-cha-cha" a novel of Politics."

His first four publications are textbooks or reference materials
in higher education, namely:

- Philippine Education: Everything You Wanted to Know About It but Were Too Shy to Ask;
- Institutional Panning and Development: A Primer
- Educational Administration, A Rational and Structural Approach; and
- Policy and Policy Making in Education.

DARK DAYS

THE ACADEME IN TURMOIL

MELCHIZEDEK MAQUISO

38 DARK DAYS
THE ACADEME IN TURMOIL

Copyright © 2021 Melchizedek Maquiso.

*All rights reserved. No part of this book may be used or reproduced by any means,
graphic, electronic, or mechanical, including photocopying, recording, taping or by
any information storage retrieval system without the written permission of the author
except in the case of brief quotations embodied in critical articles and reviews.*

*This is a work of fiction. All of the characters, names, incidents, organizations, and dialogue
in this novel are either the products of the author's imagination or are used fictitiously.*

iUniverse books may be ordered through booksellers or by contacting:

iUniverse
1663 Liberty Drive
Bloomington, IN 47403
www.iuniverse.com
844-349-9409

*Because of the dynamic nature of the Internet, any web addresses or links contained in
this book may have changed since publication and may no longer be valid. The views
expressed in this work are solely those of the author and do not necessarily reflect the
views of the publisher, and the publisher hereby disclaims any responsibility for them.*

*Any people depicted in stock imagery provided by Getty Images are models,
and such images are being used for illustrative purposes only.
Certain stock imagery © Getty Images.*

ISBN: 978-1-5320-9066-0 (sc)
ISBN: 978-1-5320-9067-7 (e)

Library of Congress Control Number: 2021902773

Print information available on the last page.

iUniverse rev. date: 02/27/2021

ACKNOWLEDGMENT

This novel is in grateful acknowledgment of the inspiration given by the fearless, outspoken and principled men and women who constituted the academic community of a state college in Northern Mindanao at the time of their struggle in 1986. Their individual actions propelled by a strong belief in justice and the right to be heard served as the fabric by which a groundswell toward collective action was woven: unafraid, doggedly determined, and incisively purposeful.

Much have to be learned from their experience.

The posthumous publication of this novel acknowledges with gratitude Prof. Expectacion Castor-Gonzales, a published book writer and an accredited editor for her thorough editorial work; Dr. Estefania Kollin, a former colleague, professor, and chief of the Publications House at Central Luzon State university for her initial commentary; daughter Tess Michelle and son Melch for their priceless encouragement, support and comfort at all times.

Thanks is also due JM and Theresa who inspired and pushed for the publication of this work.

Likewise, Its publication in 2021 offers a timely and warm welcome to the newest member of the family: Kirill Mikhail.

DEDICATION

To the 1986 students, faculty, staff and parents of a state college in Northern Mindanao who carried the torch of idealism in the struggle to assert the integrity of their academic institution, this work is heartily dedicated.

May they continue to be principled leaders who would faithfully take on the critical role of nurturing the youth for a better future.

FOREWORD

It was no mean feat to have accomplished what I ought to do for the longest time. I felt elated, relieved and proud.

Dr. Melchizedek Maquiso's second novel, "38 Dark Days" (subtitled "The Academe in Turmoil") is finally out. And what a story to tell!

I am not quite sure how novelists and book authors actually came out with their great works but I do know how my husband Mike, in his highest and lowest moments journeyed through many years of ups and downs before his voluminous manuscripts had come to form and substance. On second thought though, it had substance from the very beginning but form was definitely still undecided. Should it be a memoir? a lengthy essay? a novel?

His was a colorful journey of more than twelve thousand days which started in late 1986 when he began writing using his old reliable Olympia, got stuck with it after it was first rejected by a publisher shutting it away to gather dust in one corner of the house. He eventually got back to it in 2012 after he retired but never had that joy of seeing it take off until its publication in 2021. Unfortunately for him, he did not live long to see his dream novel get launched.

In my beloved husband's memory this work was published posthumously.

The novel was based on a true story. The plot revolved around men and women of a small polytechnic college in Northern Mindanao who stood up against political meddling and rallied behind their incumbent officer-in-charge to keep and uphold the integrity of the academe and the dignity of the profession.

The characters and setting were replete with easily recognizable traits obvious to one who had lived through the era, the setting so closely resembling the time and place the events happened. In fact, the original manuscripts carried real names of people and places. But when the decision to write a novel instead of a memoir was reached, he painstakingly showed deference to those who helped much in the struggle and to protect innocent individuals by keeping them incognito. His efforts to conceal identity was however, proven futile. He might as well had named them because his characterization was a complete give away.

Mike was earnest in his desire to reveal what actually happened during those fastidious days of what seemed to be an endless agony, struggle and battle as shown in his detailed accounts of the day-to-day occurrences. He carefully took note of every important incident or circumstance that he knew will bring the story to points of conflicts and climaxes, of turnarounds and resolutions backing them up with documents and evidences for authenticity.

The drama that unfolded said much of the state of the nation three months after the famous "people power revolution" that toppled a regime described as "dictatorial and abusive" and paved the way for the hasty crafting of the freedom constitution which justified the setting up of a revolutionary government.

It was on this ground that when he tried to offer his manuscripts to his publisher in 1987, it was turned down outrightly with a post-it note: "We don't want to be involved in controversies nor get embroiled in litigations."

It might not have occurred to him at that time that his work could possibly be considered rebellious and anti-establishment since it underscored the role of the government and the powerful people behind it in the events that followed.

Lest you forget that this is a work of fiction, I suggest you read it with caution and considerable objectivity. This novel is the narrative not of the opposition but of a man whose principles, professionalism and high regard for the academe preceded his reputation in a field where he spent the biggest chunk of his professional life. It pays tribute to the courage and bravery of men and women of a Polytechnic State College in Cagayan de Oro City to oppose the "powers-that-be" despite being scathed, bruised and hurt in the process. Nevertheless, they stood proud and tall in the victory they gained much later.

Enjoy this book and get a glimpse of the eventful past that often did not make it to the pages of history books.

TERESITA MAQUISO, Ph.D.

PREFACE

"AN EXERCISE IN FUTILITY!"

Observers, high-level bureaucrats and the rank-and-file would blurt this out with certainty when they learned that an obscure state college down south attempted to compel the President of the Republic to recall the appointment of a new college president which her executive secretary had signed on her behalf. It was worse when the "official" action was a tactical move to appease two warring politicians on one hand, and to reward the appointee for having vigorously campaigned for her in the national elections, on the other.

At a time when the chief executive had the sole authority to appoint heads of state college or university would she buckle down to the pressure?

This is an interesting topic for a thorough study not only by educational administrators, policymakers and decision-makers, but by the academic community as well, that is, if educational institutions, particularly those run by the state, would faithfully take on the critical role of nurturing the youth for a better future.

This novel is about a small state college which launched a protest to uphold the integrity of the academe, insulate it from political intervention, and support the ideals of students, faculty and staff enshrined in the College charter. The struggle, ironically happened when the country was euphoric over the "success" of the People's Revolution which claimed to have ended the regime of dictatorship and expectations of ushering in a new era of freedom and democracy were high.

The scenario began with the barely three- month old "revolutionary government" calling the shots. With the stroke of a pen, the constituents of that small college in Metro Ciudad shuddered upon knowing that their school had been likened to that of a third class municipality wherein the appointee of the deposed administration or the duly elected official had to be replaced immediately.

A new college president was appointed via the political backdoor. Done surreptitiously, the selection process bypassed the department in-charge of education in the country. Having known how the appointment was undertaken, the community filed a protest zeroing-in on three fronts: (1) objection against political meddling in the academe; (2) objection against the incoming college president; and, (3) appeal to retain the incumbent.

The roles played in the protest by the local and national politicians, educational leaders, local media, the military, the court, and the local community contributed significantly to the crises that developed. All these and their ramifications rocked the school and manifested the vivid interplay of societal forces and their consequences.

However, the crises did not end there. The consequences and the search for a new college president to follow days after, turned out to be lengthened shadows of the agony and the compromise that marked the past 38 dark days.

What happened to that educational institution in 1986 was a microcosm of the country in peril. It demonstrated that at such times, all sectors of society somehow got to be involved, even if on the surface, the problem seemed to be purely academic.

The complexities of events served as the backdrop in writing this novel. Why all these had to happen and how these had affected the institutional behavior of the community made it invaluable for students, school administrators, institutional planners and builders, policymakers, and decision-makers, all composing the bureaucracy.

-Melchizedek Maquiso-

PROLOGUE

It was quarter to six in the afternoon.

In one of the sidewalk cafés in the city, the habitués of the place, mostly the yuppies often take this time as their "happy hour" to convene, converse and have several rounds of ice-cold beer to unwind after a hard, often unexciting day at work.

The place was crowded as usual. The loud conversations were spiced with colorful language competing with the blast of rock, the coolness of jazz and the tenderness of old-time favorites. The attack on ideas and exchange of opinions were becoming spirited as more bottles of ice-cold beer were ordered and downed.

In one corner, three men were in a huddle two of whom were engaged in an animated and seemingly sensible exchange. They whispered and talked loudly in alternate fashion.

"I repeat, we are in the best of times and the worst of times," said the man with a necktie to his friends. He appeared sober. "The best of times offer us opportunities to do the good, the true and the beautiful; the worst of times impede our progress since our old bad habits have already become our second nature. We have become addicted to them," he added emphatically raising his bottle, looked at it for some time and took a big gulp.

"Hmmmm…" reacted the be-mustached man scratching his right ear. "Hmmmm…" He lighted another cigarette and took a long drag of the nicotine. "So how do you rid of old bad habits – eradicate them, erase them?"

Instead of answering directly the question of his drinking buddy, the man with the necktie launched into a melodramatic monologue.

"The problem is that every time the government changes, there are accompanying campaigns or crusades to rid the country and its people…

us, of old bad habits. In short, we equate change of values and attitudes with change of government. What happens? Because of this equation, nothing really happens. My position is this: change of values and attitudes must be pursued independent of political change. In fact the pursuit of the good must be continuing and must not hinge on change of government," he expounded passionately. "Look at Italy, its national government changes as often as twice a year on the average in the last so many years. Some local governments over there change as many as three times a year and yet, those vibrant Italians are blessed with a good life. They share an amazing dedication to the pursuit of the good life. They have "*dolce vita.*"

With that he emptied his cold bottle. "More beer!" he yelled at the bartender.

"You mean to say they are not compatible since the change in government is a question of form, and the change in values is a question of substance?" Mustache querried. "Is that why our situation remains the same? The change in both doesn't work! That's why…. hmmm," taking his cold bottle to his lips then slowly brought it down forgetting to take a swig.

"Something like that," the impassioned man agreed loosening his tie.

"The way I understand it, bad habits are those infractions that are not serious enough but irritate or piss off most people like littering, talking with one's mouth full, picking one's nose in public, coming in late during meetings and …" Mustache paused as he looked around and in loud whispery tone exclaimed, "FART…ing in public like it's nobody's business!. Ha! Ha! Farting is such sweet sorrow! Ha! Ha! Ha! Ha!" He laughed so boisterously that the men and women around them many of whom were tipsy from the beer that seemed to flow endlessly, gave him a dirty, mischievous look.

"I'm sorry," he threw an apologetic shrug of his shoulders and a sorrowful pout of his lips. Some responded with a thumbs-up, while others simply nodded. A few acknowledged him with hooded winks.

Assured that he had not offended anyone with his vulgarism, Mustache asked for another bottle thanking the girl at the counter. He almost immediately emptied it.

"You're right my friend," Necktie said after a suppressed laugh. "But you are talking about bad habits only in the micro level, the simple bad habits. There are bad habits that are serious and complex. Washing one's hand of responsibility, for instance that usually ends in passing the buck, political patronage without meritocracy."

"Daylight robbery, graft and corruption, *ganun?*" suggested Mustache.

"Yes, graft and corruption and plunder and all the manifestations of evil against humanity," Necktie couldn't contain his excitement.

"Hmmm…" Mustache wondered blowing perfect smoke rings through his mouth. He continued to add to the list:

"Distorting values, damaging culture, resorting to intellectual dishonesty, concocting lies and distorting facts, violating human rights, grave abuse of discretion. These are complex bad habits that are usually associated with the worst of times as against those usually associated with the best of times."

"Such as?" his friend asked with interest.

"Developing desirable values, preserving culture, exercise of freedom, judicious use of authority and power, pursuit of happiness and the like. How to bridge the extremes so that the center will hold the need of the hour for enlightened men and women." Mustache recited seriously drumming the table top with his fingers.

"Enlightened men and women?" Curly Hair, the third man spoke with a slur after a long silence. He snorted while trying to lift his head which was almost down to his chest. Obviously, he was drunk after gulping-in straight three bottles of the irreverent ice-cold beer.

"C'mon guys, why don't you stop all that bullshit talk. It's my birthday! Am not in the mood to talk nonsense today. Another round coming up,!" he yelled.

Ignoring him, Mustache turned again to Necktie reproving him. "I think my friend, you're making simple things very complex," raising his bottle and emptying it in a long haul, licking his lips on the bottle's mouth. He did not respond to Curly Hair's attempt to distract them from his and Necktie's intellectual fencing. The two were too absorbed to notice him who had contributed nothing to the conversation.

"Okay, let's grant that there are complex bad habits, and there are simple ones, how do you get rid of them for the good of society?"

"I think, there has to be a revolution first to shake the status quo," Necktie declared sounding serious and a little proud that his friend was following the flow of his philosophical thought. "Then let's follow that up with a program that teaches people how to rid of bad habits, all their symbols and emblems thrown out, all the evils they represent against the good, the true and the beautiful discarded… flushed down the drain," Necktie prompted with eagerness. "In a world of dismal failure, it is okay to dare to dream. All it takes is a valiant heart and a versatile mind," he elaborated with all the conviction he could muster.

Time seemed to stop when an old familiar song took over the cacophony of loud talks, jazz and the rock. The "Unforgettable," of Nat King Cole floated over the smoky cafe leading all conversations to a sudden halt. His silky voice flowed in midair—cooler than the ice- cold beer in the drinkers' hands.

"What do you mean revolution?" Mustache asked, breaking the spell of that old, familiar song, not wanting to lose the subject at hand, scratching his right ear again. It looked like a habit he couldn't give up.

"Peaceful…not bloody revolution. Revolution of the mind and heart…" Necktie almost whispered dreamily, as he nodded his head to no one in particular.

"Will the two of you stop all that chicken shit…let's drink!" Curly Hair raised his bottle to his mouth but missed the cold liquid, its content spilling into his almost untidy polo *barong*.

"Holy shit!…I'm not drunk…just enjoying…it's my birthday, that's why," he chuckled explaining unnecessarily.

"You okay, partner? Just go slow on your beer," Mustache said slightly irritated. "By the way, what chicken shit are you talking about? Chickens don't conceptualize. They only look for bits of things in the dirt, never go beyond the dust and," he paused, "in between, they shit. You know that, don't you?" He didn't get a response from Curly Hair whose head was back to his chest.

Mustache took a long swig, slapped his forehead to shake off the tipsiness he was feeling and turned to Necktie. "So what symbols and emblems should be thrown out?"

"As I was saying…" Necktie said haltingly lighting a cigarette. "As I was saying…"

"C'mon, you guy, I said, shut up your crap, okay? It's my birthday. Let's drink more. My treat!" Curly Hair shouted and dropped his face on the table. He was almost ready to pass out.

"Drinking too much is a simple bad habit on the micro level, ha! ha!."
Necktie laughed as he slapped Mustache's arm who guffawed and playfully
ruffled Curly Hair's thick black unruly hair.

"Are you saying I'm drunk? Are you saying I've gotten bad habits?"
He was whining.

"No. What I'm saying is that you're a good man with bad habits…
heh, heh! Joke only."

"You haven't even sung *Happy Birthday* to me and now you're saying
I'm drunk!, huh-huh-huh! My best friends, you are all terrorists…Huh-
huh!…" Curly Hair's whining was getting louder.

"Terrorists?" Necktie and Mustache both cried in protest.

"Academicians acting as terrorists, hah!" repeated Curly Hair. He
raised his bottle and finding it empty, tried to stand up but fell while
hollering for more beer.

Quickly the two helped Curly up, raised both his hands and announced
to the crowd, "It's the birthday of our great friend here! A toast to his
health!" Everyone raised their bottles and loudly blurted out the "Happy
Birthday" song quite out of tune.

Soon after, the dimmed lights of the small café flickered, and the
place was swathed in bright lights from a 60-watt fluorescent lamp, a
signal that the happy hour was over. The beer drinkers started to leave,
the three buddies among them. A few chose to stay to order dinner and
perhaps a few more ice cold bottles of beer after ten pm when liquor could
be served again.

1

THE AGONY BEGINS

DAY 1, FRIDAY, MAY 30
The Education Minister's Fury

DR. LUCRETIA QUILANTANG, the new education minister was presiding over the last plenary session of the Educators' Congress being held at the century-old Teachers' Camp in Baguio City. When a short break was declared, Baby Abcede, the Minister's secretary, handed her a piece of document. Dr. Moises Granada had requested Baby earlier to personally hand it in to the Minister when she gets the chance.

From the back of the packed Benitez Hall, Dr. Granada saw the Minister raised her arms in obvious dismay over what she had just read. He noticed that she showed that one-page paper to her deputy ministers seated at the presidential table. They all seemed to have the same reaction as that of their boss.

When the session finally ended at around twelve thirty, the woman chief walked toward Dr. Granada and motioned him to follow her in her office. Once they were inside, the lady Minster pounded her fist on the table exclaiming in disgust, "This is my first frustration since I took over!" Her small eyes bulged and her monotonic voice cracked. Dr. Quilantang was one of the first appointees in the Cabinet of the new government. The plump, short woman was 71 but the way she slammed that fist on the table and the manner by which she expressed her frustration, she could easily be mistaken for an angry woman of 50.

This was their third meeting during the entire Congress. The first was at the evening socials where she nagged Dr. Granada for not paying her a courtesy call since she assumed the post.

"It was also the Minister's birthday," her secretary informed him later. "All the SUC presidents were there except you, Sir. They even serenaded her."

Their second encounter was in a meeting wherein the presidency of the disputed state polytechnic college in Northern Mindanao was the main agenda. The school's academic character and integrity were being threatened by political interference. Granada was officer-in-charge of the said college. That threat finally became an undisputable reality that day.

On the first day of Congress, Minister Quilantang was not aware yet that the Executive Secretary of the Cabinet, Conrado C. Rayos had signed the appointment papers of Esteban Barrado as President of Metro Ciudad Polytechnic College. She was fuming mad upon learning of this development recalling that about five days ago, she was arguing very strongly with the President of the Republic on the phone against the possible accommodation of Barrado since she had already recommended Dr. Granada to be retained and re-appointed to full presidency.

"But it was very difficult to reason with the chief, you know," the minister said in exasperation. "It appeared," she continued, "that she has made up her mind on that day. In fact, she sounded happy" she added in obvious disgust, "because for the first time, the two political arch-rivals in Northern Mindanao, Ex-congressman Cosme Daldalen and incumbent Local Government chief Felino Mendel finally became friends by nominating just one person – Barrado," she informed the bewildered Granada.

In order to appease the obviously disappointed man, she continued quoting parts of her conversation with the President.

"If this is your final decision Ma'am, then what shall I do with Dr. Granada? Would you authorize me to look for another university for him?" the Minister recalled asking the chief executive.

"Go ahead," the President told her.

At breakfast that morning, Dr. Granada personally gave the Minister a copy of his latest book on higher education management with a dedication in his own handwriting:

> *To Dr. Lucretia R. Quilantang,*
> *Education Minister*
>
> *In sincere appreciation of your avowed commitment to uphold the integrity of the profession.*
>
> *Sincerely yours,*
> *Moises Granada*

He worded his dedication that way echoing the lady minister's speech before participants of the Congress wherein she explicitly expressed her belief that "the integrity of the profession should be upheld in the selection of a head for state college or university..." Granada remembered very clearly too that when she met the SUC presidents for the first time a month ago at the old Normal College in Manila, she spoke lengthily on the "first principle" of the new government—integrity, adding that competence and acceptability should also be paramount. On several occasions during previous interviews and in her many speeches, the Minister had repeatedly stressed that specific guidelines should be followed in the selection process before the President of the Republic approves the appointment of an institution head. These guidelines should be the tenets from which preliminary screening of candidates to the final approval by the chief executive as recommended by the Minister should be based.

While listening to the minister talked enthusiastically on the subject, Dr. Granada couldn't help but think that the appointment of Barrado blatantly violated the set guidelines. How was the so-called "integrity of the profession" upheld in this case? To his mind, the ideal was completely shattered.

Once again, Dr. Granada scanned his copy of Barrado's appointment papers, the same exact copy that Baby Abcede handed over to the Minister earlier. Bearing the name of the office and official logo of the President of the Republic, the document read:

To: Mr. Esteban G. Barrado

Thru: The Minister of Education
Palacio del Uno, Manila

> *You are hereby appointed President of Metro Ciudad Polytechnic College for a period of five years to commence on June 5, 1986. Your appointment shall be in effect for the entire duration of your term unless otherwise revoked or nullified for cause.*
> *By virtue of your qualification to the said position, please furnish this Office copies of your oath of office.*
> *So ordered.*

CONRADO C. RAYOS
Executive Secretary

Granada speculated as to why the appointment paper was signed by the Executive Secretary instead of the President herself. Was this deliberately done to avoid the ire of her own Education Minister who already had a specific name in mind for the position? Who was Esteban G. Barrado, in the first place? His name didn't ring a bell in the world of the academe where everyone knew everyone. He surmised that this Barrado could be the same "Steve" Barrado who was a co-Rotarian in the Rotary Club of Metro Ciudad where he was also a member.

If he were the one then Granada remembered him as the guy who campaigned very actively for the new chief executive in the last election. He recalled that the man in question delivered a very passionate speech extolling his preferred candidate lambasting the incumbent and his party the PMN (People's Movement for Nationalism) as the "source of all evil" that brought about the worst of times in the country's history.

———————————

Flipping through the pages of her notebook rather impatiently, Minister Quilantang finally got into a page which Dr. Granada supposed was marked "Metro Ciudad Polytechnic College..." She told him directly that she had thought of four options to offer him per the President's instruction adding that she had already discussed these with her deputy ministers. "They all agreed that the options were more attractive and desirable."

There was no doubt in Granada's mind that the Minister had bigger things for him in exchange for the MCPC presidency. He felt flattered but at the same time he was hesitant and uncomfortable. Was the Minister engaged in horse trading?

Perhaps aware of his ambivalence, she tried to convince him saying "in life, reality must be faced head-on. One way of looking at it," she continued, "is to take stock of its challenges." This was her cue for Granada to respond to a call to take on a much bigger responsibility, alluding quite clearly to a higher position which was her preference from among the other options she had offered him earlier. The older lady recalled that she too was once college president of St. Catherine's College, an exclusive private school for women until she was called upon to serve in government.

Yes, her preferred job for him was an assistant cabinet position. However, the more Granada thought about the possibility of accepting the alternative post, the more he recoiled inside. And the more he recoiled inside, the more he was convinced that the Minister was simply thinking of expedient ways not to offend him any further. In other words, the Education Minister was actually skirting away from the fundamental issue which solution called for the application of the first principle rather than simply a response to expediency. He reminded himself that this was basic instinct response since she just assumed the new role and that her guidelines in the selection of college or university president were also new. If these guidelines were not respected then certainly there was no difference between the new and the old system. Her credibility would be put in question and possibly, jeopardized.

However, knowing her reputation for integrity, Granada thought that he should not decide on impulse and should leave the matter on the table for a while. He knew, as he looked at her, that she was not comfortable with her proposed solution to the problem.

When she finally asked him for a decision, he replied that she should give him time. They agreed that the time would be on or before June 15.

Very early that morning before the first session began, Joselito "Jongjong" Prieto, MCPC liaison officer based in Manila brought a copy of the appointment papers of Mr. Barrado to his boss Granada in Baguio. He reported that the College constituents were enraged by the knowledge that some local politicians intervened in the affairs of the school. They believed Barrado was unqualified in all aspects to become their new president. The faculty and staff, as well as the deans and heads were all poised to launch a massive protest and set up barricades to make sure Barrado won't be able to enter the school's premises.

Upon hearing the news, Granada instructed Jongjong to return immediately to Manila, book him on the first morning flight of June 2 ASAP and to contact people at MCPC.

"Please tell them not to institute any drastic action until my return."

The rain, heavier in the last two days, continued to pour in the nation's summer capital. It was only about two o'clock in the afternoon but darkness had already set in as the fog engulfed the pine trees at the Congress site. Jongjong, his face worried, gradually disappeared in the rain and into the darkened horizon to catch the afternoon bus to Manila.

DAY 2, SATURDAY, MAY 31
Like Wild Fire in Teachers Camp

The news that a new MCPC president was recently appointed because of political meddling spread like wildfire at the on-going Congress. In hushed conversations, the participants asked in dismay:

"What then is the difference between the new Education Ministry and the previous one? the new government and the old regime?"

Everyone also recalled that two prominent and known associations of colleges and universities passed a resolution urging the President of the Republic to discourage and inhibit politicians from interfering in the affairs of the Education Ministry. The resolution also strongly endorsed the guidelines prescribed by Education chief Quilantang particularly in the selection of heads of higher education schools. The same was adopted by the Congress in its plenary session the next day bringing to mind the keynote speech of the Minister focusing on social transformation through education. The substance of her speech gave the attendees some assurance that better days for education in the country were not far-fetched. With the news, however, all dreams seemed to have vanished into oblivion.

"...*No political revolution is complete without an accompanying transformation of society, nor is social transformation possible without the inner transformation of the individual. More than ever before, our task as*

educators is to bring about this 'revolution of the mind and heart' to become
urgent and imperative…"

The reactions of most SUC presidents and CEOs to the "bad" news were one of apprehension. They worried that there was no longer an assurance that the criteria and the new guidelines would be followed. Political meddling seemed to be still rampant and commonly practiced. People with compunction and a sense of *delicadeza* who served government in the past resigned because they had been bypassed, their recommendations ignored and taken for granted by the highest official of the land. Former education minister Odulio Cortez exited from the service for that very reason. Would the same fate eventually happen to Minister Quilantang? Many wondered.

There was no doubt that she was sincere. This was the impression on her by the Congress attendees. But would she be firm and steadfast enough to resist political pressure, especially if the pressure will come from the chief executive herself?

Wasn't the theme of this Congress- "social transformation through education" rather pretentious, a calculated strategy to make the participants appreciate the supposedly "new era of change?" Her gospel of social transformation was seductive but little did Minister Quilantang know that it did not actually achieve its goal. To most, it was shallow and superficial. They frowned on the merit of the transformation concept *viz-a-viz* political accommodation of non-eligible, unqualified personalities to positions of trust that required academic excellence. Speculations as to why the President failed to grace the opening ceremonies were many and varied. She was supposed to deliver the keynote address, but for some unknown reason, she did not show up. The Minister told the audience that bad weather prevented her from coming over. End of discussion.

Restlessness at the Home Front

After the long distance call of Jongjong got through, leaders of the academic community in Metro Ciudad including the student leaders convened for an emergency meeting that same morning. They were utterly disappointed to hear Mr. Barrado's appointment as true. Jongjong swore that it's for real and told them that OIC Granada had given the instruction for them not to make any drastic move until his return.

The circumstances that triggered the restlessness and anxiety among the College constituents stemmed from a "rumor" that reached the school resident auditor Florence Avuen, which according to him came "from a very reliable source." Avuen, relayed the information on Tuesday, a day before the official appointment was signed (May 26) that his source was convinced that the rumor was indeed true.

Beth Sebastian, chief of planning and resource management had written an account of the auditor's morally depressing information.

> *On May 29, Avuen was again at the administration office to confirm the news. At about the same time, around four in the afternoon, a telephone call for EVP Sosimo Soriano from Mr. Barrado himself was monitored raising alarm among members of the community. Curious as to what the call was all about, I asked EVP Soriano who was quite cautious about the whole thing. He said that Mr. Esteban Barrado wanted to meet with him to find out the reactions of the faculty and staff to his appointment. The EVP said that he told the incoming president the plain truth that the rank-and-file, as well as the heads were not pleased and that he was not acceptable to them. Upon hearing from Dr. Soriano the gist of his telephone conversation with Barrado, the leaders convened and discussed the serious issue at hand laying down plans for a huge protest, a move that was against the wishes of our OIC president Granada to stay calm while we wait for his return.*

Deans and heads, including presidents of personnel and faculty associations, the alumni and the student government met in an atmosphere of agitation and frustration. They showed anger on their faces and in the tone of their voices. There was undeniably a mounting tension, probably because of the uncertainties their beloved MCPC will face if and when the new president takes over.

Once again, EVP Soriano reminded the group, "We can't do anything, his appointment has been signed and released."

Someone from the rank-and-file countered, "No, we can do something. Let's protest. Let's launch a massive rally to prevent him from coming in."

Prof. Anita Caluya, faculty association president suggested to wait a bit since she heard from some people that Minister Quilantang promised during the Concerned Teachers of the Republic convention held two weeks ago that she will keep Dr. Granada at MCPC.

"In the meantime, let's send telegrams to all concerned beginning from the President of the Republic expressing our hurt and disappointment over this development. Let's emphasize and remind her of the presence of a set of guidelines in the selection of a state college head. We shall also point out that we were never consulted at all. She may listen to us. They may listen to us," she averred.

Everyone looked at her and saw the woman's intense desire to first take the peaceful and diplomatic recourse. But the majority was hot on the trail. *"Now na, protesta na!"* they shouted.

The vice president stood up and raised a hand saying: "I'm with you. Who else are with us on this?"

All hands were raised and whistles of excitement could be heard all over the campus. The protest had begun at the home front.

Eight telegrams found their way to people who were believed to carry some weights because they rubbed elbows with the chief executive. The *palakasan* and *kapit* systems were not dead, and it seemed the MCPC people were hoping against hope that it will work.

RUSH

Her Excellency, the President
The Palace

REITERATING MCPC FACULTY AND STAFF,
DEANS AND HEADS, STUDENTS, ALUMNI

ASSOCIATION SUPPORT FOR RETENTION AND RE-APPOINTMENT OF DR. GRANADA AS METR0 CIUDAD POLYTECHNIC COLLEGE PRESIDENT /STOP/ WE NEED A PRESIDENT WHO IS FULLY QUALIFIED /STOP/.BARRADO' S APPOINTMENT BLATANTLY VIOLATED MCPC CHARTER.

Telegrams with similar sentiments were sent bearing the names of stakeholders and people of repute from the school. They were all out within that day.

It may be recalled that months before the People's Revolution took place, the Board of Trustees passed a resolution giving full authority to Dr. Granada to act as President of the College changing his designation from that of an officer-in-charge." Dr. Granada however, wanted a formal appointment recommendation coming from the former Education chief duly signed by the President of the Republic before he assumes the post. The Board said the signature of the President was only a matter of formality; his designation as OIC did not diminish one bit his authority as president of the College. They assured him that his papers were already on the table awaiting signature except that, an insider whispered in total confidentiality, "the President is very sick with an incurable disease."

———————————————

DAY 3, SUNDAY, JUNE 1
Beleaguered and Daunted

The drive down Kennon Road was slippery due to heavy rains that continued to pour. It was kind of dangerous not only because of the downpour but because rocks and small boulders were rolling downhill. Granada's driver had to keep his speed slow avoiding the catastrophic roll down by a hairline. The traffic was also beginning to get heavy. His three passengers spent the time talking about the just concluded Congress, each one expressing displeasure and discontent over what happened. The men agreed that the educators' meet was a total disappointment. "It was all promises. Nothing is new nor were there something to be excited about," commented Dr. Celo Rogelio drily. He was travelling back with Dr. Granada and another high official from a state university in Iloilo, President Tarcilo Passim. Both Dr. Rogelio and Dr. Granada were heading home to the same famous agricultural university in Nueva Ecija where the former was executive vice president and Granada's wife, Dr. Tessa was dean of CAS.

"Actually, I was thinking. What did we learn from the Congress that we didn't already know? Granada asked his companions. "Is an honest-to-goodness program on social transformation through education even realistic? Can it be done? he queried doubtfully.

"*Alam mo pare,* it's all idealism, so nice and intellectually sounding when discussed on conference tables but really… it was just a blunder," said the guy from Iloilo with a hint of sarcasm. "All talk, you know. *Bago eh, kailangang magpa-impress,*" he added closing his eyes sending a clue to his companions that he just wanted to sleep. Last night was spent at a disco bar with some co-attendees lasting till wee-hours in the morning.

Dr. Rogelio disagreed with his colleagues believing that the Minister was sincere and had some good points. "Maybe, she was just too excited about her program *na ang dating niya sa* majority was that she was trying too hard to sell her ideal concept."

"I believe the idea is good but the question remains: Could it be done?" insisted Granada. "*Alam mo naman tayo,* we can't just be budged from our comfort zones."

He went on to tell the two men about his specific workshop group's plan to hold a Mindanao conference with MCPC as the venue sometime in November to evaluate results and meeting the Congress' goals and expectations. They also agreed, he said, to undertake transformative activities in their respective schools. "*Kaya lang*, I'm not sure if I am still around to do those activities in my school," he added with a wry smile. Where would he be by that time? Granada silently asked himself, making some wild guesses in his mind.

All three men fell into silence. Dr. Granada was a bit annoyed by President Passim's snoring. He realized, the big-bellied man from the Visayas was not listening at all. He then turned to look at Dr. Rogelio who was busy writing something on his notes.

"What are you writing? he asked.

"Ah, just some thoughts that came to me now," he answered seriously without looking up.

"Like what?" Granada was curious.

"I thought maybe some were truly captivated by the call of the new minister for a revolution of the heart and mind. But they may have felt at the same time that they are incapable of bringing about its realization for the reason that their loyalty belongs to the old dispensation."

"Hmmm… that's possible," he concurred and left his friend alone to his scribbling.

Keeping to his own thoughts, Dr. Granada remembered the article of a former Ministry Consultant published sometime in April which, in a way, affirmed Dr. Rogelio's thought. Entitled, "What Beset State College Presidents," the consultant wrote that with the issuance of a circular requiring all presidential appointees to tender their courtesy resignations, many SUC presidents interpreted it as a foreboding sign that something dreadful to their career might inevitably come. This might cause the beleaguered presidents to choose to support the new administration and give up their loyalty to their former superior.

The passengers were silent for a long time as the strenuous whining of the Chevy's engine and its screeching tires took the tricky curves of the descending terrain.

While having a leisurely *merienda* at Dr. Passim cousin's restaurant in Urdaneta, the men had the chance to talk more seriously about the situation. They recalled the general impression of majority of the participabts on the composition of the new top officials of the Ministry. Except for one, they noted, everyone in the Ministry handling policy decisions was not familiar with the operation and management of state-owned higher education schools. Almost all of them, from the Minister down to her deputies came from the private sector. It was something to be wary about.

The new group seemed to have intimidated many leaders of SUCs. When before these men and women were openly and aggressively pushing their agenda— ideas, plans and programs to improve the system during past national and international conventions and conferences, the just-concluded Educators' Congress showed a group of dismayed and anxious faces, sitting silently during sessions and meal breaks unmindful and seemingly less interested on what was going on. During dinner or lunch, they often seated themselves in the farthest corners of the dining hall, looking at each other rather blankly or conversing in hushed tones. Lacking was the usual vibrancy and excitement displayed by educators on such occasions. The atmosphere, they all agreed, was one of sobriety and passiveness. It gave people at the Congress the chills.

President Passim admitted that he too was somehow afraid now that demonstrations in his school for his ouster were going on.

"All these," he said, "were instigated by agitators paid for by politicians who wanted me out so that their protégée could take my place."

Dr. Rogelio aired his assumption that trouble would surely erupt in his university if a new president is appointed from the outside.

"The situation is volatile" he said, "after President Armando Carpio decided to retire. The campus," he pointed out, "is now divided between the reformist and the loyalist groups."

"We are in the best of times and the worst of times," Passim said vigorously scratching his head as he tried to recall the literary great who said that famous line.

Granada finished it for him adding "It is the best of times because the new dispensation raises many of our hopes and expectations. It is the worst of times because there are many barriers that are present to frustrate us."

A thought occurred to him, something that he can't deny. He knew that he was not only beleaguered but that he may ultimately lose his school under the most disappointing and unfair circumstance.

Family's Stand on the Matter

As soon as the children heard the car honked, they rushed out to meet their father at their cottage's garage.

"Daddy's here now," shouted the excited youngest son, Melch.

Dad Moises was aware of his children's jubilation today. He knew too well why they were so happy and he felt kind of sad and guilty. They were all ready and excited to move with him to MCPC for the June enrolment and classes. Tessa, his wife, announced even before he could hug his kids who were all over him, that she was all set to transfer to the same school. Tessa was Dean of the College of Arts and Sciences at Central Nueva Ecija State U.

Six year-old Melch babbled about his expected enrolment at the Loyola University's elementary department in Metro Ciudad instead of enrolling at the nearby St. Josephus Parochial School, some five kilometers away from CNESU. The boy just completed his kindergarten.

Tess Michelle, their only daughter who was twelve was excitedly looking forward to attend school at Mary Cecilia College in the city. She decided not to take the scholarship examination anymore at the National Arts Center in Makiling where she had dreamt to study piano. "Anyway," she opined, "Mary Cecilia has beautiful pianos in its music department to tinker with." She had visited that school with her mother and brothers last December.

Mikhail Apollo, the eldest at 15, announced that he passed his college entrance exams in San Beda College and U.P. but had to forego those now that the family was moving to Mindanao. Will there be time for him to apply for admission at Loyola? he asked his Dad.

Dad Moises was not saying anything, just listening to his family's blabbering. He had no heart to douse their enthusiasm and excitement at the moment. He was smiling and nodding his head waiting for the most appropriate time to break the bad news. He hugged every one of his children, gave each a smack and said, "C'mon guys, Dad is hungry. Can't you at least feed me first?"

It was difficult to tell his children and Tessa that they will no longer be going to Metro Ciudad. He took all the strength he could muster to break the bad news gently to his family. It was heart-breaking to see their faces lost their glow, their smiles, their eagerness. He told them that the President of the country just authorized the appointment of another person to his post. He could not fully explain why he had to be replaced but emphasized that the new appointee was purely a political accommodation. He didn't know if his children understood that.

"But Daddy," Michelle in her usual hyped state blurted out, "didn't the new President know you campaigned for her"?

She should look at our room – it is still full of her pictures and posters!"

"No Michelle," Mikhail told his sister. "Those posters have nothing to do with Dad's problem, not even the new president's campaign stickers in our notebooks and in our car."

"Why Dad," Michelle would not give up, "did you vote for the PMN candidate?"

"C'mon Michelle," Mikhail was getting impatient. "It doesn't mean that because I want to study at San Beda I am for the president because her husband finished law there. It doesn't also mean that because I want to study in U.P. that I am for the PMN bet because he studied there himself. See?"

"You're simply wholly off!" Michelle retorted.

"Don't worry guys. I can always return to CNESU or accept a better position that Minister Quilantang is offering." He mentioned the option which the Minister preferred him to take and which he was inclined to accept.

"What about the stand of MCPC constituents on the issue Dad?" Mikhail asked.

"I think they will hold protest rallies to show their disapproval."

"But how long will that last?" his son wanted to know.

"I am not sure," he replied. "It depends."

Tessa who had been silent all along, finally said what had been bothering her. "What would your people say about you if you accept another position while the protest is going on, that you have abandoned them in exchange for something more attractive?"

"That's the risk I have to face. But since, nothing is definite yet, let me cross the bridge when I get there," he replied.

The whole family was of the belief that the upcoming protest was justified. But should Dad join the movement and stake out his future with the protesting community? That question had to be answered fast.

Over dinner, Moises, his wife and children discussed possible scenarios in the event of an active protest. His family encouraged him to abide by the instruction of Minister Quilantang to appeal to his people for patience and understanding. However, he should also find out first the final stand of the constituents on the matter and make his decision from there. If there would be a protest, he should not in any way stifle it; that if a mass action will be launched, he should see to it that this will be done in accordance with the behaviour expected of people in the academe.

As Tessa and daughter Michelle started to gather the plates, Mikhail asked: "Dad, what if you would be forcefully yanked out of the campus once the new president takes over?"

"Well," Daddy said quite taken aback by Mikhail's question replied candidly: "Naturally, I won't resist. I will exit with dignity. Anyway, I am quite sure they won't do that."

Mikhail shot back: "Dad, would you go to prison or would you rather go to the hills?"

"Like Father Baliwag?" Michelle asked, referring to the rebel priest, obviously excited.

Father and sons looked at each other for a long time. The birds in the mahogany tree in their backyard started to chirp. Time to go to bed.

———————

Jongjong told him over the phone that he had booked him on an afternoon flight instead of in the morning. Dr. Granada requested to arrange for a car to pick him up at the airport and asked that only the school's legal counsel Atty. Gael Padera and his consultant for external affairs, Nap Lopa should meet him on his arrival. The others should wait for him in school.

That done, he went to bed anxious and uncertain. "What lies ahead, dear God?"

DAY 4, MONDAY, JUNE 2
MCPC Community Took a Stand

While waiting for his flight at the domestic airport in Pasay, one of his faculty members, Christina Aglipon came up to greet him. She happened to be booked on the same flight. She told him that faculty members on study leave in Manila of whom she was one, had decided to support his retention.

"Please Sir, don't leave us," she pleaded.

"Most of us, as well as VPAA Vilar will come back to join the protest," adding that "it's just that the VPAA is in the hospital right now where he is recuperating from a minor surgery. He and Ma'am Agnes will fly home as soon as he's okay to show their support," she assured her boss.

"Thank you, I really appreciate your concern," he said humbly.

———————————

Contrary to his instruction, many from the College met him at the airport. Two placards bearing "Welcome back, Mr. President!" could be seen at the Arrival area.

As soon as he was out, everyone swarmed around him, all eager to hear news about the issue. They wanted to know his initial reaction and what he had done in response to the recent development.

"I'll be calling for a general meeting of the faculty and staff a little later. See you there," was his brief reply.

With him in the car on his way to MCPC were Atty. Padera, Nap Lopa and Beth Sebastian who briefed him on the current situation and how the community reacted to the issue. Nap confirmed that Esteban Barrado was indeed the same Steve Barrado, a brother Rotarian. "He had not shown himself yet in the College nor had he indicated the date when he will report officially for work," Nap added.

Granada kept quiet but was thoughtfully listening to the three nodding his head occasionally.

At the gymnasium, signs of an embattled campus were too obvious. Placards and streamers of all sizes and forms were displayed occupying every space of the huge lobby.

"STOP POLITICAL DICTATORSHIP!"
FREE MCPC FROM POLITICAL MEDDLING!"
"WE WANT DR. GRANADA!"

The posters were "screaming like the cayote in the wilds," printed in big, bold letters over Manila paper, discarded sacks, old newspapers, and on white cloths. These will be displayed strategically in the front gate and at the campus fence fronting Recto Avenue.

Once inside the gym, Granada was speechless, surprised at the overpowering warmth of the moment. He was touched by the rousing applause and waved back to his constituents with the same fervor. The faculty and staff were there, including the officers and members of the Supreme Student Council.

The meeting opened with a prayer followed by the briefing of EVP Soriano on the status of the community's effort to prevent the takeover. He pointed out that the academic community was one in rejecting Mr. Barrado as their new president.

The more involved stakeholders led by the faculty association, chiefs of offices and departments, student leaders and members of middle management presented their views and were unanimous in their decision to physically bar Barrado from entering. This plan, they claimed, was justified by the fact that the appointment blatantly disregarded first, their school's charter bypassing the BOT's authority, and second, that of the guidelines set by the Education Minister.

Legal counsel Padera stressed that "while it is generally known that the present government is a revolutionary government empowered by the fast and immediately constituted 'freedom constitution, said government is not actually a government of men, as some misguided followers of the new president were already showing signs of abuse and power control." He also cited Sec.1, Art. IV of said Constitution: "All existing laws, decrees, executive orders, proclamations, letters of instructions, implementing rules and regulations, and other executive issuances not consistent with this Proclamation shall remain operative until amended, modified, or repealed by the President or the regular legislative body to be established under a New Constitution."

Dr. Granada was nodding his head acknowledging what the counsel was reading. The lawyer underscored the fact that he did not know of any law which had amended, modified nor repealed said provision in the Charter. "Thus," he said forcefully, "this Charter and all its provisions still remain in force."

The gym rocked and shook from the thunderous reactions of the audience. Many shouted invectives on the absentee new president.

Atty. Gael raised his hand to pacify the now highly fired up audience. He repeated the position of the community– to protest in the strongest terms the Barrado appointment. His lengthened discourse agitated further the people by mentioning their rights to free expression and dissent, their right to gather, warning them however, on possible violations and abuses that they might commit in the process. "These," he stated strongly, "might warrant corresponding penalties and lawful sanctions."

When Nap Lopa was called to speak, he cited his experiences and observations on how pickets and barricades could fail or succeed. He offered suggestions on how the picketers could be organized and mobilized adding that the public and the media should be constantly informed of the development in order to gain support. Lopa said with certainty that he knew Barrado very well having worked with him in the Metro Ciudad Press Club and at the Mindanao Press. He was convinced that given the option, Barrado was unlikely to choose and aspire for the College presidency since he was not really trained for this. Mr. Lopa suspected that some local politicians might have encouraged the man to give hints to the President of the Republic about his interest in the post. Why they did this, Lopa said he could only guess.

After those fiery speeches, Dr. Granada was called to speak. He informed them of the meetings he had with Minister Quilantang, outlining the background which led to the appointment of the controversial figure. The audience howled at this knowledge. He relayed the message of the Minister appealing for their understanding reiterating that this unfortunate circumstance was a reality they could not get away from.

"But didn't the Minister realize that our Charter has also been violated?" they asked.

"Perhaps she didn't know that. But it was appearent that she could not do anything anymore since the president of the land has already made up her mind and authorized the appointment," he replied trying to defend Dr. Quilantang's course of action.

Noticing that their OIC had not expressed yet his thoughts on the issue, they pressed him for comments.

Dr. Granada mentioned about his family's opinion that should the community decide to hold protest rallies, he should grant them without restraint their right to dissent, respect their decision and protect them at all cost. He pointed out that since it was obvious that a mass action was inevitable, he appealed for a peaceful undertaking conducted in a manner expected of members of an academic community.

Gathering courage, he drew a deep breath, told them of the options offered to him by the Minister in place of the lost presidency and that he had up to June 15 to make his decision.

There was complete silence. It seemed they were not ready for the surprise nor were expecting such news. It was a big let down to learn that their OIC will, at all probability, be leaving them behind.

In order to lessen the obvious disappointment of the people at what they learned might probably happen, he assured them that if given a chance, he still would prefer to continue serving them.

"While I believed in your cause, I could not possibly join you openly and have to stay neutral or I could be accused of using my position to influence you to rally in my behalf." He went on saying that "if you really want me to be retained, please understand that I need to stay on the sideline and not get involved. You know, you can't do something like that without leaving some footprints," he said sounding apologetic. "I have no choice but to keep an objective distance. It is during times of crisis when the best or worst in people usually comes out," he said in parting.

"That is okay with us Sir," Prof. Pons dela Cruz declared. He was department chair of science and technology. "Just make sure you won't leave us and we'll take care of the rest. We promise Sir not to cease protesting until Mr. Barrado's appointment is revoked and you will be appointed our President."

Everyone cheered wildly at his statement.

"Does this mean that I am under house arrest from here on?" Dr. Granada asked in jest.

Someone shouted from the bench: "No, Sir. We will be barricading Barrado out and will be barricading you in!"

That remark really brought the house down.

Academic Freedom viz-a-viz Political Meddling

That same afternoon, Dr. Granada was given a copy of a letter-memo to the President of the Republic from the leaders of the protesting community. It explicitly expressed their position on the controversy.

The letter read:

> *In line with our desire for peace and quiet in the campus, in our homes and in the whole Metro Ciudad community, we have voluntarily binded together as concerned citizens of the Republic to bring to your attention our utmost displeasure over the unwarranted appointment of an inexperienced non-academician as President of Metro Ciudad Polytechnic College. We wish to ventilate and voice out our gripes, complaints and grievances relative to the said action by your Executive Secretary who, we believed did this in compliance with your instruction. We pray that you listen to our side in order to come to a fair and just resolution of the issue with optimal objectivity and rapidity.*
>
> *We wish to state without hesitation that we, the undersigned and the whole MCPC community including*

parents and friends of the school are not insensitive and very much aware of what our beloved institution is going through at the present time. We believe that we are being persecuted in your exercise of the so-called "president's prerogative". We truly expected, that as a matter of deference, you could have at least consulted us, the people who are directly affected by this decision. We feel that our academic freedom has been ignored and disrespected, to say the least.

Allow us, Madam President to enumerate our arguments that will back us up in our desire to have you retain Dr. Moises Granada, MCPC's officer-in-charge who faces the threat of replacement by someone unqualified and unacceptable:

MCPC needs a President whose qualifications are commensurate to the dignity and integrity of the position, someone who has met the stringent requirements to qualify as state college president;

The presidency should be filled up on the basis of specific policies, guidelines, rules and regulations provided for in the College's charter for such purpose; and politics and/or political meddling shall not, in any way, interfere in the process of selecting and /or appointing the head of this institution and in all state colleges and universities in the country for that matter. We, sincerely believe that we should enjoy true academic freedom, hence, any and all disruptive political machinations will be opposed vehemently to the end.

We therefore wish to state categorically that we want Dr Moises Granada, our incumbent Officer-in-Charge be installed as President.

As a collective group, we are one in thought, word and deed in upholding our choice and preference. Our sincere and professional acceptance of the man is based on respect and confidence that with his impeccable credentials and track record, he can further the growth and development of this school which only started to happen when he took over. He has practically transformed the campus into one huge communication channel which gave us a wider space for more meaningful exchange of ideas, exercise responsibly our freedom of speech, and the right to be heard. We are free to express our thoughts, ideas, plans and programs for the College to bear fruits, take form and be implemented.

His leadership style is democratic and participatory and by that, we take our roles seriously accomplishing more than what we have set. The man as an administrator works through us, not over us. He is often in consultation with his constituents bridging communication gaps between and among us.

Finally, we are of the belief that he is the president for us and your patronage of local politicians' meddling in the affairs of this esteemed institution will do more harm than good.

We pray for your kind action on this humble petition.

Smooth Turn-over: An Option

After the highly-charged meeting at the gym, Granada and several leaders proceeded to the president's official home in the campus. His men were still hungry for more serious conversations with him on the issue. There were many unanswered questions and they waited patiently, acknowledged that he must have been caught off-guard by the suddenness of the dire circumstance. They wanted to know if he was available for talks anytime they needed to see him. He said "Yes."

When the leaders left at around eight o'clock, Nap and Atty. Gael stayed behind as they have other official matters to discuss with the OIC. Earlier, Dr. Granada had secretly asked Nap when he excused himself to use the bathroom to stay with the legal counsel.

Without mincing his words, Dr. Ganada said "I am for a smooth turn-over, a peaceful transition" which nearly floored the two men. Both looked at him with widened eyes and were speechless for several minutes. They felt like a bomb was dropped on their faces.

When Atty. Gael finally found his voice, he sounded incredulous. "But the community won't like that," he remarked obviously shocked.

"But I have no choice," Granada insisted. "Minister Quilantang stressed that I have to face reality. Barrado already has the appointment."

"But does she know that our people are protesting his appointment?" Nap interjected.

"I am not quite sure. But I think the most honourable act I can do as a public official is to work for a peaceful transition. I believe this should be my course of action, do an honourable exit."

Again, there was silence.

"By taking this stand, by taking this position, I could not be accused of sabotaging the government by disobeying the President. You might accuse me of saving my neck for future repercussion but if I do not do this, how could you distinguish my role from that of the protesting community if I just stay out of it and watch from a distance?"

"Yes," Lopa said. "But how do you think they will react to your stand? I think you should clear this out with them otherwise they might think you deserted them in the middle of a fight to protect your self," he warned.

"Okay, okay," Atty. Gael cut in. "What if you just remain silent about it? Let's bid for time!"

"You could be right except that my silence over time may only create unnecessary tension," Granada explained.

"I think any kind of tension could be avoided if I'll clarify my position this early."

"You may be right there," his counsel agreed. "But where would you place yourself in relation to the on-going protest?"

"This would clearly set me apart from the protesters," Dr. Granada said. "While I am in direct sympathy with your cause, I also cannot jeopardize my own future, that is, if I still would like to be part of the system."

"What about them?" Lopa asked referring to the protesters. "What if they lose this fight? They would surely be in the mercy of the victor, whoever that victor be!"

Granada agreed that while that might be a possibility, the "victor" won't resort to some kind of harsh action against them since he would be dealing with the entire academic community.

"It would be almost impossible to prosecute the whole body," he added with certainty. "On the other hand, if I make a wrong move, I might end up the villain and all the blame later would be on me."

As they parted that night, Granada knew he just lost two of his able advisers and personal friends.

———————————

DAY 5, TUESDAY, JUNE 3
Real Political Motive Revealed

As early as five o'clock, Dr. Moises was doing his daily morning routine, jogging around the campus oval hoping to complete at least six rounds of leisurely run. He was often joined by some male faculty and the chief security during these runs. But today he found himself running alone. Instead of the leisurely run he used to have after the first two circling of the oval, his steps now were brisk and fast, lacking the same relaxed stance he used to enjoy. It was also unusual to see his face a bit dark and unsmiling. His be-mustached face seemed fixed which hid his nicotine- stained teeth.

Dr. Granada was in deep thought that he failed to notice at first, Beth's assistant Dino Cabal who was walking from behind trying to catch up with him. He had in his hand a mimeographed copy of something which he wanted to give Dr. Granada. When the OIC finally noticed him, Dino gave the paper to him saying, "we want you to read this. This has been circulating since yesterday, Sir."

"More letters?" Moises was asking himself mentally.

Finding an empty bench under a big, old narra tree, he sat down and began reading.

> *Dear Mr. Barrado:*
>
> *By now, you must have known that the entire MCPC community, including parents and alumni are strongly*

against your appointment as president of this College and are working hard to render it null and void.

We admire you as a member of the local media because you're doing a good job as one. However, we regret that we cannot accord you the same admiration to that new position in which you have allowed yourself to be appointed contentiously. This is a job that is simply not within your realm of experience and range of qualifications, hence, not for you.

You will have to agree with us that we need a President who is equipped with the experience, knowledge and skills necessary to run and manage efficiently a polytechnic college such as this. We envision a President with integrity, possessing the academic qualifications required of the position and the dynamism that can propel men to action, command respect not only from those who work for and with him but also from his peers in the academe.

We assume that you may probably have the qualifications but we need a man with the proven caliber to ably manage a polytechnic college with complex vocational-technological programs. Dr. Granada has shown he can and we look up to him as the one who can make MCPC the center of academic and technological excellence in this part of Mindanao.

We believe that you have been used by some scheming politicians who thought of themselves wielding power in this region. Unfortunately, we unwittingly helped these same politicians changed our government. We were their supporters and now we realized and regretted the wrong we did by bringing them to power.

We assure you that we have no intention of denying the President of the Republic the chance to give this country a better government because this was exactly why we rallied behind her. In keeping with this ideal, ironically, we are protesting against political intervention and meddling by the same people in the affairs of this institution. The new president of the Republic has promised us a better country, the exercise of freedom of expression and that our voices will be heard. We believe that she meant exactly this: that she will listen to us.

Your emissaries, however, have given us a negative picture of our new President and her kind of government. When informed that we were concerned about qualifications, they brushed it off and countered that qualifications are no longer necessary in a "revolutionary government." We were made to believe that this so-called "revolutionary government" is one that subscribes to a higher standard of professionalism, due process, Christian love, frowns at favoritism and political patronage, pushes for a revolution of the heart and mind. Did we understand it wrongly? Your unacceptable appointment exemplifies that under the revolutionary government these ideals are simply lip service.

Our leaders in the on-going protest have already received threats. Could you be so cold-blooded to allow intimidation that early? Do we see now how your administration will be conducted when you officially start your work? Truly, that gives us the chill.

We therefore strongly express our opposition to political intervention whether in our school or elsewhere to bring about change especially when we began to reconsider the fact that the status quo is far better than the forthcoming change. We have been here long enough to know the difference. And so we ask ourselves now: Were we wrong in fighting for change? Do we really have better people in government now or the new bunch are much worse?

We appeal to your sense of rightness and propriety to desist from assuming the post as president of this College. This way, you can still keep your self-respect and protect your family from disgrace. We are unanimous in this appeal and hope that you will consider. Running a school like MCPC is a huge challenge and you may be facing difficulty knowing that you may not get the cooperation and support of people who make up the majority, that is, if you are able to assume at all.

We have enclosed a brief resume of Dr. Moises Granada, our choice for the College Presidency, so you know what we meant by "highly qualified". Also enclosed are copies of appeals and petitions submitted to all concerned to make our desire known and hopefully, heard.
For your information and guidance.

The letter was signed by the faculty, staff, heads of departments, alumni and student leaders.

Dr. Granada was not surprised to read this. He knew, his people were so intent to let their cause be made public and reach the concerned individuals.

He looked up, drew a deep breath and let out a sigh. "Where will this protest lead us, Lord?" he said in silence.

———————————

While attending to some documents which needed his signature, Gilda, his secretary informed him that a certain Atty. Cecilo Daldalen had telephoned and wanted to invite him for coffee at "Caprice" a beach resort in the outskirt of the city that evening. Since he did not know the man personally, Dr. Granada instructed Gilda that should he call again, invite him instead to his office any time in the afternoon.

Curious as to who Atty. Cecilo Daldalen was, he asked Nap who told him that the guy was one of the brothers of Congressman Cosme Daldalen, who figured prominently in Barrado's highly contested appointment. Popularly known as "Celing," he also served as confidante and adviser to his brother's political party.

Of the Daldalen brothers, Granada knew Gerardo "Gary" Daldalen a little, who, he learned later, was to become the legal and personal adviser of the incoming MCPC president.

Nap Lopa and Atty. Gael were with Granada in his office when the expected visitor arrived. Gilda let him in while his five companions (who looked like goons) were made to wait outside. Since the president's office had glass walls, Celing's companions could see what was going on inside. This made Daldalen comfortable knowing his men were visible from his view. Granada would remember later that the same men were to become part of the transition task force of Barrado.

As introductions were made, it turned out that Nap and Celing knew each other and greeted each other like some familiar friends. Celing took his seat after shaking Granada's hands tightly.

Dispensing with formalities, Atty. Daldalen stated his purpose, citing that it should have been his brother Gary who would have come that day but for one reason or another, could not hence, he took the task instead. His purpose in coming was to inform the community and the OIC that President Esteban Barrado would be arriving from Manila on June 4 or 5 and would assume office within the week.

Atty. Gael, Nap and Dr. Granada looked at each other trying to appear calm and composed at the announcement. They didn't realize that it will be that soon. Then Granada remembered the appointment papers—June 5, 1986 as date of effectivity.

Before anyone could say anything, Daldalen launched into an incriminating narrative which revealed the circumstances that made Barrado president.

"You know, Nap," addressing his old friend, "this is really our last fall back position. The PDR (Partidong Demokratiko ng Republika) got all the juicier positions and so we have no choice but to get this."

Granada was not sure if Daldalen was referring to the College Presidency or the whole College. He gave Atty. Gael a questioning glance who asked the visitor to qualify his statement about "no choice but to get this."

"Oh the presidency of course and with that, take control of the school," he answered candidly, lost on the impact of his response. "We can't have the PDR get this as well," he said with sarcasm. PDR was the arch-rival party of the MAP for political dominance in Northern Mindanao. Partido Demokratiko was headed by Felino Mendel the former feisty mayor of Metro Ciudad and recently appointed head of the Interior and Local Government. MAP (Mindanao Alliance Party) was the political party of the Daldalens wherein Cosme was president.

"You know," Daldalen continued boasting, "I was the one who solely brokered this out with the right people in the Palace and got the signature of Exec Rayos for Steve." All three men listening to him were silently exchanging glances, not saying anything. They simply let Daldalen spilled the beans.

"That's why, you know, Moi," addressing Dr. Granada, "Steve told me he would find it awkward to meet with you. I understand you are brother Rotarians?" he said quite unsure.

"Why would Steve find it awkward?" Nap inquired.

"To be frank, Steve did not even have this position in mind. He wanted some other jobs on the national level but he couldn't get any. The same with me. Until now, I couldn't get the post that I wanted. The PDR got them all. So when I finally hitched this position for Steve, he reacted rather reluctantly since he knew Moi is the incumbent. But I was able to convince him that this is our last fall back position."

Granada kept his fists closed under his table and was itching to tell Daldalen to his face how shameless he was and how low was his regard for the college presidency. But he decided to keep his temper in check and decided not to comment at all. He simply looked at the man almost contemptuously and hoped he continued his boasting, unaware that he had given so much information which he, Nap and Atty. Gael had been wanting to know from the beginning. There was something in Celing that was not only amusing; he proved himself the infamous "Pandora's box" unknowingly revealing, spitting out information that should have been kept in confidence because they were damaging. But in his excitement, it seemed, Daldalen couldn't care less.

"Moi," he said with certainty, "I've been told in Manila that you would be given a higher position."

"I am for a smooth turnover," Granada told him avoiding what Daladalen was hoping to confirm.

"In that case there is no problem," the old man said obviously pleased at what he heard. Turning to Nap, he said in a threatening tone, "you know Nap, those people in the picket line are making a lot of noise. It would be easy for me to have them snatched. This is an educational institution. They should not do that or else…" he warned.

"You shouldn't even think about it Celing," Nap answered in an agitated tone. "They are faculty members and students on a peaceful picket. Their rights have to be respected, too."

"Oh, but they are making a lot of trouble. Their act is a shame to this city," Daldalen retorted with a snide.

With that, the visitor stood up, offered his hand to Granada who purposely did not take it, saying his goodbyes. He left unceremoniously, obviously happy at the effect he had on the three men.

———————————

In Dr. Granada's cottage that evening, the protesters were enraged upon learning from Nap that they're being watched and that there's the possibility of a snatch against leaders and initiators of the protest movement. They were also told of the same abhorrent story Granada and his two advisers heard from Celing Daldalen. This made them more furious.

"Tama lang pala na mag-rally tayo. We have all the reasons to do so," expressed Anita.

"How could a lawyer get that low?" EVP Soriano asked almost whispering. He was unusually silent and only reacted when he heard the story.

"And to think that he is a Daldalen!" someone blurted out angrily.

"No wonder the Daldalens have completely lost their credibility," asserted another.

"What I could not understand is why he had the nerve to tell Sir that he maneuvered all these and that Barrado was not keen on the position at first!"

"Well, probably he was very confident that Sir will be replaced, anyway, that's why…"

"Maybe Barrado doesn't want to appear too eager to get the position, you know, *pa-importante*," suggested another.

"Trying to make a strong statement, I guess," said Atty. Gael.

As the conversation progressed centering mostly on what happened during the meeting and about the Daldalens in general, emotions were getting higher and heated up as the night deepened.

Because of the exposed threats to the lives of leaders and protesters, plans to protect them were mapped out initially. Security measures from within included closure of the main gates while protest was going on; incoming guests should only be allowed to enter using the students and personnel entrance on the side.

Aware of the imminent danger, Granada instructed the security guards to be more vigilant in checking visitors making sure each one was properly logged in before allowing entry. Cars and other vehicles should likewise be checked, their license plate numbers also recorded.

There was a general consensus among those present that every one of them should be more watchful and wary of suspicious-looking individuals. If possible, protesters should go in pairs whenever they need to go somewhere. Threats were threats and these should not be taken lightly, Granada reminded them.

In the middle of their caucus, Beth Sebastian recalled that Dr. Soriano had recently received a note from Barrado. She looked at the vice president and asked, *"Di ba EVP?"*

The man could not immediately answer but slowly pulled out something from his back pocket and handed over a folded note to OIC Granada. The latter opened it and found a letter written in someone's handwriting. Granada wanted to know if it was written by Barrado himself. The EVP said "it was." Written in Barrado's personal stationery the missive was brief underlining his preference of Soriano as his "key" toward a smooth or rough turnover, expressing his trust in the vice president's influence and ability to control the College constituents. He also asked him to "assure Moi of my respected friendship."

After reading, Granada commented in a surprisingly calm voice: "I noticed that the note was dated June 01. Today is already June 03. Did you purposely hide it from us? Had Beth not mentioned about it, it looked like this will be kept from our knowledge. Why Susing?"

All eyes were on the vice president who was apparently upset and uncomfortable at the OIC's inquest. He opened his mouth to speak but decidedly closed it again without saying anything.

Sensing the embarrassment Soriano was feeling at that moment, Granada shifted their attention by asking if there were other threats against the community that he should know of. Anita Caluya said that now that she had learned of the threats, she had an inkling she was being followed. Beth mentioned that someone had warned her to be more careful. Some student leaders reported that several strange-looking people were seen outside the main gate who appeared to be discreetly observing their activities.

Not wanting to create panic among his supporters Dr. Granada brushed off Barrado's message as SOP and that the community should not be too alarmed. However, he advised them to be careful at all times. He said, "it was expected." At the back of his mind though, he knew somewhere, someplace, some dark intentions were being hatched.

Dr. Soriano who remained silent asked permission to leave. He left the group sad feeling he had betrayed his own people.

As soon as the older man was outside the cottage, Atty. Gael surprised everyone present when he announced that since the OIC was for a smooth turnover, he should see to it that there was going to be a real smooth turnover and not a rough one. His voice was faintly edged with hurt.

When they heard this, every one looked at Dr. Granada suspiciously, waiting for him to explain what Atty. Gael meant. Had their own OIC-president betrayed them, too?

With the untimely exposure of his plan to yield the presidency through a smooth transition, he was constrained to explain his position on the matter the way he did explain to Atty Gael and Nap Lopa.

However, after hearing his side, the leaders begged him to reconsider and abandon his plan. His consultants did not reiterate the plea of the majority. They were certain, Granada won't change his mind.

Though tired after the non-stop meetings with his leaders, Moises was wide- awake, recalling bits and pieces of the discussions they had, remembering their angered faces, their hurt. For the first time, he felt inadequate as their own leader. Should he give in to the clamor to stay and do the fight with them? What would be the upside and the downside of changing his mind, that is, if he ever does? What would be the consequences, if ever?

He tried to call his liaison officer, Jongjong in Manila but he couldn't get through. The line was just bad. He gave up trying and instead typed a telegram to Minister Quilantang. Granada will ask his secretary to be at the telegraph office as soon as it opens the next day.

RUSH Telegram for Transmission

Dr. Lucretia Quilantang
Ministry of Education
Manila

MCPC COMMUNITY STRONGLY OPPOSES
POLITICALLY MANIPULATED APPOINTMENT

OF BARRADO /STOP/ ENRAGED OVER BARRADO'S WRITTEN THREAT TO TAKE OVER CAMPUS EITHER SMOOTHLY OR ROUGHLY / STOP/ DECISION TO BARRICADE ALREADY ARRIVED AT BY ACADEMIC COMMUNITY BEFORE MY ARRIVAL /STOP/ HAVE BEEN MEETING ALL GROUPS TO RELAY YOUR APPEAL FOR UNDERSTANDING BUT TO NO AVAIL / STOP/ AM COMPELLED THEREFORE TO STAY WITH MY PEOPLE AND SEE THIS THROUGH WITH THEM/STOP/ PLEASE MADAM MINISTER THE SITUATION NEEDS YOUR IMMEDIATE AND DIRECT INTERVENTION /STOP/ WAITING FOR YOUR ADVICE THANK YOU/ MOISES GRANADA

DAY 6, WEDNESDAY, JUNE 4

First Sign of Deception

On advice of Nap Lopa, the protesters started to update the public via news bulletins hoping to gain sympathy and support for their huge undertaking. These bulletins were distributed in mimeographed copies.

BULLETIN NO. 1

JUNE 4, 1986

WHAT HAS HAPPENED SO FAR?

We have issued a manifesto affirming our belief that the academe must be free from political intervention. The appointment of Mr. Esteban Barrado which was achieved thru political manipulation, disregarding guidelines and bypassing Minister Quilantang is vehemently opposed by us.

We sent an open letter to Mr. Barrado last Monday (June 2) urging him to desist from assuming the post of President at Metro Ciudad Polytechnic College where he is not acceptable because he is not academically qualified and lacks the necessary knowledge and skills to manage MCPC. We have already sent him telegrams to this effect and hope that he realizes where he stands with us.

Atty. Cecilo Daldalen came and informed Dr. Granada that Mr. Barrado may report for work any time soon, probably today, June 4 or tomorrow, June 5. Atty. Daldalen boasted that it was his sole making that Barrado got the post by approaching and coaching the "right people" in the Palace to grant him his request. He had no qualms saying that this (Barrado's appointment) is their last fall back position since all the juicier posts have been taken by the PDR. Barrado wanted a position in the national government but none was available for the picking, hence, he had to settle with MCPC presidency. What an insult to us, treating our school like it's a junkyard!

Threats have been thrown to us from the Barrado's and Daldalen's camps. They specifically warned us of possible "snatches" of our leaders and members.

Let it be known that we are holding a PEACEFUL PROTEST and violence is definitely out of the question. Dr.Granada has pledged that if given the chance, he will continue serving the College. It is his first priority. Hurrah!

We will go on with this protest until the President of the Republic listens to our plea, until our demand is granted.

Because the picket at the College had begun to attract attention of the city populace, the leaders were often invited to speak before civic clubs and organizations, among them the Metro Ciudad Rotary Club where both Granada and Barrado were active members. Ms. Sebastian was asked to shed light on the issue during its regular Wednesday luncheon meeting held at the VIP Hotel.

Beth tackled the issue with deference aware that she could not afford to create any kind of animosity with its members for obvious reason. Unfortunately, the open forum that followed turned out to be an inhibited one. Instead, the program coordinator dwelt more on the Rotarian principles enumerating the "Four-Way Test." The MCPC issue was relegated to the background drowned by members' disinterest and indifference.

On her way back to school, Beth reminisced the hard work she did to let the Rotarians appreciate the reason for their protest. She felt that all her efforts were in vain. She drew a deep breath and exercised her left and right palms to let off her steam.

Smooth Turnover: What It Entailed

Big, bold streamers and posters lining the pavement around the MCPC campus from Gate 1 to Gate 2 did not fail to catch the attention of passers-by and commuters of the city. Standing, sitting on stools or walking to and fro were groups of students and faculty members handing out mimeographed copies of bulletin to people who showed more than the usual interest, engaging them in conversations or shaking their hands. They gathered to start their protest against Barrado's ascent into office as president by barring his physical entry into the school. The main gate was now closed. Visitors and others who wished to get inside were ushered in through the pedestrian lane of each gate.

Beth and her entourage went straight to MCPC after coming from the Rotary's luncheon. She was utterly disappointed at the indifference shown by the members to their cause. She reported directly to OIC Granada who advised her to be more prudent in accepting invitations. "We want our cause to be heard by the right people," he reminded his planning officer.

In the afternoon, Atty. Gary Daldalen phoned in to say he had a message from Barrado to relay to the "outgoing" Granada. He also introduced himself as Barrado's legal counsel. The OIC agreed to meet him in his office that evening.

At around 7:30 p.m. the guard announced via the intercom that Gary Daldalen and several others were outside the main gate refusing to have their car searched. (It may be recalled that the OIC had left strict instructions for a thorough inspection of any form of vehicle entering the grounds. The guard was simply complying with his master's order.)

Daldalen was forced to wait until Granada's older brother Ben who came that day from Iligan City volunteered to meet him at the main gate. Ben and Gary knew each other quite well.

As soon as Daldalen saw Ben he started to complain of the "embarrassing situation" he had been subjected to by the security guard and the protesters.

Seeing that the protesters were watching them, he boasted that he and the Granada brothers were friends. "Did you know that I was Ben's best man when he got married? We were roommates at Silliman University while in college," obviously trying to make an impression on his audience. Nobody said a word. "And, Dr. Moises Granada and I were close friends," he added with emphasis. Nobody seemed to be impressed. They just stared at him, saying nothing.

"Close friends?" Moises recalled that tonight was only the third time meeting Gary Daldalen. The first was when they met at Noli Tejano's place. Noli was formerly *a* columnist of *Metropolitan Times* based in Manila and now publisher of the weekly *News Express* in Metro Ciudad. That meeting was a gathering of the members of the Metro Ciudad Press Club. The second was when the lawyer spoke at the weekly Metro Ciudad Rotary Club's luncheon. It was he (Granada) who extended the invitation and made the introduction of the guest speaker. This meeting was their third. He cringed secretly when Gary claimed they were "close friends."

Unlike his brother Celing, Gary talked in a loud, booming voice, sounding like he was always in an argument. He was nonetheless, articulate and knowledgeable on political issues. Like his congressman brother Cosme, Gary also had intense political ambitions. He ran for Congress in his district last elections but lost miserably finishing last among the candidates.

"We came, President Moi," Gary said in his distinct Silliman accent, "to invite you and the picket leaders for a dialogue with President Steve tomorrow, if this is okay with you," enunciating his voice. Gary loved his voice and projected it in a manner that it almost sounded comical especially when he had an audience. "Since it is very apparent that President Steve is not welcome in this school at the moment, we propose that a dialogue be held outside."

Gary lighted his third cigarette since he came inside the President's Office unmindful of the "No Smoking" signage he saw earlier at the secretary's lounge. His hands were heavy, each finger as thick as the jumbo sausage with the left point and middle fingers yellowed from nicotine. His customary eye-rolling and grimacing stance while he continuously puffed smoke out irritated those who were in the office with them.

Prof. Caluya, annoyed by Gary's nonchalance, asked him why Celing was making threats against them to which he professed ignorance.

"Oh, did he? Sorry about that," he said casually, not sounding apologetic at all.

Anita's claim was backed by Granada confirming that Celing indeed made his threats in his office yesterday in the presence of Nap and Atty. Gael when he came to deliver Barrado's message.

"Oh…ah.." Gary was groping for words to say.

"You know what Gary, your brother and I were once co-teachers at the Liceo. We both know and understand what academic freedom is all about. That's why I can't understand why he is treating us this way. We are teachers who are on a peaceful protest, so do not expect violence to come from us." Anita remarked. She was breathing hard, her body was shaking carried away by her anger. "However, you can have me killed because I will not allow Mr. Barrado to step inside while I am still alive."

Her words were met with long, loud cheers from students and co-protesters who heard what she just said. They were milling at the lounge outside the PO curious and expectant.

Dr. Granada lightly touched Anita's shoulders telling to keep her cool.

"Let's all sit down and plan for tomorrow's meeting as you have suggested, Gary," leading the small group to his conference table.

After several suggestions were laid on the table, it was finally agreed to hold the dialogue at the Regional Office of the Education Ministry at three in the afternoon the following day, June 5.

Recalling what his brother Celing told him about his meeting with Dr. Granada, he praised the OIC to high heavens for his "noble gesture" to turn over the College to Barrado. But when the latter explained to him what it entailed, Gary suddenly became less enthusiastic and speechless for a while trying to collect himself. He could not properly light his cigarette from there on and throughout the rest of their conversation. His group left grudgingly.

Later on many suspected that what Dr. Granada laid out for him as conditions for the "smooth turnover" were undoubtedly unacceptable.

Bulletin No.2 issued later in the evening, reported on the subject of the proposed "smooth turnover."

BULLETIN NO. 2

Early tonight, Atty. Gary Daldalen together with Atty. Graciano Iner, Sammy Mejor and two other companions came to our school to talk with Dr. Granada. Present too were the picket leaders.

Atty. Daldalen came as the emissary of Mr. Barrado to arrange for a meeting between our OIC and his client to be held in the Regional Office at three o'clock tomorrow. The focus of the talks is how a "smooth turnover" of the College could be done as proposed by Dr. Granada. It seemed, Barrado's attorney was not happy hearing the conditions involved.

Terms for the turnover were laid down for consideration by the incoming.

1. *Thorough and intensive inventory of assets, monies and property of the school which may take about two weeks of work;*

2. *Identify entry points to make Mr. Esteban Barrado acceptable to this community. There is an on-going picket and before a turnover takes place, this has to be smoothened out but not in either "smooth or rough manner" as Mr. Barrado shamelessly intimated. We are an intellectual community and we cannot be forced into submission. People here do not just say "yes".*

3. *An assurance from Steve Barrado that the picketers will not be harmed, and that their positions in the College will not be threatened. (We have received threats from their end.)*

   Dr. Granada said there has to be a modicum of guarantee to satisfy all three. We should remember that the manner of appointment of Mr. Barrado is not only an academic matter; it is a matter of integrity.

In the meantime, our OIC-president assures us that he will not leave yet the College. He will see to it that the community is protected and secured from any retaliatory move from the other camp. This, according to him, is his moral responsibility over and above his basic functions as head of this institution.

He is willing to talk to Mr. Barrado outside the campus, however, he made Atty. Gary Daldalen promised to secure his life (because of existing threats) when he goes out to meet Mr. Barrado.

We maintain that it is our right to be heard and express ourselves. We cannot be treated like meek lambs. Politics in education can only mean the death of academic freedom. Let's call on God to be with us. "If God is with us, who can be against us?"

Deception in the Works

Granada was with the protesters in front of Gate 1 after his meeting with Gary Daldalen when the school's Personnel Officer, Linda Pinyan reported that she saw big streamers being printed at the *Pinoy Visual Arts and Signs* in her neighborhood. She chanced upon them on her way home. What was unusual about the streamers, she said, was that the text heralded the entry of Barrado to MCPC with the whole community allegedly, welcoming him gladly.

Alerted by the news, he dispatched his staff Danny Hibe to check on the information and find out who made the order. Jun Ilio went with Hibe carrying his camera to take pictures if necessary.

When the two returned after an hour or so, they confirmed Linda's report. They took pictures of the streamers and were able to identify who ordered and paid for them. The photographs showed clearly how the message was worded.:

WELCOME
COLLEGE PRESIDENT ESTEBAN
"STEVE" BARRADO
WE ALL SUPPORT YOU-

ADMINISTRATION, FACULTY
AND STUDENTS

They also learned that the streamers were to be put up across main streets and avenues in the city. Hibe showed them the duplicate of the receipt of payment issued to a certain "Mrs. A. Barrado".

Linda Pinyan looked sad as her report was confirmed by Danny and Jun. Linda was not only one of the active protesters; ironically she was also a first cousin of the Daldalen brothers.

"I'm here because of principles," she said, referring to her involvement in the picket. "And my close relationship with the Daldalens has nothing to do with that."

Late that night, the third issue of the picketer's bulletin came out to report about the "Welcome President Barrado" streamers being clandestinely prepared for putting up. This issue expressed the disgust of the academic community over how low the other camp could get in its bid for acceptance and how wicked was its means.

They braced themselves for more frauds and deceits from the enemy. This was just the beginning.

———————————

DAY 7, THURSDAY, JUNE 5
Face off at the Regional Office

As expected, the Regional Office of the Ministry of Education in Metro Ciudad was jam-packed at three in the afternoon. Aside from the protesting group, representatives from the military, media, and some ministry personnel were there to sit as panel of mediators and observers.

As soon as Mr. Barrado saw Dr. Granada enter the room, he rose from his seat to meet him and extended a hand which the latter intentionally avoided. He tried again for the second and third time but Granada simply ignored the man's effort on civility prompting Atty. Gary to lead his client back to his seat at the other end of the conference table.

"That's all right, that's all right…" Gary tried to console his client as the man was obviously embarrassed by Granada's overt refusal to take Steve's proffered hand. In order to calm Barrado who by now was visibly pissed off, the lawyer, whispering to his ear, assured him that such reaction was normal and a tactic to put the opponent on the defensive. "Let's wait. I'm sure he has something to say about refusing to shake hands with you," he advised.

———————————

After the usual preliminaries to commence the meeting by the Ministry's regional representative he called on Atty. Daldalen who rose and proudly showed the appointment papers of Barrado to every one present emphasizing that it was signed on May 26 by the Executive Secretary Conrado C. Rayos in the Palace. He added that his client's oath of office was administered by no less than the Minister of Justice, the honourable Leon Golez. That done, he then announced that his client, no doubt, was now the new president of Metro Ciudad Polytechnic College. No one commented from Granada's group. Their response was a deafening silence that Barrado was extremely uncomfortable. To allay his discomfort and queasy feeling in front of an inauspicious and unfriendly audience, he immediately launched on a long, direct-to-the point speech centering on five major points:

First, he wondered aloud why he was being "shabbily treated" by the academic community when he was their new president. Slighted by such reaction, he said that perhaps this was caused by the fact that the community did not really know him yet.

Second, he claimed he was "most fit and most qualified to become MCPC president" having been involved in the field of education all these years. "I was a high school teacher at the prestigious Loyola University in Manila, became dean of the College of Arts and Sciences at Metro Ciudad Capitol College and presently, director of the Graduate Studies on Public Administration at Loyola University, a position I have held for ten years now". He accentuated the fact that he had served in other capacity in practically all fields of endeavour the peak of which was when he became Secretary General, a post equivalent to the protocol rank of Deputy Minister of the National Social Action Group or NASAG, Office of the President of the Republic from 1968 to 1974.

He bragged about being offered by Minister Quilantang the presidency of the State Institute of Science and Technology, "a much bigger state institution in Manila" but turned it down because "I wanted to serve the people of Metro Ciudad than in any place elsewhere."

Third, according to him, he was highly endorsed by recognized leaders of the region namely new Interior Minister Felino Mendel, former congressman Cosme Daldalen and "by one of the most prominent educators in the country" Fr. Nestor Javieto, President of Loyola University of Metro Ciudad branch.

Fourth, because of his educational achievements and his rich experiences in both government and private sectors, Secretary Rayos hailed him as most qualified for the position of MCPC president. But above all, he said, as regional deputy campaign manager of the party of the presidential candidate now the President of the Republic, "…she did not hesitate to authorize her executive secretary to appoint me President of the College. Yes, there was even a time in the campaign when I had to face high-powered arms and deadly weapons. My life was in constant danger and so I told my children one time that they might lose a father. Yes, I risked my life for the President of this country," he declared passionately. (Huh? What was that for, a favour returned? asked by several, silently amused.)

Fifth, since he was appointed and had taken his oath of office, there was no impediment for him to assume the position. He was apologetic that another person had to be displaced as a consequence and felt sorry that there were some people in the campus who were out to prevent him from assuming the post.

But "I cannot be shaken," he warned them.

After his client's exhortation, Daldalen suggested to hear the side of the protesting community– what it had to say as a response to the speech of "President Steve" encouraging further the leaders to lay down their cards if they have something "to negotiate" with the new president.

Barrado unceremoniously stopped his lawyer from saying more. He stressed clearly that he did not come to this meeting in order to negotiate.

"Yes, if I have the time, I might listen to some of the problems but no more, no less. I am the President and that's it," he declared arrogantly.

"You are not Acceptable to Us"

That message was sent loud and clear from the other end of the conference table.

As soon as they were given the go-signal, everyone looked at Dr. Granada who, for the longest time, had not said anything. He motioned to his leaders to speak one by one.

Prof. Anita Caluya speaking on behalf of the faculty association, cited the guidelines set by Minister Quilantang. Since these guidelines were grossly violated, Caluya pointed out that the appointment of Barrado was not only highly irregular but illegal. This was one of the reasons for the protest. "I've said it before and I'll say it again. You can have me killed, Mr. Barrado but I won't allow you to come inside our campus," the professor said daringly that made Barrado suddenly stand up and point his finger at her, as if saying, "how dare you!"

"Calm down, calm down," Gerry whispered as he patted his client's outstretched arm and told him to sit down.

Sonny Aquiling of the personnel association reiterated that the association would not go for any other appointee except Dr. Granada; the incumbent High School Alumni president Julie Dayang seconded Aquiling's statement. Her association was also highly endorsing Dr.

Granada to the President of the Republic and would press for such until their preferred person for the post was appointed.

Several more gave their own thoughts and stand on the issue underscoring the whole community's sentiment not to allow Barrado to even step his foot inside the campus ground.

It was the turn of the leader of the supreme student council to state the position of the students.

Joel Angelo Lerpa, president of SSC was blunt. "This is for you, Mr. Barrado. The students in the College are one in this declaration specially after knowing how you employed means to get the President's approval: YOU ARE NOT ACCEPTABLE TO US!"

The crowd in the hall exploded with all types of reactions. Barrado turned white. He was seething but the flow of blood to his brain was restored in time to launch a counterattack. He slammed his fists on the conference table as Gary grasped his shoulders to calm him down. "That's all right, Steve. That's all right."

"No, it's not alright. I won't have them disrespect me and insult me in front of everybody," he said fuming mad.

The leader of the panel warned the young Lerpa to keep to the rules of the meeting or he will be forced to leave the room.

Reymar, another young leader whispered to Joel, "That was quite a bomb you dropped on Barrado!" The two suppressed a chuckle as Granada suggested to Joel to get some fresh air outside.

Amid the commotion, it became more evident that Barrado was getting terribly upset and Gary had to keep whispering to him to maintain his composure. Shortly after he calmed himself, the new president looked at everyone inside the hall and promised himself to keep them at the back of his mind.

While Gary was trying his damned best to put everything back to normal, Barrado cut him off a little roughly and said that he was refuting everything that was said, if only to be fair with himself. He asserted that it was not necessary for a college president to have a doctorate degree, citing that his master's degree in public administration was enough. He spoke a little softer mentioning that he "did not know there was a search committee that would screen candidates for the presidency." However, he insisted that this was no longer necessary since the "highest authority" of the land, the President herself, authorized his appointment.

Turning to Joel who was, at that time coming back from the outside, he tried to cast doubt on the credibility of the student leader since, as he pointed out, it was vacation time and he was not too sure if the position taken by the outspoken young leader was actually the sentiment of the whole student populace.

Not scared by Barrado's warning, Joel raised his hand and said as calmly as he could: "According to Christian theology, the devil is supposed to be most effective when people no longer believe in him!"

It took some time for Barrado to grasp the young man's metaphor. When he did, he roared in apparent humiliation: "Are you saying that I am the devil?"

"No, Sir. You did."

Guests seated in the panel were shocked. It looked like all hell broke loose inside the conference hall. Granada had to raise his hand to quiet the audience. It took a while before Barrado regained his composure as Sonny Aquiling upon Granada's urging, escorted Joel out of the hall.

"The problem of acceptability is inconsequential," Barrado continued almost incoherently, shaking as he swallowed hard. "I already have the appointment and therefore, the authority."

To stress his point, he said that this was precisely the reason why he risked his life in the last campaign so that the "rule of law which was violated blatantly during the dictatorial regime would be restored and democracy is returned to our country" concluding that "respect for authority was one of the essential elements of a true democracy."

Majority of the listeners raised their eyebrows, showing scorn at his statement which they thought controverted what he was actually doing.

"Then you must at least, walk the talk, Mr. Barrado!" another young man from the audience said aloud.

Meanwhile, Gary was nodding his head in agreement with what his boss uttered with feigned conviction. He was about to put his hands together for a clap but when he noticed no one followed his lead, he brought them down in haste.

"Hmmpp, okay let's move on," he said tersely.

Refusing a Handshake Set the Tone of the Meeting

All eyes were on Dr. Granada when he finally stood up. The room fell silent and an atmosphere of eager anticipation filled the air.

He began by admitting he refused to shake hands with the "good gentleman" earlier.

"Yes, I did refuse to shake Steve's hand and to me, that was no big deal. It may have come across as un-gentlemanly but I assure you, it wasn't. I think it is hypocritical to shake hands with someone you don't feel like shaking hands with and I don't want to be a hypocrite," he said without mincing his words.

The "good gentleman" was not looking at him. His eyes were cast down, his back on the chair's backrest with arms akimbo. Many were closely observing his reaction.

"As some of you may have known, Steve and I are brother Rotarians, and as such, I felt that he had stabbed me at the back," he accused the man who was surprised at the directness of his claim. "He knew all along I am the incumbent but had the temerity to justify his desire to force his way in and as a consequence, forcing me out. Why didn't he tell me beforehand that he was interested in the position so that the two of us could have talked things over.

Second, why did he write Dr. Sosimo Soriano, our Executive Vice President, who incidentally, is another brother in our own Club, to tell him that 'he is the key towards a smooth or rough turnover' when he should know that if there is going to be any turnover, that would have to pass through me? His action showed a scheming attitude that tended to corrupt an official in my group. Was Mr. Barrado actually driving a wedge between me and my Executive Vice-President, between me and a brother Rotarian? Is it true that he promised Dr. Soriano that once he assumes office, he would make EVP Soriano acting President, since he (Barrado) will be busy campaigning for the forthcoming elections? Is that not true, Dr. Soriano?" he asked turning to the vice president who sat quietly on his left.

"Ah, eh… that's right sir," he confirmed so softly that the audience had to strain their ears to hear him.

Granada continued. "Also, we have evidences to show that a certain Mrs. A. Barrado presumably Mrs. Almira Barrado, the wife of Steve paid the amount of Pl40.00 for the printing of two large streamers which are planned to be put up in strategic areas in the city worded purposely to deceive the public. The streamers say that the College constituents are glad to welcome the new president promising their support. These streamers are deceiving and of course, utterly false, to say the least. Have you not heard just now how the academic community is one in saying that Mr. Barrado is not acceptable? You must have heard that yourself, Mr. Barrado," Granada asked almost with sarcasm.

Before capping this point, he reminded Barrado of the 4-way test for a true Rotarian and wondered, if indeed he is observing with loyalty the club's philosophy.

Proceeding with the matter of "smooth turnover," Granada repeated in detail and more elaborately what he told Gerry Daldalen during yesterday's meeting. Barrado apparently did not take the conditions well and walked out of the conference angrily without reaching a compromise.

The meeting was a stand-off. It failed to accomplish the purpose for which it was held. The protesters went home disappointed but not discouraged. They knew this fight was real and they're ready to fight till the end.

––––––––––

2

THREATS TO VIOLENCE

DAY 8, FRIDAY, JUNE 6
First Order of the Day

SINCE HE COULD not get inside the campus yet, Mr. Barrado temporarily held office in his own residence. His first "official" action was to issue Executive Order No. 1 enumerating his policies on financial disbursements and management, inventory of assets, faculty and staff's demeanor and strict observance of rules and regulations while inside the campus and other policies to ensure peace and order in school.

A copy of the EO was given to the protesters by a member of his task force. It gathered a lot of comments, mostly unsavory and unpleasant coming from the faculty and staff who jokingly said that it should have been signed by the President of the Republic since it was an "executive order." Noting its content however (a bit exaggerated, repetitive and unnecessarily wordy), there was no doubt in everybody's mind that Barrado meant business. It was some kind of an "all-in-one" order, sweeping and encompassing.

EXECUTIVE ORDER NO.1

To: The Vice Presidents, Deans, Department Heads, Unit Heads, Faculty Members and Employees of the College

From: President Esteban Barrado

Please be informed that by virtue of my appointment as president of this institution by the President of the Republic and having been duly sworn into said office by the Honorable Minister of Justice Leon Golez, the undersigned has officially assumed the Office of the President as of Thursday, June 5 in compliance with the appointment issued to me.

Wherefore, by virtue of the powers and responsibility vested upon said office, you are hereby directed to effect the following measures immediately:

1. *All financial disbursements either for operational or capital expense are suspended immediately until after formal turnover of the financial accountabilities by Dr. Moises Granada, former OIC or his representative is effected. The depository banks have been advised accordingly.*

2. *All transportation and/or vehicular facilities of the College and its satellite schools are to be garaged in the nearest College compound and are going to be used only upon presentation of authorization from the undersigned.*

3. *All members of the faculty and administrative personnel are to be physically present in their respective stations and performing their job assignments at all times during office hours, unless assigned otherwise by the undersigned.*

4. *Absences without any convincing valid reason formally submitted beforehand to the undersigned will be considered an act of insubordination.*

5. *All College personnel are to insure that the on-going enrolment of students shall not be hindered nor hampered by any reason whatsoever.*

6. *The College security unit together with the elements of the contracted security agency are directed to insure that the coming in and going out of the public are not hindered while at the same time, insuring the security of College property and personnel.*

   All orders, pronouncements, and other rules presently in force and not contrary to this order will continue to be enforced.

   This Executive Order is issued pursuant to my sworn duty as President to see to it that despite efforts to create trouble within the College by some elements, all property must be secured, the normal functioning of the College must not be hampered and the atmosphere of academic freedom enhanced while at the same time, ensuring that this freedom is not abused.

   For your information, guidance and strict compliance.

Indicated in the order was the list of people (from the President of the Republic, the Minister of Education, regional directors down to OIC Granada) who were furnished copies of this EO including copies of his appointment and oath of office.

Resident Auditor Avuen felt he should have been included in the list. "He should have furnished me a copy or doesn't he know?" he said with a smirk.

Fake Appointments Hound Government

The early morning news published by a Manila-based broadsheet, *Metropolitan Times* stunned the country whose perception of the newly-installed revolutionary government was one of unquestionable integrity. With the news, however, they began to have second thoughts about the significance of the Peoples' Revolution where they took active part in bringing about.

At first, they believed that the new government was justified in taking over because the need for change was urgent and necessary. Now, with all sorts of news coming out in tabloids and in the grapevines, they were no longer sure.

The news item hit the streets of Metro Ciudad around ten thirty in the morning and became the talk of the town until evening because it seemingly confirmed their suspicion about recent appointments in government, especially in the education sector.

Fake appointments bug bureaucracy; education ministry not spared

Manila, June 6 - The haste by which officials of the deposed regime either elected or appointed were replaced by new appointees mostly coming from the private sector did not escape the watchful eyes of the public. Allegations of issuing "fake" appointments to unqualified people hound the three month-old revolutionary government. Replacing officials said to be "vestiges of the deposed dictatorial regime" has apparently not spared the Ministry of Education.

Last week, when most of the education officials were attending the annual educators' congress in Baguio City, a man who introduced himself as Esteban Barrado, came to the Education Ministry office in Palacio del Uno in Manila showing a xeroxed copy of his alleged appointment signed by Executive Secretary Conrado Rayos. The documents showed that he is the newly-appointed president of Metro Ciudad Polytechnic College in Northern Mindanao.

Mr. Barrado, accompanied by his legal counsel said they went to the Ministry to present himself to the Minister.

Dr. Vernie Ramos, Education Consultant for state universities and colleges advised him to come back with the original copy of his appointment papers adding that he would be sworn in by Education Minister Quilantang after which he can proceed to Metro Ciudad Polytechnic College to take his post. But Barrado has not returned since then, according to Ramos adding that the man did not even bother to present his credentials or tell the circumstances of his endorsement by the President.

"I haven't heard his name from Adam" Ramos who knows the 'who's who' in the academic community, remarked.

The appointment of Barrado, if indeed genuine, has allegedly short-circuited the elaborate selection mechanism set up by Quilantang in replacing incumbent heads of the country's 81 state colleges and universities.

The education minister initiated the formation of local search committees composed of representatives from the school's faculty, administration, alumni, community and local government in identifying qualified persons to replace the incumbents of some SUCs. Carlos Hidalgo

The article was the hot topic of the day. A male staff from the Accounting Office suggested that they should ask media to make their protest known in other parts of the country, Manila specifically. They should categorically state that Barrado's case was the best example. Dr. Granada countered that this was no longer necessary since Minister Quilantang herself guaranteed its authenticity.

When the interest on the news waned, the protesters sat down once again and discussed plans of action to warrant that their concerted efforts to keep Granada as MCPC head succeed at all cost. Each one had his or her own assignment in pushing their agenda to prevent Barrado from coming in and possibly, keep Granada as president of MCPC.

Military Presence in the Campus

Signs of "trouble" brewing were marked by the presence of the military in and around the school premises.

Early in the evening, Capt. Jose Ornano, Company Commander of the 421st PC Command arrived in the campus announcing he was sent by his superior, Col. Jessie Samoza, Constabulary Regional Commander to keep the peace and order in the College while the protest was going on. Also, he wanted to find out if and when Barrado would report officially. The protesters gave him a blank look indicating their annoyance at the uniformed men's presence.

Capt. Ornano assured the protesters that they were not there to stop them from what they're doing, instead, he emphasized that his men will not intervene in their activities nor remove the barricade. Their role, he said, was to see to it that the gates were open to make way for Barrado's entry. He added that it was up to the barricaders to block him if they so wished, provided the gates were open. The captain pointed out that the College as a public institution, should be kept open to allow anyone to come in and out unhindered.

"What if Barrado insists on getting through the barricade?" the protest leaders asked?

"That is up to you to block him or not," Ornano said firmly.

"What would happen if violence occur?" the agitated leaders asked again.

"That's the time when my men will intervene – to prevent violence."

Capt. Ornano, it may be mentioned was a PMA graduate, a lawyer and known to have lucrative business operations in the city of Metro Ciudad and in other cities in Northern Mindanao. He was also infamous for his "cruelty" specially to the poor protesters fighting oligarchs and men in power during rallies. He never made any effort to correct this impression about him. As a matter of fact, he seemed to bask in its connotation— a heartless captain.

Unsatisfied and suspicious of the motive, the group asked the commander if it is possible to arrange for a meeting with Col. Samoza ASAP.

"I'll see what I can do," he promised.

Later, he returned to confirm the appointment with his superior first hour the following Sunday.

DAY 9, SATURDAY, JUNE 7
Media Joined the Fray

Media had a grand day attacking and discrediting the protest movement since it started. Its leaders were subjected to public humiliation and trial by publicity by local reporters, particularly those from radio and TV. Some of their friends in the media who took the neutral position observed that this was not surprising at all since those who controlled air time were close associates or former employees of Barrado. One might recall that he was big in the media circle both in the local and national scene. Hence, one could not underestimate the extent of his influence over this group.

Anastacio Benhur, past president of the Metro Ciudad Press Club, Dolly Gamat of TV-12 *Newscope* and Anabel Borja of TV Channel 6 led the attack against the protesters.

Barrado's media blitz was proving to be quite effective. Its focal spin was that the picketers could never win because Barrado's appointment though signed by Sec. Rayos was actually authorized by the President of the Republic. The idea that this might be revoked by the very person who authorized it was therefore a wild one, a laughing matter.

Two radio stations spoke occasionally for the protesters but they were no match to the daily onslaught that Benhur and his associates directed against Barrado's nemesis. Over time, the suspicion that these media people were actually paid to do their daily broadcasts centering on putting down and maligning the movement was proven true when the College was later billed for these broadcasts.

One radio commentator took the airwaves once in defense of the protestors but was never heard off again.

The most effective "unofficial commentator" on the protesters' side was Tars Lamado, an employee of the College. Tars was a licensed broadcaster. With his short but witty repartees, he attempted to demolish the black propaganda expertly put up against them. As the days of protest went on however, Tars found it difficult to get free radio time. His rising popularity as a fierce and fiery broadcaster was short-lived as his broadcasting career was "nipped in the bud". Like the others involved in the protest movement, Tars was also threatened to shut up or face the consequences.

When the producers of "Weekender", a feature program doing regular broadcast on Saturday mornings over local TV Channel 6 were told they would have Dr. Granada and several of his leaders in the program, the former were less enthusiastic. They had mixed feelings about the interviews. Guests who took the hot seat stated "truths" that were seen as controversial and damaging to some leaders of the College who were there before Granada came to head MCPC.

Dr. Alfredo Marcos, executive director of satellite schools revealed that it was only during the time of Dr. Granada that a specific budget was allotted for these schools which allowed them to function and operate better. He announced that all the deans of each satellite were one and united in rooting for Granada.

Another controversial statement came from Sonny Aquiling speaking in behalf of the personnel association who claimed that it was Dr. Granada who paid attention to the the rank-and-file by providing a grievance machinery where they can articulate and bring forth their work-related concerns to the attention of Management.

Dr. Granada, on the other hand who was supposed to have more "talk time" was intentionally given less camera focus and lesser chances to voice out his side of the story. Once in a close-up shot, the viewers noticed he was calm and composed, a hint of smile on his lips especially when the hosts tried to avoid passing the microphone to him. Despite his diplomatic and passive front, Dr. Granada knew, he was ready to explode!

The interview didn't sit well with EVP Soriano who reacted with resentment to what was said on air by his subordinates. He was already executive vice president when Granada was assigned OIC eight months ago. He warned that unless those statements were recanted, he himself will render them false and malicious over the radio and television in order to "redeem his honor and dignity." He was furious citing that during the pre-Granada's time, he also paid much attention to the satellite schools as well as to the non-academic staff's concerns.

The threat of EVP Soriano brought some kind of crisis to the school's personnel. Fred Marcos couldn't do anything but "eat his own words." He wrote the TV station to "clarify" his previous statement in the manner that his boss wanted it corrected. Sonny Aquiling however, stuck to his original statement.

These actuations of Soriano earned him the ire and annoyance of the protesting community. These amplified their suspicion that he was actually in cahoots with Barrado and his men. His nightly "sorties" with the new president's men were monitored and kept as evidence of his disloyalty to the academic community.

As expected, in the next airing of "Weekender," the hosts were elated to announce Marcos' clarification flashing his face prominently on screen. Afar from his statement, no other statements of substance came out of the tube, not even a gist of what Granada had said during the last episode.

Meanwhile, the interviews on Mr. Barrado and Atty. Gary Daldalen occupied the screen the entire program. Minister Mendel was also asked to comment on the protesters' demand to retain Granada.

"If the protesters can show me a law that requires that a College President must be a Ph.D. holder, I will personally hand carry their protest to the President."

So much for the social transformation through education ideal, a re-education of the heart and mind. It was, without doubt, a big lie, mired in falsity and deceit!

DAY 10, SUNDAY, JUNE 8

Gearing up for the Inevitable

As arranged by Capt. Ornano, the protest leaders motored in three L200s to Camp Alagar on Sunday to meet with the regional commander, Col. Samoza. The Commander informed them that Mr. Barrado was going to take over the College on Friday, June 13 whether they like it or not. He pointed out quite brusquely that they had no choice but to accept the fact that Esteban Barrado will sit as President.

Hearing this, the protestors appealed to the PC commander to ask Barrado to give them (the protesters) time until they could get a response or a reaction from Minister Quilantang. A request for urgent action was already sent to the lady Minister, they told him. He said he can't promise anything but he will try.

In the meantime, the commander pressed for agreements in connection with the on-going protest in order to "make way for a win-win solution for both parties." He was able to get the commitment of the leaders though reluctantly, to lift the barricades and keep the gates open. The protest streamers and posters were to remain in place along the perimeter fence and the main gate.

It was a long, tedious talk that got them somewhere, in the meantime. The headstrong leaders could not be budged to compromise more since the Commander did not offer something in return except a promise that he will try his best to persuade Barrado to give them a little more time.

Of course, it never happened.

The news of the takeover in five days and its possible consequences did not discourage nor frighten the protesting community. In fact, the knowledge compelled them to move with utmost urgency because the date was so close and they had not really prepared for it. Had they not asked for this meeting, they would have been caught by surprise.

Preparations for June 13 were carefully planned in details. A steering committee was to oversee its implementation and ensure everything was in accordance with the plan. Various committees were formed that involved practically the whole constituency (except for some who chose to side with Soriano) in one way or another.

Considering the proximity of the date of the takeover, the protesters decided that several people be sent immediately to Manila to follow up matters with the Education Minister. Anita Caluya, Sonny Aquiling, Joel Lerpa and Dr. Maxwell Dumog were unanimously identified to compose the delegation. Dr. Dumog was included because he personally knew the Minister, had been her student when he took his doctorate at San Carlos University some years back.

In the meantime, the community waited in anxious anticipation for their return.

Talk of the Town

Noli Tejano or Noli T (Remember him? The guy was columnist of *Metropolitan Times* and publisher of *News Express.*) visited the campus and handed Dr. Granada a typewritten copy of his still unpublished "Talk of the Town" column for the week. His article bolstered the hope of everyone, hence hundreds were reproduced which they distributed to people inside and outside of the campus. This pre-empted its publication two days later.

Noli T was not only famous for his wit and infectious sense of humour. He was also recognized for his in-depth political analysis. This was his commentary:

Self-welcome

Maybe if I were Esteban "Steve" Barrado, I would have given up right away the ambition to become president of Metro Ciudad Polytechnic College at the first sign of resistance from the College community for the sake of "delicadeza," you know.

But I'm glad I am not Steve Barrado and he should be happy he is not me! He may insist to be where he is not wanted, and I hope he enjoys it.

On the day Steve was supposed to "take over" Dr. Moises Granada's post as president of the College, his wife reportedly tried to hang streamers welcoming her dear husband gladly to the College supposedly by the faculty, students and employees of the school.

But the ironic thing about it was that the faculty, the students and employees, and parents of the students agreed to form human barricades that will prevent Barrado's entry. It humiliated them that they were dubiously used as legitimate signatories to the "welcome" banners.

They asked Mrs. Barrado to stop putting up the "welcome" streamers as their contents were not true, a blatant lie! Wearing long, straight, unsmiling faces, they told her Steve was not welcome.

I suggest that the loyal wife should instead hang the streamers at Loyola University, that is, if the Jesuits have no objection.

I suspect that the Jesuits want him to be president of this esteemed institution so he would stop messing around Loyola. It must have occurred to them that most job-hunting professors always come home to where they don't belong, especially when they become politicians.

The Conrado Rayos-signed appointment of Steve which was reportedly instigated by the Daldalen brothers and Felino Mendel triggered the protest. The latter was only too happy to support the initiative probably because he knew what it will amount to and what undue embarrassment it could bring to his "friend" Cosme. Unfortunately, it also cuts into the personal pride of Education Minister Quilantang who was obviously bypassed, ignored, belittled and humiliated by such action.

The President of the Republic was more cautious. She deliberately absented herself from the educators' congress in Baguio City precisely to avoid questions that may be raised on the issue, and that she may forget to laugh when she said 'I wish we have never restored academic freedom in the country.' Worse if she also forgot to say 'it's a Comico-joke only.' (Conrado Rayos' middle name is Comico).

Some affected teachers were quoting my pal, Celing Daldalen for reportedly saying that Steve's appointment to the college presidency was a means to show the people of Metro Ciudad and Northern Mindanao that Cosme Daldalen still counts very much with the President of the Republic, obviously to belie Mendel's assessment that Cosme has been 'lameducked' in both the local and national politics.

But then, it wasn't the President who signed the alleged 'appointment' but C. Comico Rayos, little realizing that with a name like that, Comico can go anywhere even to a ladies' room, and say he's only joking! It's up to you to laugh if you have a sense of humor, and be damned if you don't. It's simply enough that Lino Mendel is there, at least, not only with a grin on his face but with a guffaw!

Lino, the wise and astute politician that he is, has probably always known that the presidency of state institutions of higher learning, as well as all high-rank positions in the academe were never part of the political spoils to be won or lost in any election or even revolution.

Degrees of higher learning as basic qualifications for the same were never earned through the polling of votes by an incompetent and corrupt electorate but by cramming the brain with wisdom through years of patient study and burning the proverbial midnight oil so that one may not look misplaced and ridiculous when he becomes president of an educational institution.

That is probably why Mendel was only too glad to join the Daldalen maneuvers, not really because of the fondness of the heart but to kill five or ten birds with one stone and have his sweet revenge at the same time. He draws complete satisfaction from the blushing faces of his political opponent.

And the Daldalens, my God, had walked right into the ILG chief's little trap with all caution thrown to the winds in their eagerness to please Steve who had 'risked his life' during the campaign for the President in the dangerous and bloody 'battlefields' of Loyola University's air-conditioned study rooms and conference halls where one can idle anytime from so much luxury and comfort!

Mabuhay ka, Stevie Baby!

More Deceptions Unveiled

The barricades were lifted temporarily in compliance with the agreement reached between the protesters and the Constabulary Command Chief. The main campus was still full of people despite it being a Sunday. Meetings were held here and there while others who were not in any of the meetings were guarding the streamers and posters still in place across the outer campus fence and the main gates. They were also handing out Noli T's mimeographed article.

Sometime in the afternoon, the PIB issued another bulletin which unveiled another deception, this time involving the professional integrity of Mr. Barrado himself.

Bulletin No. 5

> *We have removed our barricades after getting assurance from Col. Jessie Somoza of the regional command that Mr. Barrado will not seek entry within one week per our agreement. Col. Samoza himself confirmed that Barrado has agreed that he will not take over the campus until after Friday, June 13.*
>
> *Our emissaries composed of Prof. Cauya, Dr. Dumog, Mr. Aquiling and Joel Lerpa left yesterday afternoon to personally see Minister Quilantang and get her official reaction to our pleadings.*
>
> *Meanwhile, this protest continues and we remain vigilant, watchful and prayerful until a definite instruction from Minister Quilantang comes in order to resolve the crisis.*

PS. THIS IS VERY IMPORTANT!
In our meeting with Fr. Nestor Javieto SJ, President of
Loyola University, he DENIED the claim of Barrado that he
recommended him for the presidency of our College. He dared
the Barrado camp to present to him a copy of his endorsement.

The denial of Fr. Javieto that he endorsed Barrado to be MCPC president did not only make the academic community angry it also became a source of embarrassment for those who, in one way or another, were affiliated with the famous Jesuit school. It must be noted that Barrado was still its Director of Graduate Studies on Public Administration and Fr. Javieto, its president.

The discovery of the truth of the matter came about when Dean Luisito Buran, Beth Sebastian and Prof. Caluya went to Fr. Javieto a few days ago to verify Barrado's claim of the friar's endorsement of him. The Reverend denied he ever did, as a matter of fact, dared his alleged protégée to present to him a copy of his (Father Javieto's) endorsement. He, insisted he never did! Was Barrado "messing around with LU" to a point that the Jesuits wanted to get rid of him bringing to mind Noli Tejano's commentary yesterday?

The furor over the controversial role of Loyola University's head on the disputed appointment of Barrado was attracting the attention and curiousity of on-lookers and fence sitters. Rumors spread fast and before they knew it, had become the talk in most households in Metro Ciudad.

A Highly Questionable Offer

Early in the evening of the same day, Dr Granada had an unexpected visitor. A certain Mr. X came to offer him a most unusual proposition. The man was accompanied by another whose name the OIC could not recall. He was sure though that if he would see him again, he would no doubt, remember the guy.

Because there were several people in the small *sala* of the cottage, Mr. X suggested that he and Dr. Granada find a place where they can be alone because what he was going to tell him was "strictly confidential." Moises brought him to his study *cum* sitting room.

As soon as they were inside, Mr. X told Granada point blank that if he wanted an "immediate appointment" to the presidency in question, all he had to do was to follow his instruction: Take the first available flight to Manila in the morning of the following day to see Executive Secretary Rayos bearing his (Mr. X) personal note. He assured him that once Mr. Secretary had read it, the appointment would be his (Granada's) right there and then. Mr. X said he had a talk with the Executive Secretary in the latter's office in the Palace that morning and the moment he got his assurance, "I immediately took the afternoon flight and here I am to tell you the good news!" he expressed delightedly.

Granada's first reaction was to throw Mr. X out of the room but suspected that perhaps there was something deeper than what was on the surface. He pretended to be interested.

Mr. X continued his blabbering thinking he got Granada's interest and attention. He tried to impress him by saying he had long been observing the OIC and found him to be an honest man and a person of integrity. "That's why," he said, "I'd like to help." He boasted knowing well the Executive Secretary being his close friend when they were together at one time in the Philippine Military Academy. "Unfortunately for Rayos," he said, "he did not finish because he did not like the atmosphere there." He also claimed blood relations with Defense chief Juanito Granile allegedly a distant cousin on his mother side bragging that such relationship allowed him to be updated on the overall situation in the region.

Granada asked him about his direct connection with any government agency and asked if this visit was official. He did not answer but wrote his full name, his position and the agency where he worked on a piece of paper. Granada wondered why a man of his "repute" would not even have a simple calling card. Mr. X sensing the OIC's doubt explained unnecessarily that he had been employed in this agency for so many years now but had remained poor because in spite of the open and numerous opportunities and temptations to make a lot of money on the side, he opted to be honest and keep his integrity intact.

"Are you ready to fly tomorrow?" he asked Granada who was surprised at the intensity of his visitor's desire to make him leave MCPC as soon as possible.

Suspecting something really fishy in the man's intention, the OIC begged off in his most diplomatic manner flashing a timid smile saying he could not do that as yet. He said it was simply impossible for him to fly the next day or any day before June 13 because of the problem in the campus. "You're aware of that, aren't you?" He told him that he could not just go straight to the Executive Secretary in the Palace without passing through Minister Quilantang

"Protocol, you know. To do that," he said, "I still have to make an appointment with the Minister before I can have an audience with her. There's no way I will ignore protocol. This is precisely why Barrado got into trouble. I won't repeat his mistake even if I get that appointment tomorrow," he emphasized firmly.

Obviously listening but not convinced, Mr. X said that the OIC should reconsider the offer more seriously. He said all his friends really wanted him to become the president of the distressed College. He left his phone number suggesting that Granada give him a call within the next two days before it's too late.

———————

Two days later Beth received a totally unexpected call from Mr. X. He requested her to convince her boss to leave for Manila the soonest and see the Executive Secretary. He also sort of reminded her that the OIC should bring gifts to Sec. Rayos since this was "normal in getting presidential appointments."

Pretending to be excited for Dr. Granada, Beth asked the man the cash equivalent of these gifts. Without hesitation, he replied that the gifts should not go below six figures and should be more or less equivalent to the "usual SOP" for such important favor

Prior to his call to Beth on June 11, Mr. X sent Granada a note in his own handwriting, indicating that the courier was his son.

The note, unedited, written on an 8 x 11 brown mimeo paper was later shown to his counsel Atty. Gael Padera and Nap Lopa.

Dear Dr. Granada,

I send this note thru my son. Kindly prepare all your accomplishments from the time you assumed office at MCPC to date. Compile them or make xerox copies if possible and put them in a folder consecutively. If there are pictures, please attach some for presentation, justifications etc.

I have already contacted my friend yesterday and last night he confirmed that he is willing to accompany us to personally see Minister Quilantang and the Executive Secretary at the Palace. Please take care of our round trip ticket plus hotel bills and miscellaneous expenses in Manila as well as in Metro Ciudad. And, don't forget the SOP for the ExSec.

Thank you and ask help from God thru Jesus Christ our Lord. Amen.

Very truly yours,

Mr. X wrote his full name and affixed his signature above it.

"Weird." Granada thought. He never revealed this man's real name till the end.

Actually, this letter was no longer necessary. He had dismissed Mr. X as a hoax and had mentally rejected his outrageous offer immediately after he left the cottage on their first and only meeting. However, Dr. Granada kept thinking of Mr. X trying to figure out his role in this drama. If he were not a fixer, then what game was he playing? Was he out to bait him to give up in exchange for the offer? Was he ordered by somebody?

As the conflict was getting more complicated, Granada never saw nor heard from Mr. X again. He was advised not to associate with the man anymore and to avoid him at all cost.

DAY 11, MONDAY, JUNE 9
Students Declared Unequivocal Stand

As was their habit, student leaders Joel Lerpa and Eddie Maguz were regular visitors at the president's cottage. They enjoyed after-school moments with the OIC who was just too happy to sit with them for a healthy intellectual exchange or for a companionable *tete-a-tete*. They exchanged and compared notes and shared stories and experiences. Theirs was a collegial relationship despite their status.

Several other students like Dax Cebal, SSC vice-president, Jimmy Caoili with his camera, and Noel Ramar with his tape recorder would occasionally join them. Bebe Ramar, wife of Noel would also join the group from time to time. Because of her youth, Bebe was often mistaken as a student. In actuality she was employed as an accounting clerk in their school. Noel, on the other hand, was finishing his engineering degree program.

Ever present too during such huddles was Dr. Fe Perida, Director of Student Affairs and SSC adviser.

As the struggle was heightening, Dr. Fe and the student leaders found a reason to become closer. This kind of relationship had somehow influenced others to follow the lead. Teachers bonded well with fellow teachers and the administrative staff. They had also formed a different kind of tie with the students setting aside for a while their status and age difference.

In one meeting at the cottage, the young leaders took note of the unkind and biased treatment media gave to their cause. They were discussing means to counter the false reports media were telling the public. A nerdy-looking voc-tech student, Kiko Solano suggested that a telephone brigade be organized so that if a radio announcer or newscaster fielded fake news, he could immediately be barraged with telephone calls to prove him wrong or to appeal to his sense of fairness and fair play. "This 'conscience game' might do the trick," he said. "But we should be ready to present facts that would negate everything they say about our cause. We should not be caught empty-handed. Facts and truths shall make us free," he added with utmost conviction.

Other concerns brought up were on sustaining the picket lines, keeping everyone's morale up, soliciting help for food and other needs and prayers.

When asked how far the junior and senior students would go in this "battle", their reply was a clear indication of their sincerity and dedication to the mass action: They would not stop until the cause is won.

As the discussions were going on, Gunding Bijonsa, tasked with clipping relevant newspaper articles for the information bureau came with the *Kalayaan* issue of June 9. The newspaper bannered the rally at MCPC. Though the news did not say anything new about the protest and was merely a repetition of previously published articles in the past few days, the protesters still considered it a gain in the sense that a national daily paid them attention. They were overjoyed in knowing that while they were being "slaughtered" in the local media, the national dailies were, at least sympathetic to them.

A City Divided

In the face of tension build up inside the prime college in Metro Ciudad, it cannot be avoided that even people from the outside made their choices and support known. It looked like the situation was no longer confined to the academe, it had actually escalated to become everybody's business.

The stand on the issue taken by Linda Pinyan, first cousin of the Daldalens that joining the fight was a matter of principle rather than of personal relationship was also shared by many of those who actively participated in the picket.

On the other hand, there were also those who were vocal and obvious about their choice: Barrado for president!

EVP Soriano had chosen to openly side with Barrado after it had been established that he was indeed horsing around with the "enemy." Fiscal Jose Alarcon, a prosecutor in the RTC was a strong supporter of Barrado. Gael Padera's cousin who was also in the judiciary was pro-Barrado so were Nap Lopa's many friends in the local media. Several members of the oligarchs have thrown their support to Barrado acknowledging his being home-grown. The Granadas, by the way, were migrants from another city.

One person who was least expected to be on the side of the OIC gave Barrado his biggest disappointment when he declined to help his friend.

Abner Nostares, a known business leader in the city and president of the College alumni association, was not only a good friend of Barrado.

They were classmates too in high school. According to Abs (as he was fondly called) Barrado had, for several times, called him by phone to appeal for his support. His former classmate had reminded him of their happy days together in the past and how they went about doing silly things. Of course, everybody knew that if Barrado got the support of Nostares, it followed that the alumni association will be behind him and that would have made a lot of difference in his bid for acceptability by the academic community.

But Abs, setting aside personal ties had rejected his friend's appeal. In the first place, the alumni association had already endorsed Dr. Granada as early as March. In the second place he believed friendship had nothing to do with the presidency of the College. He was all for "impeccable credentials and everything else that go with it." Without regrets and not offering any apologies for his decision, he advised his friend: "Perhaps, Steve, you should prepare yourself to run for governor of the province later. The College presidency is simply not for you."

Many more stories of opposing nature were told and retold. Metro Ciudad, it seemed was a city divided on this controversial issue.

Pressure on Some VIP Friends

People in power had always wanted to find out the extent of their authority over some individuals. They would normally put pressure on them to get what they want or threaten them to lose the concession of being "privileged."

Some important personalities who were friends of Granada gave in to pressure. If not, they might have lost their jobs.

Census chief Kiyel Landra who was also MCPC's PTA president had asked Granada's permission for a leave of absence saying he would lie low for a while in the association. His reason– he was being pressured by some influential individuals to withdraw his support to the protest. Kiyel was very active in mobilizing the parents in coming up with several worthwhile projects for the school.

Those people knew he can make the PTA throw its support behind Granada and they didn't like it. So, they decided to "touch" him where he was most vulnerable—the prestige of the position he was occupying.

In the last presidential election, the census chief was one of those identified as having campaigned actively for the deposed president. He had denied this several times but admitted having announced to his staff that he was for the former president. He told them that they were free to vote for anyone of their choice based on the dictates of their own convictions. "I had to do that," he explained, "since I was regional director and expected to be with the administration at that time. It was good for you, Moi," Kiyel kept telling Granada "you never made your preference known."

The pressure on Kiyel was similarly felt by other high officials in government who were vocal at first in siding with the protesting community. During several discreet conversations with Granada and the leaders of the picket, these officials expressed that they wanted to openly help him but could not do it anymore. Like Landra, they too, had their jobs and families to worry about.

Snubbed by the Minister?

Later in the day, the protesters got hold of a copy of a letter which Barrado sent to Minister Quilantang and passed it among themselves.

> *June 3, 1986*
> *MINISTER LUCRETIA QUILANTANG*
> *Ministry of Education*
>
> *Dear Minister Quilantang,*
>
> *As required, herewith is a copy of my Oath of Office taken before the Honorable Leon Golez, Minister of Justice.*
> *I would have very much wanted to take my oath before you but I had to rush back to Metro Ciudad after I received my appointment papers because of a very urgent personal problem.*
> *I went back to Manila as soon as I was free hoping I could see you and take my oath, but your staff informed me I*

had to wait for several days before I could have an audience with you. However, I decided that I had to assume office immediately and so requested Minister Golez who graciously accommodated me.

I want to assure you that I shall do justice to the appointment and, within my powers and authority, translate the vision and goals of the President and our new administration into reality.

Like the numerous major changes that our President is instituting throughout the country, I'd like to follow her example. However, I am facing huge resistance from the College constituency, but I assure you, Ma'am, I am on top of the situation.

I hope to see you as soon as I can and give you a progress report on the situation at MCPC. Warmest regards.

Sincerely yours,
(SGD) ESTEBAN BARRADO

Those who had read this letter concluded that the way Barrado phrased his letter implied that he was actually "snubbed" by the Education Minister.

They saw a glimmer of hope in this.

DAY 12, TUESDAY, JUNE 10
Letter to the Students

From his private residence, Barrado wrote a very long letter to the students of the College. It was a muddled kind of missive where he appealed for their sympathy and support on one hand, boasting his qualifications and accomplishments on another, crowded it with his plans and strategies on how he would run the school. Implicitly, this letter was also his counter to the June 6 *Metropolitan Times* article on "fake appointments bugging the Ministry" that was freely circulated on campus the past week. Hundreds of copies were handed out to students who were at that time, enrolling for the incoming semester.

Many who had read it commented dryly when they saw how the letter was composed—lacking in deference and courtesy and failed miserably in its attempt to sound honest and sincere, aside from the fact that it was definitely wanting in coherence, unity and conciseness, and obviously, good editing.

My dear students,

Welcome back to school and to our College!

*First of all, I wish you to know that the new President of the Republic has **terminated** the services of Dr. Moises Granada as officer-in-charge of the College and appointed me as your new College President. I took my Oath of Office before the Honorable Minister of Justice on June 2 and thereupon immediately assumed the College Presidency.*

On behalf of the President and in my behalf, I wish to thank Dr. Granada for his eight months of service which I understand was admirably efficient. I congratulate him for a job well done.

Let me now inform you of what we are doing and some of the things we intend to do in the immediate future.

I have formed a Task Force composed of volunteers who have my trust and confidence. This Task Force shall discuss with the heads of all the academic and administrative units the best ways and means to effect a smooth transition from the old administration to the new. The Task Force members shall also prevent any possible attempt by anyone to disrupt, or in any way hamper the normal functioning of the College and its various units. They will insure that during the transition all college properties shall be safeguarded, documents and records secured. They will see to it, above all, that the interest of the students will be protected.

I am sure you are aware that there are efforts by a number of faculty members and administrative staff to question the decision of the President to appoint me. This group wants to do everything to stir up trouble. They have been feeding students and the faculty and even the public with wrong information to turn everyone against my appointment and my Presidency. They may even plan to prevent the holding of classes in order to dramatize and attract attention to themselves and create a climate of instability to embarrass our new President and her administration. They want Minister Lucretia Quilantang to be angry with the President. They want to discredit Minister Lino Mendel, former congressman Cosme Daldalen, all the new government's leaders in our area who have given their faith, confidence and trust in me and believe in my worthiness to the position and my ability to administer the State College effectively and successfully.

I know I still have to earn your trust and confidence in me. So far you do not know who I really am. I am very confident, however, that given enough time, given the same support and cooperation you gave to all past presidents and OICs I shall not fail.

My confidence springs from my track record as educator and leader of men starting as a young faculty member of the prestigious Loyola University, as College Dean, as University head of a graduate Studies in Public administration, as graduate school professor in management, and for many years head of a national office with an equivalent rank of Deputy Minister, and officer of many national organizations and nationwide movements and programs for many years in Manila.

I am told many of you think that I am not qualified to become College President because I was once a TV-newscaster. I do not see anything wrong with having volunteered to do the local TV newscast for a few years here in our City. I think I did rather well, even in that job, too.

I am told that some teachers and administrators are against me because they are Protestants and I am Catholic. I am sorry they have to drag religion as an issue in running this school which ought never to be an issue in a State College where all religions must be respected.

I am told they do not want me because I am only from Metro Ciudad. I want to tell them I am proud to be a Metro Ciudanon and I claim to be worthy of higher positions in the government.

I am told that some do not like me as President because I graduated only from Loyola University. I finished my master's degree at the University of Sto. Tomas in Manila. I also finished my undergraduate course at Loyola University and I am proud of this fact. And I believe Loyola graduates can become good Presidents. In fact, I believe that, brilliant graduates from our city's colleges like CCC, COC, and Liceo or on our own State College should not be disqualified from becoming State College Presidents now or in the future.

I am told that teachers and administrators do not want to accept me because I am an appointee of the new government and they want to retain the OIC appointee of the old regime. I am sorry for them but the men of the old regime have to go because the new President is convinced that she cannot give them her trust and confidence.

These protesters say I am not qualified for the position because I am not a Ph.D. holder. The truth is the President and her Education Minister carefully studied the matter before appointing me. Presidential appointees, like cabinet ministers, regional directors, presidents of state colleges and the like, are chosen through only one fundamental qualification — that the President of the country believes the appointee is the best man for the job, and the President is convinced that her men can best help translate the vision and goals of her administration.

I was told that they are against my appointment because I was deputy campaign manager of the party of the present government in the province. I do not see anything wrong with that. I am proud and happy that I risked my life in helping end the old dictatorial rule and usher in a new era in our nation. And if the new President wants me to be part of her administration and be her representative in running MCPC, I thank her most sincerely and pledge to be worthy of her trust.

I am told that many are afraid that I will be vindictive towards those who are opposing my assumption. Being only human, I certainly am not happy with what they have done. But I will never make any decision against anyone who exercise his/her God-given right to express dissent. Only those who persistently and stubbornly continue to commit illegal activities, disrupt the normal functioning of the College, do harm to our personnel and students, damage school properties or continuously disobey our orders, will be meted out punishment. Other than these, we must allow for human error. We must let bygones be bygones. Forgive and forget.

Let me also say that the idea of having a new College President, and my appointment as such, is precisely to effect change. Therefore there will be change.

While the past administrators have done many excellent things, there remains a lot of improvements to do. We need more equipment and facilities. We need better trained and more effective instructors. We need to be more careful in the use of our funds.

Existing facilities, like the gym must be better managed to allow for more use by the people, by the youths in the City's barangays, but most especially by our own students. It should not be preserved only for some special privileged few.

Our curriculum needs to be restudied and modified so that the skills acquired by our students in the College will truly match the exact skills needed by industries here and abroad.

The highest office, especially the Office of the President should be closer to the students. They should talk with them and listen to them more often. We have to contrite more substantially to the progress of our community, our city and our region. Indeed, we have to do many, many things for the State College which were not done before.

With your support, your cooperation, and your prayers, and with God's help, we will succeed.

Thank you, and give my love and warmest regards to your parents and to all your loved ones.

Sincerely yours,
(Sgd) ESTEBAN BARRADO
President

How would the new president feel had he seen copies of his letter crumpled, trashed, cut into pieces and strewn all over the campus? It could have been a sight enough to make one feel so small, so insignificant, so worthless.

The students vowed they would give him a reply he'd rather not have. They felt, as they finished reading it that there were a lot of wrinkles, inconsistencies and many statements needed to be refuted. They were not only misleading, full of unfounded accusations, but largely threatening in a way. These young men and women also noted that he had put a lot of imagination into his letter to win their sympathy.

"He won't get an inch of victory from us," they promised each other. "Never!"

———

The Daldalens' Might

It was a given.

The Daldalens were a force to contend with in this part of the country. The brothers triumvirate had a name recall that stuck among the marginalized electorate, hence, the sacred votes were theirs for the taking, No sweat!

To the protesters' mind, the leader of the Mindanao Advancement Party was undoubtedly the real person behind Mr. Barrado taking the post. Well for one, they've heard this truth straight from the horses' mouth when Cosme's brother Celing visited the OIC in his office a few days ago. It was an expose' that didn't shock anyone any more. However, the greater public must know of this "unholy alliance" and decided to come out with a strongly worded open letter to the brothers. It contained among others, the circumstances behind Barrado's appointment underscoring Cosme's role in this. The protesters also mentioned about their observation that Barrado could not be seen in public without Gary Daldalen and some stalwarts of the Party in tow. That Gary was the new president's legal counsel was only incidental. Their association reeked of political stench more than anything else, the protesters were certain.

After the much-vaunted participation of the oldest Daldalen in the case, he was seldom seen nor heard off often in Metro Ciudad. No, he did not go low key. As a matter of fact, he soared like an eagle conquering new horizons, this time, the venerated SAMI board room.

Having carved a name for himself in the past Congress as a staunch opposition, Cosme Daldalen was recently awarded a much-coveted director's seat in the Board of Directors of SAMI Corporation, the biggest food and beverage conglomerate in the country. As director he enjoyed the perks of a big-time mogul like a free Mercedes Benz, an unimaginable allowance, tons of beer and food. Since he stayed most of the time in Manila and had no direct hand in what was going on in Metro Ciudad he may had not known what his brothers were actually up to. Should he be included in the letter?

The protestors all agreed that Cosme should not be spared since it was he who endorsed Barrado to the President, not to forget that he was the president and chairman of MAP.

June 10, 1986

Atty. Cosme B. Daldalen
Atty. Cecilio B. Daldalen
Atty. Gerardo B. Daldalen
Daldalen, Daldalen and Daldalen Law Office
Jose P. Rizal St., Metro Ciudad

Gentlemen:

We have received word from Minister Lucretia Quilantang that she is sympathetic with our cause. After getting such encouragement, we met as a community and affirmed once and for all that we cannot accept Mr. Esteban Barrado as President of this College. Please convince him to withdraw from assuming the presidency of MCPC for the good of every one.

We wonder how a man of his self-proclaimed reputation and integrity could stand the disdain and intolerance shown to him by the students, the faculty, staff and unit heads of this school. He had called the deans and unit heads to a conference at Garden Restaurant, first last night, June 9, and then today, June 10, and not one had shown up, a clear manifestation of our abhorrence to his undesirability as MCPC's next head. We assure you Sirs that we stand united and firm in this decision especially now that we have the support of many friends as you must have heard and known first hand.

Sirs, you had our support when you worked relentlessly for the election of the new President of the Republic. We were not few. Our number was big believing we should be with you all the way during your campaigns, and we did. We took part in the renewal hoping it will lead the change in the country for the better. We do not want to think that we were wrong and all our efforts were wasted on this new government. Unwise and un-thought of appointments to key positions were telling us otherwise. This has been common knowledge since the haste by which officials of the old government were being replaced was worrying the citizens of this country.

It saddened us to know that you were more than willing participants in this untested scheme of complete overhaul of government regardless of good performance by the incumbent. While we agree that there was indeed a need to cleanse the ranks of the undesirables, there should have been at least, a systematic and fair method of choosing who should go and who should stay.

And Dr. Moises Granada is among those who should definitely stay.

We therefore reiterate our ardent request for you to prevail upon Mr. Esteban Barrado to give up the presidency which should have not been his in the first place. The integrity of his appointment has been tainted and dubbed spurious hence, invalid.

We trust that you realize that this appeal is for the greater good. Discovering an error and rectifying it is not a sign of weakness but of strength and magnanimity. We hope this does not fall on deaf ears.

Our profound respect and best regards.

That same afternoon, Noli Tejano and Robert Fernan, a reporter from *News Express* came to see Dr. Granada to warn him that the regional command personnel will not only escort Mr. Barrado when he enters the campus on June 13 but that his military entourage will not leave him until he's seated on the presidential chair inside the President's Office. They added that the military men assigned to accomplish the job even sounded tough and confrontational when they tried to ask some questions.

The "bad" news of Noli T sent shivers to those who heard it, except for Granada who looked unperturbed. He was ready for anything, he told them.

Why would the military get so deeply involved in the conflict in the College?

Were there some interests at stake?

The protesters surmised it must have something to do with a ranking officer's clandestinely-operated security agency which was interested to take over the security operations in the College. It could only happen if Barrado sits on "that chair."

"Why don't we denounce him to the Defense Minister?" some of the protesters suggested.

"We don't have the proof yet. This will all be allegations and might boomerang on us if we act indiscriminately," Granada reminded his men. "We'll wait and see what happens," he said.

"Sir was right, it will be difficult to prove the interest angle not to mention the repercussions of challenging a high-ranking military officer who certainly has strong connections not only in the military but in the business sector as well," they all agreed.

The day ended leaving many of the protesters edgy and anxious. Will the takeover be bloody? They fervently hoped not and took their posts in the picket line believing in their hearts that what they were doing was not an exercise in futility.

DAY 13, WEDNESDAY, JUNE 11
Financial Disbursements Dilemma

As soon as business hours commenced at eight in the morning, the Manager of the Republic Bank in Metro Ciudad went to see the head officer of the Budget Management Office confiding that he was confused as to who really was the person in authority at MCPC. Was it the incumbent Dr. Moises Granada or the newly-appointed Mr. Barrado? He informed the BMO chief that three days ago, Mr. Barrado and his lawyer furnished his bank with a copy of the latter's appointment papers and filed a notice that effective immediately Esteban Barrado will be the person authorized to transact business with RB as regards depositing and withdrawing funds for and in behalf of the College. The notice also indicated that all payments be suspended until after financial responsibilities have been officially transferred to his care. On the other hand, the manager mentioned that Atty. Gael Padera, the school's Legal Counsel also came to him insisting that Dr. Granada was still the person in charge since there was no formal turnover yet adding that an attestation would surely be required by the Treasury Department.

The bank chief insinuated he was being pressured by Barrado's men and said that he will file an inter-pleader so that it would be up to the court to determine who had the authority. "That way, we don't have to be saddled with this case," he said almost exasperatedly.

The manager was on his way out when he met Jun Ilio the College cashier on the hallway. He came in with a wide grin announcing excitedly that the Treasury Department just notified Barrado that his application for deputization could only be acted upon if his specimen signature card had been authenticated by the Education Minister. At this point, it was clear to the bank and the BMO that bank transactions remained on status quo which meant it could not grant Mr. Barrado's earlier request to suspend disbursement of the general fund including salary payment of all personnel of the College. Doing so would be breaking National Bank's rule on suspension. Granada remained the authorized disbursing officer.

The Picket Information Bureau came out with Bulletin No. 6 highlighting Barrado's issue with the bank.

Bulletin No. 6

Mr. Barrado tried to impose financial sanction against the protesting academic community by requesting the Treasury Department to suspend disbursement of the general fund. This request, if granted will stop, among others, payment of salaries of all personnel. We learned that the Treasury Officer turned it down following the rules on suspension. Disbursement can only be suspended if there is an overdraft by the College. Since there is no overdraft, disbursement will continue.

Barrado also applied for deputization as countersigning officer of TVAA checks. When authorized, he can control our financial disposition. But again, he learned that this application can only be approved on two conditions: (1) If he can present his original appointment and the appointment of Dr. Granada cancelled or surrendered, (2) his specimen signature card is authenticated by no less than the Education Minister.

Based on his latest actions, Barrado was bent on accomplishing two things: Cut off the life-blood of the college employees by suspending salaries; and familiarize himself with the rules on the disbursement of public funds.

*This fresh move appeared calculated to cause panic among
us and force us into submission. But instead of intimidating
us the scheme only galvanized our militancy and tightened
our resolve to go on with the protest.*

*Recent developments showed that although there is likely
a possibility of a Barrado takeover, we will win in the end.*

Onward to victory. We shall overcome!

While the ruling of the Treasury Department was clear, there was no doubt that the latest move of Barrado and his lawyer to cut off the "life-blood" of the employees had caused a wave of panic on mostly everyone.

"What if he finally succeeds?" they asked in apprehension.

Thankful that the Treasury was temporarily on their side, they however, kept thinking that the new president could employ means to coerce them into submission. Certainly, there were devious ways he could get back at them. What if he finally wins this fight?

Surprisingly, many, especially those holding middle level positions said they were not bothered at all and were ready to go if need be.

Rose Guino, the librarian, said it didn't matter. She could easily get another job.

Fely Cabale the sports director intimated that the change might actually be good for him. He could go back to his home province and live a more peaceful life. Bonifacio Letran, Chief of Budget and Finance, said he was all set to till his small farm if worse comes to worse. Others too claimed they were ready to leave rather than serve the man they could not respect.

The great majority who were wholly dependent on their jobs in the College were extremely worried though they did not admit it. They were beginning to be torn apart by the suspense of waiting.

The possibility of losing one's job and its consequences was the recurring topic of talks among them that lasted until late in the evening. The indication that they were vexed could be seen on the expression on their faces. Should they leave the picket line and join the other side because it seemed the most logical alternative to ensure they still have a life after the protest?

Doug Lustre was silently observing his fellow protesters all along and felt they were slowly losing their comrades to fear and anxiety. Casting his eyes on the ceiling he exclaimed in utter dismay: "The most stupid rats are those which leave the ship which is not sinking."

Some people sitting on the cold, cemented ground turned to him and frowned after realizing what he just blurted out. Others whispered to each other asking what Doug meant by that. The rest vigorously nodded their heads in agreement. They know they have to stick together, be in it together.

An older faculty member offered a rejoinder: "The most intelligent rats are those which never leave a ship which is not sinking for as long as there is food in its kitchen."

His message was loud and clear and the anxious among them covertly agreed letting out a long sigh. The signs of a house facing an inevitable division were already apparent.

Sparks of Inspiration

Since the start of the picket, scores of visitors would come to see Dr. Granada and offered help, gave advice on what he could possibly do legally under the circumstances. Atty. Ildefonso Taburan and wife were concerned parents of a twin both enrolled in the high school department of the College. The lawyer asked Dr. Granada why he was not filing an injunction to inhibit Mr. Barrado from coming in on June 13 as announced. The OIC saw the merit of his observation and requested that he sit with Atty. Padera to discuss in details what can be done.

Several friends brought food and contributed money to help sustain the movement. Others came to simply sit with Dr. Granada and his leaders to raise their morale by bringing real news from reliable sources. It seemed, Barrado was occupied feeding fake news to crush the protesters' spirits. But the presence of their allies from the outside was like a breath of fresh air that boosted their resolve to go on despite the looming threat of disengagement from the cause by many of the protesters.

Sometimes, people who looked insignificant and had little to offer to the cause turned out to be sparks of inspirations to those who were in the middle of the action.

The burden of serving snacks, dinner or lunch to stream of guests as well as the hungry protesters fell on six student assistants working in the College Cafeteria. Mimi, Rose, Annaliza, Gloria, Mira and Tere were always prompt to serve and did their work as if their life depended on it.

Cleaning Dr. Granada's cottage so that it would look spic and span the next day was the duty of three student assistants working in the Practice House. Alma was in-charge of keeping the sala clean and dusted while Jemima and Elizabeth took turns in cleaning the toilet. These young women knew they were doing something good for their beloved school in general and to Dr. Granada in particular.

Were they worried about the eventual takeover of Barrado on June 13?

"No, we are not worried. You'll find us in the frontline," they expressed proudly.

What would happen if they get hurt?

"We'll see to it that we won't get hurt. But if we do then there's the infirmary to go to for treatment," Jemima answered seriously.

What if Barrado succeeds and they would lose their assistantships?

"Oh...we could always look for part-time jobs somewhere else," the girls chorused.

What if they would be made to stay?

"Oh, that would be nice. But we won't cook for Barrado nor clean this cottage for him."

Then they would giggle together as if everything was a joke. Sometimes guests would tease them about having boyfriends.

"Definitely not! This is not the time for boyfriends. This is the time to fight for a worthy cause!"

But how long would they fight?

"Until we win!"

Light at the End of the Tunnel

"Take courage. The fight isn't over yet. With the support and sympathy we're getting, we see light at the end of the tunnel. Our efforts won't be in vain."

This was the closing statement of Bulletin No. 7 that once again resuscitated the despairing movement. Everyone took the news with new hope and a renewed faith to their leaders. "Never give up!" they promised themselves.

The bulletin also acknowledged a few more individuals who had openly extended help and sympathy to protesters, among them city councilor Luz Banal, Dick Lapacio, the jeepney drivers association, prominent businessmen Sigmund Lee, Carlos Siao and many others who certainly believed in the cause. Their wholehearted assistance and willingness to assist belied Barrado's contention that the protest was a lost cause.

It may be mentioned that councilor Banal was fearless in her stinging comments against the aggressor while on-air publicly declaring her thoughts favorable to the picketers. Dick Lapacio was consistent in his defense of the protesters mentioning without fail that Dr. Granada was "under house arrest by the picketers themselves" which drew laughter and appreciation from the protestors knowing he was taunting the opposite camp. Noli Tejano was of course the "Talk of the Town" columnist who from Day 1 of the protest was there to give a fair coverage of the situation. His pun about the love-hate relationship of the Daldalens and Mendel topped his bevy of stories on the protest.

Rubber magnate Sigmund Lee was a volunteer radio announcer handling the "Bantay ng Bayan" program. He was clearly in sympathy with the protesters and was one of the very first media men to present the side of the protesting community objectively in his program last June 8. Mr. Carlos Siao known in the city as the "Ralph Nader" of Metro Ciudad for waging "a one-man war" against a local electric company was relentless in his advocacy. He delivered a fiery speech against political interference before members of the academic community earlier. These people and many more had made the protesters bolder and more eager to continue with the fight.

Threat of a P1.5 M "scandal"

Late in the afternoon, a member of the Picket Information Bureau went around showing a national news report that seemed friendly to the protesting community as it lashed on political interference by some with ulterior motives.

The *Kalayaan* article turned out to be a temporary relief, for in the evening's local broadcasts, some newscasters were feasting on a "scoop" peddled by the supporters of the incoming president– that the new president was readying himself to investigate a "P1.5 million scandal" in the College. Alleged nefarious appropriation was discovered, according to his men, by Mr. Barrado when he did an "unofficial examination" of the College's financial report allegedly submitted to a certain government bureau. It was alleged that the P1.5 million was released by the College administration for "electioneering purposes" in aid of the deposed president's bid for re-election.

"They're crazy," Bonnie Letran howled. "We don't even have enough for maintenance and operating expenses! Where would the College get that P1.5 million? And he has not even laid his hands on any official records of the school to make such allegations. That's preposterous!" exclaimed Letran whose face was red in anger. This rage over the obviously concocted lies was shared by everyone. They decided, a charge should be immediately filed against Barrado for this malicious imputation.

But Dr. Granada was as always, calm and seemingly unaffected by the news.

"Let them commit more mistakes." He simply said when asked.

This passiveness of Granada over an accusation serious enough to cause him to go on a rampage, puzzled a lot of his faculty members and staff personnel. Teacher Vilma Dogan had started to quietly tag her boss "Anemic." Why couldn't he stand up and rebut all the false accusations against him, that he was a PMN through and through, that he was a usurper, and that he had caused the illegal release of millions of pesos to support his political party during the last election? Why did he always say, as they tried to imitate his faint American accent, to "let them commit more mistakes?" What solution can this statement offer to solve the problem, they would ask.

"Isn't *granada* a Spanish word for an explosive device that can blow up the enemy's bunker into smithereens?" Vilma would say with a wry smile, "Why, our Granada is a dud!"

The sentiment that Granada should fight in the open was not, by the way, confined to his people on campus. Some well-meaning friends in the city who were also friends of the other man urged him that it was time he should stop acting the role of a gentleman academician and start playing his opponent's game. He should now stand up and fight.

"Some people are beginning to believe that you must be guilty because of your silence," their voices edged with unintended mockery. "We are disturbed."

In truth, Granada had wanted to react since day 1 but kept his temper in check. He used to be like Jeremiah of the Old Testament, shouting at the top of his voice, displaying his scary side. But this was the time, he felt, when silence was the most powerful statement of all. "When your enemy takes the role of an aggressor, you have to play the role of the underdog," he said ironically. "You must not even dignify his attacks with a response."

Later when he was all by himself, he thought that perhaps, he needed some diversions…to blur his thoughts, dull his pain and quiet his fears.

"Tessa!"

He never felt so alone thinking about his wife and family so far away from him. They could have provided the cushion to buffer the pain of this struggle.

DAY 14, THURSDAY, JUNE 12
Mass Leave

June 12 was Independence Day, a national public holiday. Yet, everyone was in the campus and for a good reason.

Because of the impending take over they knew would probably happen the following day, the protesters met with their OIC early that morning to request that they be allowed to go on an emergency mass leave of absence starting on the supposedly day of take over till next week to avoid being charged with abandonment of duty. Their anticipated participation in defense of their school would have to be done in their own personal time. The leaders did not only invoke the legality of it but the moral side of it.

Dr. Granada was fully aware of the rising level of distress, the sea of anxiety enveloping the community. They needed a respite from the mounting pressure. He approved the request.

Without wasting time, PIB issued Bulletin No. 8 headlining the anticipated mass leave of faculty and staff.

Bulletin No. 8

On Mass Leave

Close to 200 faculty members and non-teaching personnel of the College have filed emergency leaves of absence to protest the announced takeover by Mr. Barrado tomorrow, Friday, June 13. This move will dramatize the vehement objection of the academic community to the ascent of Mr. Barrado to the presidency. Hopefully, this mass action will paralyze the operation of our school and render it non-functional on his first day. In a meeting yesterday, the community reaffirmed its conviction not to recognize Barrado as the new president.

We take this opportunity to thank the Governor and the City Mayor for their gestures of support to our cause. In our separate meetings with them, the two leaders expressed their concern over possible consequences of Barrado's probable

forcible entry into the College. They promised to help to
ensure peace and order and avoid any untoward incident.
  We also appeal to Atty. Gerardo "Gary" Daldalen to
keep out of the controversy which does not involve him.

"What a way to celebrate Freedom Day!" Dr. Granada said to himself
after reading the bulletin.

Media's View on Mendel-Daldalen "Liaison"

The Manila-based broadsheet *Metropolitan Times* carried an article by
columnist Lolita Mercado featuring the presidential squabble at MCPC.

Nap and Moises noted that while Noli Tejano "exposed" the behind-
the-scene differences between Minister Mendel and Cosme Daldalen in
his column last June 7, Mercado explored the political motive of the two
in coming together.

Her article centered on the unspoken rift between the high profiled
personalities despite their apparent complicity to get Barrado the plum
appointment. She wrote:

> *Former Assemblyman Cosme Daldalen and Interior*
> *Minister Felino Mendel for once agreed on endorsing one*
> *appointment, that of Esteban Barrado, but the result is still*
> *trouble.*
>   *Why are Daldalen and Mendel involved in this case?*
> *Because both know that the College is a potent political hold.*
> *Its sphere of influence is wide. It has seven extensions in*
> *strategic areas in three provinces in Northern Mindanao.*
> *With such huge base, their "future" with MCPC could not*
> *be taken for granted. And the clamor for credit should be met.*
> *Who should be considered highly instrumental is now the*
> *point of controversy. Should it be Daldalen whose political*
> *clout enabled him to pick out Barrado and worked hard*
> *for his acceptance by Her Excellency or is it Mendel whose*
> *position carried the weight for Steve?*

In the meantime, was Granada ever consulted by Quilantang? Sources said that the two met several times to try to figure out what to do with the situation. He was reported to have been offered by the minister four options – a national position in the ministry and three posts in big universities elsewhere. But it seems, he has not made up his mind yet. Still hoping for a shot at MCPC?

In fairness to Barrado (who was not available for comment), he is not without credentials. He is the director of Loyola University's master in public administration program. What the faculty and students are protesting is his having sought the intercession of politicians and for grossly violating the MCPC's Board-approved criteria not to mention the Quilantang's new set of procedure for selecting the head of any state-owned institution of higher learning. And yes, they all believed, he is not qualified.

Anita Caluya and the party she headed flew in from Manila via the afternoon flight. Everyone wanted to hear about the outcome of their "mission". They hardly had a minute to breathe when they were bombarded with questions.

Their mission to seek Minister Quilantang's intervention completely and utterly failed. While the lady Minister was sympathetic, she offered no solution to the problem but suggested that they instead see Interior chief Felino Mendel and Cosme Daldalen who, the minister emphasized, were responsible and therefore the key to solving the problem they themselves created.

The group expressed disappointment at how easily the education head dismissed them after a few minutes of audience with her.

They were asking themsekves: "Was the Minister washing her hands off the case like Pontius Pilate did to Jesus?"

Realizing that Dr. Quilantang will not be of immediate help the three decided to find Minister Mendel believing that he would be more in a position to reverse the situation.

"We kept our fingers crossed," said student leader Joel.

The search for the Minister wasn't easy. They contacted his main Office in Quezon City but none from his staff was willing to tell his whereabouts. Next they tried looking for him in his other office in Green Valley only to be informed that he had not reported for several days. The three even risked calling up the Palace but the phone just kept on ringing.

"In our desperation, we decided to go to church. Praying might change our luck," Anita said. "The nearest church where we were at that time was a chapel along Katipunan. And guess who we met on our way in? City administrator Tony Sello and his wife Mayet. We were happy seeing someone we know and so we talked briefly," she added.

"After knowing that we were desperately trying to find Mr. Mendel, they told us that Sir Tony had recently talked with him over the phone and learned that the Minister was in his home in Taguig getting ready to leave for America that evening," informed Dr. Dumog.

"So we rushed to Taguig after getting his address from Sir Tony, and luckily for us we got there before he left for the airport," Joel said with a tinge of pride in his voice.

"*Galing!*" chorused their listener. "*Tapos?*"

"We were panicking while trying to locate his house and had to take several jeepney rides before getting there. It was like, we won't ever find it," confessed Anita.

Once in the house, they begged to be heard. The old man was kind enough to give them half an hour and snacks of a bottle of coke and *Skyflakes.*

They briefed the Minister on what was happening in the College impressing on him that time was of the essence. The minister was non-committal, however, he wrote two notes – one addressed to Mr. Barrado and the other, to the Regional Commander Col. Jessie Samoza.

"Keep them confidential," he ordered the three.

As they were about to leave, Minister Mendel asked if there was a way he could meet Dr.Granada. "How could I be of assistance, if I don't even know Dr. Granada?"

Caluya volunteered to have him meet the OIC at his convenience, that is, if and when the Minister wishes. She's certain Dr. Granada would be glad to meet him after his return from the US.

"That won't be necessary. I could always meet him when I go home to Metro Ciudad," the older man said brushing off Anita's offer.

The three-man team did not divulge the content of the notes to the protesters but disclosed them to Dr. Granada when they talked to him alone.

The note addressed to Mr. Barrado in the Minister's own handwriting said:

> *Steve Barrado*
> *(Confidential)*
>
> *Dear Steve,*
>
> *Please hold your assumption of the state College presidency – until the controversy is resolved peaceably through the President's intercession.*
> *Perhaps, a delay until the end of the month will not prejudice anything.*
>
> *Salamat,*
> *Lino*

The second note addressed to Col. Samoza basically had the same content except that he mentioned asking Barrado to hold in abeyance his assumption into office in the hope that a peaceable resolution of the conflict can be attained.

Anita and the two men knew they broke the confidentiality of the notes but admitted they couldn't help taking a sneak peak at the unsealed notes.

The note was personally delivered at Barrado's residence by the three. As soon as he read it, he was silent and became thoughtful momentarily, tried to keep his composure, and told the "bad news bearers" that he would not honor the request while pacing the expanse of his verandah restlessly muttering. "No, I can't honor this."

Before the three left Barrado's house they made sure they had an evidence that the latter got the note personally.

They motored next to Camp Alagar, asked to see Col. Sanoza who, they were told was indisposed. They handed the note to his aide and asked that it should reach the colonel as soon as possible emphasizing that the letter came from Minister Mendel.

With their mission accomplished, they went back to the campus finding their co-protesters cautiously jubilant over the "good news."

"They knew! How come?" Anita wondered aloud.

"Of course it won't be kept a secret for long," replied Dr. Dumog who sat among the male faculty members.

Until late in the evening, speculations centered on whether or not Barrado would honor the instruction of the Minister.

"He really had no choice since he is Mendel's godson," commented an engineering faculty.

This was the first time that Granada heard of the relationship. The information was backed by some who claimed they were present and had witnessed the wedding of Barrado and his wife some years ago and surely Metro Ciudad mayor then Felino Mendel was among the principal sponsors.

"How can he refuse his *Ninong*," they asked, "especially now that he is the Interior minister?"

A few expressed skepticism. They doubted that Barrado will give in to his godfather's request. They knew the Daldalens and their hold on Barrado. Most likely the threat to enter the campus by force when necessary would surely happen as scheduled.

"What would be the political implications if they force their way in tomorrow?" someone asked. "What will become of the newly-forged Daldalen-Mendel coalition?"

"Back to square one," Nap Lopa opined. "Like water and oil, again."

DAY 15, FRIDAY, JUNE 13

Campus Under Siege

The campus was a beehive of activities as early as five o'clock in the morning. Faculty members, administrative staff and students were busy running to and fro, doing some errands or manning some posts. A group was securing possible entrances from the rear of the campus while barbed wires were being installed to strengthen Gates 1 and 2 out front facing the busy Recto Avenue.

Believing that the oval in the middle of the campus could possibly be used as point of entry using a military helicopter, chairs, tables and other obstacles were strewn all over to prevent landing. School vehicles were parked alternately between the rows of obstacles to assure that there was no space wide enough for the chopper to land safely. Drivers Nonie Sabal and two others were figuring out how to outrun the helicopter between the rows of obstacles in case it insisted on landing. Since last night, rumors got around that Samoza's men would bring in Barrado using a military chopper.

"No way!" the men said.

Heart-shaped stickers with the words "I love Granada" were distributed and worn by the protesters. Some wore improvised cartolina caps with the same signage.

Fely Cobala and four others were assigned to man the public address system installed on the roof of the College gymnasium. From there, the 8.5-hectare main campus, the circumferential road and the road network around it could be seen without obstruction. They were also equipped with a powerful telescope.

Prof. Caluya and Joel Lerpa alternately handled another PA system on the ground just behind Gate 1.

Some of the men led by Romy Ramar were practicing how to resist incoming intruders. Three rows deep, with their arms interlinked one to another moved in unison forward and backward to simulate incoming pressure and apply counter force by moving forward together.

Some female students and faculty members wanted to join but they were discouraged from doing so. "Stay on the sideline and do some delaying tactics," they were ordered.

Someone even suggested that the small children of the faculty and staff be brought to man the frontlines to halt the offensive group from forcing themselves in when they see the children. But Granada outrightly rejected the idea since it was too risky for the children and may endanger their lives.

Angelo Belen and Susing Onyok were practicing moving the forklift while Engr. Eric Talbi was assigned to take care of the acetylene torch to repair locks of the gates in case they were broken.

Note that despite the threat of an impending trouble, visitors, mostly students enrolling and their parents were being received and entertained. It was business as usual and members of the academic community, though on official leave, tried to downplay the escalating tension they were feeling. Chairs were arranged and the staff helped visitors to their seats.

Robert Mison and his group of 12 saw to it that Gates 1 and 2 were reinforced with steel rods and barbed wires. The women looked after the placards, posters and streamers prominently displayed in the right places while students distributed protest fact sheets to visitors and curious on-lookers.

It looked like the MCPC men and women were ready for the eventuality though they made sure that enrolment went on as scheduled. Mrs. Miguela Bonato, College Registrar supervised the activities amidst all the chaos and the disorder around. She was assisted by three of her staff who could not focus well on their respective jobs as their minds were busy imagining scenarios of the alleged forced entry.

Many of the parents and students started complaining. The service was too slow and many times, the staff were confused. Traffic at the pedestrian lane was snail-paced and the line was getting longer. Only one person at a time was allowed to enter. To accommodate parents and students who were still outside the gate, application forms were distributed and cash payments were received over the open spaces of the iron railings of Gate 1. This method somehow facilitated the speedy completion of the enrolment process.

Meanwhile, suspicious-looking men started to crowd the entrance of the lane. They bullied the students who left the line in fear. However, the security guards stood firm by not allowing them to enter. They had a hunch, they were not students but part of Barrado's group whose intention was to come in before the bigger delegation arrived. Outside, Julia Pimentel an accounting clerk of the College confronted some of the suspicious looking men.

"I know most of them. Many of them are from Pioroda and Tunasan," she later told her co-protesters. Others were from the municipality of Kulintang, infamous for being known as the "killing field" of the region where communist rebels and the military often had bloody encounters. Baby Carillo whose family was influential in one of the nearby towns tried to persuade the intruders to desist from participating in the takeover but they simply ignored her. They were loud and foul-mouthed, throwing invectives that insulted not only the protesters but the students and their parents as well. Their presence created anxiety among those present in the premises.

———————————

James Sioson and some student photographers stationed themselves on the waiting shed roof just beside Gate 1. Many students joined them not only on that shed but on the roof of the Practice House. Around their heads were protest bands of different shapes and colors.

At around ten, the students in the Practice House, the janitorial staff and utility men boiled bananas soaked in salt and water which they later served as snacks to the protesters. Some took their share as their lunch for the day.

Before eleven a.m. Col. Rico Sancho, Deputy Regional Commander for Administration arrived with his aide. His purpose, he said was to mediate and prevent violence. The protest leaders explicitly said they had already decided not to let Barrado in no matter what happened. Col. Sancho promised he would go to the other camp, relay Barrado the message and return as soon as possible. The colonel was never seen again at the scene.

From his vantage point on the gym's rooftop, Fely continued to monitor the movement of all cars, trucks and pedestrians along Recto Avenue. With his telescope, he could easily identify who was coming or going. Every now and then he would mention familiar names he saw hovering around the perimeter of the school. He also took note of the "devil's car" the protesters' code name for Barrado's pale red bantam rounding the area. Fely's voice carried by the PA system could be heard in all corners of the wide campus. Everyone was alerted by what he was reporting.

How It Happened

Seventeen faculty members and administrative staff of the College executed a joint affidavit accusing Barrado and his men of grave threats, damage to property and physical injuries. Filed before the Metro Ciudad City Fiscal's Office on June 18, the affidavit described the movement of Barrado's people early in the day to about three o'clock that afternoon of June 13.

> *At around 8:30 in the morning of June 13, two trucks – a blue Mini Elf with plate number RU314 and a large, six-wheeler white Isuzu with plate number RX453 arrived loaded with more or less 100 persons. The passengers disembarked and gathered at the opposite side of Recto Avenue fronting the College gate.*
>
> *Some of these passengers were identified to have come from the neighboring municipalities of Pioroda, Tunasan and Kulintang.*
>
> *At around 11: 00 o'clock a.m., said persons attempted to enter the campus so we blocked the students' entrance to prevent those men from coming in.*
>
> *The men retreated to the gas station nearby, ate lunch and apparently got instructions from their leader. We took that time to re-open the gate to allow students to either come in or leave the premises of the school.*
>
> *Around 1:00 p.m., tension began to rise as the "outsiders" were back threatening us with all sorts of nasty and rude comments:*
>
> *"Ang ulo sa tawo mas barato pa kaysa repolyo." (The price of a person's head in our place is much cheaper than a cabbage.)*
>
> *"Dili ta mamauli kung walay aksyon!" (We will not go home if there will be no action.)*
>
> *"Maako gyud ka kung makasulod ko diha (sa campos)." (You will be mine if I can get I inside.)*
>
> *"Kung ikaw mogawas kami sa imo manamastamas."*

"Kung mogawas ka lugoson jud ka namo."(If you get outside, we will rape you.)

They stopped for a moment and reassembled again at the same gas station. We let the students who were outside to enter the gates.

At 3:00 p.m., an unusually large number of people led by Mr. Roy Tirol and Saturno Mecina, arrived and stationed themselves outside the main gate showing weapons such as hacksaw, sledgehammer and iron bars. They threatened to use them once they receive the order. We got frightened and immediately padlocked the students' entrance.

Barrado's men gathered at Gate 1 poised to start the assault. Fely shouted over the mega phone he was holding. "THEY ARE NOW MOVING IN! THEY ARE NOW MOVING IN!"

Prof. Anita started to pray over her megaphone. "Please dear heavenly Father protect us from this senseless aggression…". She was followed by a cacophony of supplicant voices from all over the campus, on top of buildings and on the grounds. 'Hail Mary, full of grace, the Lord is with Thee…"

The protesters, including the students rushed toward the gates and the fence. Unlike other campus fences and gates, those of the College were made of vertical iron bars, about five inches apart. The protagonists could see each other eyeball to eyeball.

Dr. Granada stood in the middle of the oval about a hundred meters from Gate 1. His brother Ben, Linda Pinyan, Chris Aglipon, and a group of students formed some kind of a cordon around him. Now and then, a faculty member or a student would run to him to report that some of the men outside the fence were looking for him and were asking who and where Dr. Granada was.

Recto Avenue was now clogged with jeepneys, trucks and all types of vehicles. Bystanders lined the avenue. Media men were running to and fro, interviewing people, taking pictures, or monitoring what was happening inside the campus through their hand-held radios.

The Picket Information Bureau started to send RUSH telegrams to people in Metropolitan Manila. They sent similar messages to a *Kalayaan* reporter, to the Palace Media Bureau, to Minister Quilantang, and to some deputy ministers in the Interior and Local Government Department.

> *Barrado attempting forcible entry into MCPC campus since this morning.// Armed goons now gathering outside. // Have met with the military regional command and they pledged to arrange a dialogue but to no avail.// Armed men continued to bully and intimidate protesters now holed inside campus.// Need immediate intercession and assistance before students and faculty are hurt. HELP//*

At around four o'clock, Capt. Ornano came. Melchor Bella narrated in his affidavit what transpired during Ornano's informal meeting with the faculty.

> *"When Capt. Jose Ornano of the 421ˢᵗ PC Command arrived and talked to Mrs. Anita Caluya, he told her that it is illegal to close the gates. He insisted that the gates be opened or he would use his discretion to open them himself. He further ordered Mrs. Caluya to confer with other leaders after which, he said, he should be informed of whatever decision the group would reach. He strongly warned us that he would force his way in if nothing was done to resolve the case before sundown, that is at 6:00 p.m."*

As soon as the warning of Capt. Ornano reached Dr. Granada, he immediately instructed his administrative officer to padlock all offices.

Pandemonium Broke Loose

At about four thirty, Fely Cobala with a voice hoarsed from shouting non-stop at the top of his lungs since that morning continued to announce that Barrado, Gary Daldalen and some other men were sighted heading toward Gate 1. His voice trembling and on the edge of hysteria rose to a scream as he erupted:

"THEY ARE NOW COMING IN! THEY ARE NOW COMING IN!

'PLEASE MR. BARRADO STOP RIGHT THERE!. WE ARE UNARMED FACULTY MEMBERS AND STUDENTS! THIS IS AN ACADEMIC COMMUNITY! VIOLENCE HAS NO PLACE HERE.

The shouts of Fely were joined by Anita's call for prayers over her own PA. "Hail Mary full of grace, the Lord is with thee, blessed art Thou amongst women…"

As Barrado and company approached the main gate, the picketers roared: "WE WANT GRANADA! WE WANT GRANADA! WE WANT GRANADA!"

The students on the roofs stomped their feet in cadence with the roar of the picketers below.

Granada was talking with Jay Valle, secretary of the city mayor who came to assure him that the protesters' request earlier for police assistance was already acted upon when pandemonium broke loose. The banging of the gate was heard throughout as mattocks smashed the iron gate. Students led by Joel climbed up the gate to prevent it from being forcefully pushed inside.

Hordes of students and staff members pushed themselves toward the gate to support Joel and the rest, as rocks and stones started flying from both sides. Cries and shouts of panic filled the air.

Soon, the gate finally gave way to superior force and female students and teachers scampered for safety while the rest faced the intruders head on. While this was going on, a second wave of students and staff members from the sides and from the rear picked up chairs and tables and hurled them toward the open space while Carmelito Lesaca drove the forklift toward the same direction. With the intruders temporarily blocked, the protesters quickly re-assembled and took their original position, arms in chain.

As rocks and stones continued to fly from everywhere, some of those surrounding Dr. Granada started to pick up stones. His brother Ben shouted at them not to participate in the mayhem as he firmly gripped the arm of one who was about to throw his "missile" toward the enemy.

––––––––––––––

Joint affidavit's recount of the events that ensued.

At around 4:30 p.m. Atty. Gary Daldalen, Mr. Esteban Barrado and Mr. Roy Tirol were outside the gate and tore down a streamer. Barrado, in his threatening tone ordered us to open the gate. When we refused, his men started pulling down the remaining streamers and placards. Mr. Mecina and some men who looked like goons destroyed the gate by using hacksaws and sledgehammers. The intruders beat some students and other protesters with the use of iron bars several of who, including Joel Lerpa were injured. This was their first attack on people.

Because of the commotion, some of the protesters moved away from the gate to avoid being beaten and hurt while the rest of us bravely and courageously faced the mob. Rocks were thrown at us, hitting our co-employees Robert Mison and Mimie Saysay. They succeeded in opening the main gate, removed the iron railings and threw them outside. To stop the aggressors from further hurting us, we blocked them with chairs. Because of this obstruction they were prevented from moving further inside.

While property and human attacks were going on, Linda and Chris started crying as they tried to pull their boss out of harm's way forcefully pushing him toward the direction of his cottage across the oval.

Robert Mison came staggering from the direction of the Infirmary, his head profusely bleeding. The back of his T-shirt was already soaked in blood. He was followed by the equally badly injured Mimie being assisted by another. Her face was swollen red and she had a black left eye. Her right arm was swollen too as if smashed by steel. The College nurse who accompanied the two to the Infirmary complained that the building was locked and the doctor in-charge for the day was nowhere to be found. One of the drivers had to rush several wounded persons to the nearest hospital downtown.

From out of nowhere, a news reporter was able to get into the scene of the action and interviewed Granada who briefly described what was happening. When the news appeared in the morning papers, he found out that most of it were dubious lies.

The joint affidavit further reported the following:

> *At around 5:30 p.m., after the terrifying encounter with Mr. Barrado's men, a fire truck and a six by six military truck full of truncheon-carrying soldiers got off looking like they were ready for a real battle. The coming of the military led by Capt. Ornano paved the way for a dialogue between our group led by Mrs. Anita Caluya and Atty. Gael Padera and Atty. Gary Daldalen on the other side. The dialogue between the two groups was held at the bigger President's house.*

The brand-new pick-up of Public Highways Regional Director Efraim Hizon was cautiously approaching Granada's smaller cottage. Inside the vehicle were men who looked like they're important people and their military escorts. As that long, sleek pick-up moved slowly casting a shadow, it created a silhouette of an extraterrestrial-like being that came to lead a funeral march.

"They have finally entered!" someone cried. The female students and faculty members around started to weep.

Linda and Chris tried to persuade Dr. Granada to get inside his cottage but he stood in the middle of the driveway determined to wait for the uninvited guests.

The pickup stopped a good five meters away from where he stood. Some of the men got out of the vehicle and walked with purposeful strides toward Granada.

His brother Ben who was with him since last night warned the approaching men to stop right where they were.

"Dr. Granada is my brother! Don't come near him or else…" as he extended his left arm in a tight fist while his right went swiftly inside his shirt. Another brother Bebot, their youngest, positioned himself by Moi's right. Ben and Bebot were taller and bulkier than their brother.

The left and right doors of the pick-up opened and out came Director Hizon. It seemed ages before Mr. Barrado and Atty. Daldalen finally stepped out.

Atty. Daldalen broke the ice by suggesting that a dialogue be held between the opposing camps. Granada agreed and offered his cottage where they could all sit down. Barrado came forward and said he preferred the dialogue to take place at the much bigger President's house.

Suddenly a set of keys was brought out by someone from his group and tinkered with the door lock until it opened.

Power-sharing: A Temporary Option

The dialogue was some kind of a truce, a halt from the on-going armed conflict. It had Pastor Guillermo Recardo of the Church of Christ as moderator. Nobody knew how the pastor came to be present at the scene (as well as numerous faces both familiar and unfamiliar) but when his name was raised everybody agreed that Pastor Recardo was right for the task and was acceptable to both camps.

On the side of Barrado was Gary Dadalen, Sammy Mejor introduced as chairman of the transition team, Atty. Graciano Iner, another of his counsels, and several others.

With Dr. Granada were Dr. Max Domug, Anita Caluya, Nap Lopa, Joel Lerpa, Sonny Aquiling and Atty. Gael Padera. Beth Sebastian took down notes as requested. Ben and Bebot stayed close at their brother's side.

City Councilor Jose "Pepe" Uba, Jay Valle, and Capt. Jose Ornano, volunteered as observers since not one of them came with Barrado.

Because the "audience" were not limited to representatives of both camps, the President's house was packed to the hilt. For the second time, the protagonists found themselves under one roof facing each other squarely.

Rev. Recardo started the talk rolling by a long preliminary saying he was thankful for the trust of both camps, promising to stay neutral and objective about the whole thing since both were his friends.

Gary Daldalen suggested that the subject of turnover should start the dialogue. He recalled that Granada had mentioned it during their first "failed" meeting at the Ministry Regional Office.

In response, the good Reverend requested Granada to reiterate his three basic requirements to effect a "smooth turnover".

"I am sure, Mr. Barrado already knows by heart what I've been proposing to effect a smooth turnover. There won't be any problem if he'll just accept them," Granada said in his most cordial voice.

Instead of responding to his opponent's point, Barrado insisted that Granada was no longer OIC, his services no longer needed.

Atty. Padera mentioned that he had filed an injunction in court to prevent Barrado from taking over. Hearing this, Pastor Recardo suggested that since an injunction was still under consideration by the court, both men should be allowed to stay inside the campus until a verdict comes out.

Barrado was furious at the suggestion saying it was ridiculous. "I am the president of this College. I decide who should stay and who should go," he insisted.

"We do not recognize your authority since your appointment has not been properly confirmed and endorsed by the Education Minister," rebuked Granada.

Atty. Padera affirmed what his boss had said, stressing the fact that he was still in-charge of the school inasmuch as the appointment signed by Secretary Conrado Comico Rayos was not duly recommended by the Board of Trustees of the school as stipulated in the College charter.

Director Hizon butted in and flaunted that turnover in his department did not take long and took only a day to finish. "Papers were signed without hassle since everything was assumed to be in order."

Granada looked at him trying to figure out his role in this whole scenario. "What right has he to make such a suggestion?" he thought. "Excuse me Director Hizon. I'm sure you have no idea how big MCPC is. We are not only accounting for the main campus. There are seven other satellite schools scattered over three provinces. Just imagine the volume of work that will be required to do the inventory," Granada explicitly stressed.

Again, Atty. Padera supported Granada on his point and reminded everyone that MCPC has a charter, a law which cannot be equated with the law (if ever) of other government entities. "So, Director Hizon was wrong into thinking that turnover of responsibilities and other accountabilities is a matter of formality," making Director Hizon retreat from his seat in embarrassment. He never, anymore, said anything for the duration of the meeting.

"Is that law to be turned over to me?" asked Barrado who made everyone's eyebrow raised.

"He obviously didn't have any idea of what a College charter is all about," whispered Sonny to Anita who grinned at the "silliness" of Barrado's question.

"For your information Mr. Barrado, PD 1431 is the law governing the state colleges in the country. By the way," Atty. Padera added with sarcasm, "prejudice exists in the hearts and minds of people and it cannot be eradicated by a law."

Atty. Daldalen, feeling the heat of discomfiture at his client's "ignorance of the law" insisted their stand. "Since Mr. Barrado is now the president, Dr. Granada should get out of the College. However, if the court decides otherwise, then Steve would leave."

To this, Atty. Padera responded. "Up to this time, Dr. Granada still controls the fund of the school and therefore, still is the president of the College."

Granada added that it would be quite impossible to get the court's decision on the matter since "tomorrow is Saturday and the court will resume hearing the merits of our petition on Monday. Shall we continue with this later?"

Atty. Graciano Iner seeing the rationality of Granada's statement proposed to have a peaceful interlude between now and Monday to which Barrado conceded saying "the suggestion is worth considering."

To this, Atty. Daldalen confirmed that their group agreed to the proposal.

"There is one thing we seem to overlook," stressed Atty. Gael, "the view of the protesting community. We cannot stifle dissent," he emphasized.

"We shall continue with our protest until an amicable serttlement is reached," insisted Anita Caluya.

"I believe in expressing opinion and dissent is allowed. You're entritled to it," Barrado sounded angry. "But remember, you should be responsible for whatever comes out of your mouth," he added.

Rev.Recardo declared a break of five minutes giving Granada time to briefly confer with his team. They decided on the following for consideration by the other side: Joint decision-making on major problems and in case of conflict, the military would act as arbiter until court decides on the case; disbursements should require the joint signatures of Granada and Barrado; and no public statements for or against will be issued by both sides.

After the five-minute recess, Granada announced the three points they were proposing with the appeal that the military should be a party to the agreement.

Ornano said that he will brief the Regional Commander of the proposed agreement.

"I'll decide whether to accept or not," said the agitated Barrado.

"The proposal is only a repeat of Mejor's proposal," said Recardo.

"Therefore, all parties and leaders were to desist as mentioned," said Daldalen with emphasis.

"I hereby order my task force to put the proposal into effect," said Barrado finally.

Rev.Recardo as his pious duty required called on everyone for a short prayer of thanks. "The dialogue has been fruitful by the wisdom and grace of the Amighty.

They adjourned at 7:30.

Granada walked back to his cottage shoulders bent and suddenly tired. He nodded absent-mindedly to his supporters who bid him goodnight. His eyes were on long shadows retreating into the darkened open space. A puppy's cry echoed through the now silent night, a car honked along the avenue as lights winked in the distance.

Before he switched on the lights inside his cottage, it dawned upon him that today was the darkest ever in the history of his beloved MCPC.

3

THE COURT BATTLE BEGAN

DAY 16, SATURDAY, JUNE 14
The Aftermath

VERY EARLY THE next morning Moises and Ben went around the campus and were horrified at the devastation caused by yesterday's riot. Assessing the extent of damage to property, he calculated the losses to amount to millions of pesos.

"Either Steve or I will have a big problem trying to bring back the school to its original form," he said almost exasperatedly to his brother who was in-step with him. He felt some kind of guilt very briefly at what happened but immediately discarded the thought.

"Of Little Help"

After breakfast, Danny and Irma came to pick him and Ben up to go and meet the governor at his residence in the outskirts of the city. This was the first time Granada had accepted the idea of the need to see the governor, if only to report to him what happened to his school. Earlier, Granada felt very uneasy about going (he abhorred the idea of meeting politicians in their own turf) but it seemed he had no choice. Sometime, somehow he had to shed off his "dislike" for politicians. The moment called for it.

Moises had heard of the Governor many times before, a man of means. He knew that the man was former chair of the Mayors League of the province. In the last elections, he switched party and joined the PDR of Felino Mendel. Granada was assured by Irma, a cousin of the Governor that he would listen and there was nothing to be apprehensive about. With Irma taking him, it was easy to get past the Governor's security.

Once in, Granada was surprised by the plain and ordinary character of the "mansion." All along, he thought that the house inside the high walls was huge and grand. It turned out, the Governor's residence was less pompous and unpretentious. His attention was also caught by cages in one corner of the ground where doves scampered as they passed by. In another cage was a giant python which appeared asleep but, according to the caretaker, was actually aware of their presence. "The Governor," Irma whispered, "loves the wilds and goes up to the mountains every now and then to be closer to nature."

After about twenty minutes of what seemed to be an endless wait, the man finally came out. He was dressed casually in shorts and slippers. Except for the heavy-looking gold necklace around his neck and the cropped nearly all- white hair, there was nothing really special about him till one heard him speak. His voice was deep, its resonance echoed distinctly. No doubt about it too, the Governor was English proficient which silently impressed his visitor.

Granada began narrating what happened to the College and the dialogue held. He said he wanted to seek the governor's advice and told the older man about the destructive attack on school property and the physical injuries inflicted on some protesters.

Yes, the Governor said, he learned of everything that happened. He knew the people involved. He particularly knew Barrado, the Daldalens, Saturno Mecina, Roy Tirol, Sammy Mejor, and the others – mayors of municipalities allegedly involved in the siege. In fact, he said, he wanted to talk to the picket leaders, but he was not invited. As a politician, he said, he did not want to be misunderstood. However, the governor lamented what happened. "Politicians," he said, "should not interfere in the affairs of educational institutions, much more use dirty tricks such as forcible entries as tactics. All these belonged to the political battleground," he added with reverence as if trying to impress upon Granada that political meddling was not his thing.

He suggested to them to see Metro Ciudad Mayor Pablo Jasta. The man could be of more help since the College was under his jurisdiction. The Governor stood up, asked for his phone and called up the Mayor saying Granada and his companions were now on their way to see him at his home.

Moises thanked the Governor for his time who gladly invited him to "drop by anytime."

"I'll see what I can do to help," were his parting words.

Since it was a Saturday, Granada did not expect the Mayor' residence to be full of visitors. But it was and learned that people started trooping in as early as seven. He suggested that perhaps it would be best to see the Mayor in his office on Monday. However they were asked to wait and after about thirty minutes were allowed in.

Granada had seen and briefly conversed with the Mayor on several occasions in the city before. He was quite stocky, short, but he had this easy mien about him that would make one comfortable in his presence.

Like the governor, Mayor Jasta also said he was aware of what happened adding he also knew the people involved naming them one by one. He promised to talk with Mr. Barrado as soon as time permits hoping it could be today though he didn't specifically mention what he's going to talk with him about. The group thanked him for his time.

Recalling the meetings they had earlier, Granada realized his brief encounter with the top political figures of the province and the city was a total waste of time. It was nothing but pure reporting of the incident in his school and got no assurance of concrete help from either of the men. "I should have known better," he sighed.

———————

More than anyone, it was Granada who knew the extent of damage caused by the gory "struggle for power" by people with vested interests. Admittedly, he felt he was among them. He wondered if Barrado had thought of the aftermath and doubted if his archrival ever did. He believed that though the loss and harm done to property was huge, it was not comparable to the emotional and psychological injury inflicted on his people.

Back in the campus, the scope of destruction as a result of yesterday's chaos became apparent in the clear light of day. Dislocated iron railings were strewn all over, some as far as the middle of Recto Avenue. Debris of broken chairs and tables, stones and rocks were scattered around as if the place was hit by a powerful tornado. Torn streamers and placards hanged loosely from where they were put up earlier. The ground became a dumpsite for empty soda cans, beer and rum bottles, cigarette butts, paper boxes and packages, discarded plastic bags. The campus from the gates down to the oval was a huge mess!

Dr. Granada instructed the security guard detailed at Gate 1 to submit an official report on the damage specifically identifying badly hit property of the school.

He was glad to see a number of protesters, students and faculty members clearing the area of debris. He saw no anger nor remorse on their faces, only sadness. Or was it fear?

The spot report submitted by Security Chief Siso Berga identified the destruction made on the school gates cafeteria, and the forced opening and ransacking of the Office of the President Emeritus. Food stored in the cafeteria were completely gone and allegedly consumed by the intruders.

Chief Berga added that during the take over several men were spotted entering the cafeteria, ransacked it and ate all the stocks in there. They left the place in total disarray with upturned utensils, broken bottles, littered wrappers of bread, candies, spilled water and softdrinks, and others. No food was left unconsumed. "They looked very hungry and very angry, maybe because the food was not enough for all of them."

At lunchtime, Dr. Chuck Dulay and Rey dela Rosa, Moises long-time friends arrived with a proposal. Chuck said many private citizens were concerned and wanted to help. They would go around the city and neighboring towns and solicit signatures for his retention.

Rey, a very active civic leader and a member of professional organizations in Metro Ciudad said he could seek the help of his colleagues to spearhead the campaign. Together, he was certain, they could probably hit 20,000 signatures on or before the end of the month.

Granada was touched by his friends' concern and thanked them profusely. However, he requested that citizen's participation to the petition should be voluntary and wanted it known that he had nothing to do with it.

The Campus: A Virtual "War-zone"

With two camps rising on both sides of the campus, it dawned on everyone that the school was now a virtual "war-zone."

Granada's cottage became the point of reference or the 38th parallel which identified the portion of the area to be occupied by each camp while the truce was on-going. Barrado and his followers took possession of the left side of the cottage while teachers, students and other personnel positioned themselves on the right. The "38th parallel" roughly divided the area between the "warring" factions. Anyone who crossed it on foot experienced some kind of chill since all eyes were on him. To avoid this intimidating experience Barrado's followers would take the driveway to and from Gate 2 while the protesters, the driveway to and from Gate 1.

As he took note of the situation, Granada realized that MCPC was no longer an institution of higher learning but had been virtually transformed into a "war zone."

The intruders certainly didn't look like they were decent people with some of them stripped to the waist. Others were in slippers or in rubber shoes, sockless. Their drivers catnapped in the parked cars, had their bare feet out of the car windows, oblivious of the fact that these were marked

"For Official Use Only." They had sequestered these vehicles earlier from the motor pool for their personal use.

When Granada reported to MCPC eight months ago, he chose not to occupy the President's house for the simple reason that it was too large and spacious. He opted to stay in the smaller cottage adjacent to it since he lived alone. His family was still in Luzon where his wife Tessa was working in an agricultural university there. He reserved the President's house for important guests. Once every two weeks, for instance, graduate school lecturers from Manila came to hold graduate classes in his school. Prominent educators like the former Secretary of Education, Manila-based professors, out-of-town lecturers and high government officials were regular guests. SUC presidents in Mindanao who would fly to Manila via the Metro Ciudad airport would usually stay overnight. From time to time, the house was also used for important meetings and small conferences.

Counsel Padera informed Granada that the core group constituting the transition team of Barrado all belonged to the MAP. They were tasked with carrying out the smooth transition from the old administration to the new. As Atty. Gael alleged the specific tasks of the team, Granada was reminded of Barrado's letter to the students dated June 10. It occurred to him that his antagonist was no longer in control of the situation. For if he were, would he have allowed the destruction of College's property which he may, in all likelihood, eventually manage? If he were in control, would he have adopted the strategy of a forced takeover knowing this would surely drive the students and faculty members farther away from him?

The incoming president could have wisely adopted some conciliatory moves with the students, faculty and staff when told point blank during their first dialogue that he was not acceptable to them. But instead of taking a friendlier stance, he became retaliatory and vindictive. Why?

He could have considered the proposal to identify entry points which could have compelled the academic community to accept him with deference. But he did not.

He could have easily postponed his assumption into office and honored the instruction of his own "Godfather" Minister Mendel but he totally ignored it. Since he already had the appointment in his hands, he could have convinced himself and those around him that a little more time and a little more patience would not really make a difference. Yet he was persistent and he was uneasy.

Was his repeated declaration last night that, "I am the President" some kind of a subconscious revelation that he actually wanted to assert himself but could not?

Many of those who knew him were unanimous in saying that Barrado was, in fact, a "nice guy," that he was friendly, which helped him build a career as a media man and be known as a civic leader.

Why the sudden change?

"Barado may have intended to heal the wounds of a bruising campaign in the last election and wanted to assert his leadership," Nap alleged. "He has to move quickly before he becomes irrelevant."

Nap was not a psychic nor was exact in his supposition as some men he knew who had a talent for detecting an irregularity, but he had the eye and the gut instinct for the hidden that seldom failed him.

"It is ironic," Nap continued, "that Barrado could not accept that what he did last June 13 had sparked such outrage. For one, he is covered with superfluous superlatives by media. When he goes out of control, there is always Gary who pats his hand reassuringly and like a child that gesture always puts him at ease. Wow! Can you believe that?"

All laughed, with Nap the loudest.

"So he organized a team whose members are united largely by political expediency and spent more time jockeying for position than thinking of how to run the school efficiently. And their influence upon him was pervasive. They also do not hide their presence around him. They are definitely high-flyers without wings but are excited over the prospect of a new lucrative position in the state college. Tough luck, poor MCPC!

Everyone sighed.

All the "President's Men"

Who were the men around Steve Barrado?

There was of course the "Gang of 3", the Daldalen lawyer-brothers. They need no further introduction. Suffice it to say that in this fight, the Daldalens were his life support.

There was Arturo Cereno, once the warden of the provincial jail under ex-governor Cosme Daldalen and was mayor of a small town, Santa Cruz. It was public knowledge that Cereno was strongly lobbying to be mayor of Pioroda, the municipality north of Metro Ciudad. Many of those who participated in that ludicrous attempt to take over the school were from that town.

Jess Corola, brother of a barangay captain who was allegedly assassinated by the communist rebels in Kulintang was MAP's political strategist. He was vocal about him eyeing the directorship of food and agriculture department in the region. There was Atty. Graciano Iner, member of the legal panel of the MAP, and Engr. Efraim Hizon, known to be a Divinagracia (former vice-president and ambassador to the United States) protégée, was actually a MAP loyalist. Of course, there were Roy Tirol and Sammy Mejor, his "Loyola boys".

Was Barrado in control of the situation or were these men around him controlling him? Were they taking the reins for him?

If these men were in control, then it would not be far-fetched to conclude that it was not the College's interest that was uppermost in their minds. Barrado must have been used to further their own agenda without him being aware of it, a puppet on a string.

This became apparent when it dawned on Granada that except for Barrado who had limited experience in the academe, all the others were engaged in various types of occupations outside of the academic realm. His men who were largely politicians or politically-oriented individuals would no doubt, be lacking in skills and knowledge pertaining to higher education. Most likely, the school will be used as a tool to serve their interests, either individually or collectively.

Before the day ended, the faculty and staff went to see their OIC to let him know that they will not be reporting for work on Monday, June 16 since their leave of absence were still in effect. Instead, they would use the day to rally outside expressing in no mean words their determination and willful desire to keep Barrado out.

Upon learning of the plan, he immediately sent a telegram to Minister Quilantang reporting what happened and what his faculty and staff were planning to do. He also mentioned that the students will boycott their classes simultaneously with the teachers' absence. He said they were "praying for your direct intervention."

He waited for the reply that came a day after.

———————

DAY 17, SUNDAY, JUNE 15
A Ray of Hope

A certain "Deputy Minister" Santos Matos from the Education Ministry was announced by the guard. He came to see Dr. Granada. The OIC was not sure who Deputy Minister Matos was since he had never heard of him. Thinking that he could be a new appointee in the Ministry, Granada decided to meet the unexpected visitor in his cottage.

While waiting for the unknown deputy, Granada remembered Dr. Herminio Santos of the Planning Division whom he used to meet at Palacio del Uno before the new revolutionary government was installed. Thinking that perhaps his guest was Dr. Hermie he was relieved that he now had the chance to confide to a high ranking official in the Ministry the problems besetting his College. He reminded himself not to forget congratulating Dr. Santos on his promotion. His elation was short-lived upon realizing that the alleged deputy minister was not the man he knew from Palacio. He nevertheless, welcomed the man graciously who introduced himself as Atty. Santos Matos, Legal Assistant to Minister Quilantang. (Did he forget to mention he was "deputy minister?") As he looked at his visitor, Granada tried to recall if he saw him at the Educators' Congress in Baguio last May.

"No, I didn't see him there." He told himself. He assured the man he was glad to see him.

Faculty and staff and students started trooping to the cottage upon learning that a deputy minister had come. The OIC also kept introducing the visitor as "Deputy Minister Matos."

Matos was sent by the Minister in response to the rush telegram she received informing her of the Friday incident in the College. Atty. Matos assured them that the Minister really wanted to come but the pressing problems at the Ministry prevented her from even leaving her office. "In fact," he stressed, "she had arranged for a military plane to take her to Metro Ciudad but had to cancel at the last minute. She's sending her apologies."

The conference with Atty. Matos was an opportunity for the leaders to know first hand what the Minister was thinking about the controversy.

Caluya, Lerpa and Aquiling alternately narrated what happened as the latter took notes. He was shown photos taken during that fateful day.

It disappointed Granada and his leaders when Matos admitted he could not exactly say what the position of the Minister was on the controversy but emphasized that as far as the Education Ministry was concerned, "Dr. Granada is still the person in authority since there is no official turnover yet."

The statement was quite vague but was good enough for them at the moment. Granada forced himself to see a glitter of hope in what the Deputy said.

"You will also be meeting Mr. Barrado, right?" Granada asked. "Could you please repeat to Mr. Barrado what you just told us? Since you are the official representative of the Minister, he should know where he stands as far as Minister Quilantang is concerned."

"Yes, I will say the same thing to him," he promised to the group who cheered and clapped their hands excitedly.

Matos also relayed Dr. Quilantang's instruction to him to put in writing his decision as to which position he preferred, alluding to the four options she offered while they were in Baguio.

"I understand you were to decide by June 15," his visitor reminded him. "Just make it brief and I will hand carry it to the Minister," he said.

It didn't take long for Granada to write his decision: *If given further opportunity, I prefer to serve the Metro Ciudad Polytechnic College. I've seen and demonstrated that I can propel this institution to further develop to become the center of excellence in this part of the country and be a tool to better articulate the plans and programs of the Ministry of Education. I hope that given the chance, my administration can contribute to the renewal efforts of the new government toward change. My faculty, staff and students have given me their full trust and confidence. My future is now in your hands, Mrs. Minister.*

He folded and stapled his letter which he gave to Atty. Matos. An envelope was not available to seal it in. On top, he wrote: *"Education Minister Lucretia Quilantang, courtesy of Deputy Minister Santos Matos."*

Matos assured his host that he would personally deliver the note to the Minister as soon as possible.

The OIC offered to bring him to the bigger President's house after serving him a simple lunch.

Barrado chose to use the official residence as his temporary office while the truce was in effect. But the man was not there and so he introduced the envoy to Atty. Gary who was manning the "office."

Obviously, Matos was appalled by what he saw – men stripped to the waist, some with tattoos on their bodies in an unkempt room. He felt rather uneasy around these men. He talked briefly with Atty. Daldalen, relayed the message of the Minister and emphasized that this should reach Barrado soon.

The Deputy had to see himself out because Granada had left after the introductions for a lunch appointment. He went directly to the airport and took the next plane out.

Solidifying Forces

Lunch was at Prof. Nenita Semla's residence in a teachers' village some 10 kilometers west of the city. She volunteered to have the meeting in her place since it was her birthday and the place was relatively safe.

Many leaders of the protest were already there when he arrived. He was glad to see his VPAA Honesto and wife present. "You missed the action in the campus last Friday," he joked.

"Yeah I know, but thank God it's over for now," replied the man who obviously was still not well from his minor surgery.

"Lechon!" shrieked Bebe.

Sounds of "uhhhs" and "ahhhs" were heard when the big, fat succulent roast was laid before them. They thought it best to fill their stomachs first before settling down to serious business.

"What else are we celebrating aside from Nits' birthday?" asked Sonny.

"Victory!" they all shouted and laughed boisterously while pounding their stainless spoons and forks on the wooden tables.

"That will come eventually," said Dr. Granada with a wide grin.

Lunch as well as the lechon didn't take long to finish, the roast completely stripped to the last bone. Everybody was in a hurry to finish eating unaware that another surprise would be sprung on them before the day was over.

As the events of June 13 were recalled, they took note of those who were hurt in the encounter. Granada instructed some female teachers to follow them up in the hospital and ensure that they were well taken care of adding that the school will shoulder the expenses.

Before the meeting went further, the group asked their OIC to be honest with them.

"Sir, we want to know if you're serious in wanting to stay with us, if this fight we're doing is not a waste of time." Beth remarked.

"I think you should know what I've written the Minister today regarding my choice. Today is my deadline to make that choice. I reiterated that my preference is still MCPC."

His statement assured everyone especially those who were in doubt as to where they stand with him. Their fears that their OIC will eventually desert them were allayed. It was enough that they knew he really desired to stay even if his future at MCPC was still uncertain.

Prof. Caluya who was finishing her desert of sweetened young coconut rose from her seat and said "Let us all protect Sir. Don't you worry, Sir we won't stop until you are appointed our President."

A rejoinder was heard from beyond the fence: "Sir, once we win, I'll have my pig butchered for the celebration!"

Everyone had a good laugh over that remark from Tomas Pingol.

"We shall have a Mardi gras!" shouted Vin Elayo who just returned from Germany on a scholarship.

"No. Let's have Ati-ati-han instead," Nits shouted and the laughter continued.

After the hearty bantering among the guests, they buckled down to talk seriously. Noting what the school had lost as a result of the failed *coup* they decided to re-assess their strength and weaknesses and identified key persons who will take the front in any foreseen negotiation. The reorganization was done to solidify their forces and to ascertain who were for them or against them. The drafting of a schedule of activities for the whole month was agreed on to be reviewed regularly by the steering committee. This was necessary since they believed, the struggle was certainly going to be a protracted one.

The steering committee was strengthened with the addition of the VPAA. Romy Ramar and Dr. Elvina Tapan were kept as chairman and vice chairman respectively. Several important committees were formed headed by trusted individuals. Special assignments were entrusted to members who they thought could facilitate completion of tasks immediately and with expertise. Their assignment was generally public relations, liaison, coordination and seeking public support. They also considered accepting volunteers to do the leg work. They did not forget to detail the role of the students in the whole protest scenario. They were asked to be vigilant, keep the students on their side and encourage those who plan to defect to the other side to reconsider. In other words, students should police their own ranks. They will also be mobilized to solicit signatures to render Mr. Barrados's appointment null and void. Joel proposed the creation of an intelligence task force who will regularly monitor radio and TV broadcast, track down the going and coming of Barrado's men, and secretly list down sympathizers and "enemies" of the cause.

After the reorganization, it was agreed that the faculty and staff will be stationed in front of the main campus on Wednesday, June 19. This would give the protesters enough time to recharge, gear up and get really ready for another round of continuing struggle ahead.

The protesters stayed at Nits' place until early afternoon, refining plans and simulating strategies in between bites of the perennial boiled bananas with fermented fish soaked in vinegar and pepper. They ended the affair with high hopes for brighter days ahead.

Local Media: Not Solid Afterall

As expected, most radio and TV stations in the entire Metro Ciudad did not report truthfully what actually happened in the College on June 13. Instead, the airwaves were full of stories about Mr. Barrado having assumed office and was "happily welcomed by the academic community." While many media men had joined quite willingly Barrado's game, others stayed out of it and did not bother to muddle with the issue.

The protesters knew people of Metro Ciudad didn't believe the lies peddled by the biased media but they were still saddened and pained by the unfair treatment they got from the press. They were concerned about the effect of the news to those who had no firsthand knowledge of the situation and might have thought all's well at MCPC.

However, despite the large-scale conspiracy to hide the truth, one newspaper could not be silenced, the local weekly *News Express*. When it hit the streets sometime in the afternoon, the protesters felt vindicated. The issue carried a blow-by-blow account of what actually happened complete with photographs. The news belied what other local radio and TV stations were feeding the listeners and readers led by Mejor's minions.

Its front page headlined the upcoming teachers' mass leave with other related stories.

Barrado bullies way into school premises, 3 hurt

Deans of State College ignore Barrado's call for conference

"No confirmation yet" says Education Ministry of Barrado appointment

A blown up picture of Anita Caluya and other protesters with raised fists in front of the placards and streamers demanding the cessation of political interference in state institutions was prominently displayed.

It also featured a fresh "Talk of the Town" column of Noli Tejano.

This particular issue got the ire of Barrado which in a way caused a dent in the once solid Metro Ciudad Press and Radio Club where Barrado was not only a member, but one of its past presidents.

Another reason which caused the cleavage was published in the same issue– the denial of incumbent Club president, Ms. Chato Solis about endorsing Barrado. In fact, she was quoted saying that though Barrado was a member of the press club, she "...believes he (Barrado) is not qualified for the job."

Chato had visited Granada earlier to apologize. She confessed that she affixed her signature to a Club endorsement not knowing that it was for Barrado. She explained that this endorsement was actually a general one and did not specifically mention the College presidency. Otherwise, she said she would not have signed it. It might be mentioned that Chato was also a professor at the Liceo de Cagayan and she and Moises Granada were batch mates at Silliman University during their undergraduate years.

DAY 18, MONDAY, JUNE 16
Suit and Counter-suit

He had not gotten over the shock of the destructive "assault" of the campus during the weekend when Granada received another news which indicated the worst was not over yet. A police officer came to tell him that he had a subpoena along with five others. Charges of sedition, grave coercion, illegal assembly, prolongation of tenure of office, and usurpation of authority were filed in the regional trial court which immediately served a subpoena. Others named as co-defendants were Anita Caluya, Beth Sebastian, Romeo Ramar, Sonny Aquiling and Fely Cobala. They were ordered to appear before Fiscal Epifanio Mulino at three in the afternoon that same day.

"This is pure and simple harassment but there is no need to worry about them," Atty. Padera assured those accused when told of the charges. "Shrewd politicians commonly employ this tactic to put the enemy in the defensive," he added casually. "We need to get a lawyer for you."

When Caluya and the others were informed of the charges, they spoke boldly. If they were to be arrested, they said, they would not post any bail and instead would just go straight to jail. "It's quite clear, Barrado could not think of anything more noble than to harass us," they said in their accusing tone.

The basement of the Church of Christ was almost full for the emergency meeting of the protesters. The place was large enough to accommodate hundreds of people. The meeting was called to finalize plans for the protest rally around the city in the afternoon to decry the charges and the appearance of their leaders before the fiscal's office.

"We are charged with sedition and other charges," Beth Sebastian informed the group enumerating the charges filed against OIC Granada and five others. The protesters booed angrily.

While the discussions were being held, Granada whispered to Atty. Padera that he got word from a high official that it would be best to get a PMN lawyer to represent the group in the forthcoming trial. The said official suggested a name—Atty. Exequiel Padera. The name "Padera" made the group vulnerable to suspicion that the "disgruntled PMNs" were backing protests against the revolutionary government and getting him might not be a good idea. Gael Padera did not like its implication. Yes, he was the younger brother of "PMN boy," former Mayor Exequiel Padera of a municipality in a neighboring province but his brother was no longer a politician, he's now a practicing lawyer. However, he understood too well the group's reaction. He said "no" to the unpopular suggestion and likewise inhibited himself from officially representing the group saying he will limit his services to making legal briefs. However, he volunteered to be Granada's personal lawyer in this case and in any forthcoming cases, in anticipation of future charges. All praised Gael for his selflessness and loyalty.

After a thorough deliberation the decision to hire Atty. Ernani Amasing of PDR was arrived at. He was not only a PDR high profiled attorney but was also known as the "champion of the oppressed." Anita Caluya who knew him personally was tasked to inform him of the decision and brief him of her group's predicament.

As Granada left the venue it occurred to him that the legitimate faculty and staff of the College had not only been dislocated, they were now like the proverbial nomads, moving from one place to another without a home.

Preliminary Trial Postponed

The injunction filed by Atty. Taburan before the Fiscal's Office on the forced entry was supposed to be decided today. However, Atty.Gael opined that this was no longer necessary and could be rendered moot and academic since Barrado was already inside the campus. All they have to concentrate on now were the charges facing them.

As the group climbed up to Fiscal Mulino's sala it looked like the whole academic community was on trial. The protesters were all over the place and everyone wanted to be a witness. Atty. Padera had to explain that this was just a preliminary hearing and only those named in the complaint were to appear. In spite of their legal counsel's explanation, the protesters still followed Dr. Granada's entourage to the Fiscal' office, crowding the lobby and the reception room.

To the group's irritation, the Fiscal did not sound very friendly. He showed them the charges impressing upon each one present their alleged seriousness and gravity and sort of warned that the accused may be formally charged before the graft court. "This is a serious case," he emphasized "and the civil court is not the proper venue." When nobody said anything, he suggested to Atty. Padera l to advise his clients to settle the case amicably. The good attorney informed Fiscal Mulino that he was only standing in for Atty. Ernani Amasing who was not available at the moment. "Atty. Amasing will represent them," he said. He asked for postponement of the preliminary hearing. When the name of Atty. Amasing was mentioned, everybody noticed that the Fiscal became less aggressive and was no longer insistent. He left them for a while saying he will have to confer with Barrado and his lawyer who were in another room. When he returned, he announced that the hearing was reset at ten o'clock in the morning of the following day.

Students Gave Barrado What He Didn't Want to Hear

Students' response to Barrado's letter of June 10 had been drafted, polished and finalized.

Didn't they promise themselves that they won't let it go without giving him an answer? They made sure he got their open letter today.

Expectedly long and straight-forward, copies were mimeographed and circulated in the campus and in and around the city streets. It was significantly a public display of disgust and contempt over the series of events that could possibly "overthrow" Granada from MCPC's presidency and perceived dark days for the institution in the coming months or years.

Highlights of the letter zeroed-in on their point-by-point response to the claims raised by Barrado in his letter to the students.

> *Point 1.* *"The Task Force will insure that during the transition, all College property shall be safeguarded, documents and records secured."*
>
> **Response.** Your supposedly task force destroyed the main gate of the College when you forced your way into the College on June 13, tore down the walls of the Office of the President Emeritus where official records

and documents of this institution are kept and allowed the destruction of the padlock of the College Cafeteria to gain access to the facility, ransacked and consumed all the food stored in there. How can you now say that you have indeed secured, protected and safeguarded said documents, records and school's property? What excuse can you possibly offer to defend these contemptible acts of your men?

Point 2. *"I am sure you are aware that there were efforts of a number of faculty members and administrative staff to question the decision of the President of the Republic. This group has been feeding students and faculty, and even the public with wrong information to turn everyone against me to embarrass the President ...."*

Response. First, the "a number" refers to about 180 of the 200 members of the faculty and personnel associations. Note that the number was significantly large. We knew that those who you think were on your side are not your true followers but were simply with you because they're afraid to reject you for fear of consequences later. You have, by estimation, around 20 or less. We were aware that your invitation to a conference at Garden Restaurant on June 4 and 5 were snubbed by our teachers and deans. Dr. Soriano who has been obviously behind you and 13 others including yourself only composed the June 4 meeting. What could have been the agenda? We wonder.

Just to set the record straight sir, our teachers were not feeding us and the public wrong information. They were just telling the truth and we believed them. What were these allegedly wrong information being fed to the public?

1. That your appointment was not recommended by the MCPC Board of Trustees, a clear violation of a specific provision on choosing a president as stipulated in the College Charter. It's a fact and you know it.

2. That you did not go through the right process, by-passing the search committee of the Education Minister and her set of guidelines. Can you refute that?

3. That you yourself admitted that you obtained your appointment through political accommodation as a reward for your efforts during the last election, and

4. That we have not seen the signature of the President of the Republic on your so-called "appointment papers" made us doubt the genuineness of your appointment.

We never intended to embarrass the President of the Republic and neither did the faculty and staff of the College. On the contrary, we wanted to help her put the right people in the right posts who will support her reform platform which include social transformation, consultative decision-making, and stronger citizens' participation.

> **Point 3.** *"The faculty, personnel and students want Minister Lucretia Quilantang to be angry with the President, to discredit Minister Mendel, Atty. Cosme Daladalen and other new officials who have shown trust and confidence in me and believe in my worthiness and ability to administer MCPC successfully…"*
>
> **Response.** We were certain Minister Quilantang will not be angry at the President. She's too honorable to even think about it. We hold on to her preference and assurance to appoint the right person to the presidency of any state institution of higher learning, MCPC included. As educators, the faculty of the College are greatly concerned with preserving the integrity of the academe and protecting academic freedom so that the community will continue to entrust in their hands our development and growth as future leaders of the country. Together we, have sought the assistance of Minister Mendel who is now studying the matter and hope that he considers favorably our plea.

Point 4. *"I know I still have to earn your trust and confidence in me. So far, you do not know who I really am…"*

Response. The little we have come to know about you arising from the June 13 assault of the College are enough for us to conclude you can be scary and unreasonable. How can we trust a leader whose actions are threatening and contemptible when you choose them to be. The academic community is not the place for such horrendous behavior. We can never allow such contempt of our leader pervade in our learning environment. It is not healthy.

Point 5. *"My confidence springs from my track record…"*

Response. Without the documents to validate your claim, everything is pure hearsay. Our simple request is to provide us with your bio-data duly certified and authenticated and allow us to assess it objectively

Point 6. *"…I am not qualified… because I was once a TV newscaster…"*

Response. That point is irrelevant. There was never any objection raised about you being a media man. You are deviating from the real issue.

Point 7. *"…Some teachers and administrators are against me because they are Protestants and I am a Catholic."*

Response. Another irrelevant point as it was never an issue here. Nobody cares if you're Catholic or Protestant or INC or Muslim as religion has no bearing whatsoever to the main problem.

Point 8. *"I graduated only from Loyola University…"*

Response. We look up to Loyola University as a respectable school. It is not something to be insecure about. Again, this was never an issue.

Point 9. *"I am not qualified because I am not a Ph.D. holder."*

Response. This is true. This is one of the many qualifications a president of any state college must have. Others, if you must know, include personal qualities such as integrity, honesty, unquestionable character, preferably not a politician. As to professional qualifications, he must be an educator, an academician able to run a university, competent and productive (author of professional books) and acceptable to the community.

Point 10. "*I am told that many are afraid that I will be vindictive. Being only human, I certainly am not happy with what they have done. But I will never make any decision against anyone who exercises his/her God-given right to express dissent...*"

Response. How can we believe that when you caused injuries to three of the College's employees and several students during your failed *coup* and brought damage to government property in your attempt to take over the school. Shall we also include your filing of sedition and other charges against President Granada and five others who openly fought with you? Do no harm, do no damage, not vindictive? You are indeed a man who does not honor his own words!

Point 11. "*...we need to be more careful in the use of funds.*"

Response. The person you so desperately want ousted is a great proponent of this and sincerely lives up to this expectation. We wonder if you can even equal his honesty and integrity in handling the finances of the school.

Point 12. "*Our curriculum needs to be restudied and modified...*"

Response. We hope you know exactly what you are talking about.

The letter had an emotional but forceful message:

Sadly you started with a wrong move. You could have put your best foot forward and made friends with us instead of antagonizing the whole community. You have shown unwittingly a side of the kind of leadership you might be employing when you have the chance. And we didn't like what we saw. It did not scare us though, in fact, it prepared us to be vigilant and be on our toes more. The students look for idealism in our leaders and mentors. After what you've done, our resolve not to accept you as President of this institution has become stronger than ever.

We're sorry to say Mr. Esteban Barrado, you are not welcome at MCPC!

The entire leadership of the Supreme Student Council led by Joel Lerpa signed the letter.

———————————

DAY 19, TUESDAY, JUNE 17
The Preliminaries

The courtroom where the preliminary hearing was taking place overflowed with people who had a stake at what was going on even if that "stake" was simply to satisfy their curiousity. Protesters and Barrado's men scrambled for the best seat and the best view of the proceedings. Media men swarmed the place with cameras flashing every now and then. Even if this was just the preliminary, the deliberations and the arguments that were brought up looked like that of a full blown court trial. Atty. Gary Daldalen kept on hammering the point that Dr. Granada was no longer a public official since the appointment of Mr. Barrado rendered the former's term void and therefore he's no longer officially employed at MCPC. As such, he should be charged in the civil court while the rest, in the Ombudsman.

The drama in the entire proceeding spun to high gear when Granada *et.al.*'s defense lawyer Atty. Amasing mentioned about the confidential note of Minister Mendel to Mr. Barrado.

As soon as the presence of a note was brought out, Atty. Daldalen raised an objection warning Caluya that this could have very grave implications on her case. She should therefore not say anything about the note for she could be sued for breach of confidence by the Minister himself.

But Atty. Amasing had already trapped the Fiscal earlier to order Caluya to produce the note.

As the lady went searching for that piece of evidence (a copy showing Barrado's signature) inside her bag, the courtroom was buzzing and the fiscal had to pound his gavel to bring order and silence in the court.

As soon as Anita recovered it, she turned the note over to the Fiscal. The defense lawyer immediately moved to have it marked "Exhibit A". He then pressed Barrado to admit that the signature on the note was his indicating without fail that he did receive the original on June 12.

Barrado, on advice of his lawyer, admitted that it was indeed his signature.

Atty. Amasing then moved that the signature be marked "Exhibit A-1."

Gary Daldalen was known for his antics in court, a reputation which he obviously enjoyed. Throughout the proceedings, he would now and then face Granada with his back on the Fiscal to which Atty. Amasing pointed out that Gary was "snubbing the Honorable Fiscal." Gary denied ignoring the prosecutor saying he just wanted to look at Granada who "is my close friend since our Silliman days, and me standing as best man in his brother Ben's wedding…" He went on to narrate irrelevant information alien to the case being heard.

As a reaction to his opponent's diversionary tactic, Atty. Amasing would whisper to a friend in the sala and burst into an impish smile or laughter annoying Gary who would call the Fiscal's attention to this and complained that companero Ernani was "ill-mannered."

Sensing his opponent's discomfort, Atty. Amasing finally revealed what he and his friend were whispering about—"girls!" and let out a guffaw. A commotion in the audience was heard—was Gary Daldalen becoming paranoid?

The clash between the two was not simply a battle of legal maneuvering to put one over the other to win the case. As they tried to outsmart each other with their arguments, it was becoming apparently clear that the court battle was actually a fight for supremacy between the MAP and PDR over anything they found themselves in. The hearing turned out to be a show of might and strategy rather than of substance.

As witnesses were called, testimonies from both sides were taken and included in the minutes of proceedings. The court adjourned with both parties unsatisfied at the outcome.

As soon as Granada's group was out of the courtroom, Atty. Amasing explained several mistakes committed by his team like when Granada pointed to the witnesses every time the Fiscal asked if he knew the person sitting beside him or at his back. By pointing and identifying them, he said, Granada had actually implicated them. The OIC said he was sorry but that he could not possibly lie. Atty. Amasing said that he understood.

"Takeover" of Offices Began

While MCPC's constituents who were on mass leave were caught in the drama of the preliminary hearing in the morning, little did they know that Barrado had already ordered the forced opening of the offices in the

Administration Building. By 9:55, his men had entered the Office of the President.

It was reported that the padlock to the main entrance of the administrative offices was sawed off in the presence of Dr. Soriano, Roy Tirol, Benhur Alejo, a certain Captain Salgado and a few unidentified men. Gary Daldalen was believed to be present at the scene but had to leave early for the preliminary hearing.

Also based on the same report, the lock of the President's Office was hand-drilled by a hired keyman from *Keyer's*.

The whole incident was witnessed by the security guards on duty, some protesters and photographer Jimmy Caoili and his fellow students. As Jimmy took pictures of the break-ins, one of Barrado's men grabbed him by the arm intending to sequester his camera. The young man, however, managed to extricate himself from the man's grip and ran away with his gadget intact.

At about 1:35 o'clock in the afternoon, word reached the protesters' headquarters that the College security guards were going to be disarmed. Atty. Gael, Nap Lopa, and Patrolman Serge rushed back to the campus to verify the report. Capt. Ambrosio Dallo, manager of the security agency hired by the school was waiting for Granada in his cottage. He was apologetic, but said he had to disarm his own security men on orders of President Barrado.

Granada stressed to the security chief that he was still the person in authority and thus all orders should come from him. He reminded him of the contract he signed with the College emphasizing security services for and in behalf of the institution as paramount. Therefore, he must comply with it or be sued for breach of contract.

As Granada explained the matter to him, Capt. Dallo began to look stressed as he related that earlier, he attempted to disarm his men but they wouldn't let him. They would only allow themselves to be disarmed on orders of Dr. Granada.

"Perhaps," Granada said, "your men like the instructors and students of the College were also fighting for a cause."

It seemed he hit a chord in Capt. Dallo for the latter to say "Sir, I am also willing to die for you."

———————————

In the face of all the incidents piling up and aggravating the situation, Granada felt he was left all alone, abandoned by his superiors to sort things out by himself and later face the consequences of his action. He decided to send a telegram to Minister Quilantang.

> ADMINSTRATIVE OFFICES FORCED OPEN TODAY/STOP/ WE ARE NOW HARASSED WITH COURT CASES/STOP/OUR LIVES IN THE CAMPUS ARE CONTINUOUSLY BEING THREATENED/ STOP/MADAME MINISTER PLEASE CONVENE THE BOARD OF TRUSTEES TO HELP RESOLVE THE PROBLEM/STOP/ WAITING FOR YOUR INSTRUCTION./ GRANADA

Later, he learned that Anita Caluya likewise sent an SOS to the president of the national federation of faculty in Manila seeking assistance and support.

Protest March

The protesters wasted no time and began their protest march around the city while Granada and his counsels checked out what's happening in the campus. Carrying their torn streamers and placards they marched from outside of Gates 1 and 2 of the College in Recto Avenue occupying the entire width of the streets taking the city route via the main thoroughfare to downtown Divora. It was a good one-and-a-half hour- march that created a traffic build up but which commuters did not at all mind. The joiners distributed copies of handouts, primers on the protest, copies of the reply letter of the students to Barrado and their manifesto.

At the Divora amphitheater where they were allowed to gather, leaders took turns in delivering speeches condemning Barrado's way of setting himself up and the political accommodation he was favored with. They also decried the destruction done on the property of their school, the injuries inflicted on some of their fellow protesters and students, the rough and rude men he had picked to surround him and the composition of his transition team.

Sonny Aquiling read their latest manifesto in full. It condemned the assault of the campus on June 13, the presence of bullies, goons and alleged communist rebels inside the campus posing as Barrado's bodyguards. The manifesto affirmed their belief that the Metro Ciudad Polytechnic College should be headed by a man of unquestionable character, highly qualified as an academician, and above all, acceptable to the whole academic community. It reiterated that educational institutions of higher learning must be spared from the division of spoils of political victories and must not become "dumpsites" of mediocre and unqualified political appointees.

The manifesto ended with the members' affirmation of Dr. Moises Granada as the most qualified to bring MCPC back on track urging the President of the Republic to withdraw Esteban Barrado's appointment.

DAY 20, WEDNESDAY, JUNE 18
Granada Couldn't be Budged

Since the MCPC incident was something that can no longer be disregarded as clamor from the public for news was getting stronger, Channel 6 invited OIC Granada to appear on its late night's news program "Tonight's Balita atbp." The interview was taped in the morning and was scheduled to be shown that evening.

Even before the question-and-answer progressed to part 2 it was clear that the hosts were leading the interview toward "cornering" their guest to admit something that will jeorpardize his position on the issue. Two major questions were asked: First, why was he (Granada) still around when Mr. Barrado had assumed office as the new MCPC president? What was his stake on insisting to stay despite the presence of appointment papers awarded to Barrado? Second, is it true that he was a "royal-blooded PMN" getting support from the deposed president's political party and that the picketers were actually "loyalists" backed and financed by People's Movement for Nationalism's money?

Granada immediately realized that he was there not to be given a platform and air his side of the story but to possibly compromise his integrity by putting him on the spot and humiliate him and his group.

Gathering himself up and putting on his signature dignified, cool and calm bearing he answered the questions confidently hoping against hope that his interviewers would be fair enough to air in full his response and explanation.

To the first, he said that as early as June 5 during the first dialogue with Barrado, he already put on the table a three-point proposal for a smooth turnover. "Unfortunately," he said "Steve Barrado refused to accept my proposal."

Granada explained that he could not just leave the College without the proper turnover since he needed to be cleared of property and money responsibilities before he finally bows out. "Assets, funds, property of the school which are considered government-owned and official documents have to be secured and accounted for. The process has become more complicated after his forcible entry."

He pointed out quite strongly that Barrado's appointment had not been attested to by Minister Quilantang, thus, he could not disburse funds as yet. "The Treasury Department, in fact, requires him to have his specimen signature attested to by the Minister but so far, Barrado has not complied," he pointed out. "Atty. Santos Matos, legal assistant to the Minister visited me last June 15 and assured me that I am still the person in authority because of the absence of a formal turnover."

To the second question, he said in exasperation, "the charge is ridiculous." He denied being a "royal blooded PMN" because he was never affiliated with it or with any political party for that matter.

"Politics has no part in my entire career in education though there were pressures during the last election. I never succumbed to these," he said quite proudly. He had always been neutral and non-partisan as his position called for neutrality.

When queried further about his protesters' alliance with PMN, he was dismayed at the hosts' insulting tone.

"That's also ridiculous. I know my people and none of them is guilty of such accusation. They were given a free hand to choose whoever they wanted to vote in the last election and if there were money greasing that happened, don't look at them, look elsewhere," he said almost in controlled anger. "There's no way that PMN is funding this protest!"

Granada's concluding statement was an appeal to the local media to be objective, fair and balanced in their reporting of news and events about the College. He was frank in his observation that the reports coming out so far were obviously favorable to Barrado.

When the interview was broadcasted in the evening, the whole Metro Ciudad were glued on their television sets expectant and curious. Will Granada be given a fair share of media mileage? Will he be accorded the chance to explain his side which for so long had been curtailed?

To their total disappointment, Channel 6 did not broadcast Granada's explanation in its entirety nor was he shown while speaking. His face was flashed briefly while the newscaster was reporting on something else, mostly taking the views of Barrado and his supporters overshadowing significant statements uttered by Granada in the interview. His answers to the questions were spliced and the anchor merely mentioned that he had been invited to shed light on the issue.

As disgusting as it was humiliating, Granada vowed never to allow himself to be mudslinged by the local media again.

"To hell with you!" he cursed in utter abhorrence of their act of betrayal of his trust.

Ejection Order Gone Pfff

Because majority of the faculty and personnel of the College were on mass leave, they did not dare enter the school's premises which by now was occupied by Barrado and his men. This made them "without a home" for the time being and set up temporary headquarters in the small apartment of Beth and her husband some five hundred meters away from the campus. Many protesters stayed there during the day holding meetings, preparing bulletins and protest paraphernalia. In the evening, men volunteered to alternately keep watch.

Today, they had another thing coming. It was something they couldn't shrug their shoulders off that easily and say "whatever it is, we will overcome."

Returning from lunch at a friend's house, Granada was greeted by another agitating news: Barrado ordered that by 12 midnight, the OIC should have vacated his cottage and had left the campus for good. Security must see to it that the order was carried out without delay. In other words, he was being evicted from his official home!

The news made Granada and his counsels and close in group rushed to Camp Dagohoy to report Barrado's ejection order. There they met RUC Commander Gen. Mariano Frias.

The general was very familiar with the controversy but said he couldn't be of help since that sort of problems does not fall under his jurisdiction. However, upon the insistence of Nap Lopa whom the general knew personally and who told him that he was their last hope, the commander promised: "Let me see what I can do."

In consideration of Nap's request and upon realizing the helplessness of the group, General Frias radioed Col. Samoza at Camp Alagar to send some men to check on the situation in the campus. After getting the junior officer's acceptance of his order, he wished Granada's group good luck.

On their way out of the General's office, Granada was met by some of his friends in college who were stationed at the Camp. They wanted to volunteer to secure and protect him but Granada knew it would be quite impossible to do that since they still had to go through a chain of command before any assignment could be given. He was grateful for the offer but said it was not necessary.

Back at Beth's apartment, a telegram from his wife Tessa was waiting for him. She was worried that he had not sent word to his family in Nueva Ecija for quite some time. She was asking about the situation in the campus adding that the children were missing their dad. He immediately sent a reply assuring her not to worry as the situation was under control and that the problem in the College would be resolved soon. Granada felt guilty and sad at the thought of his family in far away Luzon whom he had forgotten in the midst of trouble.

———————

Having verbally received such ejection ultimatum, the first question was whether or not Granada should return to his cottage inside the campus now. Someone suggested that he should not since this might be dangerous. Others prodded him to go, stay there and not abandon his home. "Hold your fort," they urged him.

"If I go back there I am sure, his men won't stop me. They must have known that my deadline is still at twelve midnight tonight. So I can go back without any problem, hopefully."

It was at this time that some students arrived. They reported that the student assistants staying in the Practice House were driven out forcefully by Barrado's men. "They are now occupying the Practice House," they told the group while catching their breath.

"Where are the girls now?" Granada asked with concern.

"In the house of one of their friends in a nearby barangay, sir. They are safe," Jimmy said which made Granada let out a sigh of relief.

They also reported that about thirty minutes ago, another lawyer of Barrado, Atty. Graciano Iner went to his cottage and ordered the security guard on duty, Jonas Liwag to clear the place of Granada's things and belongings in fifteen minutes. But Liwag rebuffed the attorney saying that he (Iner) better not come back in fifteen minutes because his "shotgun, a powerful Aliwati would not respect any body, not even a lawyer."

"If that's the case," the protesters said, "we should not give up your cottage. It is the last symbol left of our struggle. We shouldn't give it up no matter what happens," they shouted in unison.

"If it is necessary, then let's all die there," the students said boldly.

Remembering Barrado's deadline, Granada dictated to Beth his reply to the verbal order. He stressed that he was not going to vacate the cottage until a formal tutnover was effected. After Atty Padera reviewed the draft, Granada requested Sonee Gumba to type it and immediately send copies to Dr. Quilantang, Col. Samoza and City Mayor Pablo Jasta. He specifically instructed that the copies for Col. Samoza and the Mayor be personally delivered and that the couriers should surreptitiously observe the reactions of the two. Dr. Fe Perida, Dr. Max Domug and Prof. Elvie Urbano volunteered to deliver the note.

Many wanted to escort him back to his cottage but Granada declined saying it could only accommodate some 25 people at the most. There were now about seven people there including his brother Bebot and Bords Mallimas, a hometown friend. His brother Ben, Danny, Sonny, Nap, Amboy Cabigao, Police officers Serge and Kiko delos Arcos, Joel Lerpa and four other students, two non-MCPC sympathizers, Atty. Padera and himself made a total of 21 persons.

Some of the female faculty members offered to go with the group saying that with them in the frontline, the chances of violence might be lessened. "They might think many times before firing at helpless women," explained Miss Salvacion, the 55-year old Home Economics teacher.

Danny and Ben decided against it saying they didn't want to compromise their safety. The women were to stay behind and wait for instructions and prepare for any eventuality.

Mumble of prayers were heard as the men headed toward the school.

It was almost dusk when Granada's group entered the guardless gates. The security guards were not in their usual station. Where were these men? There was an eerie kind of feels inside an almost deserted place and Nap sensed the hair in his arms rose. Police Officer De los Arcos got off the first car, felt his revolver in its holster and very carefully did a quick reconnaissance of the area. The rest of the back-up proceeded slowly toward Granada's cottage. About seven meters away, near the so-called 38th parallel, some 50 men were milling around the bigger president's cottage. These men looked at them curiously as they got inside the smaller house.

Once inside, Bebot and Bords warned them of prowlers they saw lurking at the back of the cottage. Atty. Gael asked if they saw PC soldiers around but the duo said they couldn't tell. All five security guards who were supposed to be at their respective posts were also inside. They said they were avoiding the provocations directed at them by some of Barrado's men and decided to get out of the warfreaks' way. "By staying alive we can help secure Dr. Granada," they said.

De los Arcos came to report that more men arrived and were stationing themselves at Gates 1 and 2. The police officer said he recognized some of them especially those with police records.

Jem Pascua a friend supporter of Granada arrived with seven companions. He told the group they came to help. All in all, there were now 35 people inside the cottage.

Granada gave clear instructions that if trouble erupted, everyone should stay calm and not panic. He made it clear that the trouble should not start from their end. They would only retaliate if Barrado's men would force themselves inside.

"Once physically inside, that would be the time to defend ourselves with blood, if necessary," he stressed.

"By the way, has it ever occurred to you that we're practically defenseless, no arms except for the ancient shotguns of these brave men here? This is suicide!" Ben uttered jokingly.

"A noble way to die, Sir," Joel replied.

At about quarter to ten in the evening, Granada got word that Col. Samoza had endorsed his letter to Barrado with notations in his own handwriting. The city mayor could not be reached.

At exactly 10:00 o'clock, a courier from Barrado's camp came a'knocking at the small cottage. He brought a letter.

Dear Dr. Granada,

I wish to reiterate that after giving you more than enough time to wind up your affairs, it has now become necessary that you immediately vacate the guest house and the College premises effective midnight today, June 19. You are required to turn over College property in your possession to my Transition Committee for proper safekeeping and utilization.

You are aware that as a gesture of good faith and fellowship, I have allowed you to continue the use of the guesthouse, a vehicle and a few facilities since June 5, when I assumed the Presidency and your term as Officer-in-charge ended. It has been twelve days since then, and it is my decision that all privileges accorded to you during your incumbency as Officer-in-charge must now be terminated. Other school officials need to avail of these.

Thank you very much and I wish you good luck in your future endeavors.

Sincerely yours,

(Sgd) ESTEBAN BARRADO
President

Granada acknowledged receiving the letter by affixing his signature. He immediately wrote his reply in his own handwriting and requested Sonny Aquiling to deliver it. "Make sure Mr. Barrado receives it himself," he told Sonny.

June 18, 1986

Dear Mr. Barrado,

In reply to your demand to vacate the premises of the College, the Undersigned will oblige only if a formal clearance of non-accountability of all monies and property, records,

*papers and other documents belonging to the College shall
have been executed properly and duly signed by you.*

*Before said written clearance is received, the Undersigned
will continue to stay inside the campus as the accountable
person in authority of this College.*

*While your demand is inhuman, unethical and highly
irregular, my appropriate response to you is in the interest of
the educational community – to ease the tension, to prevent
further destruction of property, and to safeguard the lives of
those staying in the campus.*

Very truly yours,
(Sgd) Moises Granada
Officer-in-Charge

Again, he made sure to make copies of this to furnish the minister of
education, Col. Samoza and Metro Ciudad Mayor Jasta.

Noting that his letter reply was already on Barrado hands, he sat down
quietly and waited.

Meanwhile, Col. Somoza' wasted no time in endorsing Granada's letter
knowing time was of the essence.

Steve,

*I think it is a reasonable request worth considering.
I suggest that before Dr. Granada is asked to vacate the
premises, there should be an inventory of funds and property
and formal turnover of accountabilities therefore be
accordingly made.*

Salamat.
Sgd) Col. Jess Somoza

The Colonel wrote the note below Granada's signature. This was
reflected on the Xerox copy which Dr. Perida got from the copy furnished
to Colonel Somoza. The copy was delivered to Granada by the students
about twenty minutes ago.

As the clock ticked, waiting seemed ages and forever that night. Silhouettes of men prowling at the back of the cottage were cast on the bathroom glass panes. Out front, other men were moving on foot to and from the 38th parallel like aimless ghosts in the peripheries. A lone star shone not too brightly from heaven. Everyone waited with bated breath.

Inside, the cottage started to smell of human sweat. The air condition had stopped, the hot temperature adding to the discomfort and tension felt by everyone in the room. Yet, they kept themselves locked in not bothering to open the wide windows for some fresh air.

Drifting in the wings of sleep, Granada opened his eyes as he heard footsteps. He listened acutely. A cold wind of unease stirred inside him. He thought he heard a cry, a cry from the bowels of despair. He woke up and realized he was dreaming.

At about five in the morning Joel and Jimmy remembered to boil coffee. They were surprised that they were able to fall into deep sleep. Fatigue and weariness must have put a toll on these men's tired bodies and fell asleep throwing all cares to the wind. Cooler heads must have prevailed to let them sleep in peace. Col. Somoza's note must have influenced Barrado to defer whatever dark intentions he had planned for the evening.

They got ready for another round of an uncertain day keeping their fingers crossed.

DAY 21, THURSDAY, JUNE 19
Protesters Filed Criminal Charges

After four days of hard work, Atty. Padera was finally able to come out with the necessary documents for the filing of counter charges against Mr. Esteban Barrado, et.al. on behalf of the aggrieved academic community. The main cause of the delay was the difficulty of getting the certification of barangay captains that those injured were actual residents of their respective barangays. Another source of difficulty was the delay in the issuance of medical certificates by doctors who treated the injured. Speculations circulated that these individuals were sympathizers of the other side although this was hard to prove. Nonetheless, every one was relieved when the documents were obtained and their case finally moved.

Seventeen members of the College's faculty and staff executed an affidavit dated June 18 jointly charging Barrado, Tirol, Mecina and about 100 John Does for grave threats, damage to property, physical injuries, coercion, forcible entry, and breaking a peaceful demonstration.

The joint affidavit specified the criminal acts committed during the forced takeover of the College on June 13. This was filed at the City Fiscal's office by the leaders of the protesting community.

Meanwhile Barrado hired an additional security agency after realizing that the old agency had pledged its loyalty to his opponent. Panther Security, it was learned later was contracted for one year. A full force of 35 guards were assigned on campus, two of whom were in plainclothes. The allegation that It was hired to fulfill an earlier personal commitment was proven true during the transition process undertaken by an acting president. Panther Security was owned by a military man who was with Barrado in the early days of his assumption. In contrast, the Cosmos Security which had been under contract with the College for several years now had only a contingent of ten men. Since he knew he could not void the existing contract Barrado was aware that their services naturally centered on securing Granada and his group. The OIC vowed to block any attempt by his enemy to cut off Cosmos' services.

Since regular teachers and instructors were on mass leave, the "new president" hired some teachers from nearby high schools. They allegedly resigned from their jobs since the College offered a much bigger pay. Emergency laborers to do menial jobs completed the list of new hirees. Soon the number of employees of MCPC ballooned to an unprecedented number. It had almost doubled the number of existing personnel which later became a problem when restoration to normalcy was being done. It was one of the biggest headaches of the temporary acting president.

Of course, this act of hiring new personnel was condemned by the protesters blatantly tagging Barrado hideously.

A second protest rally was held in the afternoon. They were jubilant that at this time, the crowd practically tripled when they reached the amphitheater in Divora. But they were disappointed when no one from the local media came.

"Asa pa ba tayo?" Beth dispelling the disappointment of her fellow protesters.

Pay Cut Feared

Some who chose to stay in their offices and did not join the mass leave were feeling the pressure. Barrado was determined to show them "who's the boss" now and threw his weight around without mercy.

Chief Accountant Celestina Poon reported to Granada crying almost hysterically that she could not anymore bear the pressure on her. She narrated in between sobs that she had been "in hiding" in the last several days but Barrado's men found her and compelled her to report for work. She was called to certify funds availability for certain disbursements. Not only did Barrado dishonor the earlier agreement during the truce to co-manage the College with Granada until such time that the turnover was effected, he was also insisting his "authority" to disburse the funds despite the Treasury Department's ruling.

Poon's superior Bonnie Letran and the rest of the people in the cottage did their best to pacify her and asked her not to strain herself too much. "Don't give him the pleasure of seeing you break down," they encouraged her.

Jun Ilio the College Cashier also came in looking tensed and jittery. He informed them that Barrado had threatened to strike out all the names of the protesters from the payroll for the week. He said that like Ms. Poon, he too was extremely strained to submit to the biddings of the "new president."

"Be reminded Jun, I am still the person in authority and with my lone signature in the payroll, I could disburse the salaries of the teachers," Granada stressed. "And these people, your co-workers were on official leave of absence. Barrado has no right to strike their names out of the payroll," he added angrily.

Atty. Gael reminded them that during the truce on June 13, it was agreed that all disbursements should have the joint signatures of Granada and Barrado.

"Will that still apply?" Ilio asked perplexed.

"Yes, there was that agreement," the legal counsel replied. "However, Barrado had violated every statement contained in that agreement. Dr. Granada had not been consulted on decisions reached and acted upon thereafter," he remarked aloud. "We do not want to think that you were in conspiracy with them in the disbursement of funds," pointing an accusing finger on Illio whose face turned white. He was suddenly frightened by the accusations of his colleague.

Someone whispered from behind that Ilio was scared of Barrado because of an anomaly that the latter had discovered recently. It was alleged that Jun had secretly withdrawn a bidder's bond equivalent to ten thousand pesos and kept the money for himself.

When Granada heard this allegation, he took Jun to another room and confronted him in the presence of Atty. Padera, the chief accountant, Bonnie and Lito Cabale. Granada asked him pointblank if indeed the talks were true that he withdrew somebody's bid bond.

Ilio was uncomfortable and did not give a straight answer avoiding Granada's eyes. Everybody who observed his reaction had no doubt that he did. His hands were shaking which he tried to control.

"If you were scared, it's because of your own doing. You got into an anomalous situation which you yourself has created," Granada continued. "Should Barrado win this fight, he won't spare you and surely you will be prosecuted and eventually lose your job," he was almost threatening the man. The MAP people were simply waiting on the side, ready to grab your position. You know that, don't you, Jun?" he asked softly but with emphasis.

The man didn't stir from where he was standing nor raised his head to look at Granada. He didn't say a word but kept his head bowed.

"However, *kung manalo tayo, may investigation pa ding mangyayari sa kaso mo,*" said Atty. Gael "and you might not lose your job if found not guilty," he assured him.

Lito Cabale briefly touched Jun's conscience saying that it was his moral duty to pay the salaries of teachers and staff members who were on official leave of absence. "Because of Barrado's blatant violation of the truce agreement, the joint signature clause," Lito pointed out, "was no longer in effect. Hence, the signature of sir will suffice."

Everyone agreed on what Lito said.

Jun promised that he would make available the personnel's pay the following day, Friday and asked to leave.

Later, he came back with the ready payroll that his accounting clerks had prepared three days ago.

As Granada signed the payroll the protesters were delighted but weren't as hopeful. They knew that the coming days were not promising. To them each day had become a calendar of worry, anxiety and anguish.

"It's Time for You to Go."

That same afternoon Granada received a long letter which the protesters dubbed "It-is –time-for-you-to-go, Dr. Granada" letter from his adversary, Steve.

Dear Dr. Granada,

I regret that I cannot grant your request to continue residing at the Guesthouse. This decision is made not by any desire for vindictiveness, humiliation or unkindness toward you but for the following compelling reasons.
1. Change of leadership in many government institutions and turnover of responsibilities occur almost daily everywhere

in the country and outgoing leaders do not hold on to their posts for the simple reason of waiting for an inventory and the preparation of clearances which you so stated as your reason for staying.

2. My Transition Committee whose members are working hard to achieve normalcy in the campus and ensure that the College will function in the face of constant and multifarious activities of your group to derail, sow chaos and disorder, and escalate trouble in school are really in need of these facilities to carry out their work.

3. Your presence in the Guesthouse is the one single factor that emboldens your misguided followers to continue their move to destabilize the status quo. Your continued presence gives them the illusion that you are still the highest authority in the College as well as give yourself the imagined feeling that you are still in command. Know that you are no longer head of this institution. Let us not deceive the public.

Much as I regret it, but you have to go. We must put a stop to your undeserved privileges, to this one single source of chaos, of resistance, of disorder that continue to be perpetuated by your group in the College – your presence.

Furthermore, we have full knowledge that your plan is to escalate the tension and fan the raging fires of hate and controversy to attract the attention of the community, the nation and eventually the national leadership, an eventuality which in your scenario will keep you in the helm of the College and will drive me out of it.

We are also aware that your abnormal desperation to cling on to the last thread of authority is caused by the existence of questionable transactions and irregularities during your eight-month stint as officer-in-charge. We are determined not to be a party to your attempts for cover-up.

We are therefore reiterating this official notice for you to vacate the Guesthouse at the appointed hour and look for lodging elsewhere outside the campus. We shall appreciate your turning over the Presidential car and other vehicles, office equipment and other facilities which should now be at my disposal.

If indeed, because of your present troubled state of mind, you do not know the proper procedure for a quick and normal turnover, experts composed of regional directors who have recently taken over their offices and Commission on Audit officials will be sent to assist you. They will guide you to facilitate this simple undertaking.

We want to let you know that we have not run out of patience nor kindness, nor magnanimity. Instead, our reason and wisdom prevail. For in every instance that you have appealed to our patience, kindness and compassion and we have given these to you, you have turned these to your advantage, which I am sure you gleefully watched as they fell perfectly in accord with your sinister and dark motivations.

We have finally decided to put a stop to all these. It is time for you to go.

Very truly yours,
(Sgd) ESTEBAN BARRADO
President

Granada's first reaction was one of uncontrolled rage. He was like, as his name implied, an explosive device ready to be thrown to the enemy side to blow him out into pieces.

"How dare Barrado accuse me of questionable transactions and irregularities! Fuck him!" he yelled, his voice echoing in the open campus.

But this momentary rage turned into amusement after he regained his composure and realized that Barrado was nothing but a lover of words, loved to play with big words. So it was all words, he decided.

"Think nothing of it, Moises Granada!"

DAY 22, FRIDAY, JUNE 20
Keeping the Tension Low

As scheduled, the protesters stationed themselves in front of Gates 1 and 2 in continuation of their protest. It reminded them that today marked a week's anniversary of the assault in the campus. Romy Ramar opened the activity with a prayer, invoking the Lord's intercession in settling their problem fast. They had been in agony for so long now and wanted rest from such despair.

Because the street where they were was traversed by honking vehicles and people curious about their cause, their prayers were drowned by the noises around.

"Lord please hear our prayers, amen."

At around ten o'clock many of the faculty and staff courageously crossed the oval rushing to see Dr. Granada in his cottage to complain about their names being stricken out of the payroll. It turned out Jun Ilio did not honor his word, instead, he showed the signed payroll to Barrado who in turn, instructed Dr. Soriano to sign it in his stead. Soriano's signature was acknowledged by the bank since he had been previously authorized by Dr. Granada to sign on his behalf every time he was out on official business.

Dismayed at what he learned, Granada asked those whose names were cancelled to come with him to see Barrado at the Office of the President so that they could formally lodge their complaint. But his men prevailed upon him not to go saying it was not a good idea. Goons were all over the place and any face-to-face confrontation between him and Barrado might end up in violence, they feared.

Daunted by the helplessness of his situation, Dr. Granada wrote Jun a note telling him that the signature of Dr. Soriano on the payroll was not necessary since he (Granada) was not out on official business and had already signed it. That should suffice. Jun was instructed to immediately rectify this misrepresentation or face serious consequences later.

His note was replied to immediately by Jun who admitted that he was confused and didn't know who to follow. The pressure was weighing much on him and wished he could do something to right whatever wrong he had committed. He apologized for his action and explained that it was not his intention to turn over the payroll to Barrado. EVP Soriano saw him carrying it on his way to the Cashier's Office and prodded him to first see the "new president" about this. It was inside the PO where the dropping of names from the payroll was done.

The note from Jun was handcarried by Bebe Ramar and Maria Aquino. Enclosed was cash money amounting to P9,000 which Jun proposed, could be used as emergency loans to those affected by the cancellation.

Granada did not accept the money but instead instructed Bebe to return it to Jun and to tell him how disappointed he was in him. He kept the note though.

The reactions of the protesters was one of gloom. It dawned on them that somehow they must pay the price for this fight. And what a price to pay!

"Where will I get the money to pay for my rent?"

"I have only ten pesos left here. What can I buy with this?"

"How will my family survive?"

These were the questions that nagged most of them, yet the fight had to go on despite possibilities that they may be facing a bleaker future.

The General Took Matters into His Hands

It concerned General Frias that the trouble at MCPC was getting out of hand and thought he had to step in.That same morning, a certain Major Jabe from the Regional Unified Command came to relay the message that Gen. Frias was willing to mediate between the two "presidents" if they find him acceptable.

Granada construed that the General and Col. Somoza must have been in constant communication for the colonel to suggest that his senior officer take the lead in carrying out his (Granada's) proposal for a formal turnover. He was secretly overjoyed that the RUC commander considered coming to the rescue. This move, he believed could be the key to the final settlement of the conflict which had plagued the institution for almost a month now.

It was four in the afternoon when Gen. Frias with a Pekingese puppy in his arm and his aides came. Granada presented him a copy of his June 18 letter to Barrado and the latter's reply which the general gave to his aides. "Hold these," he ordered.

The venue of the proposed talk after much argument, was decided to be at the "38th parallel" perceived to be a neutral ground. Tables and chairs as well as a working sound system were set up quickly. While both parties were arranging themselves opposite each other, Neyra Arcon came running inside Granada's cottage and into the bathroom. Bebe Ramar was close behind her trying to calm down the hysterical Neyra. The woman was shouting at the top of her voice. "it was all the fault of Jun Ilio. I worked hard on the payroll for days and nights," she cried "only to find out that I was among those whose name was crossed out. Hu huh u hu."

Gen. Frias looked curiously toward the cottage and so his aides and the media men who had now gathered to cover the event. Granada explained to them the cause of the outburst. From their reaction, he felt they all understood but can only watch.

The conference started immediately after that slight distraction. It turned out to be a public spectacle. The media who had been conspicuously absent in the past were now present with their TV cameras and other paraphernalia. People from the outside came in droves to observe, including several well-dressed ladies and decent-looking gentlemen from the "new president's" side.

"This is unusual," Granada thought and whispered to Nap Lopa if he called the press.

"No, I did not. Let's just wait and see, they must be cooking something spectacular," he whispered back.

As soon as everyone involved in the conference was seated, Gen. Frias launched into a long opening remarks.

After his introduction, the General requested Granada to read his letter of June 18. When he got into the last paragraph which said Barrado's "demand is inhuman..." the General cut him off saying that was no longer necessary. He then requested Barrado to present his response to this letter. However, the General also stopped him saying it was too long and that he should simply answer if he was amenable or not to Granada's proposal. Barrado started to argue but the General told him "not to be emotional."

"All right, General, for your sake, I agree," Barrado nodded feeling defeated.

Granada requested the presider to ask Barrado read aloud the seventh paragraph of his letter dated June 19 (which practically accused him of covering up "questionable transactions and irregularities" in the College). General Frias made a quick scan of the letter after which he curtly said "We should go straight to the point." Granada bowed his head, humbled by the wisdom of the older man.

Since the general dispensed of mentioning the root cause of the trouble saying "after everything had been said and done, it is now time to sit down and discuss the business of turnover". Those present officially agreed without further question.

"Everyone present here and taking part in this undertaking must ensure that the turnover is peaceful and in accordance with the rules and regulations of the agency involved," the General said in his commanding voice.

With such order, a turnover committee was formed with members coming from both parties. Each party was allowed to have three members who will craft and execute the plan accordingly. They were tasked to do an exhaustive inventory of the College assets which include monies, property and essential documents. The inventory must also include liabilities of the school.

It was agreed that the committee should start its task the following day, Saturday. Today, their most basic concern was to identify the members of each team which was done in haste.

Granada named supply officer Lito Cabale, accountant Celerina Poon, and Ceasar Castro, Administrative Officer. Mr. Barrado named Sammy Mejor, Atty. Graciano Iner and Public Works regional director, Engr. Efraim Hizon.

At this point, Granada questioned Engr. Hizon's inclusion in the task force. Hizon immediately declined the appointment sensing Granada's disapproval. He knew he would be in trouble if he accepted the nomination. With Hizon's refusal of the role, Barrado named Roy Tirol in the Director's behalf but insisted Hizon was still his consultant.

As the third party in the whole set up, the General named Capt. Jose Ornano his representative to the committee and designated a certain Col.

Jose Tagactac to be its chairman. That settled, everyone breathed out a sigh of relief.

"Progress!"

Or so they thought.

In an attempt to sound "know-it-all" in the area of turnover, Engr. Hizon commented that inventory could easily be done in one day citing his own experience in the Public Works Ministry. "It could even be less here, since this is a small campus," he noted.

Granada pointed out that the director had no idea whatsoever of the school. He informed their counterpart that MCPC had seven satellite campuses that were spread out in three provinces and the inventory will cover each one of them. Engr. Hizon was suddenly silent and never said a word anymore throughout the entire conference.

Since a committee had already been formally set up for the purpose, Dr. Granada got confirmation from Gen. Frias for his continued safe stay in the campus until the formal turnover was effected. The general ordered Barrado to honor the agreement this time after he acknowledged the OIC's wish.

To Granada and his group's surprise, Atty. Iner suggested that a ceremonial turnover be held right there and then with the actual inventory to follow later.

As soon as Atty. Iner made the suggestion, Almira Barrado, wife of Steve followed by some well-dressed ladies, moved to the front with a bouquet of flowers in her arms as TV cameras zoomed in on her.

Nap Lopa threw a half-grin to his boss when Granada looked at him. So, this was the "spectacular" part of it. They were actually planning a show for media's consumption.

The faculty members and students behind Granada sensing what the Barrados were scheming yelled, "Don't agree, Sir. Don't agree!"

"I won't agree yet to a ceremonial turnover Sir" Granada told the General.

"What about a symbolic turnover ceremony?" Gary Daldalen suggested, sounding very conciliatory all of a sudden. "Anyway, it would only be symbolic."

Gen. Frias agreed that a symbolic turnover ceremony was okay with him.

"You are being partial, General," Granada kind of reproved the officer who realized that any formal turnover will happen only until after the work of the committee was completed.

"Okay, no turnover yet until everything has been settled peaceably," he agreed.

He shook hands with Granada, Barrado and the others and left.

As Granada stood up to leave too, Gary Daldalen jumped to his feet and started arguing. His "friend" walked toward him and said: "That's enough, Gary. I know that when you start opening your mouth, there is no end to it anymore."

With that, Moises threw him his rascal's smile, raised his hand for a high five and lightly pinched Gary's right chubby cheek. Those fat cheeks creased in a grin until he laughed so loud his face reddened like a boiled lobster.

The protesters at the back cheered and started chanting, "WE WANT GRANADA! WE WANT GRANADA!! WE WANT…"

"No…No!" Granada said quickly, spreading his arms to stop the chant.

Reporters rushed toward him and asked what the seventh paragraph was all about.

To satisfy their curiousity, he read aloud the paragraph in question and told them that this was an absolute lie and that Barrado's statement was libelous.

In the evening news, another lie about the meeting was highlighted – that a formal turnover was held in the afternoon with General Frias leading the ceremonies.

"Tsk, tsk, tsk, biased media strike again!" Granada and his group guffawed as they watched the late night news.

4

ON THE GROUND
AND UNDER
THE TREES

DAY 23, SATURDAY, JUNE 21
Odds and Evens

BECAUSE THE PROTESTERS had no specific place to gather and meet, they needed to look for a space as agreed upon during the gathering at Nits' birthday. Several offered their own place including Attorney Taburan's big yard about a kilometer away from the College. But the modest apartment of the Sebastians was chosen because of its proximity to the school and was conveniently located in the heart of the city. It became the protesters' haven in the meantime. Funny that at the opposite corner of the same street where the apartment was, stood the imposing Baclayon Building owned by Amira's family. Figuratively speaking the protesters had a "close encounter" with the enemy. Good that Steve and his family did not live there as the building was rented out to businesses who set up offices, parlors, stores, shops and what-have-you. Among its renters was a government agency.

Beth's husband Briccio, a.k.a. Brix was the dean of the Department of Engineering. He was deeply involved in the movement as Beth was. It can be said that the couple had a big stake in keeping MCPC out of Barrado's hands.

The apartment was not big but of moderate size. It had a living room, three rooms, a small kitchen and a bathroom which thankfully, had a good flushing toilet. The bedrooms were for the couple, their 15-year-old daughter Chyna and a spare one for guests.

Since that fateful bleak Friday the thirteenth (June 13) Joel Lerpa and student council's male officers had practically occupied the guest room. Chyna's room was offered to the girl officers and occasionally used by some female faculty and staff members. The couple's room ceased to be a private room. This too became available to anyone who wanted to take a nap or refresh one's self.

Here in this apartment, the protesters got together daily if they were not out on the streets to rally or hold pickets in front of the College.

Here, Myrna Cacdan, Sonee Gumbala, Nelya Zambales and those who cared to help, pounded on their typewriters to type or reproduce position papers, primers and bulletins, affidavits, telegrams and all sorts of documents. Beth saw to it that copies of all important documents were compiled and properly indexed by the school librarian Thelma Vista.

Romy Ramar and the Steering Committee spent hours upon hours in the HQ planning strategies, reviewing past event identifying their group's good moves as well as faulty strategies committed by both camps. They kept a written record of what happened as part of documenting "history in the making." All other committees met here to submit reports to the Steering Committee and to get apprised of their next assignment.

The mood inside the headquarters was not all the time serious and gloomy. There were light moments that brightened dark days and cheered up dampened spirits. The girls, for example would suddenly bust into "sing along" using Chyna's cassette recorder. Sometimes, even the oldies would join them belting out old time favorites. Oftentimes, Joel could be heard humming or singing his favorite song, "Be My Lady." Was he dedicating this to someone special? Girls who had a secret crush on the feisty young man would be blushing.

Here too, a lot of tears had been shed. The sorrows and pain of waiting for a solution to their dilemma that looked like it was not forthcoming in the near future were weighing their spirit down. Some felt insulted because they were unduly suspected of "spying" for the other side. The female teachers who were shamelessly shedding tear for their noble cause became known as the "crying ladies of the revolution." Edgar Santocrioto, the young man in charge of the stand-by generator inside the campus poured his heart out here because of accusations of some that he was a "balimbing,"- which meant a person of many loyalties, one who would align himself where he can benefit more. "I feel so betrayed," he said crying openly.

Brix'es garage where his battered Lancer was parked became the student artists' workplace where they printed all types of placards, posters and streamers for the movement.

Most times, the clicking of typewriters, the clanging of dishes, pots and pans and the endless exchange of arguments were a daily fare. But at the end of the day, one idea stood out – fight to keep the ideals of the College alive.

Being together at the headquarters day in and day out, one thing became evident– distinction between and among middle level management people, the rank and file and students, disappeared. All had simply become protesters, believing in one cause and reinforcing each other for the sake of that one cause.

Pressure, Pressure

Lito Cabale and Bonnie Letran who sat with their counterparts in the Turnover Committee were keeping themselves from walking out of the group's meeting. Barrado's team was pushing them to the edge to agree finishing off their inventory in one day. Bonnie had to replace the accountant who suddenly became indisposed due to muscle pains and irregular heartbeat. Caesar Castro was also not available since their first working day was a Saturday and his religion barred him from doing any work during their observance of Sabbath. So there were only the two of them versus three and the military rep who was perceived to be partial to the other team.

Both Lito and Bonnie were firm in their response to the "proposal" saying it was simply impossible to finish the inventory in only one day knowing the breadth and depth of the scale of work they needed to do in order to come up with a detailed list of all assets, property and the school's financial status. They also pointed out that they still have to agree on the procedure they will employ to make the work faster, easier and orderly.

"Let me remind you again that we're talking here not of one campus alone but of seven others located in three provinces," Letran stressed in his obviously agitated voice. "There were tons of documents which we need to inspect and scrutinize and it'll be crazy for any human being or even more to finish this in a week's time, more so in a day. I am not sure if you're up to the challenge, but we're not willing to compromise time," he added in dismay. Col. Tagactac, chairman of the Committee had no choice but to ask Barrado's team to agree to hold the inventory longer which the latter vehemently objected. They angrily said they would confer with Gary Daldalen about the suggestion and left the meeting kicking the chairs that were on their way.

To get back at Bonnie and company, they were given the run-around in their next meeting. Agnes Kampil who drove the men to the supposed meeting place complained that they were fed with wrong and inaccurate information about the venue. Agnes drove from the campus to Camp Alagar believing it was where the meeting will take place. The camp was some five kilometers drive through heavy traffic toward its nearest neighboring province, Kaliwanagan. But once at Camp Alagar, they were told that the others were waiting for them at Camp Dagohoy, a good fifteen kilometers away in the opposite direction. Frustrated, they reached the Camp only to be informed, and correctly this time, that the meeting was actually at MCPC!

"Aba, ginagago ata tayo ng mga yon ah," she blurted out in sheer exasperation.

Agnes was so mad that she threw invectives left and right. Her three passengers tried to put her back to good mood by complementing her on her skillful driving which did the trick. She readily smiled and said that she would just charge all that to experience. The drive back to the campus was leisurely and unhurried. "Let them wait!" they remarked in unison.

Protest Status: "Are We Getting Somewhere?"

Dr. Granada dropped by at the headquarters that afternoon. He came to assess the situation with his leaders and to plan for further action. An honest-to-goodness evaluation of their moves and decisions was undertaken admitting where they failed and why they failed. They took account of their good moves and how they could augment support by the community. "We'd have to know if we're getting somewhere," he commented.

While brainstorming on what to do best and what-not- to- do, they came to realize that Barrado had his own dilemma and could by now be, figuratively speaking, "groping in the dark."

They assumed that first, Barrado won't be sitting College President for long because of what he did to the school. Aside from the destruction of school property, physical injuries, and attempts to deceive the public through paid TV and radio broadcasts, he had pending charges related to his "acts of violence" against the institution. With such infractions, he could eventually be booted out of the presidency. In time, the community whose support he so desperately wanted to get would lash back at him.

"Steve Barrado committed the final screw-up," Atty. Padera said with a grin.

Second, the man could never be College president without the support of the faculty and students. If the rank-and-file continue to abandon their work and students refuse to come to their classes, operation would stop and the "new president" could not legitimize the hiring of new faculty members as this would require official action of the Board. The teachers he hired, in all probability, might turn against him or leave since he would fail to pay their salaries. He could not also disburse from the general fund in the absence of a signature confirmation from Minister Quilantang. The students, on the other hand, would be firm in their stand not to return to classes since the faculty wouldn't be there. At worst, he would be leading a ghost school since its halls and classrooms will be empty and deserted.

Everyone gave a thumb's up when Dr. Granada reiterated his observation that Barrado was committing more and more mistakes every day and it would be a matter of time before these mistakes boomerang on him. They believed his advisers were not at all helpful, instead they amplified his weaknesses as a school administrator by their unsound and inappropriate advice which he would likely to take hook, line and sinker. Eventually these mistakes and errors of judgment would catch up on him.

Third, the problem of the College was already a national issue and the whole academic world was watching with interest. With professional organizations like the SCUAP monitoring developments citing violations and disregard for resolutions adopted in the last Congress in Baguio, the controversial appointment might be recalled especially so that Minister Quilantang still refused to recognize him. There were confidential observations and monitors fed to her, some personal but nevertheless considered essential if they were to deal with her correctly and on the level. For example, the lady minister knew about Barrado group's uneasiness around her. They had never seen her smile nor laugh – not even once. She was serious, straight, formal, spinsterish, with a holier-than-thou disposition. During her meetings and at the last Educators' Congress she'd been the least amused by their antics, the quickest to condemn their missteps, the slowest to forgive their lapses. They attributed this to her background being the president of an elite private college for women before she was appointed education minister. And they never overlooked the fact that she didn't have to elbow her way around nor used anyone to get that prestigious post. She was personally picked by the President of the Republic. The Minister had absolutely no reason to play their kind of game.

"And by the way, what was the real intention of that Ministry Memorandum requiring all past presidential appointees to tender their resignation? Isn't that the sword of Damocles hanging over our heads to suppress any dissent or contradictory stand that we might take against the Minister and the Ministry? Do we still enjoy academic freedom in this new dispensation?"

No one had a ready answer. Dr. Granada raised his arms upward as if in utter helplessness. "There's more to this and I don't see its resolution in the near future."

The President of the Republic was scheduled to come to Metro CIudad. The controversy in the College was not only an academic issue that had captured national interests, but it manifested quite unmistakably a political shading that involved many influential figures including the Palace itself. To dispel such suspicion, the chief executive could do nothing but to render a decision believed to be forthcoming within the next two weeks.

Two weeks? This seemed forever. Could the protesters, the already low-moraled faculty and staff and the students last for another two weeks?

Adding to the protesters' burden was the local media which always saw to it that their cause was mentioned in bad light. When before Granada was hardly covered by the press, lately he had been the target of a smear campaign.

"Why was the OIC insistent on staying when he was deliberately asked to leave? Was he trying to cover up his many 'illegal and misuse of funds?"

The reporters remembered their quick interview with Granada during that conference mediated by General Frias. Barrado practically accused the OIC of fraud in handling money matters which the latter vehemently denied. The media seemed determined to press him down on this issue.

Many times the protesters were disgusted at how radio broadcasters would berate them for questioning the power of the President of the Republic in authorizing the appointment. They hated newscaster Dolly Gamat of TV 12 who kept repeating in her regular program that the majority of the students, faculty and staff of the College were in "full support" of President Steve Barrado conditioning the mind of her listeners that really, there was no problem at all at MCPC.

"That's the biggest lie ever!" their angry voices would reverberate in all corners of the city every time Gamat would pompously air her twisted belief.

"Why don't we buy air time to counter these terrible propaganda against us?" Tars suggested adding that they could raise money to pay for that radio spot. "That is what the Barrado camp is doing!".

The Committee knew that air time was very expensive and diverting some funds they had raised so far would mean spending less for more basic needs. They appealed to Tars to continue his mission of thwarting the negative media blitz in his own little way. They praised him for doing a good job despite his lack of resources. The telephone brigade should also continue to "police the airwaves" by calling the attention of broadcasters who peddled lies and distorted facts.

The review took note of a steady rise in the number of their supporters. They were pleased that in general, they were gaining more and more sympathizers despite the setbacks and the black propaganda mounted by the other side. Fraternal ties and alumni support were getting stronger as seen in the amount of cash donations or contributions in kind. The rest came from private individuals with no ties whatsoever with the movement but were sympathetic with the cause. Others got involved in the movement as deeply as the members of the protesting community were. The husband and wife team of Waldo and Jette Valdez allowed the use of their vehicles by the members. Waldo also made himself readily available at all times to drive for them practically leaving his business to his assistants during the duration of the struggle. Students who joined the rallies sometimes slept in his store.

Nitoy Huncio, father of a fourth year education student joined Chuck Dulay and his group in soliciting signatures for a petition to be submitted later to the President of the Republic. He was able to gather more signatures and joined their group to Manila to seek an audience with the Education Minister bringing the sentiments and appeal of the community. Several public officials, businessmen, including educators were secret supporters whose names were mentioned in hush because of their preference to remain anonymous. The alumni association of the College was considered the most active organization that heavily supported the movement.

Alerted by the President of the Republic's forthcoming visit to Metro Ciudad, the protesters took advantage of the news brought to them covertly by a local executive. Mr. Custodio Guinoo informed the group that the President was definitely arriving in Metro Ciudad on July 6. If they wanted an audience with her they should better prepare for this event as early as now since the MLG staff was finalizing the schedule of the chief executive during her stay in the city. A copy of the schedule was given them with instructions not to let anyone know about them getting it from MLG itself. They carefully studied the still confidential schedule of the President's anticipated visit.

Too Many Plans, Too Little Time

Since Monday is fast approaching which meant classes will be opening, a plan to sabotage the holding of classes inside the campus was laid out. The protesters were certain that majority of the students will boycott on the first day. They planned to hold protest classes starting Tuesday at the sprawling MacArthur Park fronting the Provincial Capitol. The original plan was to start these protest classes on Monday, June 23 but since Barrado had announced that classes on the main campus would start on that same day, the protesters agreed to move theirs on Tuesday. Their reason was to see if Barrado could muster a significant number of students and teachers to report to class on Monday.

Meanwhile, the local radio and TV stations kept broadcasting that it was all normal on the campus front, that most of the faculty and staff members were back to work and that parents should remind their children not to miss the opening on Monday, June 23.

Moving with speed, the protesters divided the work among themselves. Assignments like who should solicit teaching devices like blackboards and chalks, who should gather tables and chairs and bring them to the site, who should remind the students about holding classes at the park were designated. However, after realizing that it would be difficult to bring chairs and tables to the venue, it was decided to dispense with them. Teachers would just stand while the students would squat on the ground. A permit was already obtained for the use of the park for the purpose.

Schedule of classes had been plotted earlier by the Registrar's Office and had designated areas in the park where specific classes would be situated. New posters and streamers were to be placed around the park announcing their activities and a public address system was to be installed.

The importance of securing the place to ensure that no intruder nor provocateur would be able to infiltrate the ranks was given utmost attention. Vic Salgado was charged with this task. This effort would be reinforced by SSC's "intelligence and assets" who were briefed on their assignments in the park and inside the main campus.

Behind the frenzy of preparing for the best and the worst at the opening of classes, everyone was waiting for "the day" with apprehension and anxiety.

The Soluton Was Not in Metro Ciudad

Ben Granada who had been with his brother Moises since the trouble began suggested that while protest classes were going on, it was imperative that a delegation be sent again to Manila, this time, to appeal to national media for more mileage and to heighten campaign for support. He also raised the possibility of seeking an audience with the President of the Republic pre-empting her scheduled visit on July 6.

"While I believe that this issue will be settled in due time, the solution would actually be made in Manila and not in Metro Ciudad. We shall only be at the receiving end at what they have decided either favorably or unfavorably and that's final," he stressed. "We need to lobby and make them hear our side especially so that Gary and his client are preparing to go to Manila within this week," he informed them. "We have to anticipate their move."

It did not take long for the group to consider Ben's suggestion but insisted that Dr. Granada should go with the delegation. The strategy was to approach highly influential personages in Manila to obtain their support for the cause.

Granada readily agreed saying he had been planning to see Minister Quilantang and at the same time, visit his family. "I've neglected them far too long."

To join the OIC were Beth Sebastian, Anita Caluya, Joel Lerpa and Sonny Aquiling. Atty. Gael should be left behind to oversee the activities at the park with VPAA Vilar to stay on top of the situation. Nap volunteered to join the team to Manila.

With six in the delegation, six plane round-trip tickets were needed. Ben offered to buy two, Granada to take care of his own while two more tickets were taken cared of by faculty members Trining and Chris. Nap said he will shoulder his plane fare and other expenses. Caesar said there was little cash left which could be used as their pocket money. That settled, all were set to go.

Anita thought it was wise to inform the governor of their plan to go to Manila. She and the governor's cousin Irma paid him a visit hoping to get a note or a letter from him endorsing them to some people. She was not disappointed because the governor wrote two notes: one for Minister Mendel and the other, for the chief of security in the Palace. He advised Anita and her group "not to wear anything fancy should you be given an audience with the President. I always wear a T-shirt every time I see the President," the older man said as he bade her good luck.

DAY 24, SUNDAY, JUNE 22
Meeting MCPC President Emeritus

PAL Flight 182 took off very smoothly from Metro Ciudad Airport. As soon as they were airborne, Dr. Granada asked for the newspapers. He was given copies of *Metropolitan Times* and *Kalayaan*. Both carried accounts of the development on the on-going protest. The *Metro Times* reported on the SOS telegram Granada sent to Minister Quilantang asking the Minister "to convene the College Board of Trustees to iron out the problem." So far, the lady boss had not replied to the call for help, the news item stressed.

The *Kalayaan* article highlighted the Concerned Teachers of the Republic (CTR) criticism of the Education Ministry for being "too slow" in its campaign against corrupt officials. One part of the article had reference to the protest at MCPC.

> *CTR leaders also threatened to march to the Palace if the President does not revoke the appointment of Esteban Barrado as president of Metro Ciudad Polytechnic College in Northern Mindanao.*

Granada signaled Caluya who was three rows behind him about the article. Her efforts in getting the support of CTR and other teachers' associations were beginning to pay off.

In Manila, the group immediately proceeded to Anita's friend who lived in Santa Mesa. Since the place was small they decided to leave Beth and Anita with the family who willingly offered a room for the two. Nap, Sonny and Joel together with their boss were billeted at CNESU Extension Office in Malate which became their transient home for the duration of their stay in the big city.

Dr. Granada phoned Jongjong and summoned him to come to the transient house immediately. He also asked him to bring whatever information he could share to the group.

Jongjong came with news about the situation at the Ministry. He reported that Minister Quilantang was practically washing her hands off the controversy in the College.

"The Minister was sympathetic," he stressed, "but had categorically stated that she had nothing to do with the problem. She would not also comment on the proposal to convene the Board of Trustees for a meeting," he added disappointingly.

"Why? What was her reason for not convening the Board?" asked the puzzled Granada.

"She didn't say anything except shrugged her shoulders!" Jongjong said.

"What kind of a Minister is she?" Joel burst out in exasperation.

The group tried to explain to the young man that perhaps the Minister was still feeling her way around being new and inexperienced in handling a gargantuan job. "She must have been overwhelmed and that, she did not really know l the people involved," Dr. Granada alleged.

"And perhaps because of this, she has to wait for the right time before she acts," Sonny surmised.

However, the student leader was not convinced saying a Minister, as her position dictated, should be decisive and assertive. "She should also have a mind of her own, and not a puppet of anyone, not even of the President," Joel remarked aggressively.

Granada was astonished that the spirited young man had more wisdom than most older people he knew. With Joel around, he knew theirs was not a lost cause.

———————

Meanwhile, Beth and Anita got in touch with friends who could help connect their group with their target "influentials." True enough, Anita's friend got them an appointment to meet a former solon who was appointed chair of Good Government.

They waited for news about meeting Justice Minister Granile in his office soon. The opportunity to have a one-on-one talk with Dr. Quilantang still hanged in the balance. They were pissed at her intended unavailability. The Minister made it a point that she was not available due to many commitments or that she was "not to be disturbed."

The obvious refusal of Quilantang to meet Dr. Granada sent him a clear signal: "Give up MCPC."

Two other national dailies, *Tiempo* and *Vanguard* which seldom reached Metro Ciudad featured a narrative of how the trouble began. The *Tiempo* article was revealing as well as confirming that "the solution to the problem was due in two weeks." The writer must have known that the President of the Republic was seriously considering ending the rift at Metro Ciudad thinking maybe that it had gone too far for everybody's comfort.

The *Vanguard* published a similar story, except that contrary to its report, Granada did not actually "contest" the appointment of Barrado. It was the teachers, students and the entire college community who did. The story mentioned about the mass leave of teachers and the impending boycott of classes by the students. Likewise, it reiterated that the intervention of the President of the Republic was sought by the community.

President Emeritus' Lamentation

President Emeritus Gildo Bagongsilang was glad to welcome Granada and his group in his modest bungalow in an old subdivision in Marikina. He said he was happy being retired but after knowing what was happening in the school, he was deeply bothered. Even his wife was affected by the disturbing news. The couple had good memories of the institution being the one responsible for its "rebirth". That's why the grand old man had all the reason to be disappointed and hurt. He was conferred the title President Emeritus by its Board of Trustees for his exceptional services to the College being the one responsible for the conversion of the former School of Arts and Trade into its present status. People in the Ministry and the city recognized Dr. Gildo's efforts in transforming the wide marshland in the city's periphery almost singlehandedly into an attractive infrastructure complex now known as MCPC main campus. He was also recognized for establishing the seven satellite campuses in three provinces of the region. The old man made all these possible by sheer guts and at times, by "wheeling and dealing" convincing local education officials and local political leaders to help him acquire land through donations upon which those satellite branches now stand.

"The problem with these people, (referring to recent appointees and cronies of the revolutionary government) they think they have a monopoly of this government. They must be joking. I also risked my life in fighting the old regime!"

Sonny and Joel were listening to Dr. Gildo intently, noting his every word, even the constant fluttering of his eyelids. Beth had her tape recorder on which from time to time stopped. She hoped Anita would remember everything the gentleman said.

"The problem with these people is that they also think that because they had participated in this one revolution, they can already bully and bulldoze their way around. You know...." he stammered finding the right word.

"feeling entitled?" Granada supplied.

"Yes, that's it! Feeling entitled," he conceded. "What about those who built institutions but did not actually shout and march on the streets like the so-called street parliamentarians, but who were responsible in their own silent ways in establishing these institutions?"

"I have the same question, sir," agreed Granada.

"These people will destroy that College if nobody will stop them," the former president said bluntly.

Beth asked Dr. Gildo if the rumors were true that he nominated Barrado to the post and as a concession, requested him to take care of a relative in the College. (EVP Soriano was that relative.)

The old man was furious at the insinuation and claimed he was being framed up by some people there.

"You should be the first to refute this allegation yourself," he said hurt by the directness of the question. "But in fairness to you, I'm sure you were not entertaining such bullshit rumors. No doubt, these people spreading it are being led by Sosimo," the former president said with certainty. "You know the whole story Moises, don't you?"

It was about ten months ago, right in this bungalow where he first met Dr. Gildo when he was summoned to see him personally. The former MCPC head had wired Dr. Armando Carpio, then president of Nueva Ecija Central State University, saying that he had finally found the man who would take his place at MCPC. And that man, he told President Carpio, was his own Vice-President, Dr. Moises Granada.

He had been looking for one until he came across Dr. Granada's name.

"Could you please send Dr. Granada immediately to me?" the wire said.

"Are you Dr. Bagongsilang, sir?"

"Are you Dr. Granada?"

This was their first exchange that marked the beginning of a good friendship and professional relationship between two seasoned academicians.

Assuring the group that he had done something to support the plight of the protesting community, Dr. Gildo said he had called Gary Daldalen warning him of dire consequences if the situation was not rectified soon. He also showed stacks of letters sent to people who had direct link to the President, specifically one which he sent to Executive Secretary Conrado Comico-Rayos saying his "comico jokes" were certainly not funny at all. He promised to speak for and on his (Granada's) behalf when needed.

When they returned to the transient house, Dr. Tessa and their kids were already waiting for him. For the first time after a long while, he hugged every one of them tightly and realized how much he missed his children and finally gave his wife a long, warm embrace as if he didn't want the moment to end. It was a heartwarming reunion for the family who was unnecessarily separated by the wiles of men. He brought his family out for a nice dinner at Max's by the bay.

DAY 25, MONDAY, JUNE 23
Militant Groups Pledged Support

At five in the morning the men picked up Anita and Beth in Santa Mesa and proceeded to the solon's house for their appointment. The two were able to clinch it the day before.

The road was slippery and decidedly dangerous as it was raining hard. Added to this was their car's worn out condition. It's wiper didn't work and its horn wasn't at all honking either. The car, an old Mercedes was owned by Dr. Gildo which he lent to the group warning them to be extra careful because it wasn't in real tiptop condition. "But it runs quite cooperatively," he said apologetically.

The drive to Meycauayan took longer because of the traffic they had to hurdle along MacArthur Highway with several bottlenecks in Valenzuela, specifically in BBB-Gami and Karuhatan.

The solon's place was inside an exclusive village at the outskirt of this Bulacan municipality. Nap who volunteered to drive parked the car a good distance from the front gate since several vehicles had lined up the road indicating that there were already people who arrived much ahead of them. Granada told his team to brace for a possible long wait.

The former senator, they were told normally woke up at 8 o'clock. That was a good one hour away as Anita checked her watch. Nonetheless, Beth and the rest sat and waited at a designated waiting lounge along with the rest who tried to engage them in a conversation.

Some 45 minutes later Sonny and Joel had a glimpse of the former senator already talking to some guests inside his house. Without intending to eavesdrop the two learned that the other guests were Democrat Party members who wanted to get recommendations for government positions in this or that province. (Note that as soon as the new government took over, its first agenda was to replace all sitting elected officials by appointing an officer-in-charge pending "proper" screening of recommendees.) It was apparent that this solon's "note" carried much weight with the present government. Though he claimed that he had no power to appoint, he nevertheless wrote recommendations on their behalf.

Granada's group were silently watching the scenarios happening inside the solon's house and kept their own opinion and observation to themselves. It wouldn't be prudent to express dismay over what they saw and heard that may jeopardize their mission.

Former senator Malongay was not very accommodating and listened with divided attention to what Granada was telling him. He was obviously in a hurry to finish his time with them but nevertheless, wrote a note to the President of the Republic suggesting to "spare some time to listen to the protesters from MCPC when you get to visit Metro Ciudad on July 6." This was all they got from him after waiting for hours in the hope that a more concrete suggestion can be offered by the "distinguished senator."

In obvious disappointment, everyone had not-so-pleasant things to say about their experience that morning.

"I always look up to Sen. Malongay as a man of integrity and an honest lawyer. I always idolized him because we graduated from the same high school. I should have known that I should not be trusting what I heard or read about him," Sonny said shaking his head in total dismay.

"Politicians are all the same. They appeared like they have a genuine concern for their constituents. That's part of packaging themselves," Nap interrupted Sonny, sounding sarcastic.

"Were you disappointed Joel that the people you think were genuine were actually fake?" asked Dr. Granada when he noticed the young man silently sitting at the back.

Joel nodded confiding that his plan was to take up law after he finished his BS in Industrial Education. "But I don't think I will proceed," he said. "After what the Daldalen lawyers have done and witnessing how a prominent solon could be so calloused, I don't think I'd like to join their league."

"But of course, there are good lawyers," Anita reminded him.

"Yes, Ma'am. I know but I think they're rare. But I salute the likes of Atty. Gael."

Turning to Dr. Granada, the young man was curious. "Did you ever consider becoming a lawyer, Sir?"

"I did at one time," he admitted. "But my dad didn't want me to be a lawyer despite the pleadings of my mother who wanted me to become one."

"Moi has all the potentials to be a great lawyer. His teachers cried whenever he delivered his speech!" his mother used to say proudly. Their relatives agreed strongly to his mother's wishes for him.

"No! No!" his Dad objected. "That is precisely why I don't want him to be a lawyer. Otherwise he ends up being a liar! I named him Moises, after the biblical Moses so that he will become a man of God to lead his people out of the land of tyrants."

"Nice story, sir. We didn't know that part of your life. We have always known you as the bright academician, mindful of your faculty and staff and respectful of your peers," Beth remarked sincerely.

"Now you know, hehehe," humbled by what Beth mentioned.

Where's Empathy?

Their next stop was at Palacio del Uno in Intramuros where they met Jongjong. He was there early to make sure Minister Quilantang would see him. Again, the lady minister was not available. The group suspected she tried to avoid them by going out of town. Her secretary, Baby Abcede relayed that the Palace was setting up a meeting for Mr. Barrado and Dr. Granada soon. As to when and where, she had no idea yet of the details.

Anita, Beth and Nap went to the Legal Division to inquire about requirements for filing an administrative case while Dr. Granada went up to the seventh floor to see Dr. Antonio de Dios, the new Director of Higher Education. He learned that the chief was also out and wouldn't be back until late in the afternoon.

"Do these people know I am coming and made themselves disappear?" wondered Moises amused at the thought that he may have intimidated them.

However, the thought nagged Moises and made him uncomfortable. He took the elevator down and found his group waiting for him.

On the ground floor, Anita was complaining of the "indifference" of the people at the Legal Division.

Beth added, "They seem not to be interested."

"It is useless to talk to those people," Sonny said, "They are as cold as ice."

The Legal Division was not encouraging the filing of an administrative case since their lawyer, Atty. Taburan already filed an injunction, the staff reminded them. "Soon the Court will hand down the decision as to who really is the legitimate president of your college."

Granada checked his diary and confirmed that indeed the injunction was filed on June 13 before the RTC. The case was docketed as Civil Case No. 10752.

Outside of Palacio del Uno, students of San Mateo High School were demonstrating denouncing political interference in their school. Their placards "shouted out" the injustices done to the school by a politician-appointee including the lay-off of very qualified teachers whose positions were taken by incompetent political protégées. They decried the new policies that curtailed academic freedom in the school and rules found to be limiting their growth as students. It was inspiring to watch these young people stand for their rights. One of the speakers criticized the Ministry for the indifference, the lack of empathy and its indecision regarding their plight. It had been weeks since they filed their complaint but it seemed, their legitimate complaint had "fallen on deaf ears."

"So like us," Joel whispered to Nap.

"We're not alone, after all. Should we be happy?" Nap smiled sadly.

They were about to leave when someone tapped Granada on his shoulders. It was Dr. Herminio Santos, one of the Ministry's division heads. They were actually friends. Happy to see each other again after some time, Granada told him about the visit of Atty. Santos Matos in his school and what he relayed was the position of the Ministry on their case.

They talked for a few minutes more, congratulated Dr. Hermie for having retained his post.

"Congratulations. I think keeping you is one of the best decisions she has done so far," giving the man a light tap on his shoulders.

"You know my friend," Santos said, "I've been listening to that young speaker over there. I think she is right. We in the Ministry have become what we feared to become, and I am not proud of it," he expressed sadly.

"Are you telling me that nothing has really been decided on, that no one is taking responsibility?" Granada asked incredulously.

Between long-acquainted friends, body language suggested a certain specific message. As he winked at Granada and released a weak smile, the OIC smiled back as he nodded his head in comprehension.

"Good luck, my friend" Dr. Santos said offering a hand for a handshake.

Militant Groups' Statement of Support

Teachers around the country found it necessary to form groups and associations to have legitimate grievance machineries to air their demands, requests and propositions for better working conditions, better pay and other benefits. These associations and groups by their sheer number can influence government decisions and actions, and they had, numerous times.

From Intramuros, Anita, Beth, Sonny and Joel proceeded to Normal College where they were invited by CTR and other militant teacher groups for a meeting. They were requested to apprise them of the on-going protest in their school. Dr. Granada did not join them since it was exclusive to the rank and file members. He and Nap were off to meet some people in Congress hoping to lobby some congressmen who had shown interest in their problem. What they needed at the moment was support from outside community who had the power to pressure and sway decision in their favor. Status was at play here.

In the meeting Anita and her team explained the facts of the case and laid down their take on the controversy. The press and broadcast media were invited and the team was hoping that their story will be given a good exposure. They also distributed fact sheets and other supporting documents including their position paper keeping their fingers crossed that this time, the truth about the trouble in their College would be revealed to the nation.

During the meeting, the umbrella organization, CTR decided to draft and issue a "solidarity statement" upholding the position of the protesting community in Metro Ciudad. Copies of the said statement were later sent to the Palace, to the Ministry of Education, to all state colleges and universities in the country and to concerned government agencies. The statement read:

> *We, the members of the of the Concerned Teachers of the Republic (CTR) have come together in unity to denounce the illegal and inappropriate appointment of Mr. ESTEBAN BARRADO as President of Metro Ciudad Polytechnic College in Northern Mindanao.*
>
> *Whereas, we support the cause of the teachers, personnel and student body of Metro Ciudad Polytechnic College*

(MCPC) manifested in their on-going strike and mass leave appealing to Her Excellency the President to revoke the appointment of Esteban Barrado which did not pass through proper screening and selection process as provided for in the Ministry of Education's set of guidelines and rules.

Whereas, we uphold MCPC academic community's right to be consulted in choosing and recommending the College president they will be working with as embodied in the College Charter.

Therefore, we the Concerned Teachers of the Republic and its affiliates, in the spirit of solidarity, strongly speak against political interference in appointing heads of state universities and colleges, seek to uphold academic freedom, and stop politicians from meddling in matters of education. We appeal to the President of the Republic and Minister Lucretia Quilantang to resolve the MCPC problem immediately to prevent further untoward incidents that may lead to injuries, loss of lives and destruction of property.

In witness hereof, we hereunto affix our signatures this 23rd day of June, 1986.

The manifesto was signed by 21 members headed by CTR president and other officers and officers of minor associations affiliated under it.

The group left the meeting carrying that hope in their hearts that something good was bound to happen.

A long distance call from Dr. Perida came through in the evening informing them that everything was set for the scheduled protest classes. They were happy at the news that classes held inside the campus only had 36 students and only 13 regular faculty and administrative staff reported for work. She did not fail to note that the new hirees (substitute teachers and staff casuals) seemed to increase in number every day.

DAY 26, TUESDAY, JUNE 24

Epic Classes at the Park

Classes held at the park was well-attended with 95 percent and 97 percent attendance of faculty and students noted respectively. Concerned citizens of Metro Ciudad who were intrigued by the bold action of the group donated chalkboards, boxes of chalks and erasers and everything they thought would be needed by the teachers and their students. The park was filled with people who wanted to help as well as those who simply nosed around. They, however, let the classes went on uninterrupted.

The protesters made sure that officials in the national level were informed of this. Dr. Max Domug sent telegrams to the President of the Republic and Minister Quilantang reiterating their appeal for immediate and appropriate response to their request. The local government provided security but emphasized that this was standard operating procedure to prevent any untoward incident that might cause public disturbance.

Surprisingly, the classes proceeded with less hassle despite the irregularity (or was it oddness?) of the situation. Schedules had been plotted carefully to avoid overlapping or confusion in time, subject and teacher assignment. Twenty classes with at most 40 students each were conducted with a certain amount of efficiency and seriousness. There was a concerted effort to prove to Barrado that classes will go on as usual without him taking charge.

The idea of holding protest classes to dramatize the mass action was brought out by Mario Inciong, basketball coach and cultural consultant of the College. He suggested this in one of the meetings of the Steering Committee. He impressed upon the members the effectiveness of protest classes over other means like the "sit down" strike by the students or by delivering fiery speeches. Protest classes outside of the school were epic in themselves and were likely to attract more attention, more heightened interest and could gain public sympathy on the spot. Holding classes under the most unusual condition will teach students the importance of learning and using time wisely despite what seemed to be an insurmountable problem.

MacArthur Park was readily selected as venue for its many tall shaded trees and cooler ambiance. Located in front of the Provincial Capitol, the park was spacious and accessible enough for the students who came from different parts of the city and neighboring towns. Also, of the three public parks in Metro Ciudad, this was less vulnerable to heavy traffic compared to the City Central Park in downtown Divora or the Bastion Park in front of the St. Pancratius Cathedral where evacuees from the feared town of Kulintang (known as the "killing field" of Mindanao) took shelter when they fled their homes due to non-stop communist insurgents and military skirmishes. They were later found mingling freely with the protesters, observing around or talking with anyone who cared to listen to their stories. They seemed to have found people who shared and empathized with their sad plight.

Meanwhile, President Barrado was incoherently urging EVP Soriano to do something about the classes being held outside. He was worried that they were attracting much public attention or sympathy. He also knew that a few news reporters were there to cover the event.

"Do whatever you can, Soriano. I can't have it that my students were outside attending classes under the heat of the sun," Barrado said feigning concern. He was actually furious at the thought of his students defying him too.

Earlier, EVP Soriano and his team including Atty. Daldalen were at their heels finding out how the classes could be stopped and compel both students and teachers to go back to the campus. For now, they could only watch their boss threw his rage at them.

That same day, Anita made possible the personal meeting of Carlito Payos, national president of SUC's faculty association and Dr. Granada.

This was necessary, according to her to gain the sustained support of the association to their cause.

Carlito Payos whose name was synonymous with campus protests and teacher militancy looked frail. But what he lacked in good physique was obviously compensated by his intellect and strong commitment to fight the injustices committed against teachers– poor salaries, uncomfortable working conditions, and political interference in giving teacher-appointments.

He came, he said when they were seated face to face in a small restaurant along UN Avenue, to find out exactly where the OIC stood in the controversy.

Granada explained to him that as head of the institution, he had to keep an objective distance, and therefore, should not really be part of the protest movement. However, he added that his involvement became inevitable in the face of the evolving circumstances. Still, his official position was for a smooth turnover and was continuously and strongly pushing for it. While he agreed with the position of the protesters giving them advice when asked, he could not actually question the authority of the President of the Republic in authorizing her executive secretary to sign Barrado's appointment. He admitted wanting to remain part of the educational system but was confident that before the turnover happens, the teachers, staff and students of the College would have already been vindicated.

"Do you mean to say," Payos asked, "that your stake is actually a tactical or strategic move rather than official?"

"It is both," Granada replied, "considering the circumstances that led to the appointment of Barrado, the unequivocal stand of the academic community, the disgust of Minister Quilantang over that appointment, and the authority of the President of the Republic on the matter."

He emphasized that he had to balance all these adding that perhaps history would later prove him right.

Payos nodded as a gesture of politeness but Granada sensed he was not convinced. His body language and his look of disapproval at what the OIC had explained were tell tale signs. Granada knew that the leader wanted a much firmer commitment, in fact, if it were only possible, Granada should categorically side with the protesters.

"But don't you think, Sir," he pointed out, "that your proposition for a smooth turnover would only jeopardize the protest?"

"I hope not, but it could, admittedly. However, if the movement wins, then all those in the College, including the Minister of Education, would be vindicated."

As Payos bid goodbye to the OIC, he expressed hope for another meeting with him. He pledged his organization's and other militant groups' unqualified support informing Anita and the others that they were going to stage a picket in front of the Palace within the week to amplify MCPC's call for the revocation of Barrado's appointment. Their handshakes were firm and tight and assuring.

Late in the day, Dr. Tessa was back at the transient house without the kids. She had sent them back to CNESU so as not to miss the school opening. Moi promised to see them again before he flies back to Metro Ciudad.

Dr. Tessa wanted to know more about what was going on in her husband's school. She asked a lot of questions sounding worried.

"I feel you were keeping a lot from me," she accused her husband, pouting.

He smiled down at her and put his arms on her shoulders. "Oh, but there's no point in worrying you, my dear. After all, everything's under control," he said in his usual calm tone.

"Under control? But what about these photos?" She was aghast seeing the photos of the June 13 disastrous "invasion" of the College. What she saw made her afraid and uneasy.

"Oh! But they they were simply like your days at UP. You were even worst during your time," Moi was trying to humor his wife. "Nothing really serious happened."

Not wanting to worry her boss' wife further nor complicate the discussion, Beth shifted the topic to their meeting with Senator Malongay. Joel lightened the mood by mimicking the old senator's mannerisms. Every one had a good laugh. They ended the day with Tessa treating them at *Little Quiapo* feasting on its famous siopao and halo-halo.

DAY 27, WEDNESDAY, JUNE 25
No Solution in Sight

Atty. Fulgencio Torana, Assistant Executive Secretary was set to meet Granada's group in his office at the Palace. Baby Abcede advised them not to miss the three o'clock appointment with the assistant secretary, wishing them good luck as they left her office.

The group was optimistic and tried to convince themselves that the solution to their problem was finally at hand. But were they correct in their optimism?

At exactly three in the afternoon, Dr. Granada and his team were ushered in at the receiving room of Torana's office and were asked to wait. After 25 minutes Granada was summoned to come in alone. The others were left outside who were obviously disappointed and apprehensive. They wanted desperately to hear firsthand how and where the discussion would lead.

Ten minutes later, Atty. Santos Matos arrived and went inside the secretary's office followed by Mr. Barrado and Atty. Gary Daldalen. On his way in, the controversial "president" threw a swift, contemptuous glance at Anita and the rest while Gary Daldalen acknowledged the two women with a slight nod.

Inside, Granada was happy to see again Atty. Matos, the "deputy minister" and shook hands with him heartily. He briefly acknowledged Barrado and Gary with a brief nod. They waited for Assistant Secretary Torana to begin the conference.

The Secretary turned out to be a big man but ironically, was thin with words and disappointingly lacking in deference. His sole interest, he said was that there should be no trouble when the President of the Republic visits Metro Ciudad. He then pointed at the conference table in his office and instructed his guests to discuss among themselves and come to an agreement amicable enough for both. He casually informed them that he was too busy to sit down with them. With that he left the men who were dumbfounded at the awkwardness of the situation.

"Fend for themselves?"

Obviously, this was not what they expected. The men looked at each other, not knowing how to start or where to start.

Granada's first impulse was to leave the room. However, he was prevailed on by Atty. Matos to stay and take the opportunity for a real heart-to-heart talk.

He rose and made himself a cup of black coffee which the staff made available for the guests. He was entertaining thoughts that perhaps Secretary Rayos would just barge in, tell them of the President's decision or that perhaps, though this was kind of remote, they would be called later by the President herself. He braced himself for a "talk" that he predicted would not accomplish anything.

As expected the meeting did not proceed according to its purpose and intent. It spiraled out to be a verbal clash between Atty. Matos on one hand, and Barrado and Daldalen on the other. At one point, Matos threatened to leave the room, telling the two that there was no use continuing since Barrado obviously was not listening to him. He was insulted when Barrado exclaimed "Please Santy, open your mind…"

"As far as we (the Ministry) are concerned, you have not as yet assumed office because there has been no formal turnover yet," Matos intentionally accentuated the fact. He was noticeably highly agitated reminding Atty. Daldalen that as Barrado's lawyer, he should "…warn your client about those government property that are now in his hands and are freely being used without the benefit of proper accountability. The cars you are using are driven by unauthorized persons. You just be careful that no accident happens because he will be in big trouble."

Atty. Daldalen took offense of the staunch reminder sayng that his client did not really mean to offend him. He nudged Barrado secretly to apologize at the angry "deputy minister."

Granada suggested to talk about his proposed "smooth turnover" to get something done at least, to which Daldalen and Barrado agreed. But Atty. Matos declined saying they could work on that at the Ministry and perhaps, with the Minister joining them. He informed the men that a draft for the turnover agreement had been written and was ready for deliberation.

"There are so many people in this world who are simply ignorant of how government operates," Matos was mumbling to himself on their way out of the Palace.

Agreement Draft Inopeative

While waiting to be called inside the Minister's room for the finalization of the turnover agreement, Granada was engaged by Dr. Vernie Ramos in a little *tete-a-tete*. He recalled the time when Barrado came to his office to show his appointment papers. "...maybe to legitimize his claims. This was actually picked up by the *Metropolitan Times* and came up with an article critical of the present government's policy on appointing people to important posts especially that of state-owned institutions."

"I remember reading that article, sir and it gave us some hope that more people still believed in keeping the highest standards and the integrity of the academe," Granada replied. He thanked Dr. Ramos for presiding over the College's Board of Trustees meeting last January in Metro Ciudad wherein he stood in for former Minister Cortez who could not make it that time. In that meeting, Granada's position as Officer in Charge was changed from OIC to that of College President "with full authority to govern in the best way he saw fit. This was the spirit of his designation by the Education Mininster," Dr. Ramos said, mentioning that Granada passed the tight screening through a fine-tooth comb besting seven other candidates for the position. However, Granada chose to keep his OIC title while waiting for the former President's signature on his appointment papers. Unfortunately this did not happen because the new government took over unexpectedly.

Inside the Minister's office, the content of the turnover agreement was deliberated on with inputs from both sides. Atty. Matos eventually came out with the revised draft.

AGREEMENT

In sincere desire of the parties represented herein to work toward peaceful transition, ensure the protection of the interest of the constituents of Metro Ciudad Polytechnic College and to preserve the integrity and academic atmosphere of the said College, a committee composed of the following is hereby formed.

The Budget officer
The Supply officer
The Administrative officer
Chairman, Transition Committee

The Executive Vice-President
Member, Transition Committee

The Committee to be chaired by the Ministry of Education's Director for Region X, is constituted for the purpose of effecting the clearance from accountabilities of the incumbent Officer-in-charge, Dr. Moises Granada, on or before July 4.

It is the intention of this Agreement to settle any dispute and/or disagreement peaceably, hence, all charges and countercharges raised before any court or courts in connection with MCPC shall be withdrawn by their respective complainants.

During the period determined by said Committee both parties have mutually pledged to help restore normalcy in the College and hold themselves personally responsible to the Minister of Education in this regard. Likewise, both parties agreed to maintain their presence in the campus to carry into effect the provisions contained herein. However, official matters which need to be acted upon immediately such as disbursements of funds for teachers' and staff's salaries, signing of official documents and the like shall be, in the meantime, the responsibility of the Regional Director.

This agreement shall take effect upon signing by both parties.

MOISES GRANADA   ESTEBAN BARRADO

After reading the draft, Minister Quilantang ordered that July 4 be changed to July 3 emphasizing that the turnover should have been done before the visit of the President of the Republic to Metro Ciudad on July 6.

Granada rose to object to her order saying that July 3 was not a good idea since the volume of work entailed a longer period.

"Madam Minister it would be physically impossible to accomplish the job within the given time frame. If the inventory were to start immediately, June 26, Sunday not included, this would mean a total of nine days only," he said hoping that the lady minister will see the merit of his objection.

But the Minister refused to listen and insisted that her "suggestion" be taken. Granada, knowing it would be futile to argue with the lady minister, slid into silence. She asked Atty. Matos to finalize the draft who left the room quickly, wanting to get away from the "broiler" as fast as he could. He knew her too well to want to stay a minute longer.

In an effort to impress the lady minister, President Barrado boasted that classes in the College were now back to normal and that the majority of the faculty members were likewise back to the classrooms.

Granada simply told him, "Please don't distort facts. You are talking to the Minister. You know that is not true."

Dr. Quilantang chose to ignore Barrado's attempt to give him her attention. She instead went back to the pile of documents on her desk without commenting but showed signs of irritation.

When Barrado could not be stilled by the older woman's disinterest in what he was saying, she snapped at him sternly. "I don't need to listen to your blabbering Mr. Barrado. Shut up."

Sensing that the Minister was starting to get upset by his client, Gerry Daldalen pulled him aside telling him to do as told.

When the final draft was presented again to the Minister, she did not bother to read the whole document but verified that July 3 was the date indicated.

"You don't need to sign this today. Why don't you sleep over it and if necessary make suggestions to improve it. Come back tomorrow for your formal signing before this office," she commanded.

When everyone had left her office, Granada asked that he be granted a few more minutes with the Minister. He had something important to tell her.

"Make it fast," she said as she went back to signing some papers, her small eyes darting from one pile to another.

"Thank you, Ma'am for your time," Granada began as soon as the door closed.

"Ma'am did you receive my telegram last June 17 in which I suggested that you convene the Board of Trustees of the College..."

"Yes, I received your insulting telegram," the Minister cut him brusquely. "I cannot and will not convene the Board just because you said so. I am too busy attending to so many problems. And besides, I think the problem is now beyond the Board – it is already with the Office of the President."

"Ma'am, I didn't mean to insult you. The telegram was a sincere request to help resolve the problem in the College..."

"Resolve the problem in the College? Don't you understand Granada that because of your stubbornness and the insistence and wild ambition of what's-his-name Ba-bar-bas-stardo, the problem has been aggravated twenty more times!"

"Barrado, Ma'am...Bar-rad..."

"I don't care and I don't care about your suggestion. It doesn't have anything to do at all with the political interference accusation that has now become a pain in the ass in this Ministry."

"Ma'am, why don't you give my suggestion a second thought..."

"Now, Granada..." looking at him with those shrewd tiny eyes, "you are no different from Barrado, you keep on insisting and you don't listen. Can't you see that I'm too busy right now? Please close the door after you as softly as you can. I can't stand doors being slammed shut!."

Like a humiliated mongrel Granada left, his face unreadable, his chest heaving. He was furious but kept his feeling nicely hidden. However, his group knew his silence meant "danger."

On their way back to the transient house, Granada reviewed the draft, noticed that the names of Anita Caluya, Beth Sebastian, Sonny Aquiling, and some others, including that of Gerry Daldalen were now included and listed. In essence, they became signatories to the agreement which should have been just between him and his nemesis. He remembered not seeing these names on the first draft. Would Anita and the rest be agreeable to signing this and as a consequence, withdraw the criminal charges against Barrado and his men? He wanted to know.

"Never, never, never!" they chorused with firmness. "We've been hurt by Barrado and his men and they have to pay for it. The Ministry has nothing to do with our case against these dubious men."

That same night, Granada wrote Atty. Matos that upon review, he found the final draft simply unacceptable. He stressed that there was a need to modify it. Among others, he pointed out, the names of Anita Caluya and the rest should be deleted since they were not present during the deliberation. He also made mention of his group'ss refusal to drop the charges against Barrado, et. al. He ended his note by saying that he was making his suggestions following the Minister's instruction that the final draft be reviewed first before they affix their signatures.

———————————

Reading Granada's note, Dr. Matos knew all along that the OIC would not be amenable to the terms stipulated in the agreement. He gave out a long sigh.

"This is going to be trying times."

Little did Granada also know, till much later, that his refusal to accept the terms in the agreement despite his explanation, would earn the ire of the obstinate Quilantang.

Setting a Precedent

An article in the *Metropolitan Times* caught their attention before retiring to bed that night. It played up the efforts of the members of the CTR to protest the current "contemptible" practice in appointing heads of state-owned educational institutions in the country.

Mass protests hit state-owned educational institutions
by Ryenette Ocampo

Disgruntled students, teachers, and staff of at least eight state colleges and universities around the country and one public high school in Metro Manila have begun a series of mass protests by boycotting classes and holding indignation rallies to decry alleged political patronage by the Education Ministry in the appointment of state college and university heads.

Raul Viagose, CTR chairman, identified the schools coming from seven regions in the country.

Viagose hinted that Education Minister Lucretia Quilantang has the tendency to gloss over the qualifications of alleged political nominees by recommending their appointment instead of subjecting them to the selection process she herself proposed. Her criteria include professional integrity, competence and acceptability by the academic community where the appointee will be assigned.

The CTR chair cited the case of a state college in Metro Ciudad in Northern Mindanao where students, faculty and staff had launched a protest against the appointment of one Esteban Barrado as its new president.

Viagose said the plight of the said school is also experienced by seven other schools which he learned, are as equally determined to rid their institutions of politicians trying to lord it over their campuses.

After reading the article, Granada wondered aloud if their own protest had somehow emboldened other SUCs to come out in the open and staged their own with MCPC setting a precedent.

Sonny, however, looked at it differently. "But Sir. Theirs is a different case."

"What do you mean different?"

"Well, theirs is a different case," Sonny reiterated "because they are protesting against their incumbent. In our case, we are protesting against the incoming president in order to retain our incumbent."

"Well sir, do you still agree that our protest is at least setting a precedent?" Joel joined in.

"Perhaps, that is true. If we succeed in causing the revocation of Barrado's appointment, then we would surely be setting a precedent. From thereon, politicians hopefully, will keep their distance."

As they went on discussing the pros and cons of the issue, it occurred to Granada that what was actually at stake was not the revocation of Barrado's appointment but how the educational system would behave if the revocation had been carried out.

In that case, he concluded, Barrado and the protesting community and himself were but players in a game that was being played: Barrado was the willing pawn in the political chessboard while the protesting community and him, the sacrifice.

———————

DAY 28, TUESDAY, JUNE 26
"Love Affair" with Politicians

Ben Granada used to tell his brother Moises that if he can only be a little patronizing of politicians, feeding their bloated egos at times, dancing to their music, he could have been spared of such troubles as what he was now experiencing.

As early as mid-March, the rumor was rife that Granada was going to be replaced because the new administration was bent on ridding government of all vestiges of the deposed President including those associated with him. Many of his friends close to the new "powers-that-be" volunteered to bring him before their *padrinos* to secure, in their own words "his position from being grabbed by another."

Granada was thankful but refrained from being carried away by the tempting offer. He believed that the Office of the College President should not be subjected to such indignity– beg politicians to secure his position. It was just too much for him.

Granada's friends who were sincere and well-meaning tried their best to convince him that he should be realistic and forward-looking. "Get real man. This is a different era."

He countered their point by saying that people had different perceptions of reality and his own view of reality in education was far different from theirs. They had to leave it at that. His latest book had a whole chapter on political lobbying and meddling which underscored its negative effects on education. "It would be a shame," he said "if somewhere along the way, I would be a party to its perpetuation. It would be awkward and very difficult to explain to students who use my books or to my children why, I, of all people, will apply and practice what I strongly denounce."

"Know what Moi, I wish you're not blinded by your high idealism. You cannot reach the top in this country if you have no political connections."

This was always the line his friends took. And as usual, they only got a smile from him and a pat on their shoulders enunciating his point: "Well, we should at least exempt the academe. The people who should be assigned are those with merit, professional integrity and proven performance. Those are my bottom lines."

"What bottom lines?"

"If you don't have a bottom line where you are prepared to stand on, you won't get very far in this system of political patronage deprived entirely of intellectual integrity."

"But you can create political connection without jeopardizing your educational values! There are several ways of doing that…"

Sarcastically or sincerely, he usually ended up saying, "Oh yes…and bastardize the system." Then he would amusingly add that at the time when most trooped to Intramuros to pay the new Minister their respect, he didn't go. He didn't want to be misunderstood that he was lobbying for his retention.

When Moises Granada assumed as MCPC officer-in-charge some eight months ago, President Emeritus Gildo Bagongsilang already had a schedule written out for him. Top heavy in this schedule was to do a series of courtesy visits to local politicians. When he politely told the old man that he found this task rather discomforting, the latter assured him not to worry about it. He would take care of every thing mentioning that in all his six-year stay in Metro Ciudad, he never had any trouble dealing with politicians. They were all his friends and they never meddled in the affairs of the College.

"You should know," Dr. Gildo added, "that the Palace said the President would never sign an appointment unless the nominee is endorsed by a local politician. That is the hard reality, Moi, a part of the political system that has been with us for ages. But don't you worry, they will not bother you. I wasn't," he affirmed.

"Why won't Minister Cortez do the endorsing himself? Isn't he the Education Minister?" Granada didn't know at that time that he was already endorsed, that his appointment papers were indeed on the desks of the President, considered "priority", ready for the chief executive's signature. But those papers were not acted upon because the President of the Republic was terribly sick and was bedridden. His health condition was hidden from the public known only to a few trusted men like Congressman Rodelo Cordio from his city.

Granada didn't realize that he was sort of giving in to the wishes of Dr. Gildo until he found himself walking behind him on their way to see the Congressman.

Cordio expressed gladness that Granada was finally coming back to his own province after a long absence "to serve his people."

"Long overdue," he said as he shook the OIC's hands firmly. Granada felt the genuineness of his handshake.

After a few amenities, Granada asked the lawmaker point blank what his (Cordio's) interests were in the College to the embarrassment of Dr. Gildo who bowed his head knowing his face was all red.

"If you want me to become an effective college president, then I should be left alone to manage the institution," Granada stressed.

Upon realizing what he just said, he looked staright at the man and thought that he would drive him out of his office and for a good reason— he was outrightly imprudent and kind-of offensive.

To his great surprise, Cong Cordio was calm but unsmiling. He answered him just as frank.

"The gym. My only interest in that College is its gymnasium – to develop sports in this city and the province. You know that that gym is the biggest in the region. I also worked hard to get the funds to have that built. Gildo knows that."

The old man nodded his head vigorously at the same time thanking him profusely for all the help he had extended for the improvement of the College. The former MCPC president also reminded Granada that Cong Cordio was Vice-Chairman of the powerful Committee on Appropriations of the Legislative Assembly.

"That's my only interest, the gym, that is, if you would allow me to use it every now now and then for sports development," the man sounded hurt. "As for the administration and operation of the College, all that belongs to you."

He called for his secretary, dictated an urgent telegram to the President through the Executive Secretary and another for the Education Minister requesting to facilitate the appointment of Granada as president of MCPC, asap!

It seemed no matter how much he wanted to avoid politicians, Granada was fated to cross paths with them, It was ironic that these men played a significant part in his ascent to MCPC's Office of the President.

Mayor Exequiel Padera of a municipality south of Metro Ciudad was actually the first person to mention Granada's name to Dr. Gildo when the two met in a hotel lobby in the city. Dr. Gildo was at that time about to retire and was looking for a successor. Mayor Exequiel remembered Moises as one of the region's outstanding awardees during Metro Ciudad's golden anniversary as a chartered city.

In a chanced meeting with the mayor accompanied by his wife Tessa and Dr. Gildo, Moises asked Mayor Padera practically the same question he asked Congressman Cordio when the prospect of him being appointed president came up.

What was his interest in him? in the College? Did he expect him to play a specific role in the forthcoming election?

"C'mon," Mayor Exequiel said. "We are not like the Toknenengs of the North and other political warlords of Luzon and the Visayas. We are clean politicians."

Padera was interested in him because he did not only possess the necessary and appropriate qualifications but that he was also a homegrown Northern Mindanao boy.

"You have been in Luzon for so many years now," he said. "Don't you think it is now time for you to come back to your roots and serve your own people? We need people of your caliber here. Mindanao has been neglected for so long."

The Mayor expressed his concern for his own region as well as the other regions comprising their island. "Critical positions here must be occupied by qualified people from Mindanao," he stressed. "The Luzon people, not to forget the economic imperialists from foreign lands, have been, for centuries exploiting our rich natural resources. It is now time that we Mindanaowon should stop this wanton ravaging of our patrimony!"

Moises was touched by the mayor's intense passion to "save Mindanao" before it's too late. He agreed after being assured that the local leader had no intention of getting involved in the affairs of the state college.

"Tessa, your wife here, is my witness. Besides, what do politicians like us know about running a school? That's your domain, your forte."

Minister Felino Mendel as Himself

It was this so-called "allergy" to politicians, his loathing for follow-ups to secure personal favor, his strong suspicion that politicians would eventually intricate themselves into the affairs of the school as a means of paying them back for favors granted, his abhorrence of political meddling that had stifled the creativity of many educational administrators who he personally knew, and similar feelings of disgust and vehemence that made Dr. Granada hesitant to go with the group to seek out Minister Mendel. Added to this was the fact that the Minister was one of those who nominated Barrado. And wasn't he also one of his wedding principal sponsors?

Granada was aware that Lino Mendel was controversial, if not the most controversial minister in the new cabinet. He had of late been getting all the flaks because of his "questionable" appointees in local government units on an OIC capacity without the benefit of qualifying them first.

There was no doubt that Felino Mendel was a political dinosaur, the rest were midgets.

These apprehensions raced through Dr. Granada's mind as he was deciding whether or not to seek an audience with the powerful man. When he looked at the tired faces of Anita, Beth, Nap, Sonny and the young Joel, he could not help but feel depressed himself. Obviously, they were now exhausted, too exhausted from the the stresses and the struggle had caused upon their psyche. How long could they hold on? He sensed he could not disappoint them further by choosing not to meet the Minister.

Then he remembered Dr. Quilantang, the sinister old lady who had practically given up on them. She was obviously not interested to find solutions to the problem from her own end.

He made up his mind.

The group learned that Minister Mendel was scheduled to arrive that day from the U S. They were thinking where to find him since they had no previous appointment. Anita and Sonny were banking on the minister's promise to see them again when he got back from his trip. They were taking chances, a hit and miss action. Should they wait for him at his residence in Taguig? at the airport? hold him before he could even board his Land Cruiser? Nah! Surely, many would probably meet him there.

They tried his residence anyway, only to be told that none from the househelps knew their master's schedule. He could either be in Manila or in Davao for the annual PDR convention. It was like looking for a needle in the haystalk until an old acquaintance told Dr. Granada in confidence where they could catch him.

Caso "Nono" Ponce, Assistant to the Minister for Information and Public Relations led them to Hotel de las Ayalas in Makati. "He was scheduled to address a national conference of the Local Water Administrators at seven o'clock tonight. If you were lucky," Nono said, "you could possibly wrangle a few minutes with him. I'll see if I can squeeze you in after his speech." He advised the group to be at the hotel lobby before seven.

Granada and his team came much earlier and had waited for about forty minutes in the lobby before they saw Minister Mendel got out of his car followed by his personal aides. Nono signaled Granada to stand by his side as the Minister waved to his assistant to follow him. Engr. Ernie San Gabriel, Metro Ciudad water district general manager whiispered to Granada to join him on the second floor conference hall where the Minister would be speaking.

After cocktails and a short dinner, the Minister took the rostrum and thanked the person who introduced him. He was impressed at the emcee's intro that he joked he was tempted to appoint him as another OIC. That really brought the house down. While delivering his speech, he was interrupted every now and then with shouts of "Lino for President!" followed by laughter and a round of applause. (Now, that's how you boosted someone else's ego.)

On a serious note, the Minister stressed two points in his talk: First, politicians only deal with numbers, thus, if there was no organization or party to back him up, a nominee or applicant would hardly be paid attention to or be completely ignored; and, second, he did not believe in political interference, although, he believed that if he had a qualified protégée, he saw no reason why his or her application should not be given due attention. Granada, who was intently listening to the man's talk, took careful note of those points.

With so many prospective (and hopeful) OIC governors and mayors milling around waiting to be noticed by the minister, Granada was beginning to doubt that he would ever have the chance to sit with him before the night was over. Photo sessions and press interviews occupied him that Granada thought would never end. He felt his patience was running thin and had to pretend to be busy reading the program. Sonny had a feeling, his boss was trying his damned best to keep his cool. Then unexpectedly, Minister Mendel signaled Nono to take Granada along while walking down the hotel lobby and toward the coffee shop.

As they entered it, Mendel raised his hand to stop all those who were following him, announcing that he had an appointment with Dr. Granada. The OIC was momentarily flattered, feeling complimented especially so that this was their first time ever to meet. They were not even formally introduced.

Minister Mendel set the tone and course of their conversation limiting the issues on three things: (a) guidelines on the selection of a college president; (b) Barrado's deportment and behavior since his appointment; and, (c) Granada's qualifications, place of origin, and political affiliation.

As Granada explained the guidelines, the Minister took personal notes to make sure, he said, that he got the guidelines correctly.

He acknowledged that the first three steps (screening of a nominee by the Search Committee, election of the best candidate by the Board of Trustees, and recommendation of the Education Minister, *before* the formal appointment by the President of the Philippines) were indeed violated, marking these on his notes.

As to Barrado's attitude, he seemed to have already been briefed about this earlier and appeared to give it little attention. However, the Minister showed displeasure when Nono pointed out that Barrado did not only ignore his personal note but in fact, tended to throw it away after reading its content. "This information was relayed to me by those who delivered it, sir."

Going through Granada's brief resume', he was glad to note that the guy was not only from Mindanao but that he hailed from his own region. Barrado's propaganda machinery had been spreading false information—that Granada was from Luzon and that he was a GI, a "genuine Ilocano" and a royal-blooded PMN. The Minister promised to remember those info if ever he meets the man.

Mendel asked Granada of his political affiliation to which he honestly replied, "I have none, sir." Yes, there were pressures to get him involved in the last presidential election but he politely said "no" to them. He recalled that during the presidential sorties in Metro Ciudad, he turned down all invitations to attend the rallies held for the purpose. He even convened the Administrative Council of the College to announce that he was not endorsing anyone and that they can choose their own candidate based on the dictate of their own conscience.

The Minister wanted to know the importance of a doctoral degree in choosing an institutional head. "Why is a doctorate degree a necessary requirement of the position?" he asked with interest.

Feeling more confident now, he explained that any search committee would prefer a Ph.D. over an M.A. or an M.S. holder. If the institution's graduate program could grant the highest degree which is Doctor of Philosophy shouldn't it follow that the College President himself possess it? Granada mentioned that his school had several Ph.D. holders at the moment and in three years time, his faculty line up would be beefed up by an additional 15 more doctorate graduates adding that a stonger faculty and staff development program had been put in place and would be pursued in earnest.

He also mentioned the College's graduate program wherein professional lecturers and visiting professors all with Ph.Ds. from Manila universities and from the Education Ministry come on weekends to handle the program. With such a distinguished faculty line up, it would put the non-Ph.D. head to an uncomfortable and awkward position. Unless one had a post graduate stature, it would be difficult and discomforting for one to even think of aspiring for the highest post of a state-owned institution that required the most stringent requirement.

Throughout their conversation over black coffee and munching peanuts in between, Granada got the impression that the Minister had a way of making one unravel himself into his confidence. He was an intense listener and never in the entire conversation did he show any sign of disinterest or lack of focus.

Anita came to their table to show to Minister Mendel some pictures of the June 13 incident in the College. He asked questions giving Moises and Anita the hunch that he was familiar with what happened on that day. He was surprised however, when he saw the photo of Public Highways Director Hizon in front of the gate with his new service pickup in the background.

"What was he doing there?" referring to Hizon.

Anita quickly responded. "The Director actually played an active role on that day, Sir. In fact, it was his pickup which drove Barrado through the gate and inside the campus."

Granada saw the Minister shook his head in obvious disgust. He knew the photos made their point loud and clear.

"We have more photographs to show, Sir if you wish to see them," Granada said softly.

The old man didn't respond but ordered, "Wait for me here in Manila until Saturday," he said. "Nono will tell you where to contact me." He finally stood up, shook hands briefly and left immediately.

For the first time since they arrived in the big city, the group saw a glimmer of hope and prayed that their efforts, sacrifices and hard work would eventually pay off.

———————————

DAY 29, FRIDAY, JUNE 27
Taking a Bad Grip of the Situation

Last night was quite thrilling for Granada's group. Everyone can't stop smiling (for the first time after almost a week in Manila). His meeting with Minister Mendal took them to a new level of hope. It was complemented by news reports from various national dailies showing interest in the fate of MCPC now that the President of the Republic was finally taking a hand to resolve the conflict. They were also happy to note Dr. Perida's report that classes continued to be held at the park despite orders from EVP Soriano to go back to the classrooms or face the consequences of their action. The vice president threatened them with insubordination which the teachers blatantly disregard.

Also, Barrado was back in the college snapping at those who opted to report for work including the newly hired. It seemed, the new president was now troubled, unsure of his status as far as the Ministry was concerned.

On invitation by CTR President Viagose, the group attended a meeting of several militant teachers' groups at the Teachers' Lounge of the Normal College in the morning. Its agendum—to prepare for the holding of a picket at the Palace condemning the Ministry's inaction on call for the stoppage of political interference in appointing new officers-in-charge of supposedly beleaguered schools. Representatives from these schools were expected to join the scheduled activity on Monday, June 30. This information was mentioned in a news article by *The Daily Herald*.

As the meeting progressed, it was evident that those present were disappointed and furious at the way Minster Quilantang was handling the situation. Viagose bluntly said that "the Education Minister tended to wash her hands off this problem explaining that search committees were assigned to screen applicants for the topmost position in any college or university. He further opined that the criteria of integrity, competence and acceptability were seeminglt ignored allowing in the process, "the appointment by the Palace of unqualified and unacceptable state college presidents."

Representatives of various affected schools cited their respective cases. One informed that in his college, a search committee was created by the Minister herself but in the end, the ranking made was completely rejected by her, justifying her decision that she suspected said ranking was partial on one candidate.

"Please note," the rep said, "that it was she who created this committee."

A lady professor from another institution disclosed that a search committee was also assigned by the Minister but when pressured by the Governor to change its membership, she acceded by making herself and the Governor sole members of the so-called "search committee."

"Funny that the governor was also a member of our Board of Trustees. Isn't the Minister making fun of her own decisions and actions? She's in fact, ridiculing what we have done and have been doing by her indiscretion," she said furiously.

Still another rose and in obvious disappointment narrated how the search was made in his school: The father of a candidate was picked by the Minister to sit in the committee despite her knowledge that his son was in the running for the presidency. As expected, the father-member built his son up citing qualifications which, unfortunately were sorely lacking and wanting. The rest of the committee members agreed without raising any objection. It was to be expected since the old man was not only close to the Minister, he was also the patriarch of one of the most powerful families in the province where the university was located.

As Carlito Payos of SUCFA, Eric Torre, CTR vice-president for Luzon and representatives of schools were plotting strategies for the forthcoming picket, Viagose walked up to Granada and asked if he had not changed his mind, if he was still for a smooth turnover. He feared this stand of the OIC might put the mass protest of the College in jeopardy.

Granada explained his position on the matter reiterating what he told Payos when he met him three days ago. And like Payos, he suspected Raul was likewise unhappy about his decision. But he can't help it. He was certain it was the best alternative under the circumstances.

———————

Minister Quilantang known for eluding the press as much as she can found herself in the limelight as media turned their cameras on her. They had to hunt her, she was a good copy at the moment, sensationalizing her denial that her decisions (to recommend and/or retain people for top posts in universities and colleges) were influenced highly by political patronage. An article by *Metroplotan Times* carried her statement on the issue.

Quilantang denies decisions
were influenced by politics

Education Minister Lucretia Quilantang yesterday stressed that she has not bent to political pressure allegedly influencing her decision to retain 50 of the 78 school heads in state colleges and universities.

She gave her reactions to allegations made by the Concerned Teachers of the Republic (CTR) president Raul Viagose that she has practically allowed politics to creep into the Education Ministry by delaying her decision regarding the issue on 78 current school heads believed to be on a wait-and-see status. The minister said she has forwarded her recommendations to the President retaining 50 out of the 78 after what she called a "thorough study" of the matter. She added that integrity, competence and acceptance have not been set aside but were in fact, given much weight in the evaluation of candidates.

"I did not compromise these values which were basically enshrined in the new guidelines which I, myself, proposed. It would be foolish to violate my own rules," she told reporters.

She made special mention of the case of Metro Ciudad which she believed could be resolved by a dialogue between the newly-appointed Esteban Barrado and OIC Moises Granada. It maybe remembered that Barrado was charged by students, faculty members and Granada with forcible entry of Metro Ciudad Polutechnic College where the latter was officer-in-charge. The incident happened last June 13.

She also said that the President has been informed about the strong opposition against the appointment of Barrado and hoped that when the chief executive visits Metro Ciudad on July 6, she will be able to address the problem to everyone's advantage.

Several other tabloids and broadsheets carried similar article accompanied by photographs of the take-over, the mediated conference between the "warring" factions and other photos related to the protest.

"Neither Granada nor Barrado"

The idea of a third party suddenly popped up from out of the blue. It was not clear whether Minister Quilantang had that in mind for quite sometime now or it came out hastily out of sheer desperation. She was being "pushed against the wall" recently and had to find a way out.

"What do you think of having a third party—that is, neither Granada nor Barrado would sit as president, but another person?"

The lady minister surprised Anita and Beth with that question when they dropped by her office that afternoon. They looked at her with open mouth, unable to answer the question sprung on them unexpectedly. They thought she was really pissed off, agitated and impatient because the issue had been dragging on for several weeks now. It was beginning to get on her nerves and it showed. She was doubly angry because Granada refused to sign the agreement she approved two days earlier and she felt betrayed.

"Sir, the Minister was so angry because you did not sign the final turnover agreement she had approved. Maybe that was what made her say that she is now entertaining the idea of a third party," Beth confided.

"I didn't know what came to us, but we agreed with her. We were so despondent when she told us that you did not sign the agreement," admitted Anita.

"Did you tell her that I have a note attached to the returned draft? I suggested to Atty. Matos that the draft has to be modified first before I sign it." Granada clarified.

"But we didn't know about the note," the two said, looking perplexed.

"I suggested that the draft has to be modified because, among others, the two of you were included as signatories when you were not at all present during the deliberation. Also it called for you to withdraw the cases you filed against Barrado and his men. Would you consider doing that?"

"No, we won't do that!"

"I got that much reaction when I asked you on our way back here. You said "never." Did you forget?" he paused looking at the women. "You should be consistent in your stand if you expect to win the fight under any given circumstance. Please, don't embarrass yourselves further. It does not help to be impulsive," he said in a firm but kind voice.

"We're very sorry, Sir. We were carried away," said the two who were by now in the verge of tears.

"That's okay. I guess it's the stress," Granada said gently. "Now smile…"

Their faces gradually broke into a smile. It wasn't very big but their smile pierced Granada's heart secretly.

On his advice, the two started calling their peers in Metro Ciudad to find out what the community might think about a third choice for the presidency. The lines continued to burn to and from Manila. The message from the headquarters was abundantly clear: they would not settle for an alternative. It has to be the OIC! They reinforced that stand with eleven telegrams to Minister Quilantang including the messages from the student council and the non-academic staff association.

Thinking it was but prudent to apologize to Minister Quilantang for their earlier concurrence to her suggestion, Anita and Beth contacted her via her hotline to inform her first, that the entire protesting community was absolutely not amenable to any third party and second, to say they were sorry to have agreed with her while in her office.

"Ma'am, Beth and I were very sorry because we were not honest with you this afternoon." Anita's voice was shaking as she searched for her handkerchief inside her bag. "We agreed with you when you said you were entertaining the idea of having a third party probably because we were under considerable stress, were exhausted and could not think rationally anymore. Please understand us. We apologize."

Anita, whose fierceness was envied by many finally broke down. She was sobbing. Beth helped her put the telephone down.

"Fuck you, Quilantang!" Sonny uttered in total dismay while Joel slumped himself on the floor mumbling. Moises had left them and went inside his room after saying a faint "goodnight."

Nono Ponce phoned in to say that Dr. Granada should meet Minister Mendel at the Manila Domestic Airport at eight thirty in the morning of the following day.

"The Minister is flying to Davao City so please don't be late," Nono said.

DAY 30, SATURDAY, JUNE 28
Light at the End of the Tunnel

The PASS van sped through Roxas Boulevard. At exactly 8:20 Granada's group was already at the domestic airport. Ten minutes later, Nono arrived saying, as he gasped for air that the Minister would "be here any minute now."

True enough, they saw the Minister's convoy entered the gate. As soon as the big, black car stopped, the aides jumped out of their vehicles and surrounded him, preventing people who were apparently waiting for him to get near nor approach him. The aides hustled the Minister through the eager crowd until they got to the airport's lobby. The maneuver to get the Minister out of the crowd fast practically caught Granada in the middle of a highly excited horde of people. He tried to extricate himself out but the people continued to gather in large number and closed him in further. He thought it was impossible to catch the Minister with him literally trapped when he felt a strong hand held him by his left arm. Bong Rodriguez, chief aide of the Minister was pulling him out. "C'mon Doc and fast!"

With Bong leading the way, it was easy as their path automatically cleared when they passed.

They caught the tail-end of the Minister's entourage in time to get through the airport security and the glass doors closed behind them. Many of those who wanted to meet the Minister missed the chance for the second time. Granada recognized them as among those who were at the hotel in Makati milling around Minister Mendel last Thursday evening.

After talking briefly with some "aspirants" who were able to get inside the airport lounge the Minister's aide motioned to Granada to come by the old man's side. He quickly followed the aide who exuded an "air of authority."

He sat beside the Minister on the couch who told him in confidence that he had already advised Exeutive Secretary Conrado Rayos to recall Barrado's appointment. He further informed him that Rayos had already talked with Minister Quilantang about the matter. "I tried to contact Lucretia after that but I could not get her on the phone."

The Minister suggested that he flies back to Metro Ciudad and waits for him there. "I'll be going back to Manila from Davao but will be in Metro Ciudad on Tuesday," he added.

Granada was glad at what he heard. When he shared this information to his group later, their joy and feeling of triumph could not be contained.

Sonny, Jongjong and Joel exchanged high fives and patted each other's back. Granada got a pat too from the young Joel saying "this is indeed good news, sir.

The two women, Anira and Beth who hadn't laughed for days broke into wide smiles and giggled and later, into laughter of pure joy.

It was day to celebrate. The words of Minister Mendel gave them something to hope for as they were beginning to see a flicker of light at the end of the tunnel.

As they cruised Roxas Boulevard again they thought that the sea breeze of Manila Bay was fresher and so very soothing. They looked at the seaside and realized for the first time, that the baywalk was a great place to relax and savor that piece of victory that was almost at hand. But they went on, anyway, not wanting to waste precious time.

Time to pack their bags and head home.

DAY 31, SUNDAY, JUNE 29
Breaking the Wall of Resistance

OIC Granada's first meeting with the protesters last June 2 was emotion-filled and intense. He had sensed that his faculty and staff were serious enough to put their jobs and lives on the line for him. This gesture touched him deeply and for a long while threw him on a state of hesitation and indecision. It became difficult for him to even think of turning his back on his people but toyed with the idea of "fighting" with them till the end. Yet, after much contemplation and inner struggle, a choice had to be made for the College's benefit. It had to be resolute, well founded and solid enough to restore peace and order and allow the College to re-function and operate normally as any higher education institution should. Dr. Granada appealed for understanding for whatever action he might be arriving at in the end.

It was EVP Sosimo Soriano who first declared in that meeting that he was not in favor of Mr. Esteban Barrado taking the president's position. In fact, he was one with the community in condemning the irregularity of the selection process and showed interest in launching the protest at the start. But this did not last long after his silence over a letter from Barrado created doubts and suspicions among his peers and subordinates. Eventually, Soriano couldn't anymore hide his personal relationship with the new president and came out openly to the chagrin of the rank-and-file and his fellow middle management leaders.

For his action, the EVP was ostracized by his subordinates to a point that he had to stay inside his cottage in the campus most of the time avoiding unnecessary personal encounter with his co-workers in the school. His association with them only remained official and within the bounds of his responsibility as vice president.

The community was aware that he snuck out stealthily to be with the Barrado camp in their nightly frolics. As his involvement with him became more open, he was hated and sneered at by many, tagged unpleasantly which he certainly didn't relish but accepted with a shrugged shoulder.

He also had to live with less respect from his own people, suffered the indignity of being called names that shamed him. Still, he couldn't care less wielding his authority over them officially.

Dr. Soriano, a distant relative of former MCPC president Gildo Bagongsilang was being groomed by the latter to become the next president after his term. Dr. Gildo however, found out later that he could not trust his own kin. He received information that when he appointed him officer-in-charge while he was on a Fulbright-Hays grant in the United States in 1983, Soriano spent more time sowing intrigues and was busy besmirching the president's name instead of working hard to keep the College running smoothly. It was also during this period that the rank-and-file was divided into two factions— one faction sided with the EVP, the other with the VPAA. The factions remained until Dr. Gildo retired in 1985.

It did not take long for Dr. Granada to realize that something was amiss, that factionalism was something he had to address immediately when he first reported to MCPC. He knew that this split was indeed potent and had taken roots. The growing dislike for each other could not be denied. In school gatherings, for example, they avoided each other— camaraderie and working together in unity were conspicuously absent. After the activity or a meeting, one group would stand in one corner and the other in an area far from them. They often left separately and only the "neutrals" would be left behind shaking their heads in disappointment. He knew he had to do something fast and conciliatory.

Because Granada had a wide range of experience dealing with people of diverse backgrounds and temperaments he employed means to bring together "warring" members of his new community. He knew it would be difficult to work under a climate of personal differences and uncooperativeness. In order to repair the damage caused by the division, he strived to build a different perspective of service to their institution forgetting self-interest and pride. In five months' time, the new OIC successfully erased any trace of divisiveness made possible through consultative meetings, shared responsibilities, participatory management and collegial decision-making applying his time-tested personal touch approach. The entire academic community thanked him for creating an atmosphere conducive to harnessing their professionalism and bringing the College to a new level of academic excellence, maturity and growth.

The climate change within the school became known far and wide. Prominent residents and business leaders of Metro Ciudad including other professionals took notice and were awed. They praised him for transforming the school into adopting a culture of unity and harmony in a short period of time. The atmosphere of oneness and cooperation was now evident and Dr. Soriano seemed to have been caught in the whirlwind of change taking place. On several occasions, he was quoted as saying that he was now happy in the College and in his job because "...Moi does not treat me like a child."

So it concerned Granada when Soriano finally decided to defect to the other side. His first reaction was to leave the man alone believing he was entitled to his own choice. The protesters advised him to watch his back as far as Dr. Soriano was concerned because they said, he could not be trusted. A man of his character who would not and could not look into another person straight in the eye, was a sign of a very calculating man.

This repulsion toward EVP Soriano grew to plain hatred during the protest due to his actions detrimental to the welfare of the employees. He aided the attackers in the destruction of the gym's door which led to the administrative offices in the adjacent building to give access to Barrado. He also allowed the enrolment of "substitute" students without proper credentials and admission requirements to give a semblance of normalcy inside the campus, that there were indeed students attending regular classes inside. These actions, they said, were outrightly hideous and abhorrent.

In hindsight, Soriano was doing all the dirty job for Barrado and for what? Was it all worth it? The spot in which the EVP found himself had become rather complicated. He was suddenly gripped with apprehension and fear.

First, he was aware that majority of the College's constituents had nothing but contempt for him, losing all respect for his person and position. They were brutally frank telling their hatred to his face. Worse, they even booed him in public to his consternation.

Second, he felt that Barrado's men never treated him with deference. To them, he was not a high official of the school, but a lameduck with the new president's task force and Gerry Daldalen calling the shots. Soriano was beginning to feel disillusioned. His role in the whole scheme of things after the takeover had become nebulous. It appeared that his role was reduced to that of a "servant" who was expected to feed the president's people when they come to his house during mealtime to the disgust and humiliation of his wife Juliet.

Third, those who kept their loyalty to him were now closely watching him. These few followers who were bonafide College employees were in a state of fear like him, not knowing where they will be headed after the struggle, unsure of their fate in the face of this uncertain time— win or loose. If Barrado stays as president, his followers would naturally play the dominant role. If he loses, they would surely face what Soriano was now experiencing in the hands of their colleagues. In their mind, it was never a win-win situation.

As Granada analyzed this messed up situation that Dr. Soriano had allowed himself to be stucked in, he acknowledged that his vice president was indeed in the throes of a dilemma.

Always the rational person that he was, Dr. Granada was considering to have a heart-to-heart talk with Dr. Soriano in the hope of reinstituting self-respect and dignity to a fallen colleague. Ultimately, he wanted to bring back that spirit of trust he had earned from him before Barrado's entry into the picture. He wanted to regain Soriano's trust on him.

He decided to talk to his EVP despite the protesters' wish not to have anything to do with him anymore. Their reaction was one of displeasure when they learned of his plan.

"Why do you need to do that, sir? It's going to be futile," they growled. Reconciliation with Soriano was simply a waste of time and was unwise. They frowned at the idea and insisted he shouldn't do it.

However, Granada went ahead after assuring the protesters that he was not meeting him on their behalf. "This is purely personal," he stressed.

Granada requested Soriano's secretary Myrna, who was at first hesistant, to arrange for a clandestine meeting between himself and her boss. He learned that the secretary was active in the protest and that Soriano's wife was trying to recruit her to their side which she flatly refused.

Granada explained that he had a very important message for Soriano and it was important that she should make this meeting possible.

"You are my closest link to Susing. Tell him, I want to have a talk with him."

Later in the day, Granada was informed that the meeting had been arranged. They will meet at seven in the evening of the same day on a secluded room in the warehouse of her mother-in –law in the outskirt of the city. She wrote the address in a small piece of paper.

By 7:30 Moises, his brother Ben and two others were at the meeting place. With Soriano were his wife, Juliet and their 25 year-old son. Myrna was there as well sitting with Nap and Ben at a discrete distance. Outside where their car was parked, Anboy Cabigas stood to watch.

At the beginning, the atmosphere was icy and Soriano and his wife were obviously fidgety. They had no idea where this meeting will lead them.

Granada tried to put the couple at ease saying that this meeting was nothing but a friend-meets-friend again after a long time. "That is, if you regard me as a friend, Susing," he said meaningfully.

The man in front of him didn't answer but kept his head bowed. He couldn't look straight into Moises eyes. He was too embarrassed to even try.

"Despite everything that happened, I treasure the times we were togtether working for the College. And I thank you for your comment over one TV show where you said 'Dr. Granada is a good man.' I'll remember that often," Granada said sincerely.

Still, Soriano remained silent, looking down and noticed his shoes were dirty. He bent down to clean them with his fingers. He felt this was an excuse to avoid Granada's gaze.

Realizing the agony of the man in front of him, Granada very slowly broke the news he got firsthand from Minister Mendel. "Barrado's appointment is going to be revoked soon."

The information made Soriano raise his head and gave him an astounded look. Juliet let out a nervous shriek, her face drained of color. She was as pale as a ghost. She began to rub her eyes. Her son sat speechless, not saying anything and reached out for his mom's hand to calm her.

It took sometime before Soriano reacted. His gaze was nailed to his trembling hands. He braced himself for more heartbreaking news. None came.

When he finally spoke, his voice was cracked and whispery and asked if there were options available for him to get himself out of this rut.

"What do you think will be the best choice I could possibly consider?" he asked earnestly.

"Perhaps it would be best for you to to go on an indefinite leave of absence."

"Leave the school? But…"

"You have to get away for a while. Spend time elsewhere, away from those people so that you can see the problem from a safe distance," he suggested. "If you can make a clean break from Barrado, the better. This option," Granada explained, "would somehow appease the academic community although there was no guarantee that this would happen since I am not representing the members in this meeting."

"What about those who sided with me? What will happen to them when worse comes to worst?"

"I cannot do anything for them at this point in time," Granada answered. "You deal with them as I deal with you. That's one of the pains of a leader, his ability to weather the storm and survive," Granada said. "Sometimes it's like malaria. You never really shake it off."

Their conversation went on that led to his asking why Soriano shifted loyalty.

"Barrado had the legal appointment," he admitted.

Granada did not comment nor press him for an answer to his proposal reminding him to make that decision since there were only a few days left before Barrado was to be pulled out of MCPC presidency.

"I'll seriously think about it," he said meekly.

"Remember that the revocation of his appointment is not confidential. It has been decided by the higher authority. You can report this to him if you wish."

Granada stood up, offered his hand for a handshake which the EVP took and after a few words to his son and wife, left.

Soriano suddenly realized, he was alone and abandoned. He broke into silent tears.

DAY 32, MONDAY, JUNE 30
Pressures and Reactions

Growing up as a pupil, Dr Granada saw only two instances wherein classes were held literally under the trees. First was when he was in elementary when on one very hot day, his teacher took her pupils under the sprawling acacia tree near their Gabaldon -type school building. The other, he saw in a movie documentary that captured school life during the Japanese occupation.

The memory came back as soon as he saw his students slumped on the ground, listening intently to their teachers despite the heat and noise at the city's popular park that Monday morning. He came to witness for himelf how some thirty different classes of about 30 to 35 students per class were being conducted under the towering and shady mahogany trees. It was a gloomy sight – makeshift chalkboards of all size and shape, placards and streamers carrying the protesters messages of dissent hanging around the park, and teachers and students holding their session as if it was the most natural thing to do. He sensed, however, that both were extremely uncomfortable.

Capturing the attention of snoops and the curious was a collage of photographs of the June 13 incident prominently displayed on a plyboard set up on one side of the occupied area. This became one of the main attractions that made people flock to the park.

———————————

The protest classes were not without detractors and hard critics. Leading the pack of those totally against the "occupation" were the local media who constantly lambasted the protesters for 'appropriating' the park for their own use.

"The park is a public place and people of the city should not be deprived of its use. They are entitled to it. What's happening is that those people who wanted to take a stroll are now robbed of their privilege. Mac Arthur Park is no longer as available as it used to be," the media derided.

"Why don't you go home to your College where you belong instead of taking over that park which belongs to the people of Metro Ciudad," the announcers often blasted the protesters on their radio and TV programs.

But more than the rants of media and the displeasure of a number of residents, including parents of students, it was the poor condition of the set up that worried the teachers and students. For one thing, it was rough for both of them —students squatting on the grass while teachers standing all day long and having difficulty writing on the makeshift chalkboards mounted on wobbly improvised stands. Laboratory classes that needed lab and shop equipment had to be deferred due to the absence of such equipment and devices. While the area sort of guaranteed peace and order because of its proximity to the provincial capitol, vehicular noises along the busy Velez Street were a nuisance which caused loss of concentration on both. There were instances of distractions brought about by unexpected, unusual fracas on the side of the park which will stop classes unnecessarily. Though regular policemen were assigned on the beat and the protesters had their own watchers manning its perimeters, still their presence did not deter untoward incidents from happening. The condition was hard and almost impossibly manageable, yet the defiant students and their mentors persisted.

All these made some parents uneasy and half-hearted in their support. Some of them, in fact, pressured their sons and daughters to return to the campus and join regular classes there. They wanted them to concentrate on their studies instead of sympathizing with the protesters. Some even strongly urged their children to give the new president a chance to prove himself, but to no avail.

Their children would reason out that since there were no teachers in the campus, who would teach them? Although there were new recruits, the students had no confidence that they will do well since many of them were high school teachers recruited from nearby secondary schools.

Adding to the students' worries was Barrado's hired goons who, they claimed were sowing fear among those who chose to stay inside. No, it was not time to go back to the campus, not until this problem was settled, they insisted.

But there were those who gave in to parental pressure. They either went back to the campus or stopped going to school altogether.

Dax was a third year BSECE student who was "pressured" by his parents to return to the campus. He was a close friend of Joel and was one believed not to abandon the cause at all cost. Unffortunately, he did. Later Dax wrote Joel telling him what was happening inside.

Only a handful of students are actually inside. Because the instructors are few and inadequate, we don't have formal classes. The administrators are confused and obviously do not know what to do. The whole campus is a graveyard. The goons are all over the place as if they own it, as if they have the right to such things.

Another student, John Guerrero who was forcefully pulled out by his parents from the protest but refused to return to the campus also reiterated his thoughts:

> *If we will just sit down and do nothing you could never expect us to be worthy citizens later. The College called for our help and we responded. Our participation is very much needed because we are the ones directly affected. If our school has a good leader, naturally it would also produce good and competent students. Now, if we will let **B** govern our College, what do you think will happen? We all know that he's a big liar. Remember the way he lied and twisted the facts while being interviewed on radio and TV? Should we allow a man like him to be our President? No. we shouldn't! We have suffered much already. Staff and instructors suffer even more because they are not getting their salaries.*
>
> *We are both fighting for the same principle: Appoint an honorable man and let politicians keep their hands off MCPC.*
>
> *We all know we shall prevail.*

Early that same afternoon, words came to Granada that Barrado along with Soriano and a few others were to visit the Governor in his office at the Capitol. They waited for them to arrive and watched from afar, saw his entourage climbed the cement stairs of the Capitol in hurried steps.

Moises wondered what EVP Soriano might be thinking at that moment. He looked troubled. "Has he decided?", Granada wondered.

Later, they confirmed through the Governor's secretary that his boss had turned down Barrado's request to intercede for him with Minister Mendel when he comes to Metro Ciudad. He wanted to see the Minister the soonest and only the Governor can make that happen.

The old man, Granada learned, flatly refused saying that Barrado's request for intercession on his behalf was not only too late but also inappropriate. He mentioned that he and the others fought along Minister Mendel in toppling down a dictator. "But you, armed only with an appointment paper had already abused your still unconfirmed authority by forcing your way in despite protest by teachers and students," he growled at the stunned delegation. "Manipulation of power," the Governor elucidated pointing his forefinger to him "tells us that failure to use it can be just as dangerous as using it unwisely."

Soon after, he dismissed the group despite pleading by the flustered Barrado.

The news Granada heard put him on a more hopeful stance. "The horizon looks brighter," he thought trying to convince himself.

DAY 33, TUESDAY, JULY 1

Debunking the Big, Fat Lies

Classes at the Park were closely monitored noting students' as well as faculty attendance. Wendy Decasis of Personnel and some student assistants made their regular rounds every 10:00 o'clock in the morning and at 3:00 o'clock in the afternoon not only to check the list but also to find out what hits, snags and problems were encountered. She reported these religiously to the Vice President for Academic Affairs who kept details of the situation. He felt these information will come handy when the time comes.

Anita Caluya and Beth Sebastian arrived on the 10:45 flight from Manila. They were left in the big city to do other tasks and waited for developments. The duo headed straight to the park where Granada had gathered the academic community as well as invited parents for an update on the situation. The group that went with hin to Manila were now complete. They were hoping that Minister Mendel could have a few minutes with them since he promised Moises that hewill be in Metro Ciudad on July 1. However, he was not on the same plane with Anita and Beth which landed in the city that morning. It was the only flight available for that day. The probability that he might use the presidential jet was definitely nil and Granada felt a little disappointed at the prospect of him not coming at all. He dispatched Romy Ramar to check with some people in his residence and came back with news that Mendel was definitely coming the next day. He was delayed, according to his wife, due to pressing concerns he had to attend to in the big city.

Meanwhile, parents started to arrive in the park. They were eager to hear what OIC Granada had to say on the issue as this directly affected their children. They hoped that the controversy would be resolved soon as they can't wait for their sons and daughters to return to the campus and attend classes normally. Specific concerns common to all were brought up during informal conversations that ensued while gathering up. There were trivial ones like the makeshift chalkboards that wobbled and the warm climate. There were some pretty sensible comments like the Daldalen-Mendel fight for political supremacy and how this would affect business and the economy in the region.

The alumni association leaders with some teachers and staff were tasked with entertaining the guests while waiting for the meeting to start. They allowed the conversations to flow freely. All the time that these talks were going on, Granada was silently taking them in.

VPAA Vilar stood as moderator when the meeting finally took off. He assured the parents that this briefing will clear the air of a lot of misunderstanding and false information. "This way, you can better understand the problem. Also, there are rumors being spread around by some who thought they are doing the College any good, but in fact, are contributing to the unrest in the community. We hope to debunk these lies and set the record straight. So please, stay until the end of this meeting," he requested.

Using a megaphone, Joel Lerpa was first to speak. He explained why the students ended up joining the protest; related the circumstances up until the assault of the College on June 13 which led to their unified action. He was himself hurt on that day, including some of his fellow students, he informed their guests.

"We had to do this," he emphasized, to rally for a cause which they believed justified their action.

Some parents were touched by Joel's passionate speech. They were unconsciously agreeing with the young man.

Prof. Caluya spoke on the strong support of militant teacher organizations in Manila saying they held demonstrations in front of the Palace demanding revocation of Barrado's appointment. She added that these groups also came up with manifestos calling for the same. She was confident this action of the teachers' groups will bear fruits favorable to them.

To better appreciate the underlying reason for the protesters' dislike of Barrado, Dr. Granada had to explain the stringent process required by the academe in the selection of a college president underscoring qualifications, considerable educational experience, acceptability by the academic community and endorsement by the Board of Trustees. "And yes, he has to be recommended by Education Minister Quilantang (which she did not do) and approved by the President of the Republic. All of these," he pointed out, "were not met by Barrado, hence, the protest."

Granada looked at his audience and knew they were waiting for more, especially about that "declaration" that came out in a local tabloid that morning. He was very well aware of it, and in fact, had it as part of his agenda.

The declaration appeared on the *Local Star* as paid advertisement. It was, without doubt, fabricated, false and made to appear genuine with the declarers' authentic signatures affixed with Dr. Soriano leading. Why they did it, after knowing that Barrado may be removed from office anytime soon was anybody's guess. Why, indeed?

The declaration which was ironically published "in the name of truth" was in reality, malicious and repugnant. It was definitely a big lie!

SO THE PEOPLE MAY KNOW THE TRUTH

Due to an orchestrated campaign to mislead the President of the Republic, Minister Lucretia Quilantang, Executive Secretary Conrado C. Rayos and the general public, the following facts are laid down in the interest of truth.

** The protest, demonstration and boycott against the newly-appointed College President Esteban Barrado are participated in by only 160 students and 30 teachers and administrative staff. Regular classes have been going on in the campus and all college operations and activities are functioning normally.

** The protest was carefully organized by the outgoing OIC and his group long before the appointment of President Barrado. It was carefully planned to ensure the retention of OIC Moises Granada who was assigned in the College two months before the presidential elections as endorsed by PMN officials.

** President Barrado did not employ goons, and there was no violence when he took over the presidency of the College. He fulfilled the agreement made with the protesters that he will not enter the College within one week of the effectivity of his appointment. When the period was up, Mr. Barrado, accompanied by some faculty, students, media and

some friends, went to the College and politely asked to enter its premises. After repeated requests were denied, he ordered to force open the locked gate by breaking the padlock and the chain, removed the piled chairs while a military contingent watched to avert violence. President Barrado and his companions entered the campus with no untoward incident.

** President Barrado was one of the top organizers of the political campaign against the deposed president in Metro Ciudad and in the province.

** In two audiences with the new President of the Republic, the provincial campaign staff conveyed to her their desire for Barrado to join the administration. The President acceded and after several meetings with former Assemblyman Daldalen, Minister Felino Mendel, and Minister Lucretia Quilantang from March to May, the President decided to appoint Mr. Esteban Barrado president of Metro Ciudad Polytechnic on May 26. President Barrado took his oath of office before the Justice Minister on June 5.

On the day President Barrado received his appointment, he immediately composed a Transition Committee to dialogue with the outgoing College administration for a smooth and orderly turnover. Every invitation by President Barrado to a dialogue was spurned by unreasonable demands by the protesters.

While all avenues for redress or complaints have been left open to the protesters, they chose to drag the 160 students and prejudiced their studies by paralyzing classes to retain the former OIC and continue their domination of the State College.

With help from his leaders including Atty. Gael Padera, Nap Lopa and the VPAA and several others, Granada debunked the claims, patiently explaining in details and supported by witnesses' statements and photographs taken during the siege what actually happened. He opened the floor for questions and further clarifiications. His openness and straightforward replies to querries devoid of drama and sentimentality won the trust of the audience, who, in the end promised support now that they understood the issue fully well.

After giving the parents assurance that the problem would be resolved within the week, Granada apologized for the inconvenience the protest brought upon their families. He concluded by saying that the young students' participation in this protest was, in fact, one rare opportunity in their life that no ordinary classroom could ever teach them.

Later at night, Granada asked himself if what he said to the parents gave the impression that he actually encouraged the students to join them. He was beginning to be aware that it seemed he was getting deeply involved.

"Am I?" He was not sure now.

Looking back at the events of the day, Granada recalled the protesters snide over the names they saw in the declaration.

"Such foolish men, trading their honor and dignity for something so selfish as keeping their job and professional gratification. Tsk, tsk, tsk," they sighed in disappointment.

What could be the motivation into signing that declaration without considering the possioble consequence? It was obvious that EVP Soriano and his followers were promised "something more" by Barrado in exchange for issuing that declaration.

A quick review of the "motivation" behind the signatories involved proved their point:

Antonio Lacruza was simply overwhelmed by his new designation as "dean of engineering" when he was not even an engineer.

Clod Orani was supposed to be on study leave and was promised the position of dean of a non-existent Technical-Vocational Department. Yet he affixed his signature as head of that ghost entity. This has yet to be created under the 10-Year Development Program.

Sidro Cantar was named "Director" of the secondary laboratory school of the College of Industrial Education when that school didn't even have a principal.

Others who allowed themselves to be used were either protecting their interests since they were not truly qualified in their job or were caught for their insidious activities in the past like Jun Ilio. They had no choice but to bite the bait dangled before them.

Before turning off his light, he mumbled a little prayer: "Lord, grant me the courage to do what you think is right and beneficial to my people, amen."

5

FROM THE HIGHEST HOPE TO LOWEST DESPAIR

DAY 34, WEDNESDAY, JULY 2
Message of Hope and Joyful Anticipation

METRO CIUDAD WAS in an unbelievable state of jubilation. The air of restlessness and frantic expectation seemed to have left the whole community. It was replaced by an upsurge of wild energy all directed to welcoming a special guest.

Politicians of the city, the province and region couldn't be stilled. They moved to and fro, ensuring that a proper welcome to a distinguished visitor was in place, checking out streamers and banners and all preparations to a T. Who wouldn't be excited and eager? Afterall, it's the "man of the hour" who's coming to visit the city in his official capacity. It was also some kind of a homecoming for the local boy who turned himself into the proverbial "golden boy."

Classes that morning though still going on at the park were being disturbed by the noise and the excitement of the moment. The leaders decided to suspend them and asked students to help in hanging the "Welcome, Minister Mendel" streamers and banners.

Not long after, the much -awaited visitor arrived with the Governor, the City Mayor and a host of local politicians and new presidential appointees in tow. They proceeded to the "Farmhouse," an open conference hall located at the back of the Capitol building. Throngs of city people followed his retinue each one trying to catch a glimpse of their *kababayan* Minister as he took his seat among the local dignitaries. With his bearing, he was undeniably the center of attraction. Was he trying to look oblivious to the attention showered upon him? But he was smiling to his ear, obviously pleased at the warm reception he got from his own people!

From where he was seated, Minister Mendel saw Dr. Granada in the crowd. He asked his aide to call the man and requested that he sat beside him at the presidential table. The Governor and his companions stayed behind the two, leaning their backs on the stage apron waiting for any sign that the Minister had noticed them and probably call them to join him on the table.

Before the program began, Granada and he had a casual talk, the latter whispering to the OIC that he (Mendel) would not announce the decision (about Granada's fate) himself publicly fearing he might be misunderstood. Instead, he said Minister Quilantang would do the announcing herself when she arrives on Saturday, July 5. Wanting to know what the decision was, Granada asked Mendel in hushed tone who assured him that Barrado's appointment would be definitely revoked.

"What about me? What plans do they have for me" he asked, uncertain.

"You would be retained," he simply said.

The program had started and protesters were given some time to present their side briefly. Dr. Domug, Prof. Caluya, Sonny Aquiling, Prof. Romy Ramar and Joel Lerpa stood before Minister Mendel and explained why he should consider pushing for Barrado's recall of appointment. Julie Dayang of the alumni group and Genito Rubitan of the parents-teachers association said likewise. Dr. Ric Limbao, presented over 20,000 signatures solicited from concerned citizens of Metro Ciudad and the surrounding towns and cities of the region, which Dr.Limbao said called for the revocation of Barrado's appointment and the retention and consequent appointment of Dr. Granada as MCPC President. Minister Mendel was listening intently. One of his aides was taking down notes.

When the Minister walked toward the microphone to give his response, Public Works Director Efaraim Hizon sat by Granada's side smiling and looking friendly all of a sudden. It did not take him a fraction of a second, however, to realize that all eyes were on him, glaring. (What- the-heck-are-you-doing-there? looks were unnerving.) Feeling he was not wanted, he stood up and disappeared in the crowd immediately.

Minister Mendel spoke in his native Cebuano for the benefit of his fellow locals thinking that speaking in their dialect would get his message across fast and clear. (An English translation was provided.) His speech which lasted for less than an hour was interrupted several times by loud and long applauses, stomping of feet, shouts of laughter, audience's emotional outbursts and other distractions. He paused from time to time to let the wild applause die down, the audience sober up.

> *My friends. At the outset, I would like to say that while I*
> *am saddened by what has happened to our state college, I am*
> *at the same time happy that you, the students, especially you,*
> *the teachers, have shown that you cannot allow yourselves*

to be oppressed by any one. To stand for your rights is an indication of an honorable people who love freedom. We should encourage honor and freedom to pervade especially now that we are in the midst of a new government wherein all of us should strive hard in order to make it work. It is therefore imperative that we continue to take a stand to protect our rights because people who continue to abuse their authority and people who continue to be subservient to "evils" have no place in our society.

I also would like you to know that there is nothing personal in my involvement with your present problem. Steve Barrado is in fact my godson. But for me, the interest of the majority, the interest of the people, shall take precedence over all other interests and surely not above personal relationships no matter who is involved.

In truth, Steve would have failed to get this appointment had I not used my "little voice" to support his application. But my friends, forgive me for I did not know that there were specific requirements to be followed before the presidency of a state college is given to anyone. All I know is assigning OICs related to local government units like governors and mayors. In this case, even if one has no adequate education, he can be appointed as OIC. (Laughter.)

It is for this reason, that on the day I left for my last trip to America the president of your student council, as well as the presidents of your faculty and personnel associations and several others, came to see me in my home in Manila and explained the situation. Thus, I immediately wrote Mr. Barrado advising him to hold in abeyance his plan of entering the College in any manner especially if he will force himself in, egging him to settle the problem peaceably, because I believe that if people with goodwill will simply, you know, deal with one another in all sincerity, then I think any problem can be solved in a nice way instead of using force. Unfortunately we now have a troubled situation just because my request was ignored.

I say to you my friends that I uphold your conviction that education shall be for the people and that academes should be run by educators. Education is too important— a matter not to be left in the hands of politicians.

May I inform you that because of this present situation, your concern was partly discussed by Minister Quilantang during the last Cabinet meeting. I believe she will be here two days from now—that would be July 5, before the President of the Republic comes on July 6. I believe further that she has a solution to your problem. This solution has already been cleared with the Office of the President. I am not in a position to announce what that decision will be. All I can say is that it will be to the best interest of the constituents of your school.

By the way, do not anymore associate your school with the symbol of the political party of the past administration. By god, that symbol is an anathema to my eyes and sensibilities! (Laughter.)

Before, that symbol might have been appropriate but now that times have changed, it is also time that we change that symbol. I do not know what you want to name it. I couldn't care less. Any other symbol – paraphrasing Shakespeare— "A rose by any other name would smell just as sweet."

So whatever you decide, erase that symbol because that is one of the bad habits of the past. (More laughter).

And so my friends, I beg you to maintain your cool. Just don't be too in a hurry in trying to achieve what you want because I will be behind you. I will continue to be behind you in your search for a just solution to the problem that has confronted you and your College.

This much I can assure you with all sincerity because I love Metro Ciudad. This is our city. If we cannot maintain unity here then where else can we achieve unity? We need to deal with each other in the spirit of fairness and equality.

Lastly, may I again say that on July 6 the President will arrive in our city. Minister Quilantang should have been here a day before and as far as I know, she has with her the

*solution to your problem. And I believe, this solution will
make all of you happy.*

*Until then, I look forward to meeting you again under
happier occasion.*

Thank you very much.

That speech earned the Minister a standing ovation. It did not only
raise the protesters' hope many times over. It also somehow, cautiously
concretized the abstract idea "victory", of rising above adversity.

Everyone who could reach him shook Mr. Mendel's hand. Granada
was profused in his thanking him. The local politicians saw to it that they
had their pictures taken with him.

As the protesters left the "Farmhouse" hall, rain suddenly fell. It was
high noon.

"This is a good sign," everybody thought. Never was there rain in the
last few weeks.

"The heavens heard us," they shouted joyfully while dancing in the
rain.

DAY 35, THURSDAY, JULY 3
Erasing Traces of the Past

Minister Mendel's mention of "that symbol" prompted Granada and his leaders to take cognizance of the suggestion. In fact, they realized that as far back as the day when the former president was removed from office as a result of the People's Revolution they already thought of ridding the school of symbols that pertained to the old regime. They believed it was the most sensible thing to do under the circumstances.

Now that Mendel had mentioned it and in deference to the new government, it was wise to consider especially so that they were seeing signs of a favorable outcome.

Nap Lopa, consultant for public relations drafted a resolution proposing to drop or end the use of the PMN symbol or ensignia in all the school's official correspondence, activities, signages including the school uniform. it was agreed that a resolution be drafted for consideration by the Board of Trustees.

The idea of obliterating the use of the PMN symbol in the College sprang a week after the ouster of the former chief executive and the takeover of the new government. Since then the faculty and staff stopped wearing their school uniform because they claimed to have been shamed in public places by those who "helped overthrow the old government." The PMN logo was not only embellished in their college uniform but its banner flew alongside the national flag in the school's flagpole. After what happened, they felt compelled to let go of the symbol which up to the present time was still distinctly present in the College. Nobody had noticed it until Mr. Mendel's reference to it.

Sometime in March an opinion poll on the rationale of removing traces of PMN's presence in the institution was done per OIC Granada's instruction. The Planning and Monitoring Office of Beth Sebastian conducted the poll covering representative sampling of students, faculty and non-academic staff. It's result was an overwhelming "yes" which gave the College Council the authority to issue a policy statement on the matter. This policy statement was supported by the PTA of the school which came out with their own resolution upholding the action and decision of the Administrative Council. However, from then on, the issue seemed to have been forgotten as the whirlwind of events put on hold the normal College operation.

Anchored on the same policy statement adopted by the Administrative Council in March and the resolution of the PTA Board referring to the same purpose, Atty. Gael in close consultation with Granada, Nap Lopa and the members of the Administrative Council came out with the final copy of the resolution. It also proposed to furnish copies to Education Minister, all concerned government agencies and instrumentalities including the Palace.

Granada was requested to personally submit said document to Minister Quilantang since she was the Chairperson of the College Board. Copies were to be provided the President of the Republic and Minister Mendel as soon as they meet.

At 11:00 o'clock, Romy Ramar announced that July 4 was a holiday since it was Philippine-American Friendship Day. However, make up classes will be held on Saturday, July 5 as usual in the park. He also reminded the various committees to follow up their assignments for the forthcoming visits of Minister Quilantang and the President. He was optimistic that Minister Quilantang indeed had good news for everyone as announced by Local Government chief yesterday.

A Tinge of Doubt

Inspite of the optimism shown by Romy, many began to question the veracity of Mendel's announcement. Who would eventually solve their problem was repeatedly asked by the protesters oftentimes with irritation. This was a reaction to news items that came out today in major national dailies which reported on the latest pronouncement of Minister Quilantang on the controversy. Said statement drew the intense interests and skepticisms of everyone especially the protesters. This interest however, grew sour when they could not find any clue to the supposed "solution" to their problem. Their fear was slowly taking form.

Three national dailies *Day's Express, Metropolitan Times,* and *Tiempo* reported varying versions of the MCPC protest but hinting on a common assumption— that Education Minister Quilantang had adopted a "hands-off" policy with regard to the revocation of the appointment of Barrado since she was repeatedly quoted saying "that was the handiwork of politicians, and therefore, they should be the ones to solve the problem."

As they read and re-read the articles and the statement attributed to the lady Minister, the more puzzled they became of her stand. This seemed contrary to Mendel's "good news" yesterday.

"Wasn't it a paradox," they asked, "that while she evidently abhorred political interference, she threw back the problem to the same politicians when she was given the authority to resolve the issue?"

Granada stood in defense of his superior arguing that maybe she was just consistent with her position. "Given the embarrassing situation she found herself in, she must have lashed back by giving these political animals a dose of their own medicine. Thus, when the Palace turned over the problem to her, she used this as an opportunity to get back at them."

The protesters were not convinced.

"If the politicians will solve the problem then they will apply a political solution. If Barrado is ousted, doesn't it follow that another political protégée will come in? Isn't this very logical?" they asked in utter disgust.

"But then, that might lead to the resignation of the Minister," Granada speculated. "Or if she would not be allowed to resign, consequently, she will have complete control (in the selection and appointment of higher education institutions' presidents). I think the Minister is taking a very calculated risk. Let's give her more time. I think she knows what she is doing."

"Yes, but its painful for us," somebody said. "Do we have to go through this all over again? What about Mendel's announcement yesterday that she has the solution in her hands? Did he lie to us?

"I don't think so. He must have said that in good faith knowing appropriate protocols have been observed. Yes, it's painful," Granada said, "especially if we take it personally.""

"This position of Quilantang" another said, "is rather nebulous. I find this whole thing rather perplexing."

"No, I think, its rather simple," commented another. "It's known in confused management situation as passing the buck."

"So, what's going to be the stasnd of the Ministry if the chief distances herself from the issue? Isn't this a manifestation of lack of a central authority when it isn't clear whose hands are on the steering wheel?"

The question remained unanswered.

In the evening a copy of a petition signed by 36 barangay capatains of the city standing behind Steve Barrado came into the hands of the protesters. The striking statement of support said that "with Barrado as President, the State College will become truly an instrument of the new government."

"Here we go again, the penultimate political solution!" someone shouted in dismay.

DAY 36, FRIDAY, JULY 4
Mounting Apprehensions

Despite the announcement of "no classes today," MacArthur Park was teeming with students and protesters. No doubt, the park had become some kind of a second home for all aside from the Sebastian apartment-turned-headquarters.

Another upsetting news came to the Steering Committee which was at that time reviewing its plans for the anticipated visit the next day of Minister Quilantang. The deans of satellite schools, except for Dean Eugene Regenio of agriculture of the Alubijid satellite campus had "defected." Dean Regenio confirmed it and informed the group that Dr. Soriano was having a meeting with the deans at that very hour in the main campus adding that he turned down the invitation for him to join them. He preferred to come to the meeting of the Steering Committee at the Park. He also mentioned about an earlier meeting held on July 1 called by Soriano allegedly to find out the salary status of their faculty members. It was obvious, Ramar observed that one way of getting their support was to offer them an incentive tempting enough to change their mind.

However, Regenio pacified them by saying that not all were eager to do Soriano's bidding. In fact pressure had already been applied to his faculty in the Alubijid campus. Ruben Genata, recently designated by Barrado as director of all satellite colleges (which Dr. Marcos presently holds) named a mere instructor OIC-dean in place of Regenio but said appointee refused and told Genata that she would only accept if the designation came from Dr. Granada himself. Genata was also reported to have visited other nearby campuses trying to obtain endorsements for Barrado but failed to get the cooperation he needed. Teachers and instructors from Alubijid and Jasaan were not keen on Genata's overtures. The five other satellites could hardly be reached due to distance. It took days to get there. However, a few of their deans were already sold to accepting Barrado as their new president.

These information alarmed the Steering Committee and was suddenly gripped with apprehensions. What if the rest of the satellite deans and faculty and staff switch loyalty? As a whole, the satellite campuses' rank–and-file population constituted 37% of the total workforce of MCPC.

This knowledge had a strong bearing on the fate of the on-going protest including the protesters' state of morale.

The discussion on satellite schools was set aside for a while to prepare for the grand announcement on the fate of their protest by the Education Minister the following day. They had to impress upon her the urgency and impact of her decision on the life of the College.

Everyone was excited, expectant and hopeful. Were they to receive the good news of redemption as announced by Minister Mendel yesterday?

They kept their fingers crossed.

The Insinuation of "Mr. Y"

Today seemed to be a day of surprises, which the protesters thought would be better if they did not get them at all.

While at the HQ, Aurora Ella, Language Area Chairman of the College assisting Beth in the information bureau told her colleagues that a family friend whose identity she hid in the alias "Mr. Y" visited their home the other night and made at first, casual talks about the protest's status. He was interested to know if the academic community would be open to having another person as their president as long as it was not Barrado. Slowly and a bit hesitant to go on, she said Mr. Y wanted to know what possible reactions they might have if he would aspire for the College presidency.

Auring was not sure if the man was joking and could not believe at first what she just heard. However, he sounded serious and so she pretended, she said, to be interested if only to find out the real motive behind Mr. Y's revelation. In the course of their conversation Auring's husband suspected that their friend was telling the truth. "In fact," she said, "Mr. Y kept repeating that if I am sure he would not be acceptable, he'll back out. He said he was not like Barrado, unreasonable and unyielding."

The "news" Auring brought to the group disquieted everyone. It did doubly confuse them when Mr. Y claimed, according to Auring, that he was doing it on the prodding of Minister Mendel that he mustered enough courage to see her and pry on the situation.

"Mr.Y surely was certain that neither Mr. Barrado nor Dr. Granada would get the presidency. He supposed that Mendel had to scout for one who could fill the vacuum left by the two. And he, according to him, was the Minister's choice."

When the leaders heard of Mr. Y's story, their apprehensions about the fate of their struggle intensified. No, it was not only the coming of Mr. Y into the picture. Rather, it placed the "positive message" of Minister Mendel in a more questionable status.

"Was Minister Mendel really sincere when he said we'll just have to wait for the good news?"

Despite the mounting misgivings some still gave the local government chief the benefit of the doubt.

"The Minister might have accommodated Mr. Y just like any politician would. As an astute politician he could not possibly displease those who seek his help especially the likes of Mr. Y."

Others claimed they knew the Minister too well and said such qualms were emotionally-driven. They insisted that when the Minister made a commitment (in his speech last July 2) he would go all the way to fulfill that commitment no matter what happened.

"If Minister Quilantang has washed her hands off the problem and Minister Mendel has his own man in mind, then what would happen to us now?" asked the others baffled by what they were hearing.

"The situation has become more muddled!" the rest observed in total exasperation.

"Stop it! Don't get yourself freaked out by overthinking," advised Granada, who from the time their fears and doubts were articulated had kept to himself, silent but listening. He dared not comment on anything. As usual, his calm and composed front was on display. He suggested that they listen again to the tape recorded speech of the Minister for their peace of mind.

The recording was played again and again until late evening at HQ. As their ears were glued to the recorder they wanted to confirm if the Minister had hinted something that would make them think twice as to his sincerity.

Since nobody could point to a plausible clue, Granada said they really had no choice but to have faith in the man. If they didn't have that, then there was nothing else to hope for.

Quoting his favorite verse from the Bible he said such words kept his faith at times when things get to be very difficult: *"Faith is the substance of things hoped for the evidence of things not seen."*

When Granada left his leaders that late evening, he was aware that the euphoria to Mendel's message of hope yesterday had gradually shrunk into the depths of despair.

On his way out he was greeted by the students working at Brix's garage. They were finishing the WELCOME banners and streamers for Minister Quilantang. It would not be till early dawn before they're done. In Granada's watch, it said five minutes past 1:00 o'clock. "Good morning, Sir!" they chorused as he saluted back. He felt the gentle breeze outside and inhaled deeply.

———————————

DAY 37, SATURDAY, JULY 5
Agony Hits Breaking Point

It took the teachers and instructors much effort to keep their students attentive and focused on the lesson. That Saturday was no ordinary day and everyone knew why: A VIP was coming to town and she was bringing in the good news (or so they believed)!

Every now and then, everyone would look at the direction of the airport, expectant and anxious. They were waiting for the return of the reception committee who went to the airport to meet Minister Quilantang. They yearned to hear the announcement that the Education chief had agreed to meet with them even briefly. Earlier, the Regional Office had confirmed the Minister was definitely arriving from Manila on the morning flight. Would the committee succeed in bringing her from the airport to the park?

When their colleagues finally showed up, it was no doubt from the looks on their faces that their mission fell short of expectations. Anita Caluya told the group they didn't have the opportunity to approach the Minister as she was swarmed by Barrado's and the Mindanao Advancement Party people.

"It was simply impossible to even get near her," said Ramar who headed the protesters' delegation.

Worse, they overheard the Minister declared that she did not come to Metro Ciudad to solve the controversy in the College reiterating that "that was for the politicians to resolve."

Without a word or a hint whether she would meet the protesters or not (or even Dr. Granada), she took off in a light plane for Bukidnon along with an aide and President Jaima Orlege of National College of Bulidnon. They heard that trouble was brewing in that school.

"She did just that, didn't she? How insensitive, how incompassionate! What kind of an Education Minister is she?" The protesters were enraged. They were furious and insulted at her intentional snubbing of their plight.

Students assigned to hoist the WELCOME streamers in the highway from the airport also arrived shouting angrily: "Let's change this to QUILANTANG RESIGN!'"

Many did not respond to queries thrown at them. They dropped on the ground exhausted, hurt and bitter.

Student leaders Ed Maguz and Jimmy Caoili were cursing and apparently mad for feeling they were treated shabbily by the very person who should have given them at least, a wave of recognition. Instead, they got an upturned nose and an infuriating attitude. The female students were loud and sarcastic. "Even if they pay us next time, we would not be coerced to repeat such a stupid thing!"

They had been in their area of assignment since six o'clock that morning all eager and enthusiastic only to be ignored and taken for granted. Worst, they had not had breakfast or drunk a glass of water. A few were ready to faint until some well-meaning people handed them a packet of hot *pandesal*. Sonny Aquiling and two others who were assigned to take care of the welcome delegation could not do anything but sat with the students silently. They felt guilty knowing they were the ones who dragged these young people to the streets.

"How dare she dismissed us as some kind of a nuisance!" Joel exploded in frustration.

VPAA Vilar was disappointed but remained calm, speculated that perhaps the Minister would find it in her heart to drop by and meet them after coming from Bukidnon. "Let us be patient," he appealed to every one. "If we lose her... that would be our end."

"That's what we get for having an old woman as education chief," a male faculty member said. "Hell hath no fury than a woman scorned!" Little did he know that his Shakespearean quote would be used by the protesters to describe the Minister from then on.

"A woman scorned indeed!"

Justifying their mean allusion, they assumed "the Minister was bypassed by politicians, hence her contempt for them. She was also, in a way, snubbed by Dr. Granada by not paying her a courtesy call when she officially took her seat as Minister and surely, she kept that at the back of her mind."

"Not only that!" a high-pitched female voice rang. "It's really the fault of Sir. Imagine, he was also not present when the SUC executives serenaded her on her 81st birthday! You can imagine the tantrum of a senile person. It's worse than a child whose candy had been snatched!"

"*Huy, Inday.* She's only 71, not 81!" corrected her friend who playfully slapped her arm.

"Seventy-one or 81 there's really no difference. Either belongs to the world of the forgetful and the forgotten."

"Why, the old woman must have missed the heart-thumping baritone of "Sir.""

"This old woman might have felt humiliated, thus her open derision to all those who frustrated her and that includes Sir!"

"I don't think it's the woman scorned," said a young male faculty in the group. "It may be her post-menopausal frame of mind – whatever that means!"

Everyone had a momentary laugh at what he said. They soon went back to griping again bringing out all sorts of reasons for doing so.

A senior dean said that if no solution will be offered by the next day, he would consider disappearing from the scene. Several echoed his sentiment and said they might just do the same.

Almost loathing, Dean Elvi Ogaoan of the College of Industrial Education asked in abhorrence: "What kind of example is the Minister setting for our students? In class we teach them not to dilly-dally on their decision-making. Yet, we have a head who refuses to do something about a big problem in her hands. She not only refuses to solve it, she runs away from it!"

Sighs and groans could be heard as they all sank in an almost depressed state, their hope suddenly falling apart. The misery had turned to agony especially when it dawned on them that their efforts and sacrifices would eventually turn to nothing.

"If Sir Granada is the Minister, this problem would have been solved a long time ago," joked Jimmy.

Before Dr. Granada could react, someone said: "Or we will all be demonstrating against him!"

Granada shrugged. He was offended but kept himself in check. He should not turn emotional before his people. Calmly, he advised his group "to wait, the day's not over yet."

Media people from Manila were milling around, looking for human interest stories to serve as sidebars to the main story. They talked to disgruntled students and protesters. They heard stories from parents of students, from members of the community. Some had visited the main campus and confirmed their suspicion: Only very few students attended classes for the week wherein most of the teachers were the newly-hired substitutes.

In the early afternoon a general meeting was called by the steering committee with the leaders taking turns in appealing to everyone to have a little more patience. They reminded them of Minister Mendel's words that all should be "cool" and that they should not "be in a hurry" in seeking the solution to the problem because he would be "behind" them.

Students and protesters booed saying "it was all bullshit, and a big lie." They tagged Quilantang "an alien from outer space," and accused her of being so cold-hearted that she could not empathize with them at all.

Granada didn't bother to speak like the rest. He stood on the farther end of the crowd and watched with hawk-eyed clarity the reactions and body language of the protesters. Most heads were bowed, most shoulders stooped. For the first time, it occurred to him that what they were fighting for would definitely be lost if a solution to the problem wouldn't be presented between now and tomorrow. If there was no recourse, then probably most of them who had fought in the last 37 days would find themselves reporting to the main campus by Monday. Barrado would be in glee! He'll feel like he just won the lottery. The leaders of the protesting community, he was afraid, would be the first to get the ax.

When Joel Lerpa stood to speak, the audience were suddenly attentive. Granada had observed this young man since the struggle started. Every time he spoke, the crowd responded eagerly. His easy countenance, boyish grin and youthful confidence made him lovable not only to his peers but also to the faculty and staff. But today as he approached the microphone, Granada noted his grim face and tired and listless demeanor. It was quite clear his self-esteem was at its lowest.

When Joel began to speak, lacking was the same enthusiasm which used to be there. He started to appeal to his co- students to be a little more patient but got murmurs, subdued hisses and expletives instead. It was evident that the young ones were no longer willing as they used to be. They were not angry at him but were swearing at the absentee Minister whose name they associated with arrogance and heartlessness. Joel called for volunteers to line the streets the next day for the arrival of the President of the Republic. Not a single hand was raised. He did not force commitment from his peers. He knew too well why.

The meeting ended without Granada addressing the audience. An emergency meeting of the steering committee soon followed at the headquarters. Granada joined them since he was invited.

It was apparent that the mood of the leaders was not pleasant. Tension seemed to fill the air. Beth asked why Joel called for volunteers when it had been arranged that faculty, staff and students already had their assignments. Joel shot back saying that the students were already exhausted and so disappointed that to expect them to work on their assignment was wishful thinking. "They will come if they want to," he said flatly.

Arguments went back and forth endlessly heightening the tensed atmosphere which Granada did not dare mediate. He excused himself to stretch and have some fresh air.

Outside, he found some members of the faculty who confided that the general feeling was one of defeat, that many of them may not be able to hold on for long. Much that they wanted to stay and keep the fight going, they realized they had already sacrificed too much and founnd themselves penniless, running out of money leaving their families without means to live normally. Many had secured loans to get by. Others had been inconsistent in their coming to join the protest because there's no money for fare and for basic essentials from the time their pay was cut. A number admitted they had no other recourse but to "swallow their pride" and report back to the school on Monday. This decision, though unwillingly on their part, was triggered by Minister Quilantang's "heartless countenance" to understand their predicament. There was therefore no more reason to lengthen the sacrifice.

Granada did not try to persuade them to "hang in there a little more." He knew that it won't work anymore. He apologized.

Meanwhile, after the tension had died down, the committee proceeded to finalize plans for the President's arrival. They also wanted to know if Quilantang will spare time with Dr. Granada when she comes back from

Bukidnon late in the afternoon. They prayed incessantly for the old lady to come to her senses and grant him a few minutes, at least.

———————————

Back at the Park a group of students scrambled to tell the others that Barrado and his followers were marching their way to the VIP Hotel where the Minister would be billeted for the night. They proudly carried their "Welcome" banners.

As Barrado's entourage walked along Recto Avenue the protesters noted there were only 37 students, 12 staff members and some children who were unmistakeably enjoying the march alongside these men and women.

President Barrado and Dr. Soriano followed in their respective cars.

"With such a small contingent they should have marched with them," criticized the protesters, adding "they were only showing to the public the exact opposite of what they had been claiming all along – that he had the majority of the College constituents on his side."

"Barrado's funeral march!" exclaimed Noli Tejano, the former's fiery critic who happened to be watching with some press people. He guffawed and thought it looked funny. When Noli let out a hearty laugh, everybody else guffawed like a horse.

The "Injustice" of It All

Late in the afternnoon, words got to the protesters that Minister Quilantang was willing to give Granada an audience that evening.

"Finally!" they let out a sigh of relief.

Despite his appeal to his leaders not to accompany him, there were a number of them including students who insisted to come with him to the hotel. They said they wanted to give him encouragement and support.

The VIP Hotel main lobby was already swarming with people when they entered. These people were there to be seen or probably grab the chance to be interviewed by the national press. Atty. Gael learned that the Minister was at the hall in the Mezzanine talking to several higher education heads one-on-one. He told Granada to proceed to the ante-room to wait for his turn.

The OIC found a seat among the others who, unlike him, were anxious and fidgety. His eyes searched specifically for Barrado but he was not in the room. He wondered if he was conferring with the Minsiter at that time. He learned a little later that he was not.

Waiting in the smaller room were Dr. Beloy Cordola and wife Heidi who was granted time to bring to the Minister his case. Dr. Cordola was former president of Central Mindanao National University (CMNU). He was requesting to be reinstated in order to "seek justice" for himself after being removed unceremoniously from his post by the past administration.

Dr. Beloy and Dr. Moises knew each other quite well. They worked together at CMNU twelve years ago where Granada was VPAA and was OIC of the University every time President Cordola was away. He later transferred to CNESU and left Dr. Beloy who, a year later was having internal troubles with his faculty, staff and students. After a long, persistent call for his ouster by his constituents, he was finally removed from office by the Education Minister of the deposed regime. Dr. Cordola contested this decision and brought the case up to the high court whose decision was still to be served. He was doing consultancy work at one US university when the new government took over. He believed that this was his chance to be vindicated and redeem his tarnished reputation.

Shortly before the trouble at MCPC began, Dr. Beloy went to see OIC Granada with the news that Quilantang's search committee had ranked him number 1, with twenty-seven points higher than the candidate who ranked second. He intimated that the lady Minister had already "reserved" the polytechnic college in Metro Ciudad for him in case he failed to make a comeback at CMNU.

Aware of his former colleague's lack of decorum and delicadeza, Granada was silent about his school being reserved for him, but expressed considerable skepticism on Beloy going back to CMNU again as its president.

"I'll bet five cases of beer Moi. I'll get back the presidency hands down."

"Call," he said amused.

His reminiscence of the past was cut at that moment when Dr. Cesar Caperal emerged from the room beaming. He was just named new CMNU president by Quilantang.

Taken aback at the unexpected bit of news Dr. Beloy was shocked, turned all red and slumped back on the sofa his strength leaving him. He could not believe what just happened.

Granada tried to humor him by mentioning their bet. "Five cases of beer remember?"

But Cordola pretended he did not hear him as he rattled on saying the Minister just picked Caperal from nowhere to the consternation of the search committee members.

He desperately wanted to get inside, see the minister and asked her about her "despicable" decision. But he was prevented from doing so. He sat in one corner with his nervous wife who kept telling him to leave now to avoid further embarrassment. Dr. Beloy did not heed his wife's bidding, his face dark and mutinous.

Dr. Nick Pamatong who lost his bid to head the State University of Mindanao in Lanao del Sur was called in next. A Fulbright-Hays grantee he lost his bid because Quilantang allowed herself to be pressured by the political bigwigs of the city and province of the region. In the last Educators Congress in Baguio City, Pamatong was the most vocal advocate against political interference in state educational institutions and his paper on this which he presented was greatly hailed by Congress' participants.

"What if the Minister would not listen to you? Granada asked while they were waiting.

"In that case, I would go to the hills. If you won't be vindicated yourself, would you go to the hills with me? My men are just waiting for my instructions, you know."

Nick was Muslim and belonged to one of the largest royal families in his province.

And there were many more who were hoping to have an audience with the Minister. They all waited patiently. Some were obviously happy and excited, the others, somber. Still Barrado did not show up.

Atty. Gael, Nap Lopa and the rest paced the lobby of the restaurant frequently that the waiters were annoyed. None of them placed any order but asked for "a glass of water, please."

Joel, Eddie, Max and the other student leaders were deep in sleep around a corner table, too tired and too exhausted to be hungry. Their heads seemed to be nailed into the table's surface. It was quarter to nine in Nap's watch.

Suddenly, they saw Minister Mendel walked out of another room followed by reporters and some political personalities. Walking briskly to keep pace with him was Barrado with his mugged expression. Apparently, he had a talk with his *ninong*-benefactor about his status and it looked like the news was aggravating.

"He must have been told the bad news," Atty. Gael whispered to Anita.

Soon, it'll be Granada's time to be summoned as Cordola, Pamatong and several others came out of the room one by one either ecstatic or feeling doomed.

Granada was ambivalent. He felt his chances were fifty-fifty and for now, that's good enough.

One-on-One with the Minister

Atty. Santos Matos who was assisting the Minister during the whole time that she was meeting prospective appointees whispered a sincere "good luck" to Granada when he was called in. As he strode inside, Minister Quilantang raised her head, looked at him sharply, sending a message that she wasn't happy to see him. Granada could sense she was trying to impress upon him (and maybe to others too) her feminine imperialism. He noticed her eyebags hanging like barnacles which pushed back her small bulging eyes. She never invited him to sit so he remained standing.

And gave his greetings.

"Good evening, Ma'am."

"Uh, huh. Dr. Granada," she replied briefly.

"Madam Minister, first of all, I would like to apologize if I gave you the impression that I deliberately misled you into believing that I am not really for a turnover."

"So you have realized that now Dr. Granada. You could have easily whispered to me that you were not really for a turnover. I am sorry, but I have lost complete trust in you. You are no different from Barrado afterall, hmp."

"Madam Minister, I admit it looks that way, but please allow me to explain," he begged.

"What is there to say Dr. Granada? The fact that you refused a turnover is an indication of your stubbornness and wanting to keep the post," she accused him.

"No, Ma'am. My stand has always been that. It was not only because I know I will be vindicated eventually but holding on a bit was a tactical move to defuse the escalating tension in school. I sought advise from my lawyer who said this was a good move toward that end," he continued.

"I see, a tactical move! Well you can have all the tactical moves and designs for all I care, but know that I don't go for such stupidity." slammed the old lady. "You know I have always been a frank and candid person. I say what needs to be said. You simply don't have my ttust anymore, Granada."

That's why it became my moral responsibility to ensure that their lives are protected and their positions in the College are secured. Third, the turnover also requires that we identify with Mr. Barrado the entry points to effect his acceptability by the faculty and staff. You know the reason for the picket. Right from the beginning, he was not acceptable."

"I get to know that," she admitted.

"I proposed this to him as early as June 5 hoping to create an opportunity for him to be finally accepted by the community. But he rejected the terms of the turnover without commenting on any one of them. He insisted he's president and it is up to him to listen or not to any proposal and said that over and over again."

"So... why didn't you tell me these before?" she asked sounding a bit irritated.

"I relayed all of these to Atty. Matos when he visited the College last June 15. I thought he would tell you," he replied.

"Then why did you make me believe that you were really for a turnover when you last visited my office by not signing the agreement?" she retorted.

"Ma'am, you told us to 'sleep on it,' remember? So I studied it again and wrote my reactions to the draft in my note to Atty. Matos last June 25, believing I could put the message across. I literally took your suggestion that we didn't have to sign the agreement on that day, I think that was June 24. It gave me the assurance that you understood all along."

"Okay, okay. Now, what do you suggest?" Quilantang felt her question actually boomeranged on her.

Noticing that she was actually looking up at him and he, looking down on her, she asked him to sit down to cover up the awkwardness of the situation.

"Sit down please. You must be tired standing."

"Thank you Ma'am," he said taking the chair across her.

"Go on."

"Ma'am, the protesting community was informed by Minister Mendel last July 2 that you will be announcing your decision today."

"Now, c'mon Granada, I've been saying this many times: I have nothing to do with this problem. Since the politicians started it, therefore they should be the ones to finish it. I told the President that Rayos knows my stand on the matter. I also told Lino Mendel that."

"But that was not what I've been told, Ma'am."

"Now Granada. Remember what I said earlier in this conversation? I am a frank person and I say what I mean to say. Don't let me say it again. It's getting on my nerves!" remarked the old lady angrily. It took her a few minutes before continuing. "By the way, they say, you are a PMN. But I don't care. There are as many PMNs as there are many with bad habits in this government."

"But Madame, that's ridiculous! I should not be labeled as such just because I served under the past administration. I'm apolitical, never had any political affiliation all my life," his voice rang out in humiliation.

"Anything else?" cut the Minister who did not attempt to contradict what Granada said.

"Yes, Madam Minister. Could you spend a few minutes with the leaders of the protesters tonight? They are waiting outside."

"And what will I tell them? I will be practically telling them what I just told you right now!" Suddenly she felt pressured by the unexpected request.

"Please Madam, these people—the rank-and-file and the students are not only up against political meddling in the academe but they are also fighting for you so that your policies are upheld. I hope you realize that."

"Yes...I realized that," she said lamely.

"The protesters are aware that the President of the Republic promised to look into our problem when she comes to visit us tomorrow. She was quoted by a national tabloid. So I hope she fulfills her promise."

"Well, multi-sectoral groups are meeting with her for consultation. Your leaders can be there," she suggested.

"I'm sorry Ma'am but they would be tackling general issues and our presence there would be a waste of time. We want to bring to her our specific concerns with the hope that she may be able to offer the ultimate solution. Actually, the protest leaders had tried to arrange with Father Javieto for a special audience with the President but their request was denied since a similar request by Mr. Barrado and his group was denied earlier."

"But don't you think it is rather too late now to make such an arrangement?"

"Ma'am, if the protesting community is denied an audience with the President then I think, and I very well know, that this government will have more dissenters in its hands. All the protest leaders and their followers will be disgusted and I won't be surprised if some of them will go to the hills."

"Are you threatening me now Granada?" she asked slightly raising her voice, but soon calmed down. "All right, I see what you mean. I'll do the best I can. I'll also ask Lino to help."

"Thank you, Madame Minister… and if you don't mind, I have one last request to you."

"What is it this time?"

"Please restore whatever trust and confidence you had of me before, in the same manner that my full trust and confidence in you as my Minister have not been lost."

It seemed ages before Minister Quilantang could reply. She was touched by the sincerity of his appeal. Finally, she looked at the man in front of her with those small, shrewd eyes. She slowly nodded.

"Thank you, Ma'am. It means a lot to me."

Granada extended his right hand for a handshake. She took it and clasped her cold hand in his. It was brief but warm.

"Thank you, Ma'am," he lowered his voice to the timbre of a very special prayer. Men don't cry but his heart was bleeding.

Bracing up for the Inevitable

Granada came out of the room and went down to the lobby where his group was waiting. They leaped to their feet upon seeing him and surrounded him asking all sorts of questions.

"What happened?"

"What's the decision?"

"Sir, you had the longest session with the Minister."

"Sir, please tell us."

"Let's go home," was his reply.

Gathering around the mini tape recorder Granada pulled out from his pocket, everyone was holding their breath as they listened to the conversation. They were all huddled in that stuffy room in Beth's apartment.

What they heard angered and dismayed them. They were frustrated that the Minister did not have the "good news" they were expecting.

"So Minister Mendel made fools out of us by falsely raising our hopes," exclaimed Beth in disgust.

Some growled, the men threw a fist at the cemented wall and hurt themselves. They were too angry to keep still.

Granada tried to calm them by implying that he suspected Minister Mendel may have not been told that despite their agreement, the lady minister remained adamant to change her mind. "He may have been surprised himself," Granada continued in Mendel's defense.

"Let us pray. Let us have faith in the Lord…let us seek divine guidance" as Anita fell on her knees. But no one joined her on the floor, no reaction whatsoever, not even a whimper.

Their agony had reached breaking point. Tonight is a time of reckoning. Act now before time runs out. There was no point in grieving over Quilantang's inflated ego and pride and brazen self-importance. Pinning their hope on her that she might still reconsider was a crazy idea, they all agreed. They regretted the fact that they were too bureaucratic, too observant of protocols, always following the order of things.

"Since you said Mendel may have been deceived into believing that Quilantang will bring us the good news today, then let's go to him and beg him to help us. We know his words also carry weight with the President. If it is necessary to pledge our votes for him in the coming elections, so be it!"

They would do that without batting an eyelash as long as their cause can be given due recognition and solution as soon as possible. They had been in torment for length now that "selling their soul to the devil" was a thing they could do in exchange for favorably settling their messy situation.

Everyone rose, determined to wake the Minister up even if he's in the middle of his sleep. They seemed to have thrown all cares to the wind.

"Bahala na, let's do it!" putting their hands together to seal their decision.

It was already 11:20 in the evening. Irma, Danny and Bords got reliable information that the Governor was driving Minister Mendel from "Caprice" resort to his residence and must have been on their way by now.

Granada hesitated momentarily to go with the group not because it was already late at night but was concerned that he might be misunderstood as kowtowing with politicians. He knew too well that his fate and future were hanging in the balance. But when they begged him to go with them saying this could be his last opportunity to help, he acceded thinking less of the consequences.

"Let's do it!" he agreed.

Anita's husband Sesinando, National Bank manager in Metro Ciudad was with the group. He talked to the overseer of the Minister asking him to make possible the meeting between his boss and the protesters even briefly. The guy who knew the Caluyas ushered the group inside the waiting area of the Minister's residence.

"He would be arriving in a few minutes," he said and asked them to wait. Some twenty people were also waiting outside.

When the Minister arrived his security men cordoned him off from the crowd as he strode toward the group curious as to why they were there at that time of the night. "Shouldn't you be home sleeping?"

Anita took the lead and told him directly that Minister Quilantang did not have the decision "you told us she will have." She was disappointed that the lady minister was completely washing her hands off the problem.

Granada narrated what transpired during his talks with her emphasizing what he (Mendel) had told the *Metropolitan Times* earlier that this problem was under her ministry and therefore she should be the one to find the solution for it. "But she would not budge an inch and insisted on what the politicians responsible for this fiasco should do."

Minister Mentel made Granada repeat that to make sure he heard it right. "I'll try to see what I can do when the President comes tomorrow. I'll play it by ear" he promised. "It's rather late and you have to let me have a little sleep," while facing the others who were also there to see him. The statement was a signal for everyone to leave.

At the headquarters, others were still patiently waiting. It was Anita, Sonny and Joel's task to inform them of the outcome of their visit to Mendel.

"He did not promise much. He just said he'll see what he can do tomorrow," they reported.

"What if nothing happens tomorrow?" someone asked.

All eyes were on Granada who gave them a sad smile.

"Sir, if you decide to go to the hills, we will go with you," the men said.

"I can survive in the jungle," Granada suddenly found himself seriously saying.

Sleep didn't ccome easy for Moises who kept on replaying the events of the day in his mind. He didn't see a solution coming and was actually acutely aware that the President of the Republic may not have a solution either.

"Would a compromise be the best option if none is offered?" he was thinking aloud. "Right, the solution would most likely be a compromise. Somewhere in its complexity both sides would have to give."

As this thought raced through his mind, Granada decided that if he would ever have a chance to talk with the President, he would insist that foremost in the list of concerns would be the welfare of the students, faculty and non-academic personnel who believed and joined the struggle. If they lose this fight, they would be made to suffer because surely, Barrado's threats would be carried out.

Moises couldn't help but admit to himself that he's partly to blame. Inevitably, he would also get axed.

As he tossed and turned in bed the recurring thought was the shape or form the compromise could possibly take. He struggled in his sleep until he heard the cock crowed to announce daybreak. The rumble of vehicles in the city streets reminded him to brace himself up for another uncertain day.

Would he eventually seek a compromise to gain leverage for his people? Will there be risk, potential for damage and too little to gain in the process?

If a compromise was inevitable what sacrifice would it entail?

Granada drew a deep breath as he put on a nice necktie for the benefit of the two important ladies of the time.

———————————

DAY 38, SUNDAY, JULY 6
Day of Reckoning

Very early that morning Moises, his brother Ben, Danny and Irma were at the Governor's house pleading to include Granada and the protest leaders in the list of those whom Her Excellency the President will receive and grant an audience. They told the Governor that they had placed similar request to Ministers Quilantang and Mendel but explained they just wanted to explore all avenues to personally see and talk with the President.

Since the Governor was in a rush preparing to leave for the airport as head of the welcoming party, he suggested that they see the wife of the city mayor and request that they be included in the city sector list.

"Let Anita talk to her, she knows Mrs. Jasta very well," the Governor advised.

It took awhile before Danny found Anita who was already inside the Sports Center with the MCPC protesters' group. Danny explained what she needed to do and without wasting time, hurried out and sought the already stressed Mrs. Jasta.

When she returned a little later, her news downed the spirit of the group. They could no longer be accommodated since there were already twenty groups officially listed under the City Sector and each one would only be given no more than fifteen minutes to air problems or present proposals during consultation. The group was so disappointed that they thought they might just try their luck inside the sports complex where the chief executive will be speaking before the crowd.

It was quite easy for them to enter the packed hall despite the multitude who wanted to get in. Irma who was one of the receptionists did not only provide them with gate passes. She also seated them nearest to the VIPs.

Inside, the Center was overflowing to capacity. On the bleachers sat the ordinary people including some of the protesters. On the extended stage were the ministers, deputy ministers, governors, mayors, and practically all the important people of the city and the region, both in government and the private sector.

The north and south rafters of the Center were also filled up. The oval itself where the president's helicopter was expected to land was teeming with people carrying WELCOME banners and streamers. Noticeably absent were banners from Granada or Barrado's contingent. They were both advised not to put up one.

At around nine, the President's chopper landed on the farthest end of the oval with the crowd cheering wildly. When she was driven toward the stage in a heavily tinted vehicle, the people on the ground ran with it while the audience shouted, clapped their hands and stomped their feet. A reverberating chanting of the president's name filled the air…. "Sionnie… Sionnie…Sionnie…"

As she entered the hall, everyone stood up, craned their necks hoping to catch a glimpse of the small woman with short, curly hair dressed in her signature color—lemon. The atmosphere was charged with excitement. It was clear that the people were ecstatic to welcome the new President of the Republic.

However, the euphoria of her coming was doused by the less-than-ten-minute inconsequential speech she delivered before the expectant crowd. That was not the kind of address they had expected from a lady famous for her tirades and attacks during the campaign. Her talk sounded obligatory, the usual hackneyed and trite *"Thank you for the warm welcome- I am glad to be here today"* kind of message, forgetting to mention even in passing about her new government, its policies and programs and plan of action, at least for Mindanao. It was without meat and substance, frivolous and trivial. The general feeling of the audience was one of disappointment.

"Yun na yon?" (That's it?)

Some were grumbling in the mad rush out of the Center. They came, they said, as early as six in the morning just to get a good seat and be able to hear her speak to them. Many got crushed in the scramble for seat, went hungry, suffered the heat, etcetera, but heard absolutely nothing to ponder on and hope for.

Others who were more patronizing gave her the benefit of the doubt.

"She may not want to pre-empt what she'll gonna say to us later. We still have a chance to hear her fully during the multi-sectoral consultation this afternnon at Loyola U."

Dr. Granada and his group proceeded to the headquarters after that short, uneventful gathering at the Sports Center. Like the others, they thought it was a big let down, a despairing talk instead of inspiring. They were seeing signs of failure, even doom!

A lady reporter from the Palace Press Corps came with Nap Lopa wanting to interview Granada. Nap and Gel Duque had known each other when the former was still a reporter in Manila. She wanted to know the status of the protest and Granada gave her an idea where they were at the moment.

"What would happen if a solution to the conflict is not forthcoming?" Gel asked. She also wanted to know how SUC presidents in similar situation would react.

"Basically the same, I guess." Granada explained. "While the problem seems local it actually has a national impact and implication. At the Educators' Congress in Baguio City held last May, the fear of being unjustifiably replaced sooner or later had already seeped into the consciousness of the school heads including school superintendents, assistant superintendents, and middle-level bureacratic heads. That was why," he paused, "the Ed Congress passed a resolution reproving political meddling and interference in state educational institutions."

"Are the SUC presidents encouraging you to go on with the picket? Are there some who support you?" Gel stressed.

"Yes, in more ways than one they were, but not openly because they also need to be careful so as not to jeopardize their jobs. In fact many offered support like foods and anything that could help boost the morale of our teachers and students."

"Is Minister Quilantang supporting your picket.

Granada fell silent momentarily, looked at Gel and admitted mentally that for sometime now, had toyed with the idea that the Minister was, in her own way supporting this picket if only to get back at politicians. But he held back articulating this. Instead, he said "She needed strong support to back up her policies such as her newly-formulated guidelines in the selection of school presidents. Unfortunately, she isn't getting any. She must be in shock to realize her Ministry is kind-of- inutile when it comes to dealing with politicians. Now students and teachers are vocally condemning this blatant disregard of her Ministry's rules. Isn't this the best opportunity for her to explore and use this to her advantage?" Granada paused to let that sink in.

Gel checked her tape recorder as she prompted Granada to continue.

"Earlier, Minister Quilantang was quoted by several national dailies that she would join teachers' pickets to raise their salaries. But she had not been quoted in the context of joining pickets against politicians. Not yet. Her stubborn stance not to have something to do with us here at MCPC averring the politicians were responsible was puzzling us. Isn't she engaged in a protest of her own against a mightier force that is undermining her authority and the power of her Ministry?"

"You think so?" Gel asked almost in a whisper.

"Yes, I think she is, in one way or the other because she was quoted that she would join teachers' pickets to raise their salaries, support students and teachers in airing grievances and right to free expression."

"Since Mr. Barrado's appointment was authorized by the President, isn't the picket in your college a defiance of that authority?"

"The authority of the President is clearly and absolutely recognized in the guidelines set by the Education Minister, being the last step in the selection process," Granada said in a voice full of conviction. "But there were other steps that need to be done before this last step. Sadly, they were not followed but were grossly violated. This hideous disregard pushed the academic community to rise vehemently in protest. In this context, the picket therefore is not a defiance of the President's authority."

Silence.

Gel searched for her pack of cigarettes inside her bag, lighted one and blew rings of smoke which she watched with interest. She offered one to Granada.

"No, thanks," he declined.

"Do you think the educational system can be free entirely of political interference?" she inquired further.

"Most unlikely," Granada replied quickly.

Noting the reaction of the lady reporter, he continued. "Is it hard for you to believe that? You see, when the President affixes her signature on an appointment, although in our case it was the Executive Secretary who signed it by virtue of her authority, such an act was clearly and absolutely a political act, not political intervention. It was simply delegation of authority which the President can do whenever she wishes. But when this political act doesn't at all conform with the official guidelines set for the purpose, then that act becomes a simple case of political meddling, not to mention that it is an insult to the Education Minister and a slap to the integrity of her Ministry which happens to be an extension of her (President's) own office. Political interference must only be employed to reinforce the Ministry not to sabotage it!" Granada was vexed at his own words. "Otherwise what is the use of putting people there expecting them to function properly and with integrity if such hideous act is bound to happen again and again when whims and influence of politiciaans get in the way?"

Not knowing how to react to Granada's outburst, Gel reiterated her earlier question. "What happens if no solution is offered today?"

"I guess most of the protesters would have to swallow their pride and report back to school mainly for financial reason and to see to it that they keep their jobs. However, if things do not change nor normalize, I'm sure they will continue with their struggle. I told Minister Quilantang frankly that if the protesting community will not be heard, there will be more dissenters in this government and it could happen that some might choose to go to the hills."

"Was she alarmed?" Gel asked suddenly curious.

"She just promised to see what she can do. That's all she said," he exclaimed a bit frustrated.

There seemed to be nothing more to ask Granada so Gel started to check her tape recorder to ensure that their conversation was recorded in full. At that moment, Joel was approaching Dr. Granada who took the opportunity to introduce him to Gel.

"O Gel, this is Joel, the SSC president. Pwede mo siyang interview-hin. He's a gold mine' you know," he said half smiling.

The Compromise

At Beth's apartment where they all gathered after that humdrum of an event in the morning, the group felt tired and weary all of a sudden. It was almost noon and everyone was hungry. They were getting ready to have lunch when Dax came dashing in looking like he just crossed the finish line in a running race. In between catching his breath and rattling off he told them that Dr. Granada was wanted at Loyola University where the President's entourage was received.

"I learned from Narciso that the President's staff have been paging you for about an hour now. The President wanted to see you ASAP, Sir!" the student was almost breathless in his excitement.

Granada didn't wait for the rest of Dax's blabbering. With his leaders, they scampered out of the house and covered on foot eleven blocks of badly paved streets in less than ten minutes. Loyola University was a bit far from where Granada and his leaders were. It was an adrenalin rush moment. Their feet seemed to have wings!

Because of the need to reroute vehicles several intersections were blocked. These were manned by military police so cars and other vehicles couldn't get through. Granada decided it was wise to proceed on foot instead of taking his car.

The staff who met him at the gate of Loyola was muttering and gasping for breath as she rattled off asking where Dr. Granada was all this time.

He responded by saying he had no idea that the President will call for him that early. He apologized though. They were given gate passes urging him to "hurry up, the President's waiting."

They maneuvered their way through the throng of humanity and noticed that security were all opver the place.

On their way in, he saw several placards and streamers of the Mindanao Advancement Party wagered by its followers shouting "OUST MENDEL" and calling out the Governor to "RESIGN NOW". Granada came to know later that Father Javieto had a shouting match with Gary Daldalen over the rants his people were staging in front of the University. The incident was witnessed by Finance Minister Miro who pacified Father Javieto and decidedly pulled him away from an equally raging Daldalen.

After he was introduced to the security men at the gate, Dr. Granada was whisked off to the building where the President and her company stayed. There he met and was introduced to the President's Aide-de-Camp, Col. Alerto Payton who brought him up to the conference hall where the chief executive was meeting members of the Federation of Catholic Schools. His leaders who were with him were not allowed to join him after Col. Payton told them that it was only Dr. Granada who the President wanted to see.

Minister Quilantang rushed out of the hall to meet Granada. She was frantic. "Where were you all this time?"

He told her he came to know of the call only a few minutes ago.

"You would have to wait. She's having lunch with her guests right now," she said.

Turning to Col. Payton she requested that Granada be the first audience as soon as the President resumed her order of the day. "There will be no more time before then since she will be presiding over the multi-sectoral consultation at two."

From the balcony of the second floor, Granada saw his leaders waving at him, saying something which he could not decipher. Nonetheless, he knew they were wishing him good luck.

Due to excitement, he felt his stomach twerked. "I must be nervous," he told himself and realized he missed taking his lunch. He looked around hoping someone would offer him a glass of water. No one did. He braced himself for what's to come.

The security was very tight upstairs. The elite Presidential Security Group were posted in all corners of the building. He felt a little encouraged when he saw General Frias who acknowledged him with a nod. They had a brief talk wherein the older man said he had a feeling the decision that would be arrived at would probably make him happy. Granada thanked the General for his kind words.

He also saw Minister Mendel got out of the conference hall. When the latter saw Granada near the door, he hollered assuring him that the President will see him for sure and hear his side. He wanted to at least shake his hands but the Minister hurried out to conduct a business meeting with Filipino-Chinese businessmen. He would go back to the hall later to witness Granada's meeting with Her Excellency.

Dr. Quilantang's head popped out of the door as she signaled Granada to follow her inside. "Granada, follow me..." she said in her soft but obviously strained voice.

He quickly followed her inside and noticed that despite the strict security, people were going in and out of the hall where the President was. Obviously, there was not much time left for his talk with the Chief as everyone was in a frenzy. There were reminders about the consultation session to be held soon. How much time would he have with her, he can only guess.

While trying to gather his composure in one corner, he recognized Sister Jackie Belez, the young nun who was part of his discussion group in the Educators' Congress last May. He remembered her as very active during deliberations and contributed novel ideas which her group mates thought were invaluable.

"You should tell me what happened later," she whispered to him as she inched her way out of the crowd.

As soon as the room was cleared and the door closed, Granada was introduced by Minister Quilantang to the President who told him to take his seat opposite her in the round conference table. He seated himself confidently.

As he looked at her from across the table, it felt strange that he was not awed nor overpowered by her presence. He did not feel intimidated at all. It was her plebeian simplicity that rather surprised him. The President projected the mien of a "common man" as media liked to tag her. With that in mind, he looked forward to this face-to-face encounter with confidence.

With them in the room were Minister Mendel who came back immediately after briefly addressing the business group, Minister Quilantang and Col. Payton who firmly stood on the side watchful and alert.

"So, you are Dr. Granada. I am very disappointed that you do not recognize my authority," she said in her thin, faint voice. "I'm sure you are aware that I authorized Secretary Rayos to sign the appointment papers of Mr. Barrado. What were you thinking Dr. Granada?" the President remarked sounding irked. "Anyway, I'd like to hear your side."

Did the President call for him to scold him? Granada asked himself as he tried to read the expression on her face. He couldn't see any anger there although he noticed her voice was slightly quivering. Was she tired after her more than an hour flight and the series of meetings she had so far done?

"I wish to apologize Madam President if that was the impression you got. I have always recognized your authority and it would be beyond me to defy you," he responded humbly.

"If that's the case, then what is this commotion all about? Your protest has been going on for over a month now. How do you explain that?"

"Madam President, after I've learned of Mr. Barrado's appointment, I immediately came back here to inform my constituents of the news and relayed Minister Quilantang's appeal for patience and understanding. By that time, Ma'am, the community had already planned the protest even before I arrived," he explained. He looked at the President who was silently listening to him. She said nothing but signaled him to continue.

"When Mr. Barrado showed me his appointment papers on June 5 during our initial meeting at the Ministry's regional office, I presented a three-point proposal for a smooth turnover."

"But what happened? Why the big trouble?" the President asked without raising her voice. It was so passive that Granada wondered if she was getting the picture at all.

"It was unfortunate that Mr. Barrado didn't like the terms of the proposal, so he turned it down saying he didn't have to comply because he is now president," Granada emphasized. "He wanted a 'no fuss' turnover, a quick one without the hassle of doing an exhaustive inventory."

Again, the President was silent. She did not comment on what Granada was telling her.

He continued.

"On June 13, he employed quite a number of men who forcibly entered the campus, the consequences of which were destruction of property of the school and physically injuring some of our students, staff and faculty."

Granada sensed that the President deliberately ignored his account on the "take over" and went back to the issue of turnover.

"What did the turnover entail?" she asked simply.

He narrated in details what he told Minister Quilantang when he had his meeting with her. These were the same requirements he mentioned to Minister Mendel earlier when they met in Manila.

"Is that correct Lucretia?" turning to her education minister for confirmation.

"Yes Ma'am," she responded quickly.

"One basic issue here is that Minister Quilantang has not confirmed Mr. Barrado's appointment. As such, he could not disburse funds because the Treasury Department would not recognize his signature without the Minister's attestation as to its authenticity," he offered the information which made the President looked at her minister again quizzically.

Granada had a hunch the President didn't know about Quilantang's refusal to solve the problem at her level. He kept quiet.

"Is this true Lucretia that you have not confirmed Barrado's appointment?" she asked sharply.

"Er... I was in Baguio at that time, Madam President," Quilantang said haltingly throwing Granada a veiled look for putting her on the spot.

For the first time, it became very clear to him that the Minister was really against Steve Barrado. However he could not fathom why she had to make such a trivial and hollow alibi. She could have confirmed Barrado's appointment after Baguio. There was plenty of time for that. Yet up to this day, she hadn't done so.

He observed that the President did not even chide her for her negligence and left it at that.

"Hmmm," she murmured thoughtfully. "But we have this problem on our hands. I think it won't be solved if both of you are around. What do you think Lino?"

"Ah, eh Madam President," the surprised Lino could not immediately say anything. He was caught off guard by the sudden shift of attention to him. As soon as gathered back his wits, he said that a third party would be a good idea.

There it was. The President had finally said it. A new person, not him not Barrado!

Before Granada came to this meeting, he had considered the possibility of a compromise as the most feasible solution to a conflict of this magnitude. However, he was aware that the compromise wouldn't come easy. There had to be a price to pay, a sacrifice. And the sacrifice, he realized now, was him! If he insisted that he be retained and Barrado be consequently re-assigned elsewhere, this might be too much for the President to even consider. Also, there was not much time for arguments.

He looked at Minister Quilantang. Wasn't this idea of a third party actually her idea? He covertly examined her poker face. It was not betraying her. He turned to Minister Pimentel and was surprised at his quick response that a third party was a good idea. Didn't he whisper to him when they met four days ago that Barrado's appointment would be revoked and that he was going to be retained? How come the President was following a different line of thought?

"To normalize the situation, I think you are right, Madam President. A third party could be considered. I am amenable to your suggestion," Granada found himself agreeing.

"Yes, I think so too. To normalize the situation, we shall have a third party," repeated the President.

For the first time, Granada saw a hint of relief as her face lit up.

Now, he was certain that Barrado's appointment would finally be rendered null and void. And that's what mattered. Again, Granada looked at Minister Quilantang. Her expression told him she was also relieved. He noted a slight nod directed to him. Minister Mendel however, had been silent after he reacted to the President. Granada wasn't sure what he was thinking at the moment. He even avoided his eyes.

"Madam President," addressing her boldly "I hope this time, the guidelines set by the Ministry will be honored and followed to the letter. Please note that ignoring them in the case of Barrado caused this problem in the College," he said frankly.

"Guidelines?" she asked raising a pencil-enhanced eyebrow.

"Yes Madam, guidelines in the selection of higher education institution presidents," he stressed. He briefly enumerated the four-step set of rules of the Ministry as well as similar provisions indicated in the College charter.

"Is this correct, Lucretia?"

"Yes, that's correct Madam."

Without commenting on the response of Minister Quilantang, she turned to Granada. "About that third party, do you have an executive vice-president?"

"We have Madam, as well as a Vice-President for Academic Affairs. That would be Dr. Sosimo Soriano and Dr. Honesto Vilar."

"Would anyone of them do?" she asked.

"None of the two would be acceptable to the community. They belonged to different factions. It won't be wise to appoint someone who will not be hundred percent accepted by the community," he explained objectively.

"Who do you suggest then?"

"I think Minister Quilantang can designate someone on a temporary capacity until the problems in the College are resolved and peace and order restored. It is also important that he or she should be impartial and acceptable to both camps," he reiterated.

"Why not Dr. Sylvia Matupon of Loyola University? She's the vice president here and I can assign her as transition president at MCPC until situation normalizes," Quilantang blurted out. "She can stay there while a search committee is screening possible candidates for the position," she added in her unusually controlled voce.

Granada was surprised at the speed by which the name of Matupon was brought up. He wondered if this had been planned by the Minister ahead of time. If the name's an afterthought, that would be bad, indeed!

Turning to Granada, the president asked, "Is she okay with you Granada?"

"Why not? If the Minister chooses her as acting president temporarily, I think she's alright," he agreed less enthusiastically.

"What do you think Minister Mendel?"

"I have no problem with that," he replied quickly.

That settled, the President ordered Minister Quilantang to prepare for the immediate designation of Dr. Matupon.

"Yes Madam President will do that," she confirmed.

"What do we do with Dr. Granada then?" she asked.

Addressing Granada, she said, "I was told you have a PhD. In what?"

"Educational Administration with institutional planning and development as major and network analysis as minor, University of Alabama, Ma'am," he replied humbly.

"Dr. Granada was a Fulbright-Hays grantee, Madam President," Quilantang added like she was proud of his background.

"Let's give Dr. Granada a better position. Where were you connected before?"

"Central Nueva Ecija State University Ma'am."

"How long did you work there?"

"About ten years. First as consultant for planning and left the University as vice president."

"Is the presidency there vacant?"

"Former president Dr. Armando Carpio has recently retired, so it's vacant. We can actually assign him there Madam," responded Quilantang swiftly.

"Hmmm, what do you say, Dr. Granada?" throwing him the question which startled him briefly.

In reality he was not keen on the offer. He thought of his MCPC family who might think that he had finally abandon them. He also remembered his conversation with his children who commented "wouldn't that be horse trading Daddy?"

He looked straight into the chief executive's eyes and said apologetically, "Thank you Mrs. President, but I won't take it."

The President stared at Granada as if she hadn't heard him. CNESU was one of the biggest state universities in the country and turning down the opportunity to lead it would be foolish. Many had in mind CNESU as their dream university.

Had the President asked him why he refused, he would have told her that he wanted a small, dilapidated school which he can help transform into something like CNESU, a model regional university in agricultural education or like MCPC in Mindanao which he developed into a polytechnic college of note in a short span of time. He wanted an unknown and obscure school to lead because for him small is beautiful.

Again, the President didn't seem to mind Granada's turning down Quilantang's proposal. "Are there other better positions available, Lucretia?"

"I had offered him the directorship of the bureau of higher education, but he also turned it down, Madam. I had to give it to somebody else," she told her a bit annoyed.

Granada had a personal reason for his refusal. Dr. Dimla, its former head was a friend and a colleague whom he respected much for his bright and useful ideas. He knew he could not allow it that he be the reason for his friend's displacement.

As he was pondering, he closely watched the President knitted her eyebrows. It occurred to him that the she might be probing into his thoughts, wondering what he really wanted and possibly asking herself why this fellow was depriving himself of these great opportunities.

Again, Granada wanted her to ask him "why?" so he could tell her that his decision was a matter of professional integrity; that the college or university presidency was not a question of accommodation, of exchange, or for that matter, horse-trading.

She didn't bother to find out his reasons for refusal and left it at that.

Instead, she asked off-handedly, "How about Mr. Barrado? Do we have a position for him?"

At that point, she shifted her position, inhaled deeply and darted her sight to Minister Quilantang who appeared to be getting uncomfortable.

"I'm sorry but I've not thought of that yet, Madam President," she admitted.

"Well then. What's important is that we found a solution to the protest problem. I hope Dr. Granada will cooperate in bringing about normalcy in the College for the sake of the students and workers," she said firmly.

"I will issue the necessary directive Ma'am," Dr. Quilantang remarked.

"I'll do my best Madam President. And thank you for the time," Granada said extending his hand which the President took. They shook hands briefly.

Outside, Minister Quilantang asked Granada to meet her at three o'clock in the office of Dr. Matupon. She'll be arranging a meeting with Mr. Barrado so that the three of them could issue a joint statement to the press.

The meeting with his leaders and the protesters that followed was emotional. Instead of telling them himself how the dialogue with the President went, he once again produced his mini tape recorder and made them listen to it.

No one spoke as everyone listened with bated breath. Only the voices of the President, Dr. Granada and occasionally that of Minister Quilantang could be heard until the tape screeched to a stop.

While Granada explained how they arrived at a compromise and the sacrifice he had to do, the protesters were sobbing which eventually broke into loud cries. He too was choking. Beth gave him a glass of water.

After he had calmed himself down, he asked "Don't you agree that entering into a compromise was the best concession we could have gotten from the President of this country?"

No one was bold enough to comment. The silence added more heat to the already stuffy apartment.

"Don't you think that under the circumstances," Granada continued, "there was no other option but to go for a compromise?"

"Yes, Sir," a few voices responded but they were so faint that he could hardly hear them. Perhaps, it was because of the noise outside.

That day, the protesters were uncertain. "Did we win or did we lose?"

Back at Loyola University, Barrado's men continued to bark outside the gate articulating their own demands. Unfortunately, their outcry was drowned by other protests from several militant groups.

Dr. Sylvia Matupon was incredibly surprised at the news that she was picked by Minister Quilantang to temporarily head MCPC as a result of the dialogue. She, however, took it graciously but nervously admitted she doesn't run away from a challenge such as this despite the fact that she had no experience running a government school and lacked the competencies and knowledge required to fully understand its operation. She requested Dr. Granada to stay for a while and help her sort out the tangled situations in the College. She was afraid the personnel would not be happy welcoming her even temporarily. He promised her that he will.

Their meeting scheduled at three proceeded without Barrado who could not be contacted. Later, they were informed that the man had tendered his resignation at the Regional Office. This was his way of exiting "honorably" avoiding the embarrassment of having his appointment revoked by no less than the President of the Republic.

In the meantime, Minsiter Quilantang led the drafting of the joint statement for the press. Granada suggested that it should be worded carefully to give the semblance of a "mutually voluntary withdrawal" on the part of the concerned parties. Quilantang acceded and did the task of facing media to make the announcement.

Granada was on his way out of Loyola when his brother Bebot caught up with him. The younger Granada was with a distinguished-looking man who was smiling to him as they approached.

Bebot introduced Rev. Dr. Donald Nicholson saying he was his economics professor at Loyola U and had been with the University for quite some time.

"It's a pleasure to have finally met you, Dr. Granada. I have heard a lot of good things about you and has yet to hear people say something bad against you," said Rev. Nicholson while firmly gripping his hand.

"Oh, thank you Father. I'm glad to meet you too. I am sorry that I did not meet you sooner."

They talked for a few minutes with the professor obviously impressed with him.

"I hope this is not the first and last time that we will see each other Dr. Moises" remarked the professor.

"I hope so too, Father."

"I just would like you to know that it is very difficult nowadays to find a man of your magnanimity, Dr. Granada," he finally said, complementing him sincerely.

"Why, thank you, Father. You are very kind," he said smiling, wondering what in the world did he do to deserve such compliment from a man whom he barely knew.

"Rewards come in different packages," he murmured to himself as he peacefully walked away.

EPILOGUE

Bringing MCPC back to normal wasn't easy. It was, in fact, chaotic, nerve-wracking and problematic. It would be difficult to imagine that the once smooth-running, peaceful and developing polytechnic college in Metro Ciudad would suddenly find itself in a mire confronted by numerous problems that had outrageously grown in proportion.

True to her fear, Dr. Sylvia Matupon received a cold welcome from the still suspicious faculty and staff. "Why her?"

It was a good thing Dr. Granada was around to help out the acting president untangle the mess the College was in. In the short period that Barrado assumed office, a lot of problems were created which were left for the College to resolve.

Newly-hired teachers from neighboring secondary schools demanded that they be paid salaries equivalent to those of college instructors and professors. Non-teaching casual employees wanted to occupy administrative staff positions even without civil service eligibility bringing the total number of newly-hired to a staggering 100 percent increase. This dramatic rise in number was aggravated by the ballooned count of security guards from ten to forty five. The school had to employ two security agencies—the former contractor and Panther Security owned by one military man who helped Barrado during the siege.

The College was also constrained to pay for air time from TV and radio stations including honoraria for broadcasters and reporters guaranteed by a written contract. This confirmed the protesters' suspicions that the media propaganda against them were being paid for by the College's money.

Dr. Granada had a difficult time accounting for lost and destroyed school property and facilities, office supplies, and equipment as a result of the takeover. Accusations and counteraccusations as to who were responsible were endless which brought altercations that ended in fist fights and rumbles that frightened the community. What with wooden clubs and home-made weapons and occasional drawing of handguns (thank God no one got shot) the atmosphere was frenzied and agitated. MCPC was at its worst and Dr. Matupon threatened to leave. She had had too much of the troubles! Dr. Granada asked her to sacrifice a little bit more giving her all the support while Minister Quilantang dangled before her the presidency of a state college in Bukidnon which was, at that time, needing a new head after its former president retired to keep hert at MCPC until such time that the College had healed and up on its feet again.

(Instructors and students of the said school in Bukidnon rose in protest when Matupon finally assumed her post. They abhorred the idea that the new school president did not pass through a Search Committee; was unskilled and unknowledgable in government schools' operation; and was basically an "outsider" coming from a private institution. They hated the fact that she was chosen by the Education Minister without subjecting her to her own guidelines ignoring the many qualified and experienced administrators from state higher education institutions to choose from. It was appaling that the Minister did what she despised most. Well the prevailing revolutionary government couldn't care less.)

It took the duo over a month before things slowly got back to normal. The faculty and staff resumed their work and students attended regular classes. With difficulty, the newly hired had to be terminated by virtue of the nature of their appointment and repair of destroyed property was done immediately.

In the meantime, the search for a new president was on-going.

By this time, Dr. Granada was ready to leave the institution. He gave instructions to Atty. Gael to follow up their cases filed in court. He left the discretion to the lawyer to settle the disputes in consultation with the affected members of the academic community.

A feast was being prepared for his despedida. Many of the protesters especially those who were with him during their journey were sad and down-hearted. Dr. Granada was leaving that day on an aftrernoon flight. He was going back to his family at CNESU. Was he excited to see them again after missing them for over a month?

"Looking forward to it," he assured his MCPC family.

Demetrio Castro, automotive shop aide approached him to speak to him. He was one of those who "abandoned" the protest and reported back to work due to dire finanacial needs. Protesters during that time were not receiving their salaries and had to suffer much financially.

He stood in the middle of the room while being eyed with open hostility by his fellow workers. They were angry at him for abandoning the cause. Unfortunately for Demetrio, those who were with Barrado didn't also appreciate his reporting back to school and avoided him whenever possible.

A female staff at the back twirled her finger around her ear as if saying "He's nuts!"

Demetrio was aware of the stares from his colleagues but took all the courage he can muster to speak. With a quivering voice, he began.

"Sir, I came to tell you that I am sorry to have left the protest. I've been unfairly accused of being a traitor to the cause and it pains me. Sir, I was one of those who installed the barbed wires to secure the barricades, joined all rallies and demonstrations in the city and helped put up those stands of chalkboards at Mac Arthur Park. If I had my way, I won't be turning my back on our group. It was purely for financial reasons. I have four children to feed and my wife is sick of tuberculosis. She has stopped working as an occasional laundress."

He paused for a while and noticed his fellow workers were unaffected at what he was saying.

"Sir... when I reported back, I was completely ignored. I was not given any assignment so I stayed in my shop and worked there alone."

Dr. Granada pulled a pack of cigarettes from his front pocket, lighted one and offered another to Demetrio.

"Thank you, Sir but I don't smoke anymore," took a deep breath and continued. *"You know Sir, I always remember what you told us the first time you met us. Your words rang clearly and they stuck. 'Love your work because if you continue to love your work, you will make this small College beautiful.' So even if I had to endure their unkind treatment of me I persist because I remember what you have told us. Sir. Love your work and help make this small College beautiful. Those words will never leave me. They will continue to be my inspiration as long as I live. Have safe flight Sir."*

Before the party ended there were short speeches, expression of thanks and gratitude. Others gave tokens "for the kids and Ma'am Tessa." The invited students took endless photos of the occasion, of them with him, of him in his most unguarded moments. There were cries and hearty laughs as he bid them goodbye.

Anita handed him a folded paper and whispered, "please read it while you're on the plane."

He smiled down to her and put the folded paper in his pocket.

"I won't forget," he promised.

As his taxi slowly climbed the ascending well-paved highway to the airport, the skies suddenly opened and poured down the richness of heavens wetting the thirsty landscape of well-tended residential gardens and the mahogany trees lining the avenue.

Moises Granada slid the car window by his side as the late afternoon breeze engulfed him. He inhaled deeply and filled his lungs with the sweet aroma of the wind.

"A good sign," he muttered to himself.

The sun hid itself in the far distance of the horizon in order to rise and brighten the day in another part of the world.

"Such is ls life. We don't have the monopoly of night and day."

ABOUT THE AUTHOR

Melchizedek Maquiso (Mike) worked in the Office of the President in Malacanang Palace, Republic of the Philippines as Presidential Assistant for the Urban Poor and concurrent Chairman of the Presidential Commission for the Urban Poor with the rank of Undersecretary. He was awarded a Presidential Medal of Merit by His Excellency President Fidel V. Ramos.

He finished his PhD (major in Institutional Planning and Development with minors in Higher Education and Network Analysis) from the University of Alabama as Fulbright Hayes scholar in 1973. His AB and MA both in literature were obtained from Siliman University as an Osborne scholar and a Graduate Fellow in 1964 and 1968, respectively.

Most of his professional life was spent in the academe. He rose from the ranks starting as instructor to becoming full professor while occupying administrative positions in the process (Central Mindanao University, Central Luzon State university, and Don Mariano Memorial Polytechnic State College or DMMPSC). He was college dean, vice president, and OIC president in the latter.

He was serving as executive director of the Center for Interinstitutional Research and Policy Studies-Development Council of State Colleges and Universities, Region III, when assigned to DMMPSC in Cagayan De Oro City.

He was consultant for institutional planning and management in various state and private educational institutions, and the Philippine Charity Sweepstakes Office, among others.

This "38 Dark Days" is his sixth book and second novel. The other four are textbooks or reference materials in higher education, namely *Philippine Education: Everything You Wanted to Know About It but Were Too Shy to Ask; Institutional Panning and Development, A Primer; Educational*

Administration, A Rational and Structural Approach; and Policy and Policy Making in Education.

His first Novel is entitled: Cha cha cha: A novel of Politics.

38 Dark Days is published posthumously.

38 DARK DAYS (THE ACADEME IN TURMOIL)

The novel 38 dark days is a story lifted from the true to life experience of an academic institution in Northern Mindanao whose faculty and staff members struggled from political intervention and boldly fought against threat to academic freedom. Their act of bravery and firmness to speak out and fight for the issues they strongly believe will take the readers back to 1986 of the Philippine History, the People Power Revolution! To recall, during this time, millions of Filipinos sought for social change and demanded for a new government that is people-centered and values the essence of democracy. Sharing the same grief felt by Filipinos during that time, the experience of the college's personnel as they carry out the month-long protest was also filled with uncertainty, struggle, sacrifices, pain, blood, loss of hope, and test of faith. Nevertheless, they remained hopeful and positive that the turmoil will eventually reach the phase of stability, and so it did.

As I read thorough it, the novel conveys a clear message that the choices we make not only reflects who we are or the institution we are representing, but more importantly it lays out the foundation of our tomorrow and the future generation. In agreement with the author, we often associate the change of government to change of values, attitudes, and way of living. However, change in government cannot deliver social change alone. Rather, social change is a result of conscious involvement, participation and shared efforts from all sectors of the society. And this was clearly portrayed in the book.

While the story is focused on the dilemma faced solely by the college, the author was able to expound and explain how complex the society is, and so is the process of addressing societal issues. The novel explains that all sectors of the society (individuals, household, community, government institutions, private companies, and multi-stakeholders) are interrelated and interdependent, regardless of jurisdiction. Hence, it is important that we follow the set guidelines, and must act accordingly and responsibly as we fulfill our duties and responsibilities as public servants.

I also admire how the author emphasized the importance of integrity in the nature of public service. As he slowly unfolds what were in the 38 days of the protest, we will be reminded that integrity not only concerns the education ministry but it should be uphold by all sectors of the society. As they say, one can never go wrong from doing the right thing.

Aside from integrity, the importance of humility amidst the presence of overwhelming fame and power was also given strong emphasis. People's trust, support and respect are not voluntarily given. They are earned by toil, hard work, and purest intention to serve as perceived through one's decisions and actions. Idealistic as it seems, but it speaks the truth. Decisions shall be made in a participatory approach and must not be jeopardized by our personal interests and personal affiliations, nor weighted by corresponding gains and benefits. It is only right that we prioritize the welfare and well-being of our people and not only consider what is beneficial to oneself.

When one is overwhelmed with power, they often forget the need to consult their people and let their side be heard. We need more of this book to remind us of the true essence of development or social change. That it can truly be achieved if we do it "for the people, with the people and by the people", this book serves that purpose.

EDGAR A. ORDEN
President
Central Luzon State University
September 21, 2020

of this in the United States
By Bookmasters

Printed in the United States
By Bookmasters